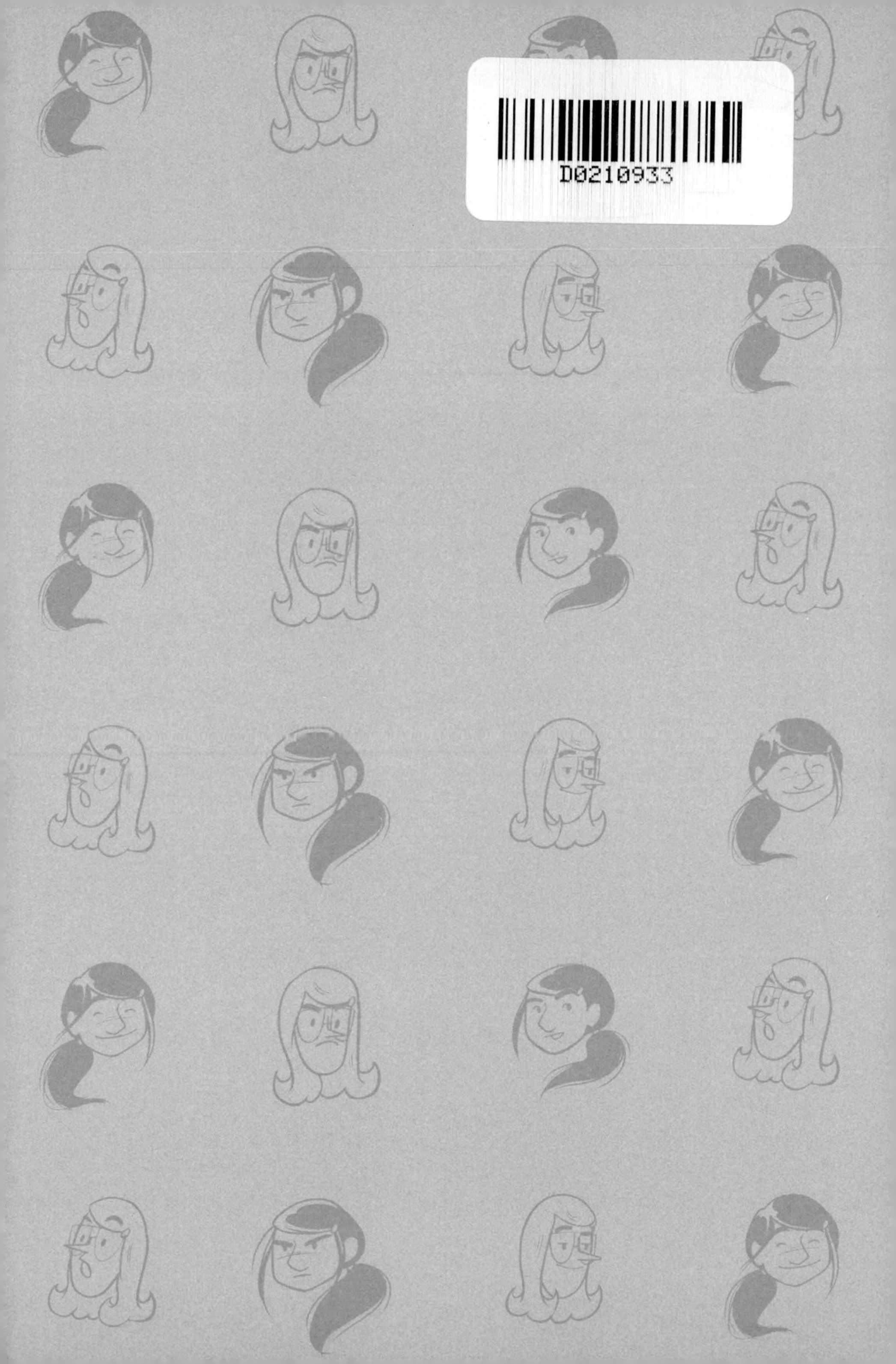

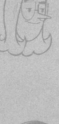

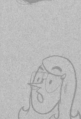

SHIRLEY & JAMILA'S BIG FALL

by Gillian Goerz

 Dial Books for Young Readers

DIAL BOOKS FOR YOUNG READERS
An imprint of Penguin Random House LLC, New York

First published in the United States of America by Dial Books for Young Readers,
an imprint of Penguin Random House LLC, 2021
Copyright © 2021 by Gillian Goerz

Library of Congress Cataloging-in-Publication Data
Names: Goerz, Gillian, author, illustrator. Title: Shirley & Jamila's big fall / Gillian Goerz.
Other titles: Shirley and Jamila's big fall | Description: New York : Dial Books for Young Readers, an imprint of
Penguin Random House LLC, 2021. | Audience: Ages 8-12. | Audience: Grades 4-6. | Summary: Starting a new school in
the fall with her friend Shirley, everything is going well for Jamila until Shirley pulls her into a new assignment: stop Chuck
Milton, a school bully who is using blackmail and intimidation to become school president—an assignment that will involve
a bit of breaking and entering. | Identifiers: LCCN 2021015245 (print) | LCCN 2021015246 (ebook) | ISBN 9780525552888
(hardcover) | ISBN 9780525552895 (paperback) | ISBN 9780593405413 (ebook) | ISBN 9780593405406 (ebook) | ISBN
9780525552901 (ebook) | Subjects: LCSH: Best friends—Comic books, strips, etc. | Best friends—Juvenile fiction.
| Schools—Comic books, strips, etc. | Schools—Juvenile fiction. | Bullying—Juvenile fiction. | Bullying—Juvenile fiction.
| Extortion—Comic books, strips, etc. | Extortion—Juvenile fiction. | Graphic novels. | CYAC: Graphic novels. | Best
friends—Fiction. | Friendship—Fiction. | School—Fiction. | Bullying—Fiction. | Extortion—Fiction. | LCGFT: Graphic novels.
Classification: LCC PZ7.7.G6533 Sj 2021 (print) | LCC PZ7.7.G6533 (ebook) | DDC 741.5/973—dc23
LC record available at https://lccn.loc.gov/2021015245 | LC ebook record available at https://lccn.loc.gov/2021015246

Manufactured in China
ISBN 9780525552895 (pbk)   10 9 8 7 6 5 4 3 2 1
ISBN 9780525552888 (hc)   10 9 8 7 6 5 4 3 2 1
RRD

Design by Jennifer Kelly and Gillian Goerz
Text set in GG Sans with permission of the author

Produced with the support of the Ontario Arts Council.

ONTARIO ARTS COUNCIL
CONSEIL DES ARTS DE L'ONTARIO

an Ontario government agency
un organisme du gouvernement de l'Ontario

FOR RAMONA QUIMBY.
YOU'RE MY FAVORITE, EVEN THOUGH
YOU'RE PRETEND. ALSO FOR THE LATE
BEVERLY CLEARY, WHO INTRODUCED US
AND IN DOING SO, IN A VERY SLOW WAY,
MADE THIS BOOK HAPPEN.

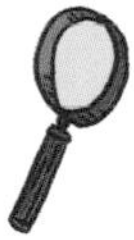

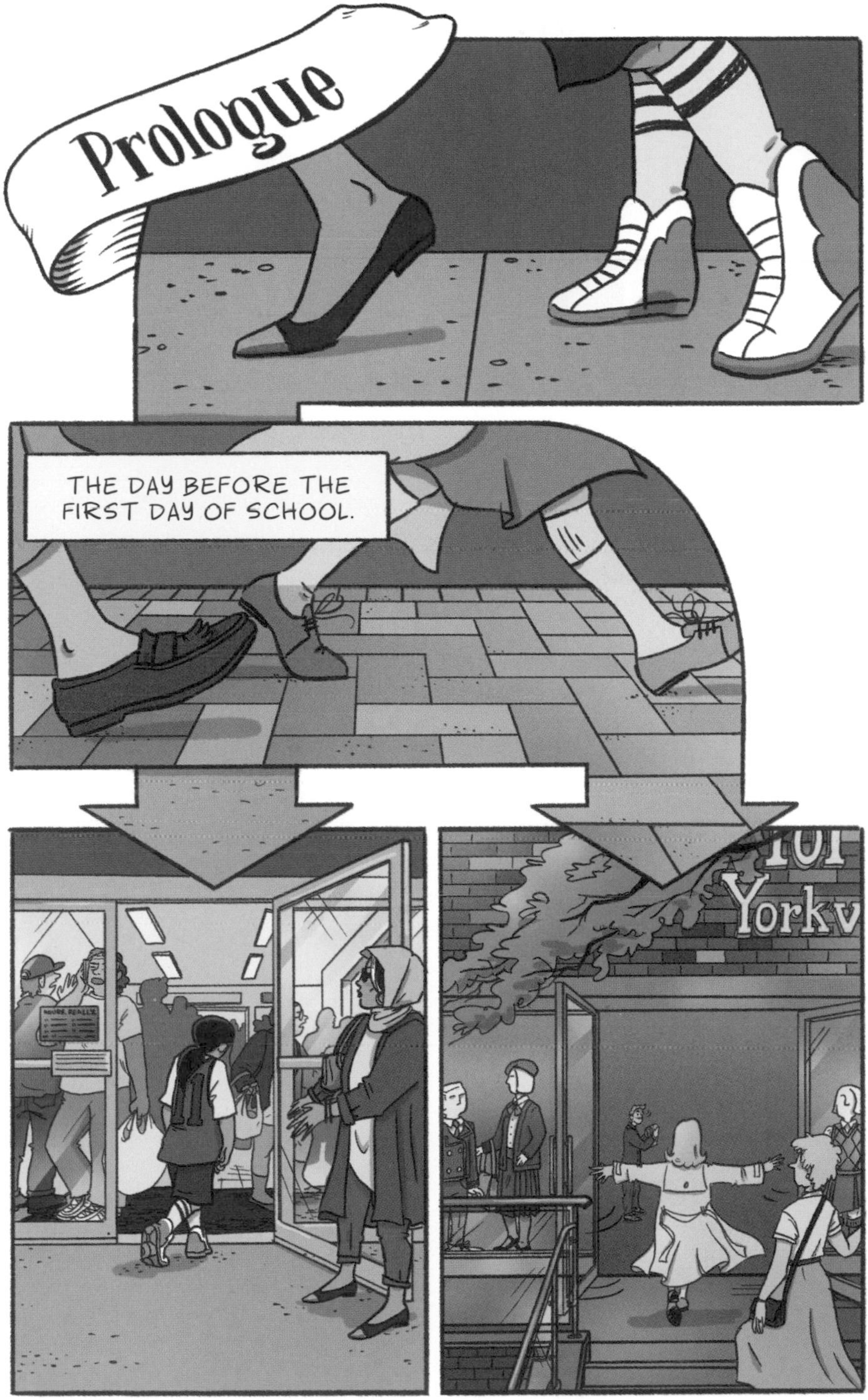
Prologue
THE DAY BEFORE THE FIRST DAY OF SCHOOL.

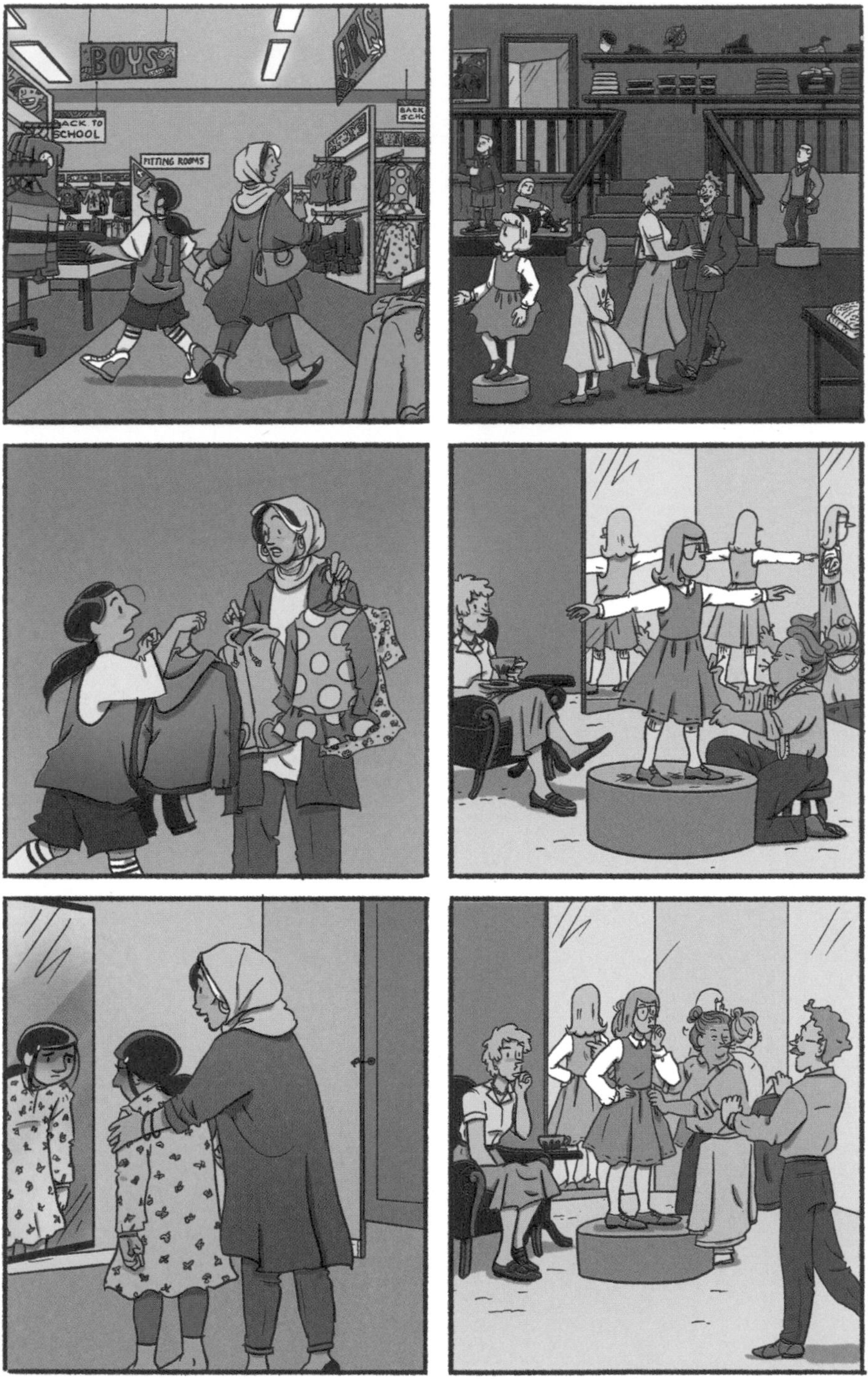
BOYS
GIRLS
BACK TO SCHOOL
FITTING ROOMS

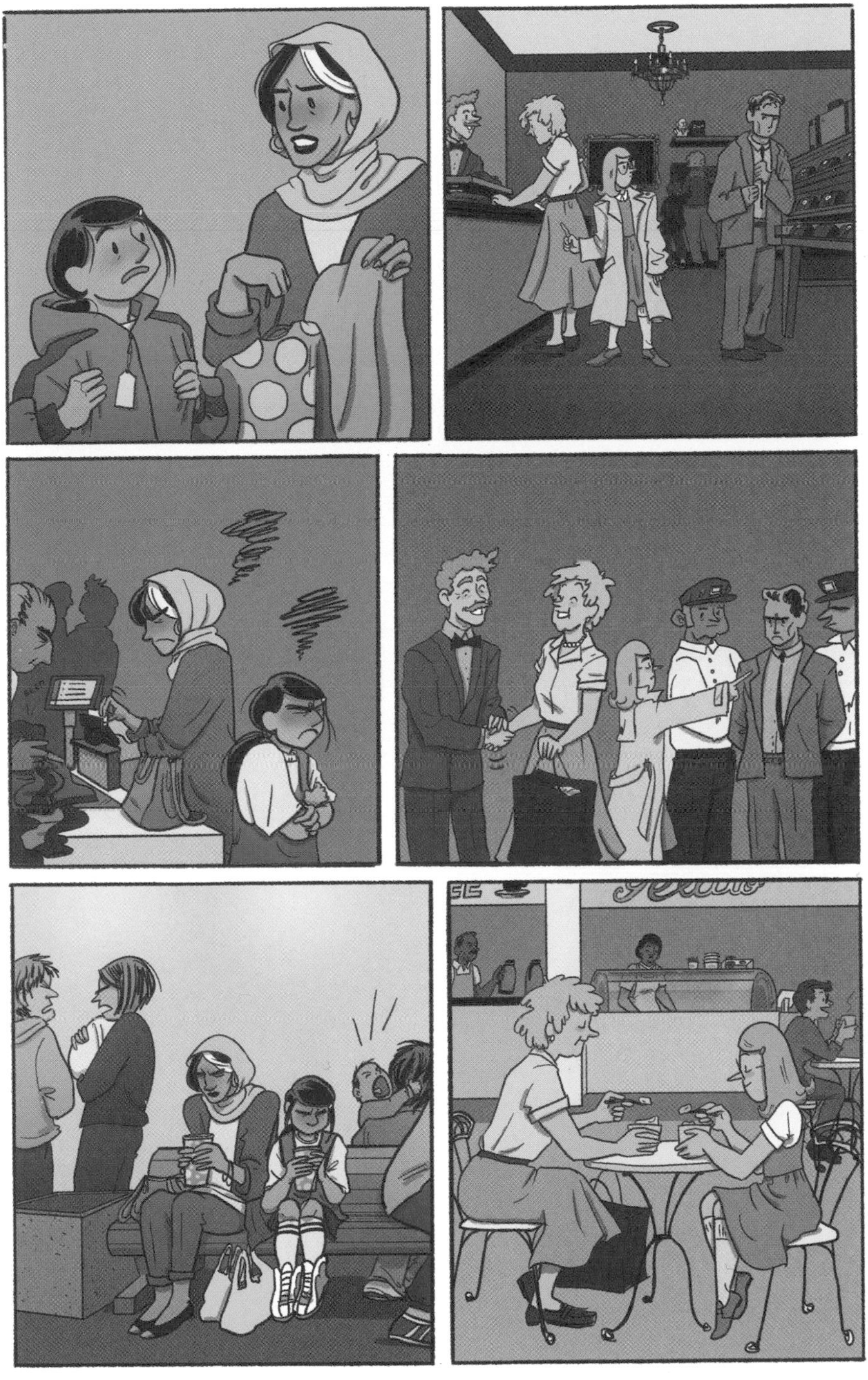

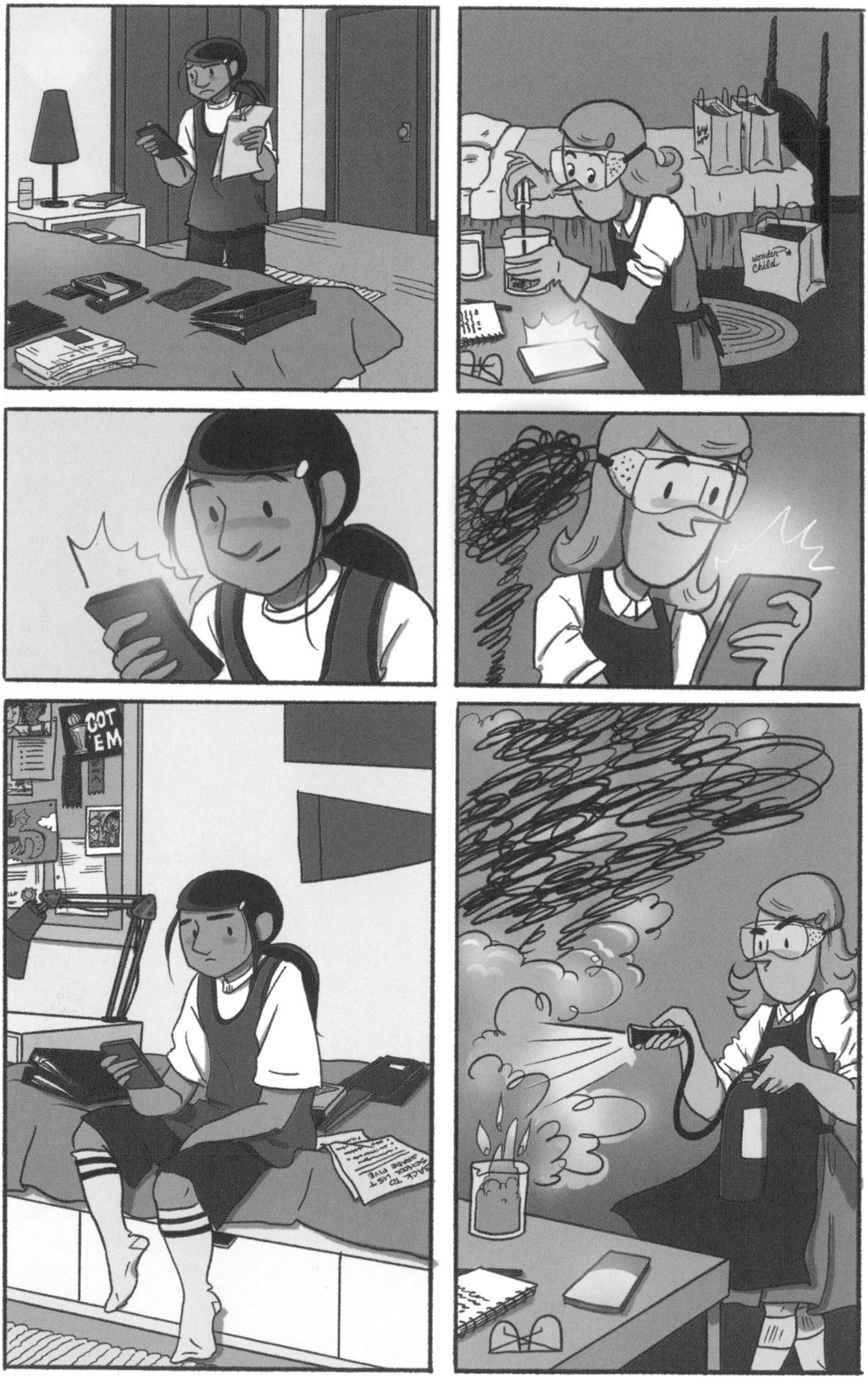
wonder Child
GOT EM
BACK TO SCHOOL LIST
GRADE FIVE

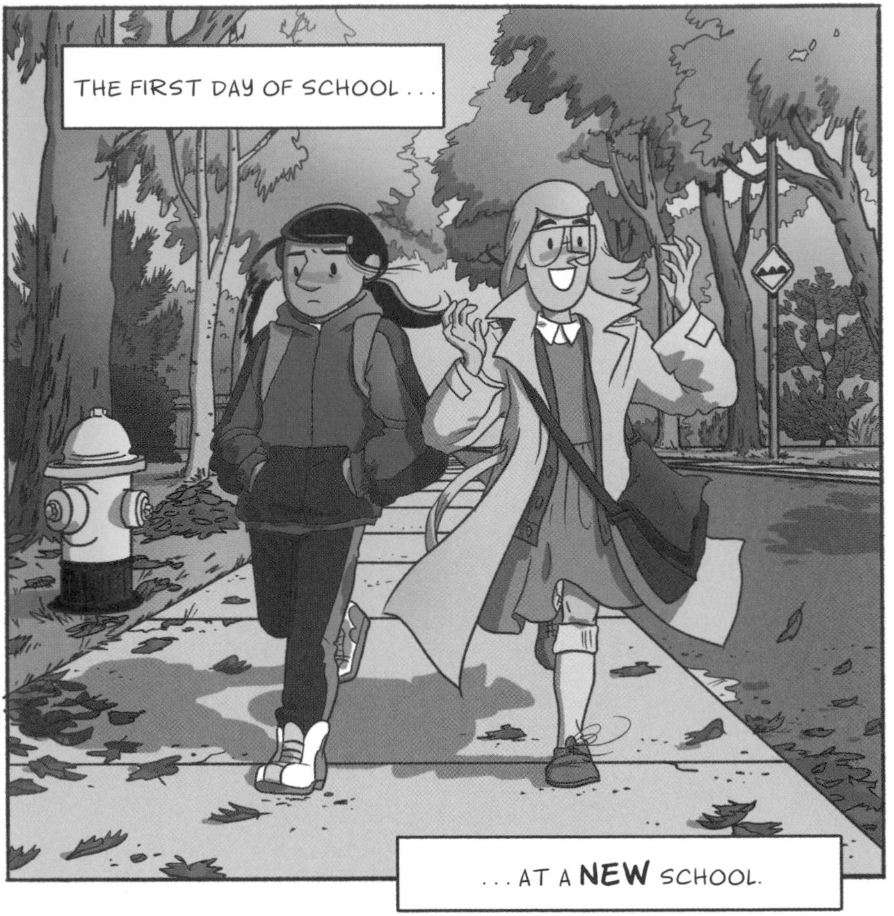
THE FIRST DAY OF SCHOOL . . .
. . . AT A **NEW** SCHOOL.

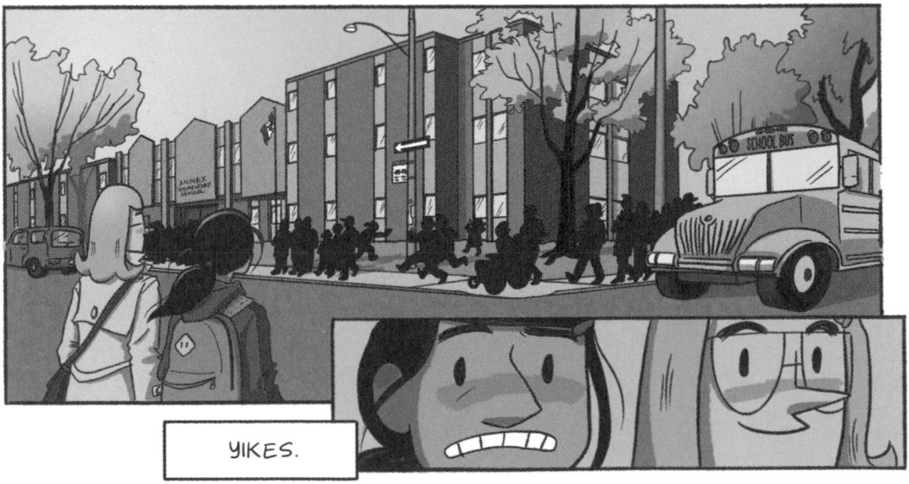
SCHOOL BUS
YIKES.

MRS. LEZAMA, THIS IS JAMILA WAHEED. SHE'S NEW.

I WAS EXPECTING YOU! SO GLAD YOU'RE HERE!

MY TEACHER WAS NICE. AND HAVING A FRIEND THERE ALREADY SURE HELPED.

BY THE TIME A WEEK HAD PASSED, I FORGOT I'D BEEN NERVOUS AT ALL.

BASKETBALL TRY OUTS

THE WILD WORLD OF STUDENT GOVERMENT

INTERNATIONAL LUNCH CLUB

ANNEX ELEMENTARY

IN A WAY, IT WASN'T THAT DIFFERENT FROM OUR SUMMER.

IT EVEN FELT FAMILIAR.

7

Chapter 1

SCHOOL WAS WELL UNDERWAY WHEN THE STORY I'M ABOUT TO TELL TOOK PLACE.

I WOULDN'T BE TELLING IT NOW IF THE KIDS INVOLVED COULD STILL BE HURT (OR GET IN TROUBLE) BY THE TRUTH COMING OUT, BUT THEY'VE ALL MOVED AWAY OR MOVED ON.

STILL, IF I FUDGE A DETAIL OR TWO JUST TO MAKE SURE, I HOPE YOU'LL UNDERSTAND.

LIKE I SAID, AT FIRST SCHOOL DIDN'T CHANGE THINGS THAT MUCH FOR SHIRLEY AND ME.

WE SOLVED CASES TOGETHER.

WE HELPED KIDS OUT.

WE EVEN SNUCK AROUND A LITTLE.

IT WAS GREAT.

TEACHER'S LOUNGE

BUT SUDDENLY, THERE WAS OTHER STUFF TOO.

THERE WERE VIOLIN LESSONS.

THERE WAS BASKETBALL.

I MADE THE SCHOOL TEAM **AND** A COMMUNITY TEAM.

THERE WAS HOMEWORK.

THERE WERE ALSO OTHER KIDS.

IN SUMMER, SHIRLEY AND I SPENT ALMOST EVERY DAY TOGETHER.

NOW WE WERE BUSIER.

MY COMMUNITY BASKETBALL TEAM PRACTICED AT THE NEARBY REC CENTER AFTER SCHOOL A FEW DAYS A WEEK.

COMMUNITY GIRLS LEAGUE PRACTICE TODAY!

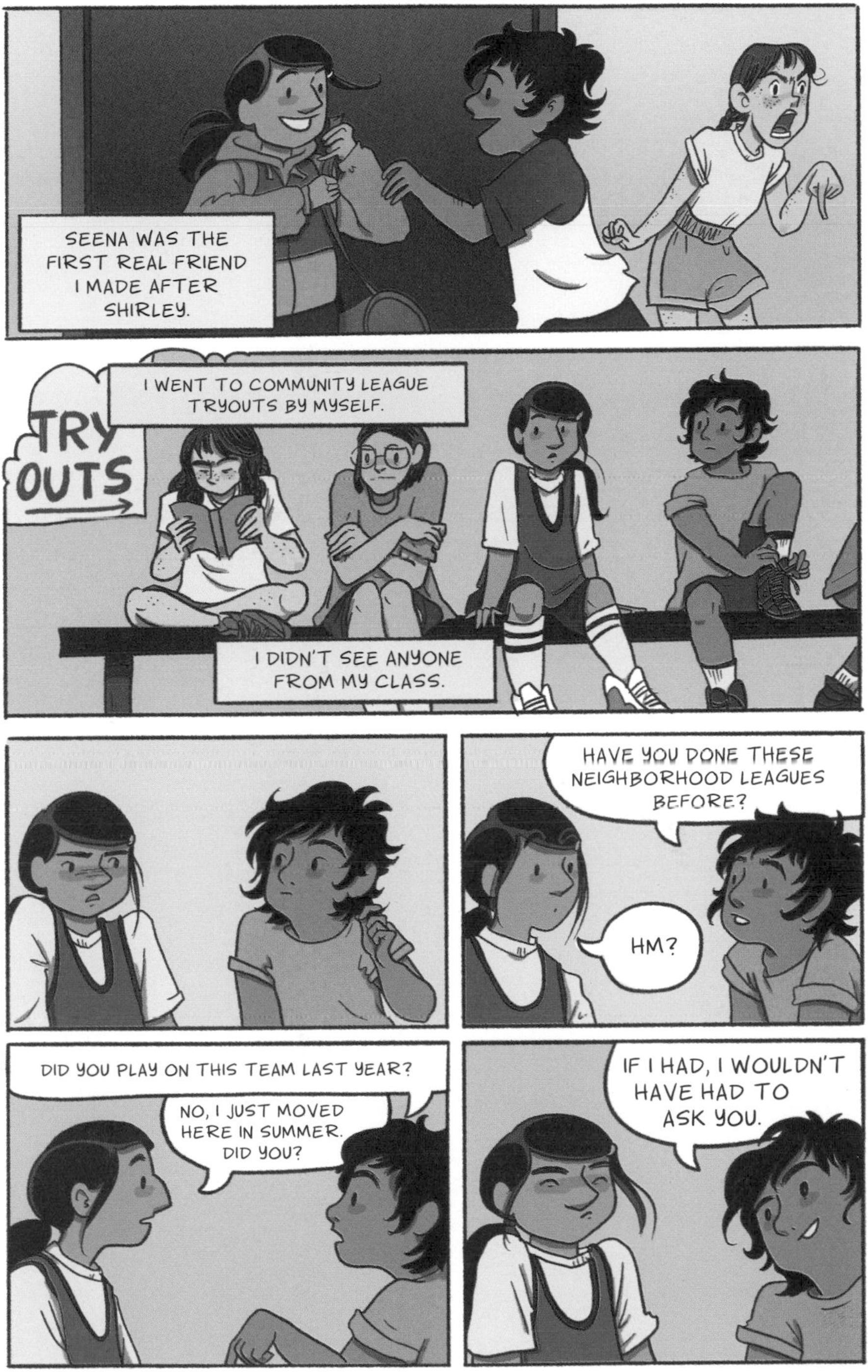
SEENA WAS THE FIRST REAL FRIEND I MADE AFTER SHIRLEY.
TRY OUTS
I WENT TO COMMUNITY LEAGUE TRYOUTS BY MYSELF.
I DIDN'T SEE ANYONE FROM MY CLASS.
HAVE YOU DONE THESE NEIGHBORHOOD LEAGUES BEFORE?
HM?
DID YOU PLAY ON THIS TEAM LAST YEAR?
NO, I JUST MOVED HERE IN SUMMER. DID YOU?
IF I HAD, I WOULDN'T HAVE HAD TO ASK YOU.

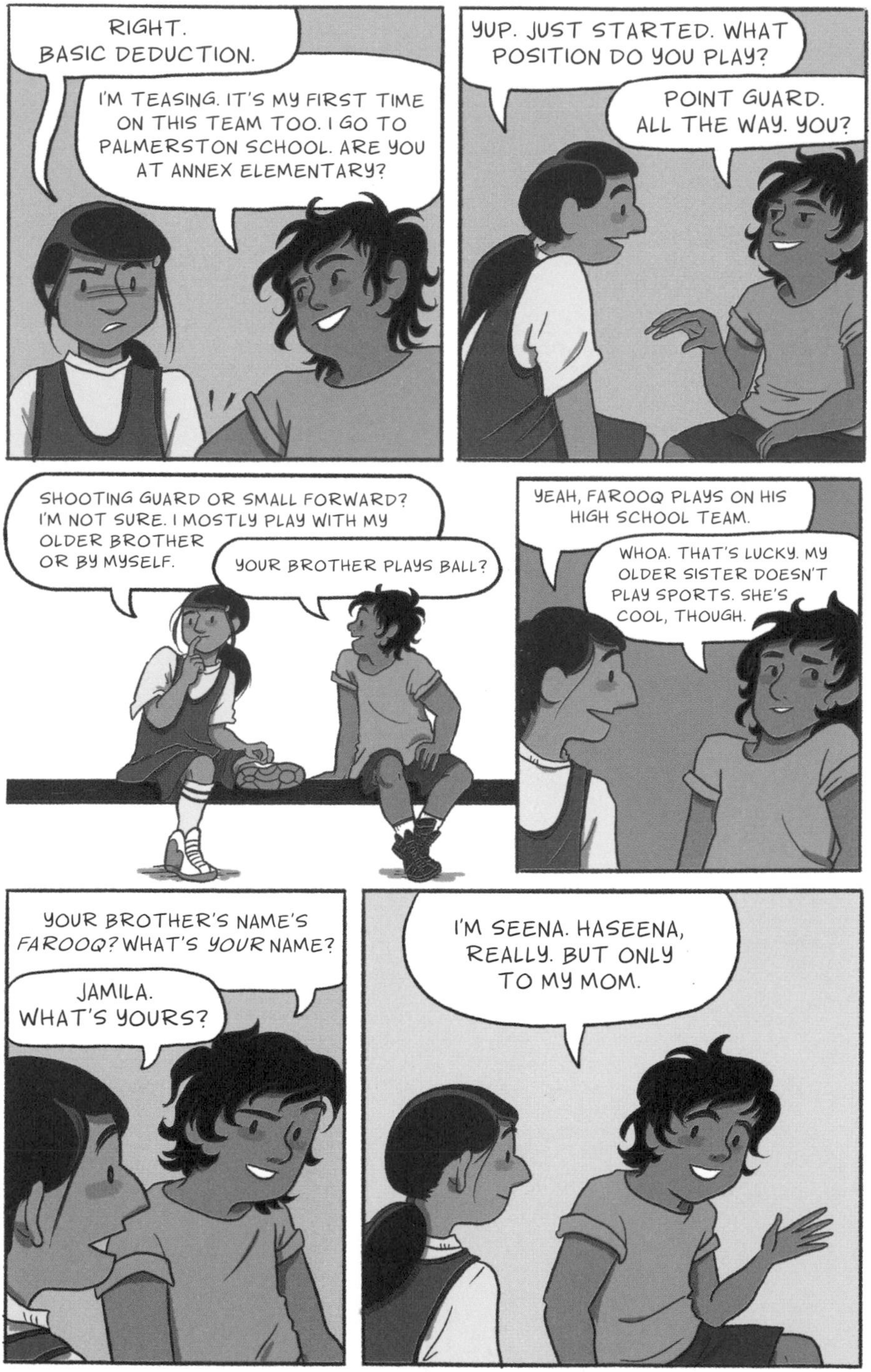
RIGHT. BASIC DEDUCTION.
I'M TEASING. IT'S MY FIRST TIME ON THIS TEAM TOO. I GO TO PALMERSTON SCHOOL. ARE YOU AT ANNEX ELEMENTARY?
YUP. JUST STARTED. WHAT POSITION DO YOU PLAY?
POINT GUARD. ALL THE WAY. YOU?
SHOOTING GUARD OR SMALL FORWARD? I'M NOT SURE. I MOSTLY PLAY WITH MY OLDER BROTHER OR BY MYSELF.
YOUR BROTHER PLAYS BALL?
YEAH, FAROOQ PLAYS ON HIS HIGH SCHOOL TEAM.
WHOA. THAT'S LUCKY. MY OLDER SISTER DOESN'T PLAY SPORTS. SHE'S COOL, THOUGH.
YOUR BROTHER'S NAME'S *FAROOQ?* WHAT'S *YOUR* NAME?
JAMILA. WHAT'S YOURS?
I'M SEENA. HASEENA, REALLY. BUT ONLY TO MY MOM.

ARE YOU PAKISTANI? I HAVE AN UNCLE FAROOQ ON MY DAD'S SIDE.

MY PARENTS CAME FROM PAKISTAN, BUT I WAS BORN HERE. IS YOUR UNCLE FAROOQ A SIXTEEN-YEAR-OLD GOOF-OFF WHO LIVES AT MY HOUSE? BECAUSE IF HE IS, WE ARE RELATED.

AUNTY JAMILA?!

YES, BHANJI! IT IS, I, YOUR AUNTY. I'M VERY DISAPPOINTED IN HOW MUCH TIME YOU PLAY BASKETBALL.

OH AUNTY! IT'S JUST YOUR EYESIGHT! I'M NOT EVEN PLAYING BALL! I'M STUDYING RIGHT NOW!

WHERE ARE YOU? I CAN'T SEE! FIND MY GLASSES!

HA HA HA HA HAHAHAHA HA

WHERE ARE SEENA AND JAMILA? YOU'RE UP NEXT!

THAT'S US!

HERE! WE'RE HERE!

SEENA WAS FUNNY.

15

SEENA WAS **GOOD** TOO.
WE BOTH MADE THE TEAM, NO PROBLEM.

COACH TRIED ME ON DIFFERENT
POSITIONS, WHICH WAS FUN
AND KIND OF SCARY. I'D NEVER
PLAYED ON A BIG TEAM BEFORE.

SEENA WAS A POINT GUARD ALL RIGHT.
THAT'S SORT OF THE LEADERSHIP POSITION.

THEY DRIVE THE PLAYS. THEY PASS
A LOT—NO BALL-HOGS—AND THEY
GOTTA REALLY HOLLER AT EVERYONE
TO KEEP TRACK OF WHO'S WHERE.

SEENA WAS GREAT
AT ALL OF IT.

RIGHT AWAY,
EVERYONE WAS KIND
OF IN AWE OF HER.

ME INCLUDED.

BUT IT TURNED OUT SEENA AND I HAD SO MUCH IN COMMON.

MY MOM REALLY LIKED YOUR MOM.

REALLY? SHE CAN BE PRETTY TOUGH.

SHE SAID YOUR MOM IS REALLY FUNNY.

ARE YOU SERIOUS?

UH-HUH.

HER MOM'S AFGHAN AND HER DAD'S PAKISTANI, SO WHEN *MY* MOM INSISTED ON CALLING **AND** MEETING IN PERSON BEFORE I COULD COME OVER, SEENA TOTALLY GOT IT. HER PARENTS HAD INSISTED ON THE SAME THING THEMSELVES.

I GUESS SHE'S KINDA FUNNY . . .

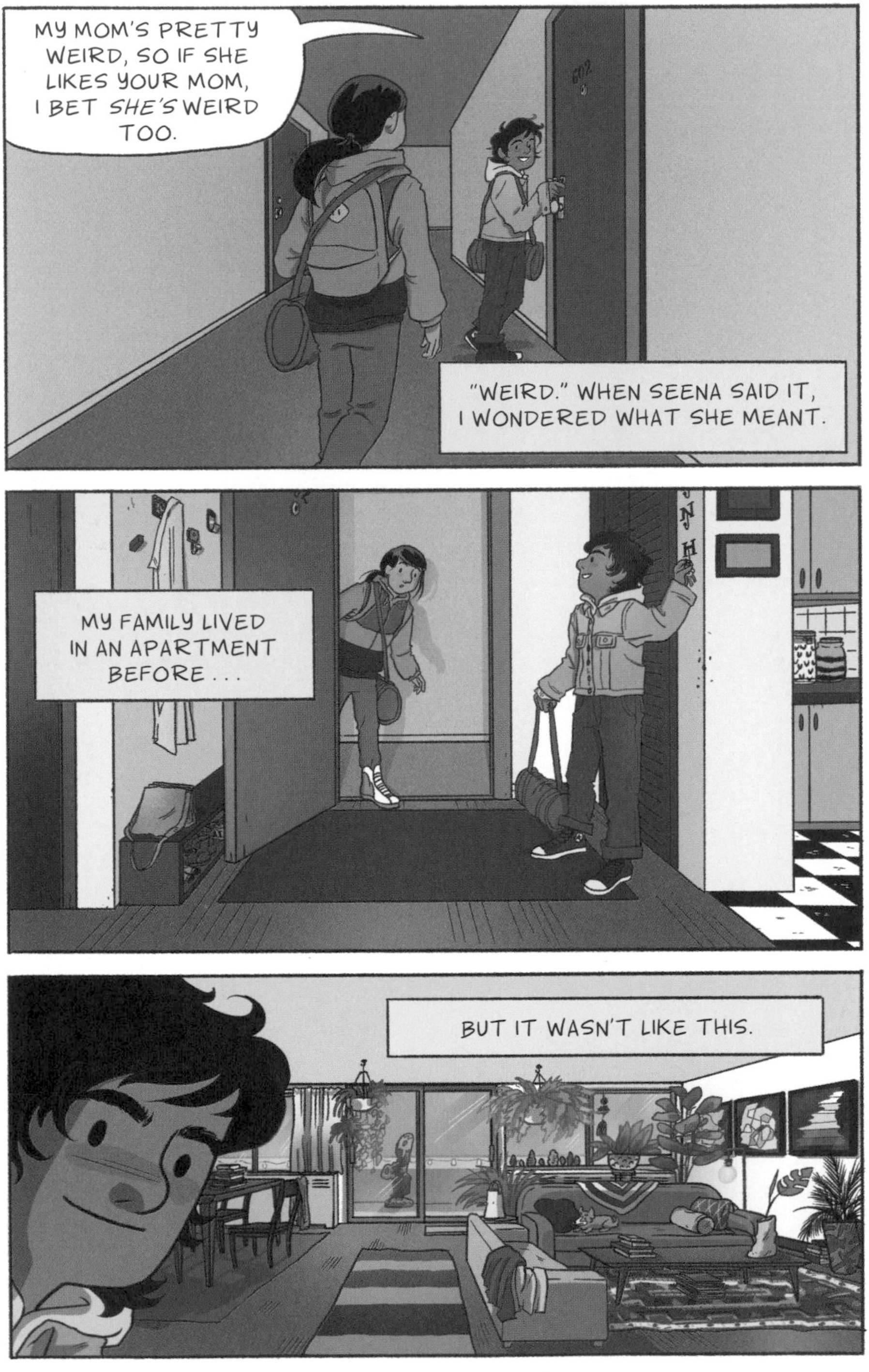
MY MOM'S PRETTY WEIRD, SO IF SHE LIKES YOUR MOM, I BET *SHE'S* WEIRD TOO.
"WEIRD." WHEN SEENA SAID IT, I WONDERED WHAT SHE MEANT.
MY FAMILY LIVED IN AN APARTMENT BEFORE . . .
BUT IT WASN'T LIKE THIS.

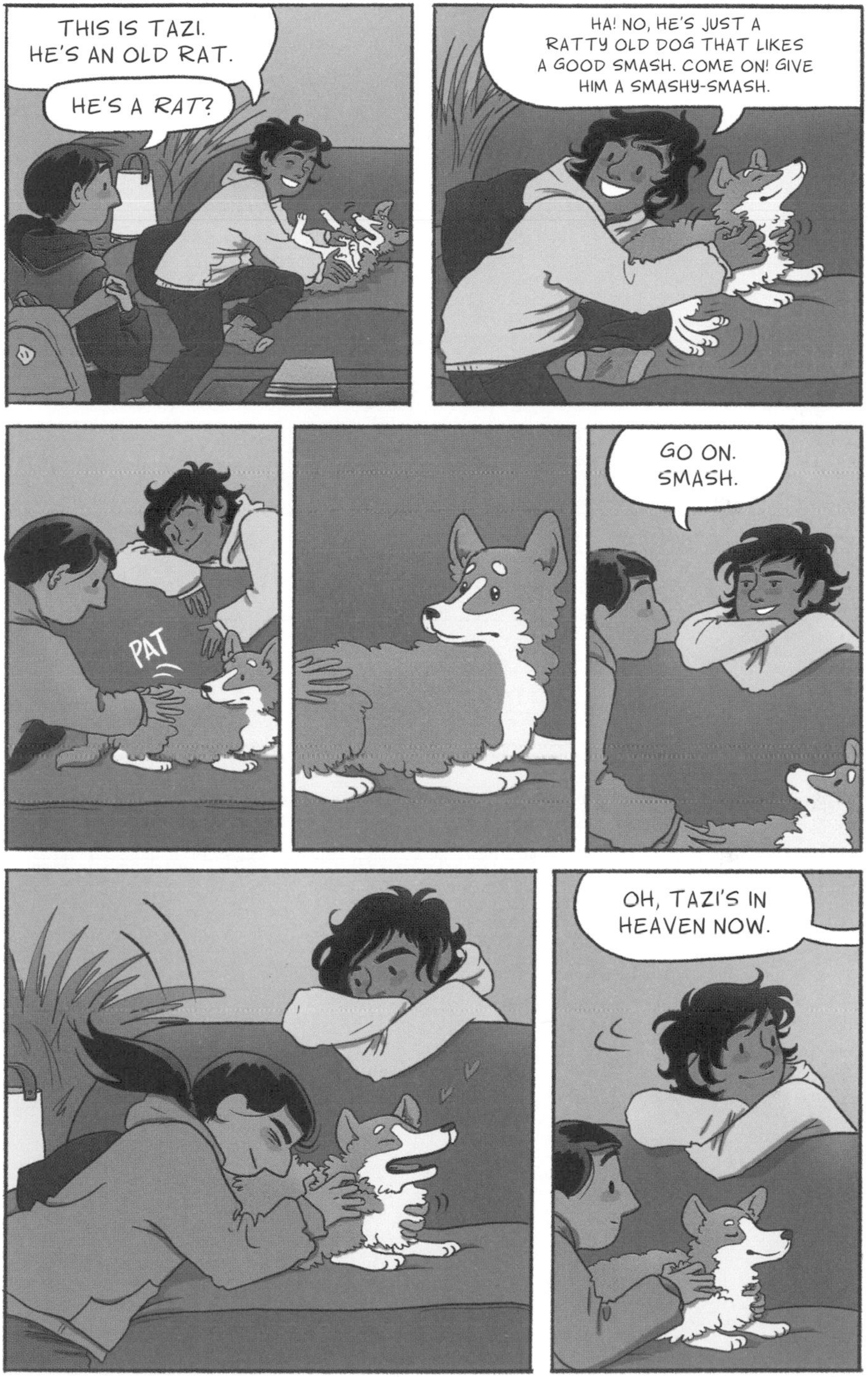
THIS IS TAZI. HE'S AN OLD RAT.
HE'S A *RAT*?
HA! NO, HE'S JUST A RATTY OLD DOG THAT LIKES A GOOD SMASH. COME ON! GIVE HIM A SMASHY-SMASH.
PAT
GO ON. SMASH.
OH, TAZI'S IN HEAVEN NOW.

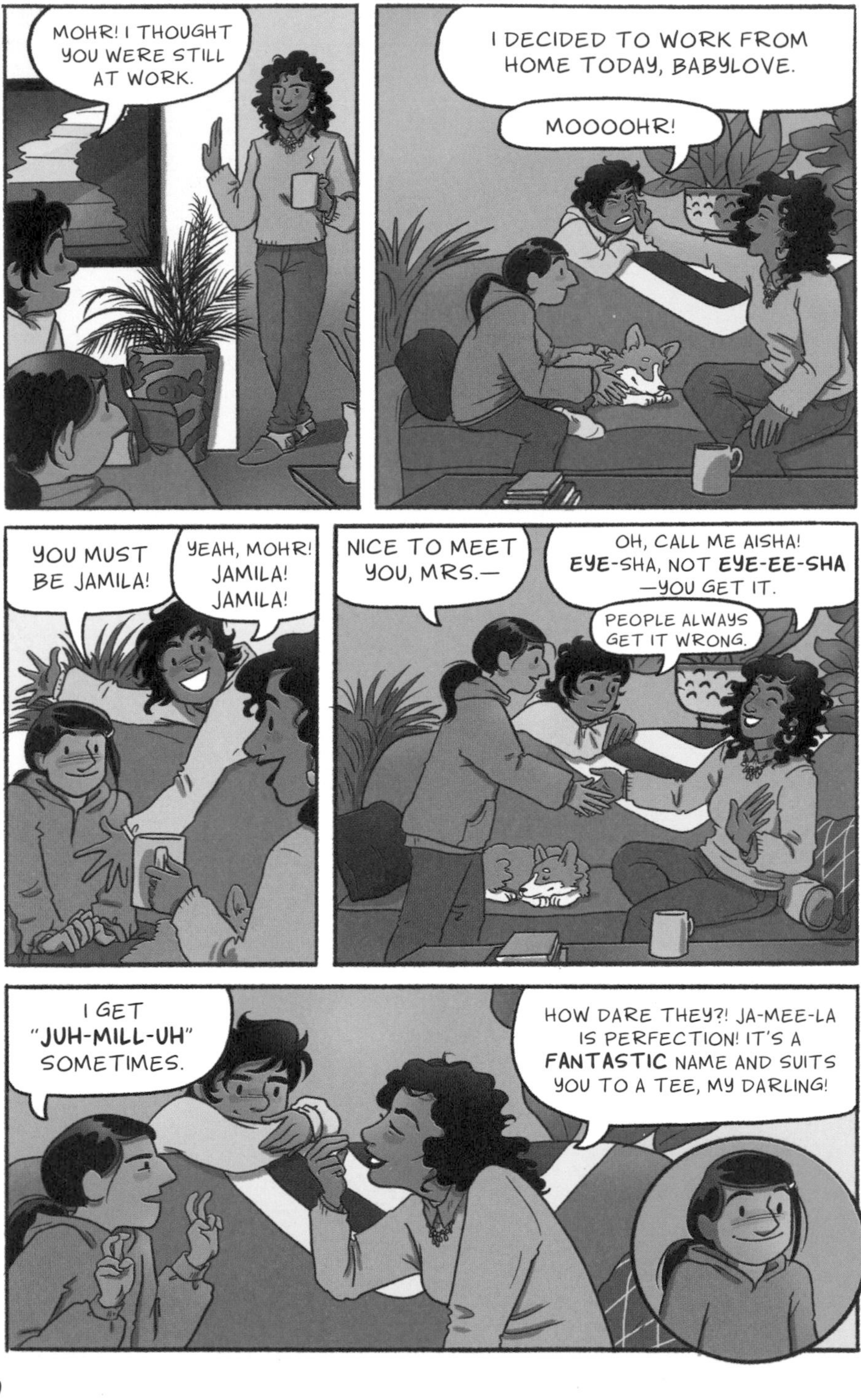
MOHR! I THOUGHT YOU WERE STILL AT WORK.
I DECIDED TO WORK FROM HOME TODAY, BABYLOVE.
MOOOOHR!
YOU MUST BE JAMILA!
YEAH, MOHR! JAMILA! JAMILA!
NICE TO MEET YOU, MRS.—
OH, CALL ME AISHA! **EYE**-SHA, NOT **EYE-EE-SHA** —YOU GET IT.
PEOPLE ALWAYS GET IT WRONG.
I GET "**JUH-MILL-UH**" SOMETIMES.
HOW DARE THEY?! JA-MEE-LA IS PERFECTION! IT'S A **FANTASTIC** NAME AND SUITS YOU TO A TEE, MY DARLING!

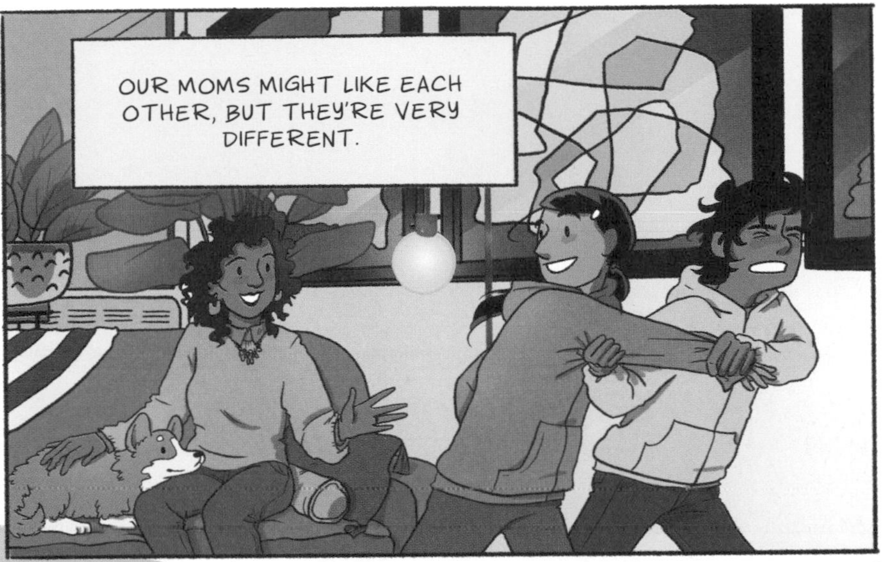
OUR MOMS MIGHT LIKE EACH OTHER, BUT THEY'RE VERY DIFFERENT.

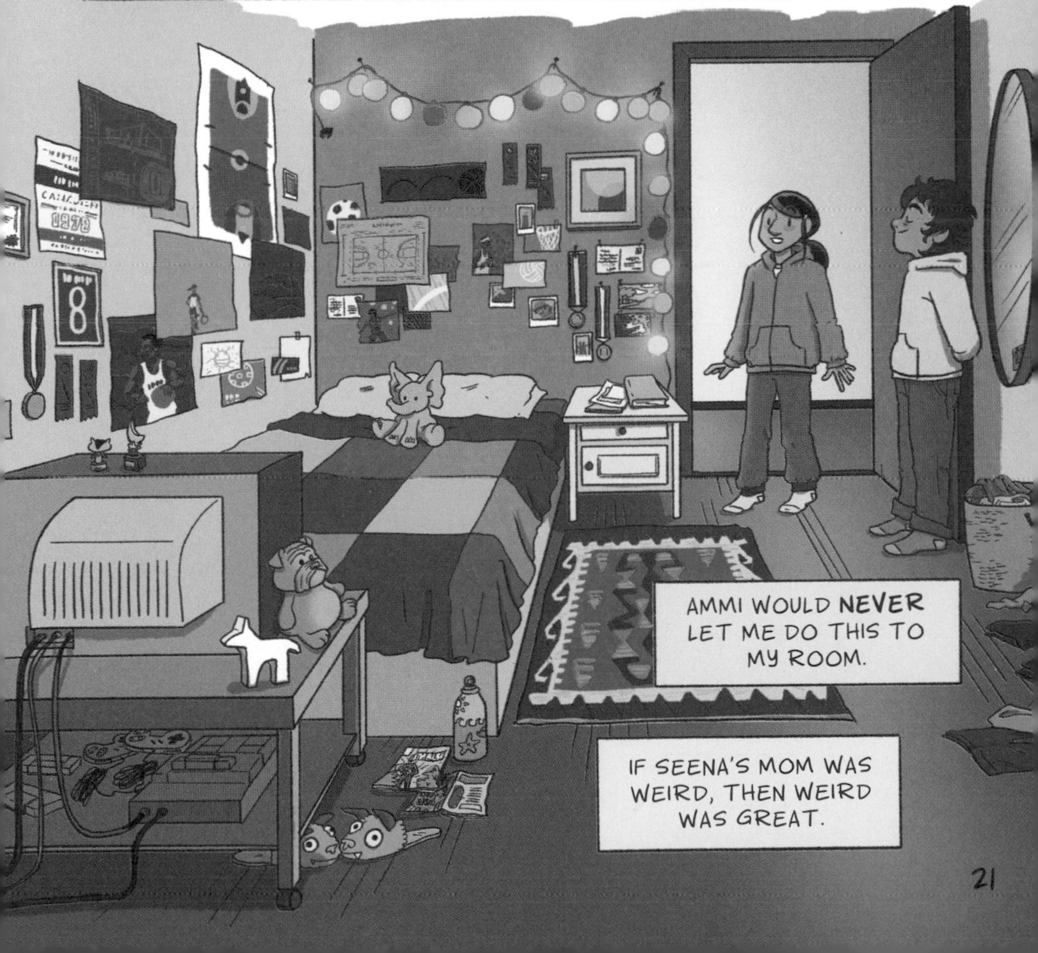
AMMI WOULD **NEVER** LET ME DO THIS TO MY ROOM.
IF SEENA'S MOM WAS WEIRD, THEN WEIRD WAS GREAT.

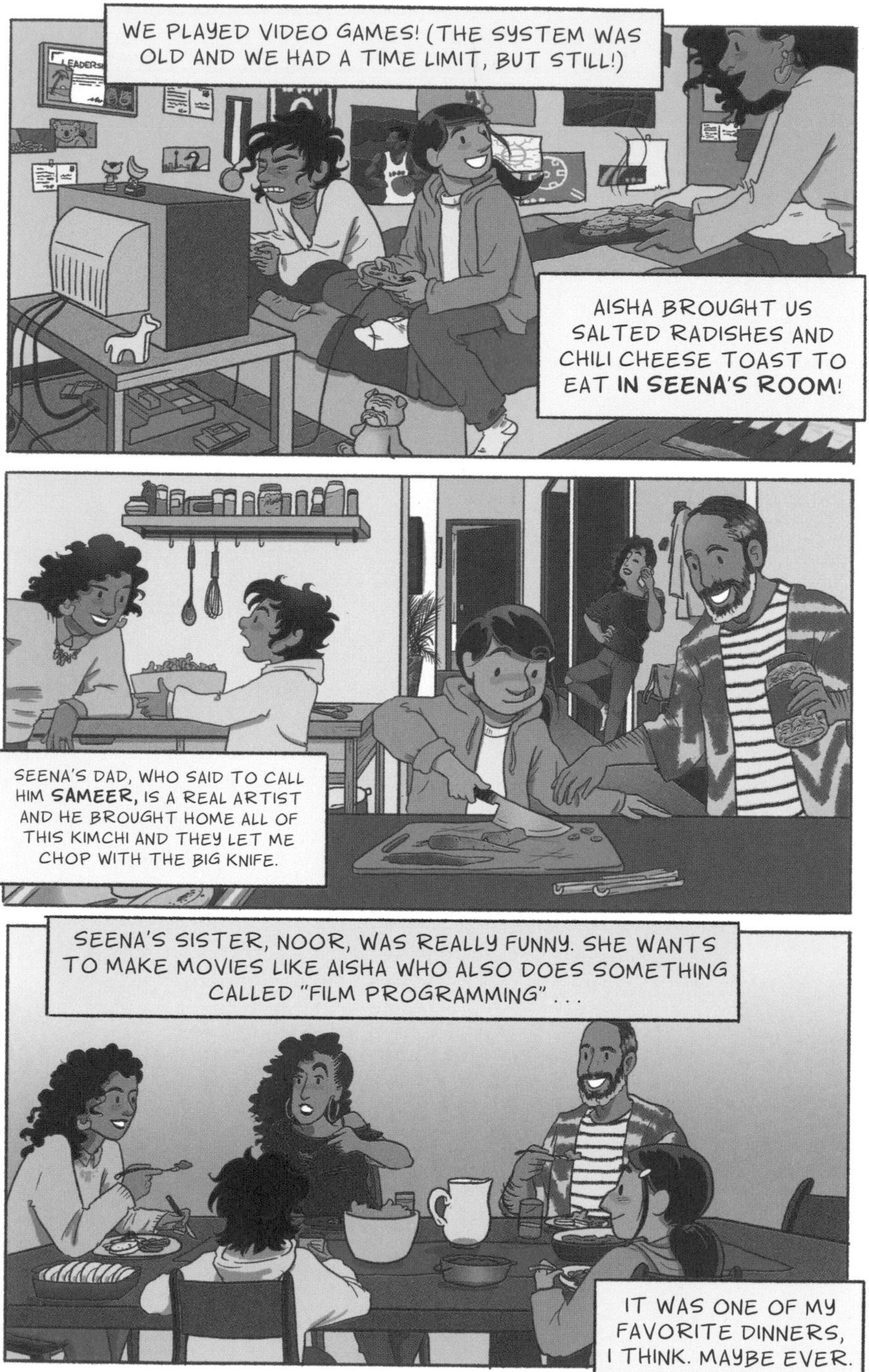
WE PLAYED VIDEO GAMES! (THE SYSTEM WAS OLD AND WE HAD A TIME LIMIT, BUT STILL!)
AISHA BROUGHT US SALTED RADISHES AND CHILI CHEESE TOAST TO EAT **IN SEENA'S ROOM**!
SEENA'S DAD, WHO SAID TO CALL HIM **SAMEER,** IS A REAL ARTIST AND HE BROUGHT HOME ALL OF THIS KIMCHI AND THEY LET ME CHOP WITH THE BIG KNIFE.
SEENA'S SISTER, NOOR, WAS REALLY FUNNY. SHE WANTS TO MAKE MOVIES LIKE AISHA WHO ALSO DOES SOMETHING CALLED "FILM PROGRAMMING" . . .
IT WAS ONE OF MY FAVORITE DINNERS, I THINK. MAYBE EVER.

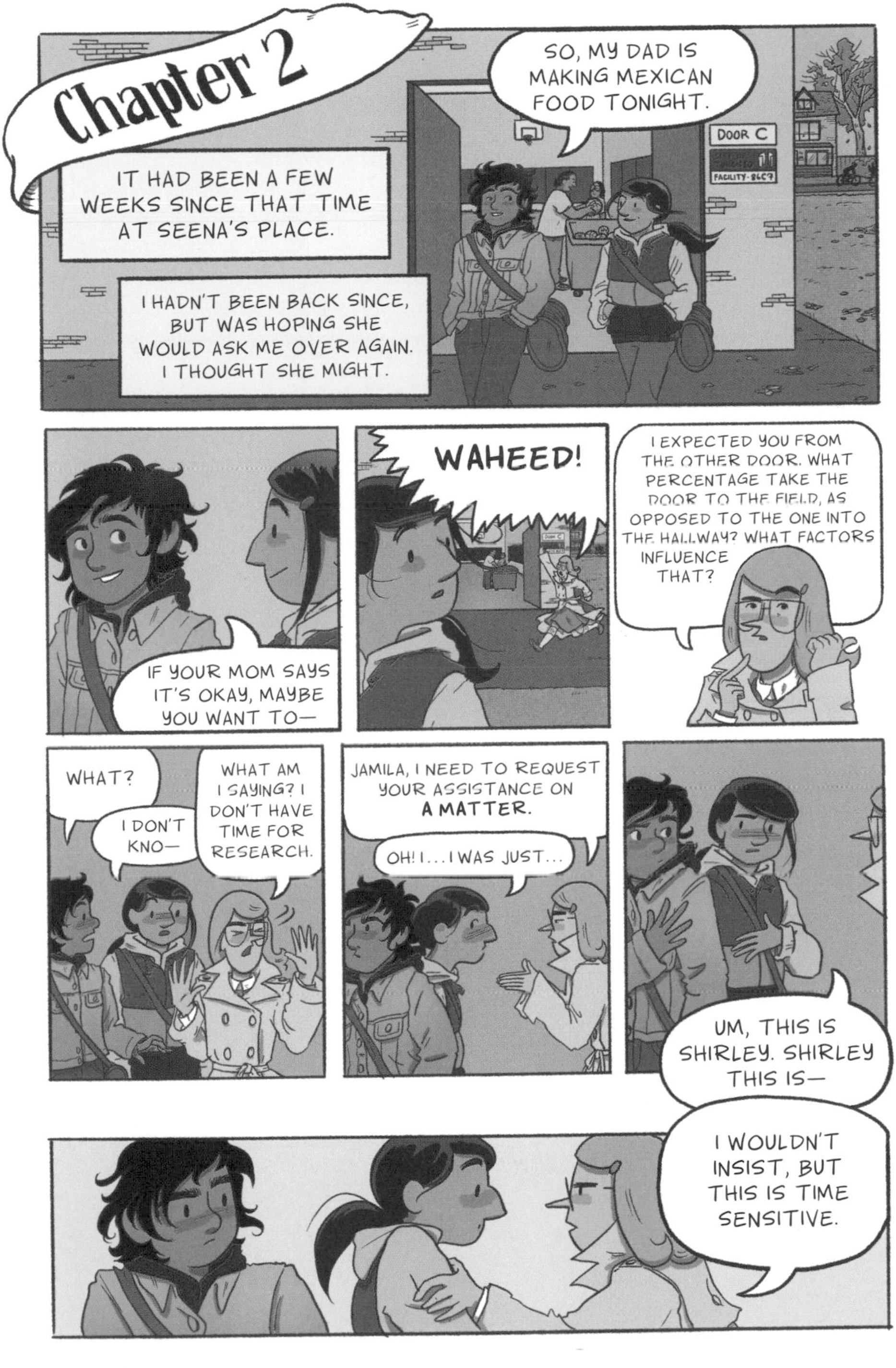
Chapter 2
SO, MY DAD IS MAKING MEXICAN FOOD TONIGHT.
IT HAD BEEN A FEW WEEKS SINCE THAT TIME AT SEENA'S PLACE.
I HADN'T BEEN BACK SINCE, BUT WAS HOPING SHE WOULD ASK ME OVER AGAIN. I THOUGHT SHE MIGHT.
DOOR C
FACILITY-86C7
IF YOUR MOM SAYS IT'S OKAY, MAYBE YOU WANT TO—
WAHEED!
I EXPECTED YOU FROM THE OTHER DOOR. WHAT PERCENTAGE TAKE THE DOOR TO THE FIELD, AS OPPOSED TO THE ONE INTO THE HALLWAY? WHAT FACTORS INFLUENCE THAT?
WHAT?
I DON'T KNO—
WHAT AM I SAYING? I DON'T HAVE TIME FOR RESEARCH.
JAMILA, I NEED TO REQUEST YOUR ASSISTANCE ON **A MATTER**.
OH! I... I WAS JUST...
UM, THIS IS SHIRLEY. SHIRLEY THIS IS—
I WOULDN'T INSIST, BUT THIS IS TIME SENSITIVE.

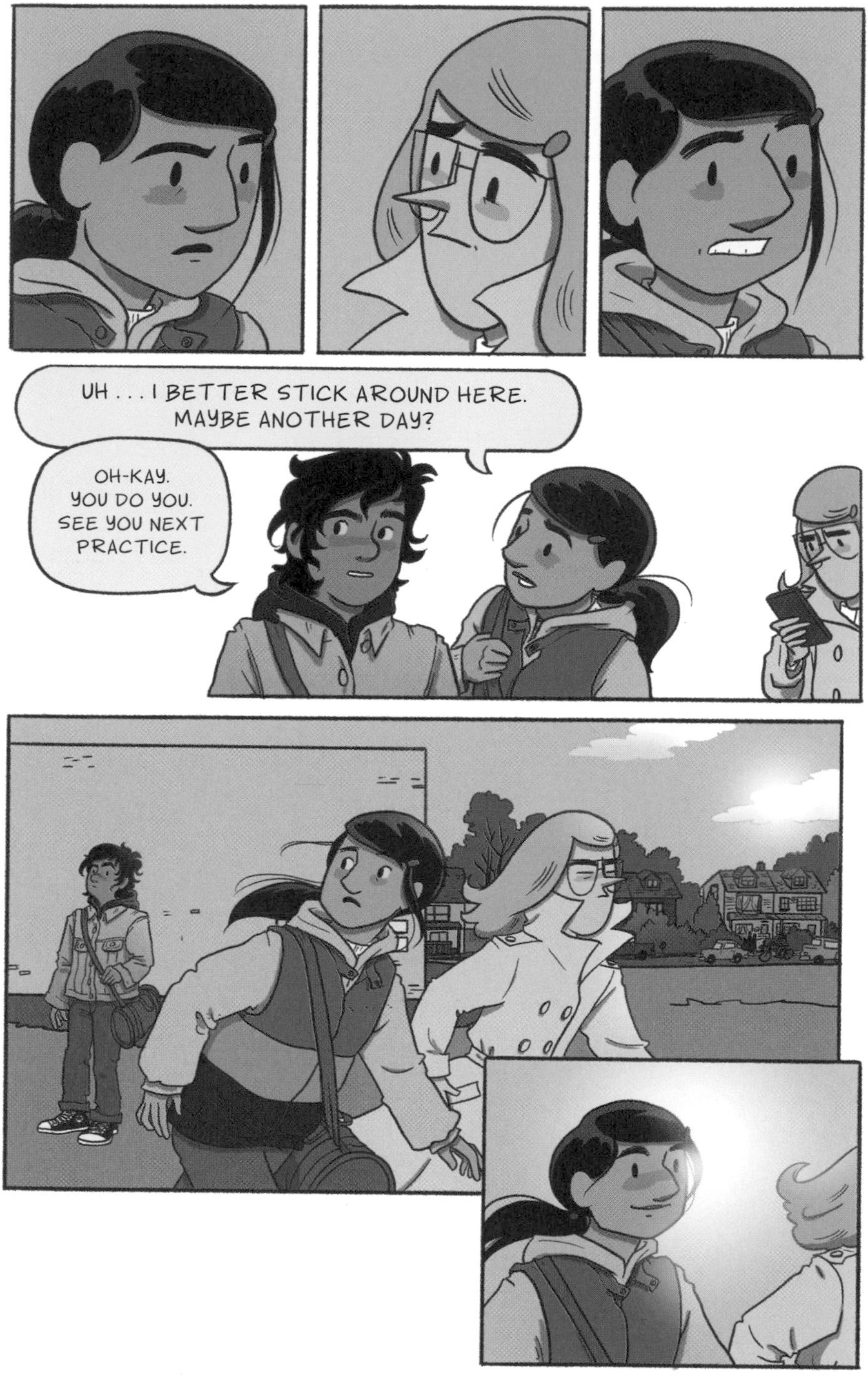
UH . . . I BETTER STICK AROUND HERE. MAYBE ANOTHER DAY?
OH-KAY. YOU DO YOU. SEE YOU NEXT PRACTICE.

25

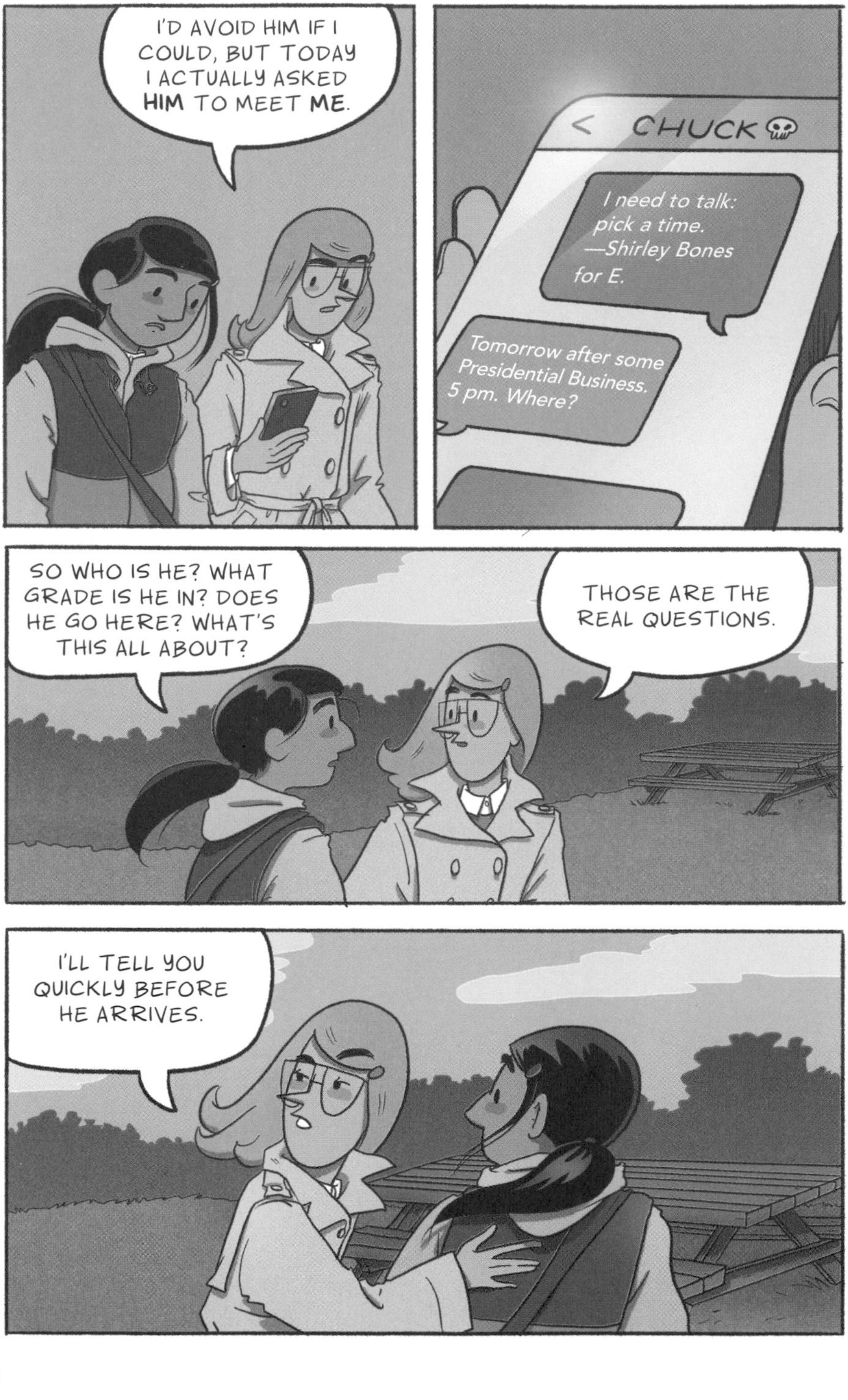
I'D AVOID HIM IF I COULD, BUT TODAY I ACTUALLY ASKED HIM TO MEET ME.
< CHUCK
I need to talk: pick a time. —Shirley Bones for E.
Tomorrow after some Presidential Business. 5 pm. Where?
SO WHO IS HE? WHAT GRADE IS HE IN? DOES HE GO HERE? WHAT'S THIS ALL ABOUT?
THOSE ARE THE REAL QUESTIONS.
I'LL TELL YOU QUICKLY BEFORE HE ARRIVES.

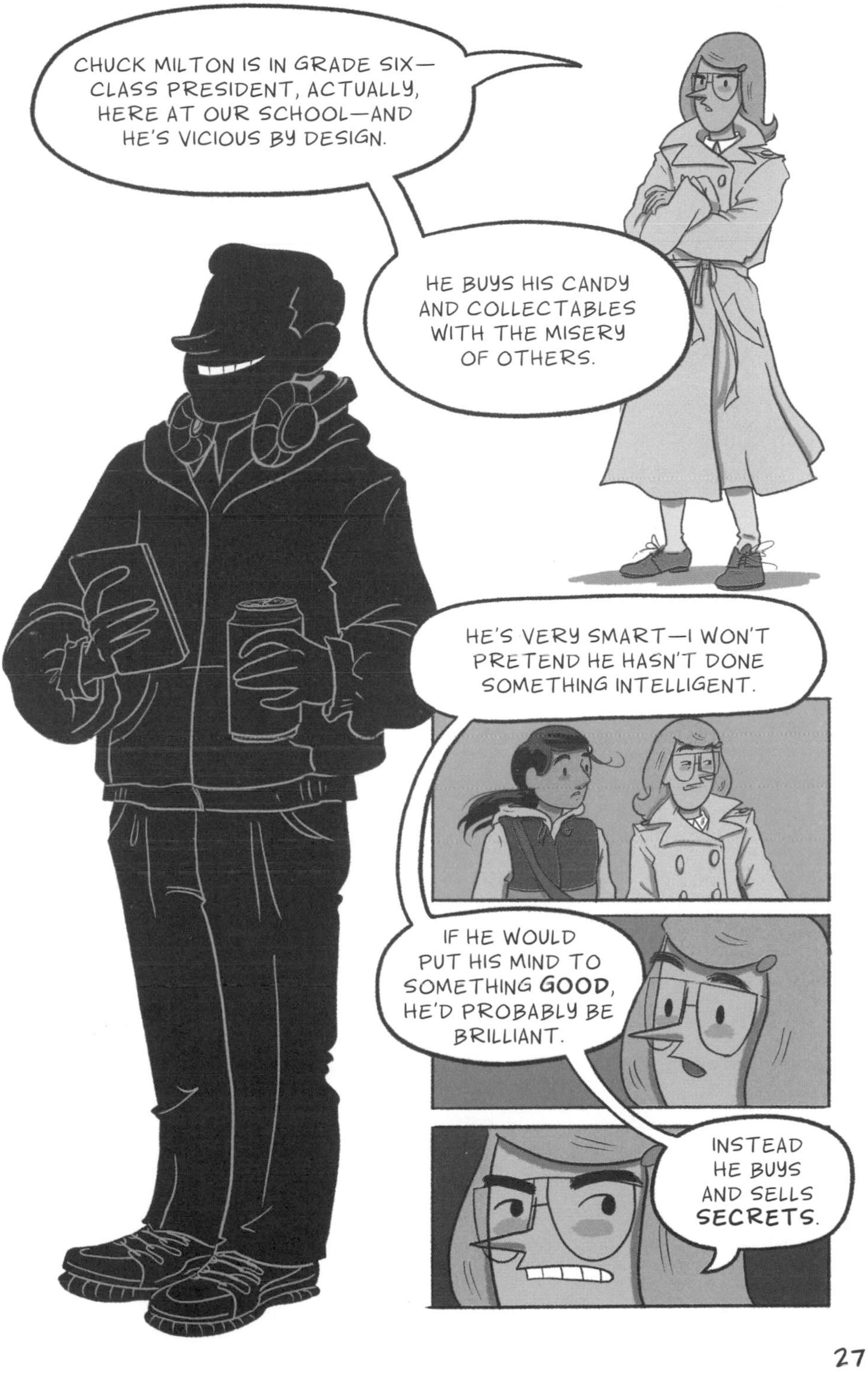
CHUCK MILTON IS IN GRADE SIX—CLASS PRESIDENT, ACTUALLY, HERE AT OUR SCHOOL—AND HE'S VICIOUS BY DESIGN.
HE BUYS HIS CANDY AND COLLECTABLES WITH THE MISERY OF OTHERS.
HE'S VERY SMART—I WON'T PRETEND HE HASN'T DONE SOMETHING INTELLIGENT.
IF HE WOULD PUT HIS MIND TO SOMETHING **GOOD**, HE'D PROBABLY BE BRILLIANT.
INSTEAD HE BUYS AND SELLS **SECRETS**.

28

29

CHUCK HELD ON TO A JUICY NOTE FOR A WHOLE YEAR JUST TO SAVE IT FOR THE WEEK BEFORE THE SCHOOL PLAY.

IF IT WOULD HAVE GOT OUT, IRIS ACOSTA—YOU DON'T KNOW HER—WOULD HAVE LOST THE LEAD ROLE.

HE COULD ASK ANY PRICE HE WANTED.

YOU CAN BET SHE PAID.

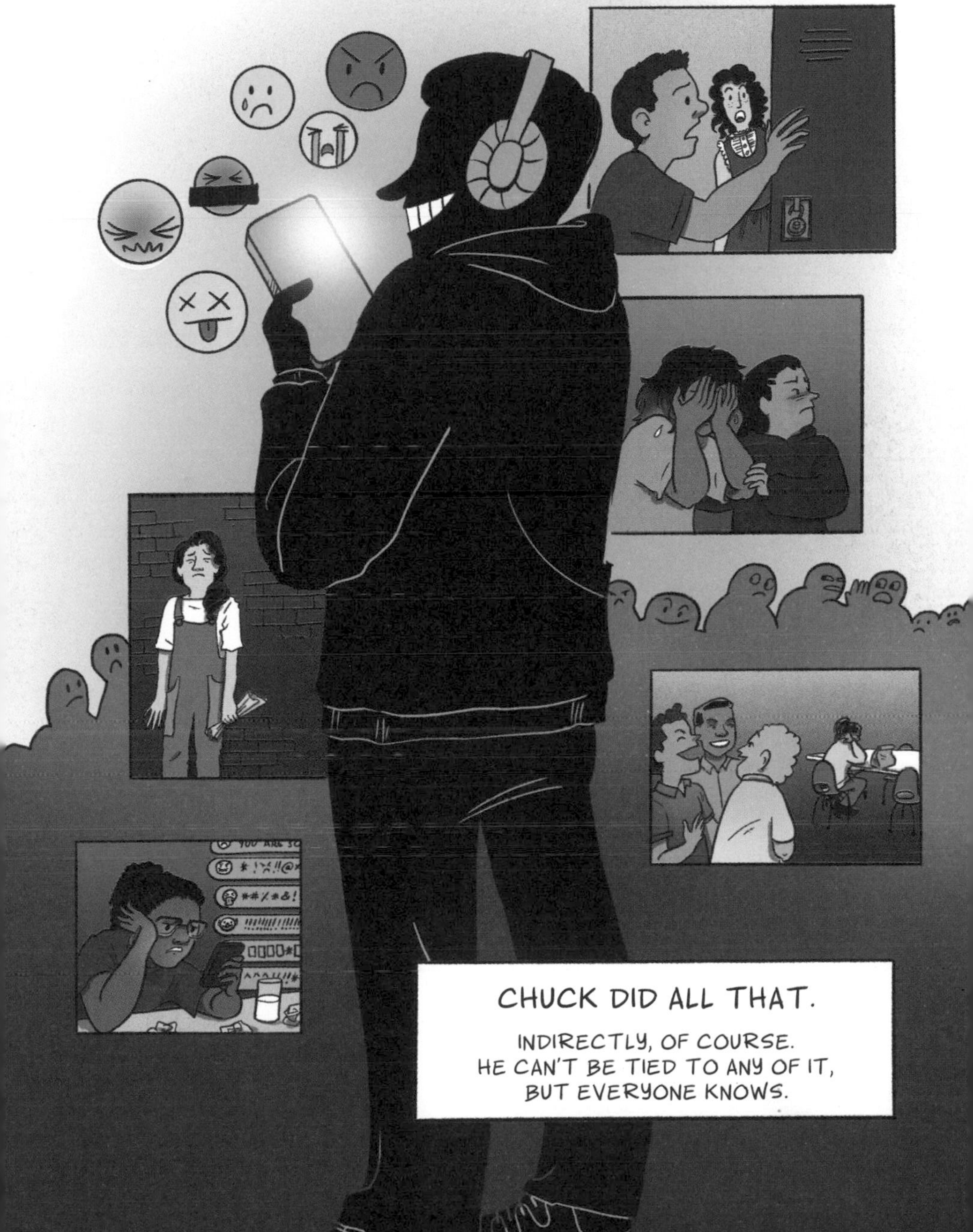
CHUCK DID ALL THAT.
INDIRECTLY, OF COURSE.
HE CAN'T BE TIED TO ANY OF IT,
BUT EVERYONE KNOWS.

THERE ARE BULLIES AND JERKS THAT WILL TRIP YOU AND STEAL YOUR LUNCH WITHOUT THINKING TWICE, BUT IT'S A SPECIAL KIND OF KID WHO TORTURES OTHER KIDS FOR THE FUN OF IT— WHILE THE TEACHERS GIVE HIM STRAIGHT A'S.

SHIRLEY DIDN'T GET THIS FIRED UP VERY OFTEN.

AND NO ONE TELLS ON HIM?

THEY WOULDN'T DARE.

HE ONLY BUYS REAL DIRT THAT KIDS DO NOT WANT OUT THERE. WHO CARES IF HE GETS A WEEK OF DETENTION IF EVERYONE STILL FINDS OUT YOU PEED YOUR PANTS ON THE SCHOOL TRIP?

HE DOESN'T ATTACK PEOPLE WITH NOTHING TO HIDE. EVERYONE ON HIS LIST HAS A REAL SECRET, SO HE HAS ALL THE POWER.

SO WHY ARE WE MEETING HIM?

32

BECAUSE MY—**OUR** NEW CLIENT, IF YOU WILL...

I WILL.

NOD

...HAS ASKED FOR HELP.

DO YOU KNOW EVA MAKWA? SHE'S IN GRADE SIX WITH CHUCK, AND A SENSITIVE NOTE OF HERS HAS FALLEN INTO HIS HANDS.

I TRUST HER AND SHE ASSURES ME THIS NOTE COULD MAKE SCHOOL A NIGHTMARE FOR HER.

CHUCK WILL SPILL THE BEANS IF EVA DOESN'T PAY UP. SHE'S SCRAMBLING TO BABYSIT AND BORROW, BUT SHE CAN'T GET ENOUGH.

SHE'S ASKED ME TO TALK TO HIM, AND SEE IF HE'LL ACCEPT WHAT SHE'S GOT.

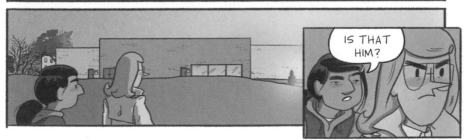

IS THAT HIM?

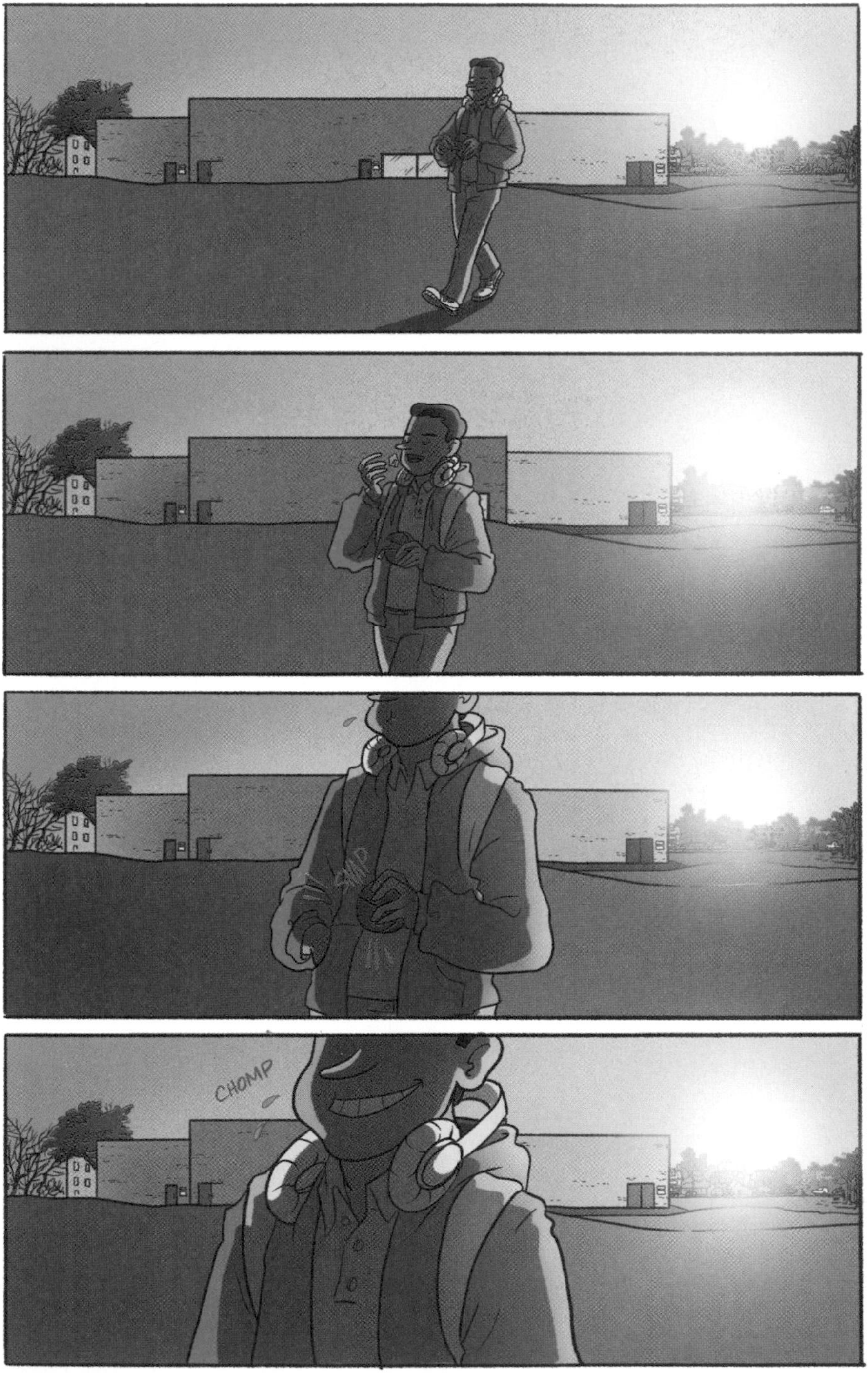
CHOMP

CANDY UPDATE

BUBBLE TAPE:
A FOOT OR MORE OF
ROLLED UP FLAT GUM.
GREAT FOR SHARING.
HYPOTHETICALLY.

POP

SORRY I'M A BIT LATE. I HAD A TEXT THAT ABSOLUTELY DEMANDED MY ATTENTION.

HE TALKED LIKE HE WAS A LAWYER OR SOME KIND OF RICH GROWN-UP ON TV. AND DRESSED LIKE WE'RE IN PRIVATE SCHOOL.

SHIRLEY? I'M CHARLES, BUT YOU KNOW THE KIDS HERE USUALLY CALL ME CHUCK AND WHO AM I TO SAY NO? HAHAHA

36

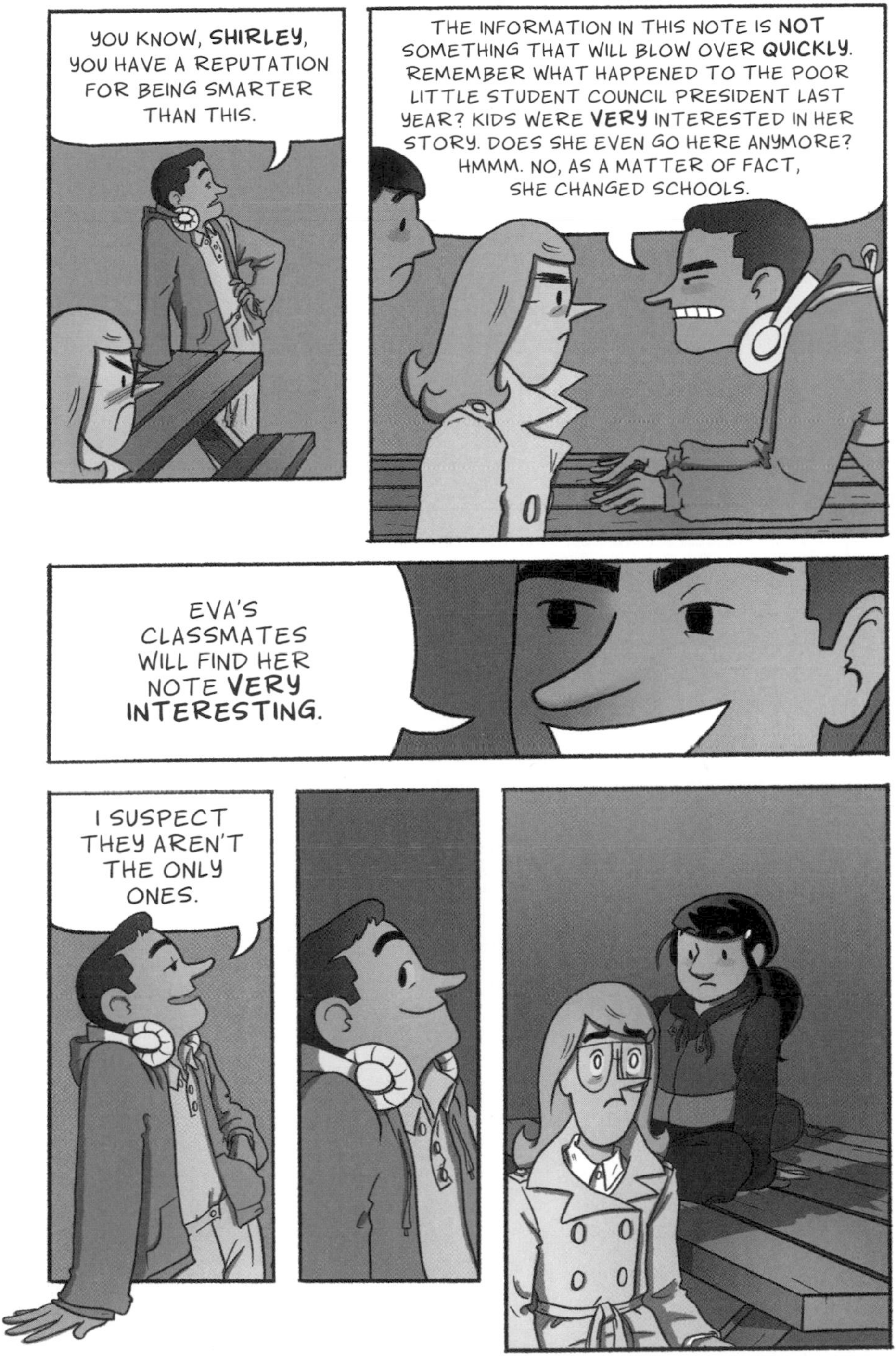

YOU KNOW, SHIRLEY, YOU HAVE A REPUTATION FOR BEING SMARTER THAN THIS.
THE INFORMATION IN THIS NOTE IS NOT SOMETHING THAT WILL BLOW OVER QUICKLY. REMEMBER WHAT HAPPENED TO THE POOR LITTLE STUDENT COUNCIL PRESIDENT LAST YEAR? KIDS WERE VERY INTERESTED IN HER STORY. DOES SHE EVEN GO HERE ANYMORE? HMMM. NO, AS A MATTER OF FACT, SHE CHANGED SCHOOLS.
EVA'S CLASSMATES WILL FIND HER NOTE VERY INTERESTING.
I SUSPECT THEY AREN'T THE ONLY ONES.

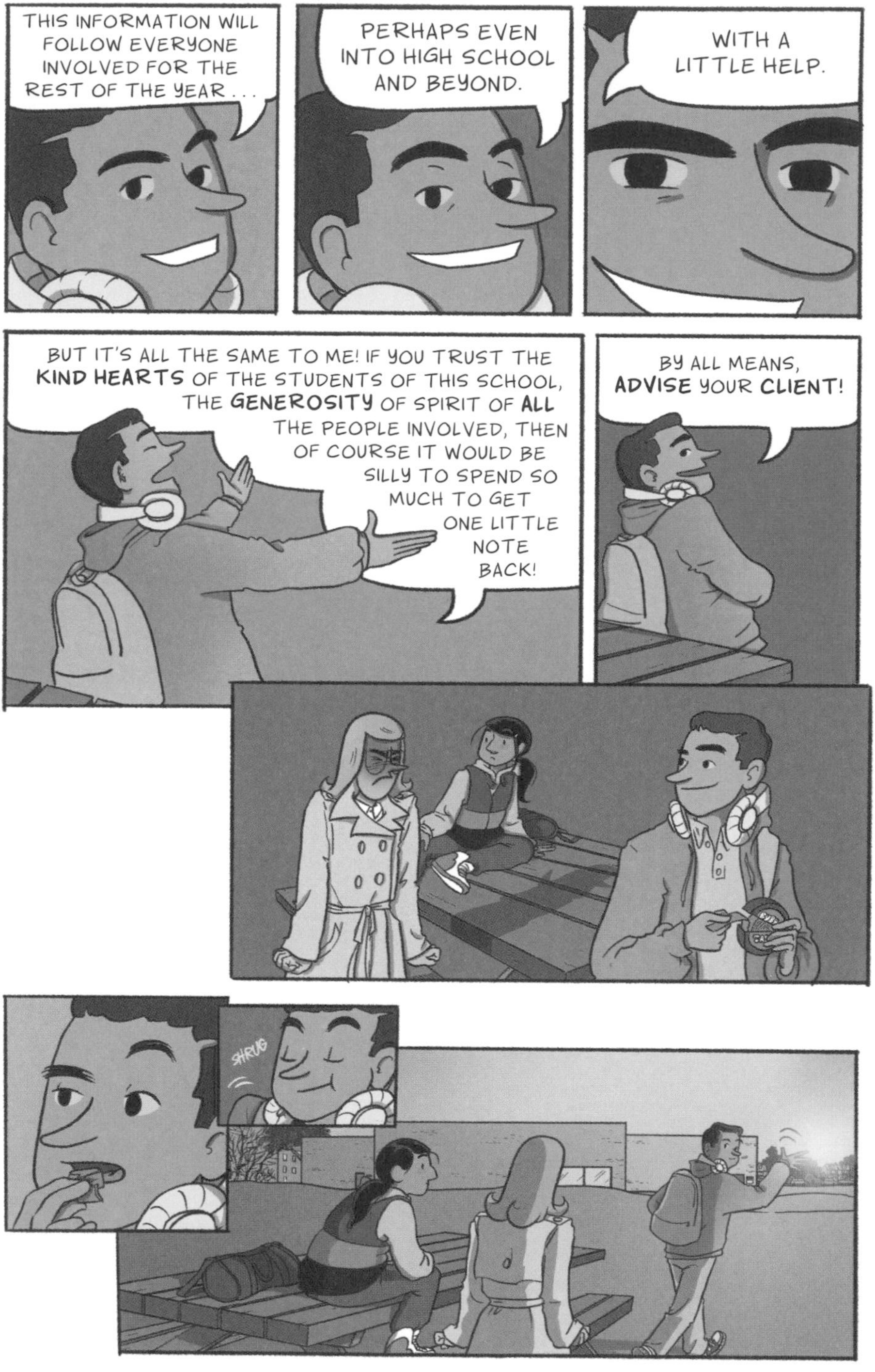
THIS INFORMATION WILL FOLLOW EVERYONE INVOLVED FOR THE REST OF THE YEAR . . .
PERHAPS EVEN INTO HIGH SCHOOL AND BEYOND.
WITH A LITTLE HELP.
BUT IT'S ALL THE SAME TO ME! IF YOU TRUST THE **KIND HEARTS** OF THE STUDENTS OF THIS SCHOOL, THE **GENEROSITY** OF SPIRIT OF **ALL** THE PEOPLE INVOLVED, THEN OF COURSE IT WOULD BE SILLY TO SPEND SO MUCH TO GET ONE LITTLE NOTE BACK!
BY ALL MEANS, **ADVISE** YOUR **CLIENT**!
SHRUG

WAIT.

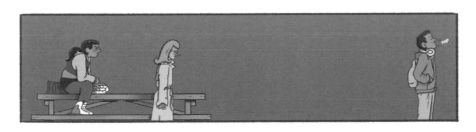

NO NEED TO RACE OFF. WE AGREE IT IS A CAREFUL ISSUE. THAT SHOULD BE TREATED CAREFULLY.

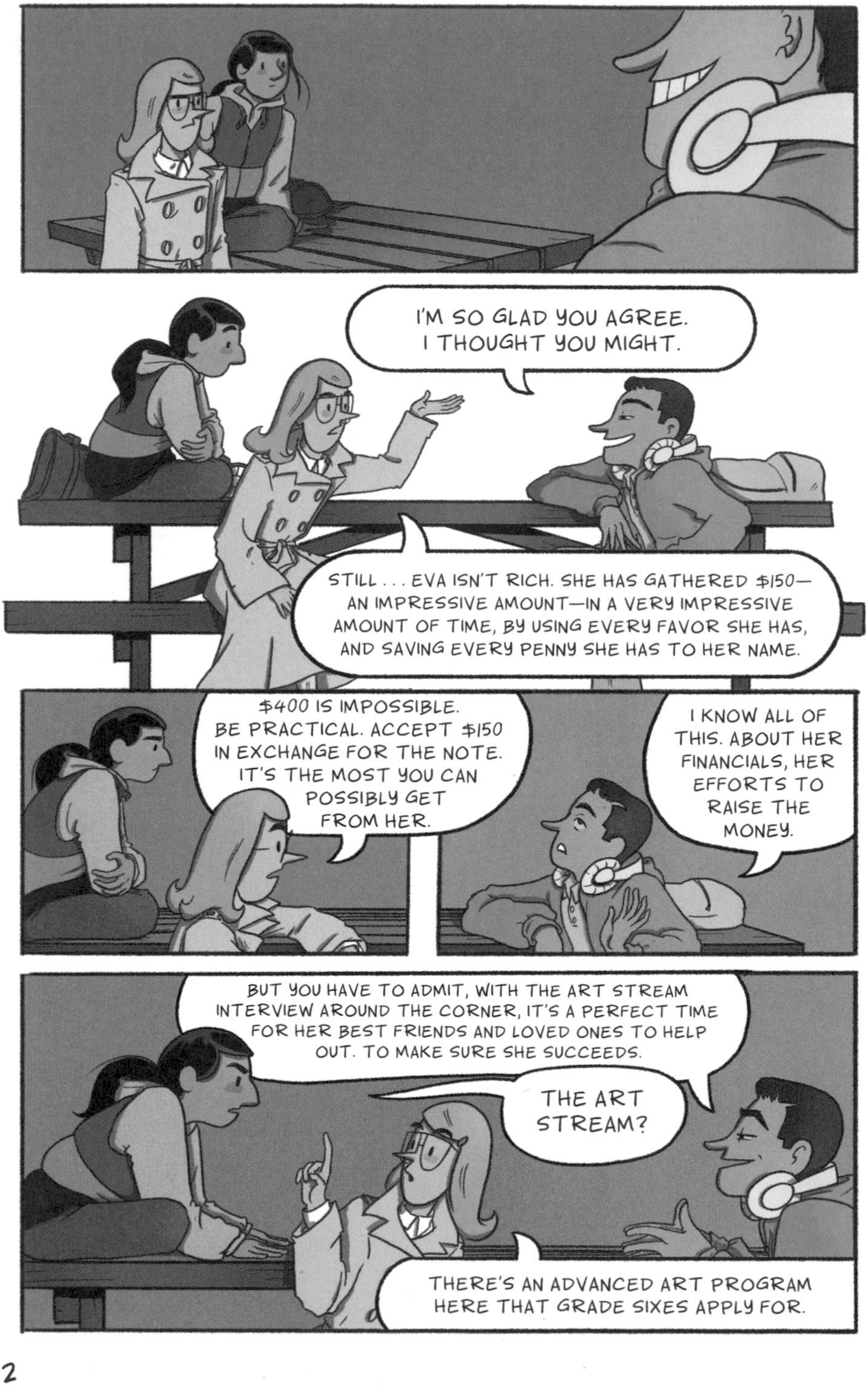
I'M SO GLAD YOU AGREE. I THOUGHT YOU MIGHT.
STILL . . . EVA ISN'T RICH. SHE HAS GATHERED $150—AN IMPRESSIVE AMOUNT—IN A VERY IMPRESSIVE AMOUNT OF TIME, BY USING EVERY FAVOR SHE HAS, AND SAVING EVERY PENNY SHE HAS TO HER NAME.
$400 IS IMPOSSIBLE. BE PRACTICAL. ACCEPT $150 IN EXCHANGE FOR THE NOTE. IT'S THE MOST YOU CAN POSSIBLY GET FROM HER.
I KNOW ALL OF THIS. ABOUT HER FINANCIALS, HER EFFORTS TO RAISE THE MONEY.
BUT YOU HAVE TO ADMIT, WITH THE ART STREAM INTERVIEW AROUND THE CORNER, IT'S A PERFECT TIME FOR HER BEST FRIENDS AND LOVED ONES TO HELP OUT. TO MAKE SURE SHE SUCCEEDS.
THE ART STREAM?
THERE'S AN ADVANCED ART PROGRAM HERE THAT GRADE SIXES APPLY FOR.

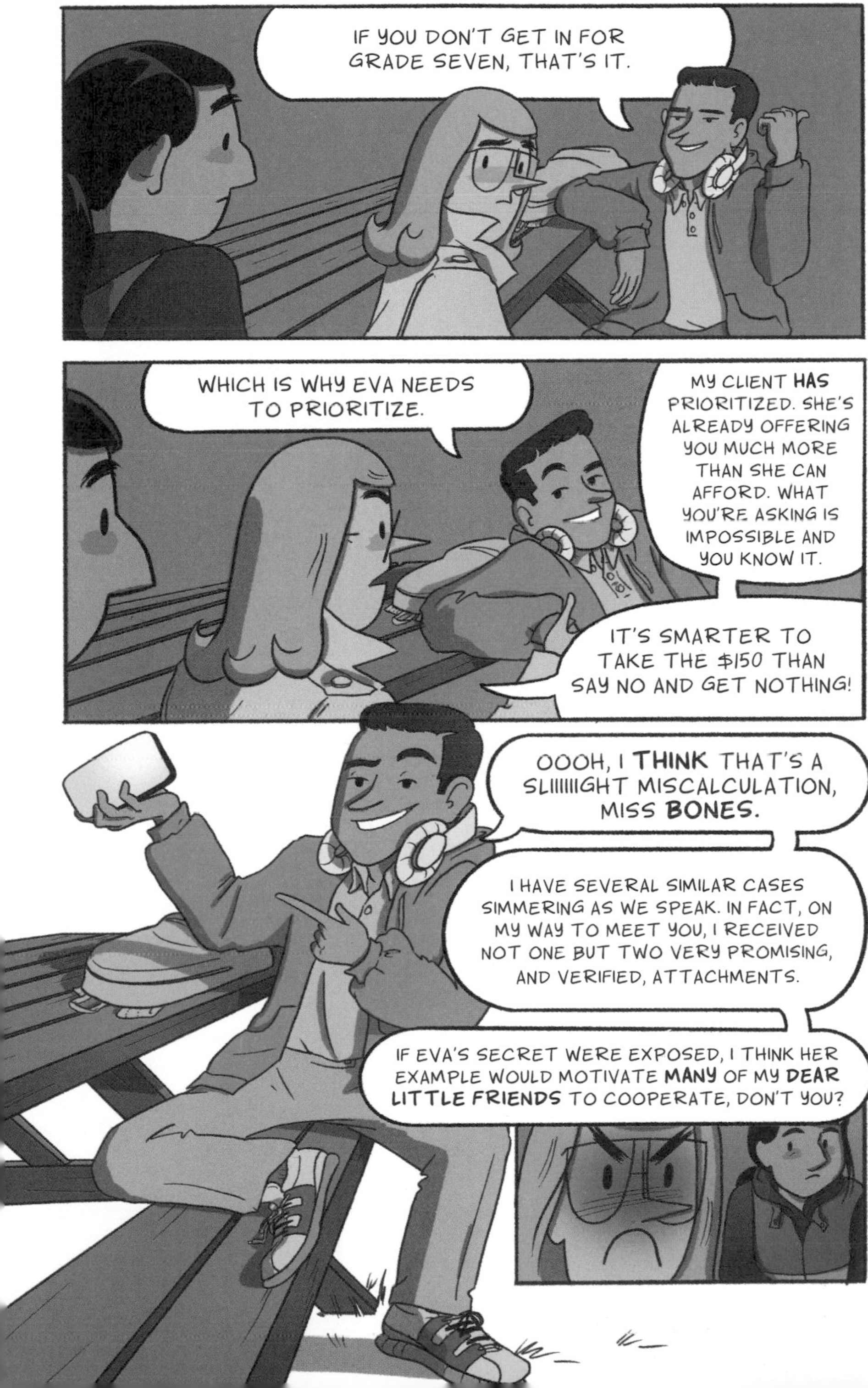
IF YOU DON'T GET IN FOR GRADE SEVEN, THAT'S IT.
WHICH IS WHY EVA NEEDS TO PRIORITIZE.
MY CLIENT **HAS** PRIORITIZED. SHE'S ALREADY OFFERING YOU MUCH MORE THAN SHE CAN AFFORD. WHAT YOU'RE ASKING IS IMPOSSIBLE AND YOU KNOW IT.
IT'S SMARTER TO TAKE THE $150 THAN SAY NO AND GET NOTHING!
OOOH, I **THINK** THAT'S A SLIIIIIGHT MISCALCULATION, MISS **BONES.**
I HAVE SEVERAL SIMILAR CASES SIMMERING AS WE SPEAK. IN FACT, ON MY WAY TO MEET YOU, I RECEIVED NOT ONE BUT TWO VERY PROMISING, AND VERIFIED, ATTACHMENTS.
IF EVA'S SECRET WERE EXPOSED, I THINK HER EXAMPLE WOULD MOTIVATE **MANY** OF MY **DEAR LITTLE FRIENDS** TO COOPERATE, DON'T YOU?

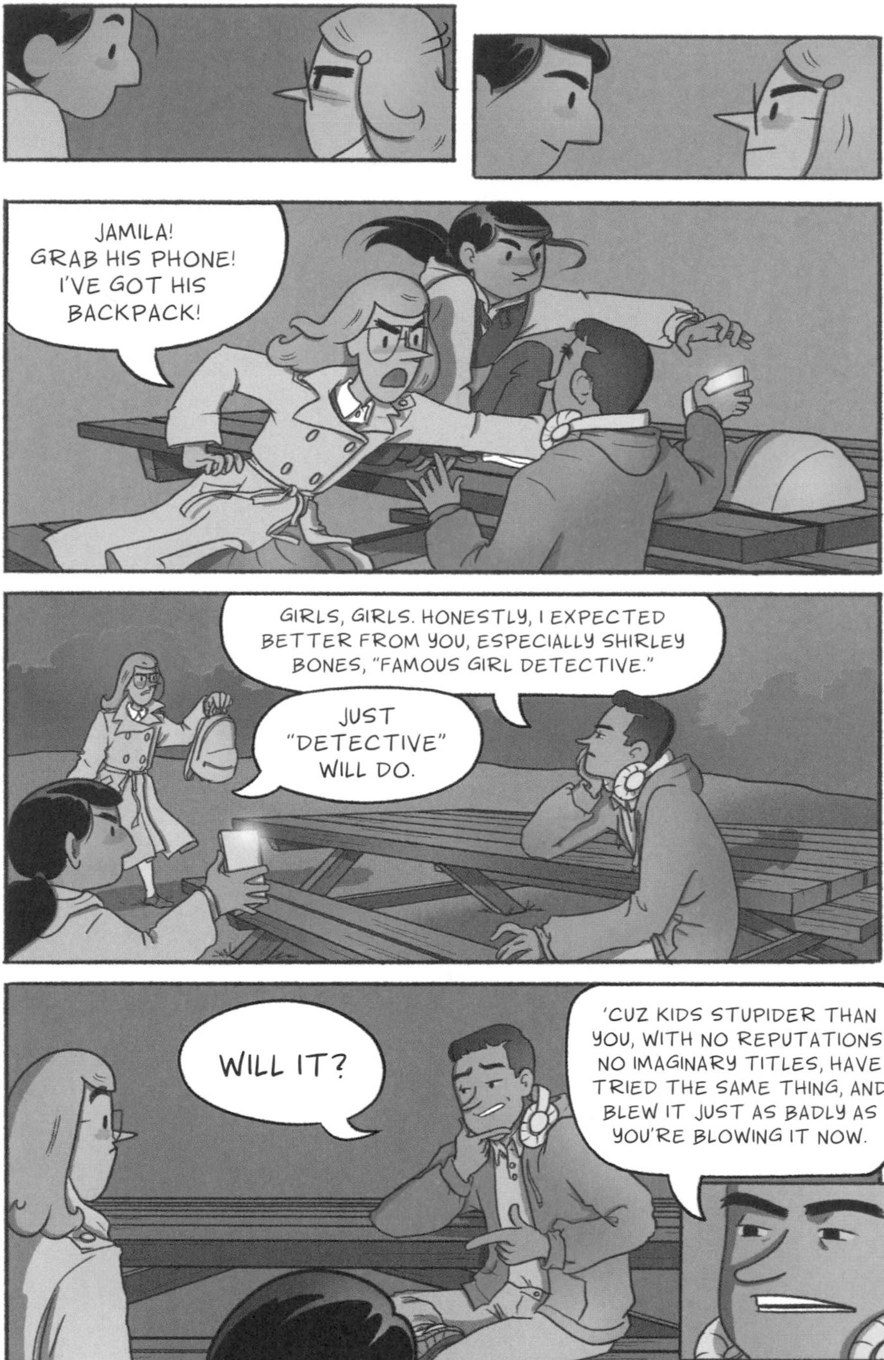
JAMILA! GRAB HIS PHONE! I'VE GOT HIS BACKPACK!
GIRLS, GIRLS. HONESTLY, I EXPECTED BETTER FROM YOU, ESPECIALLY SHIRLEY BONES, "FAMOUS GIRL DETECTIVE."
JUST "DETECTIVE" WILL DO.
WILL IT?
'CUZ KIDS STUPIDER THAN YOU, WITH NO REPUTATIONS, NO IMAGINARY TITLES, HAVE TRIED THE SAME THING, AND BLEW IT JUST AS BADLY AS YOU'RE BLOWING IT NOW.

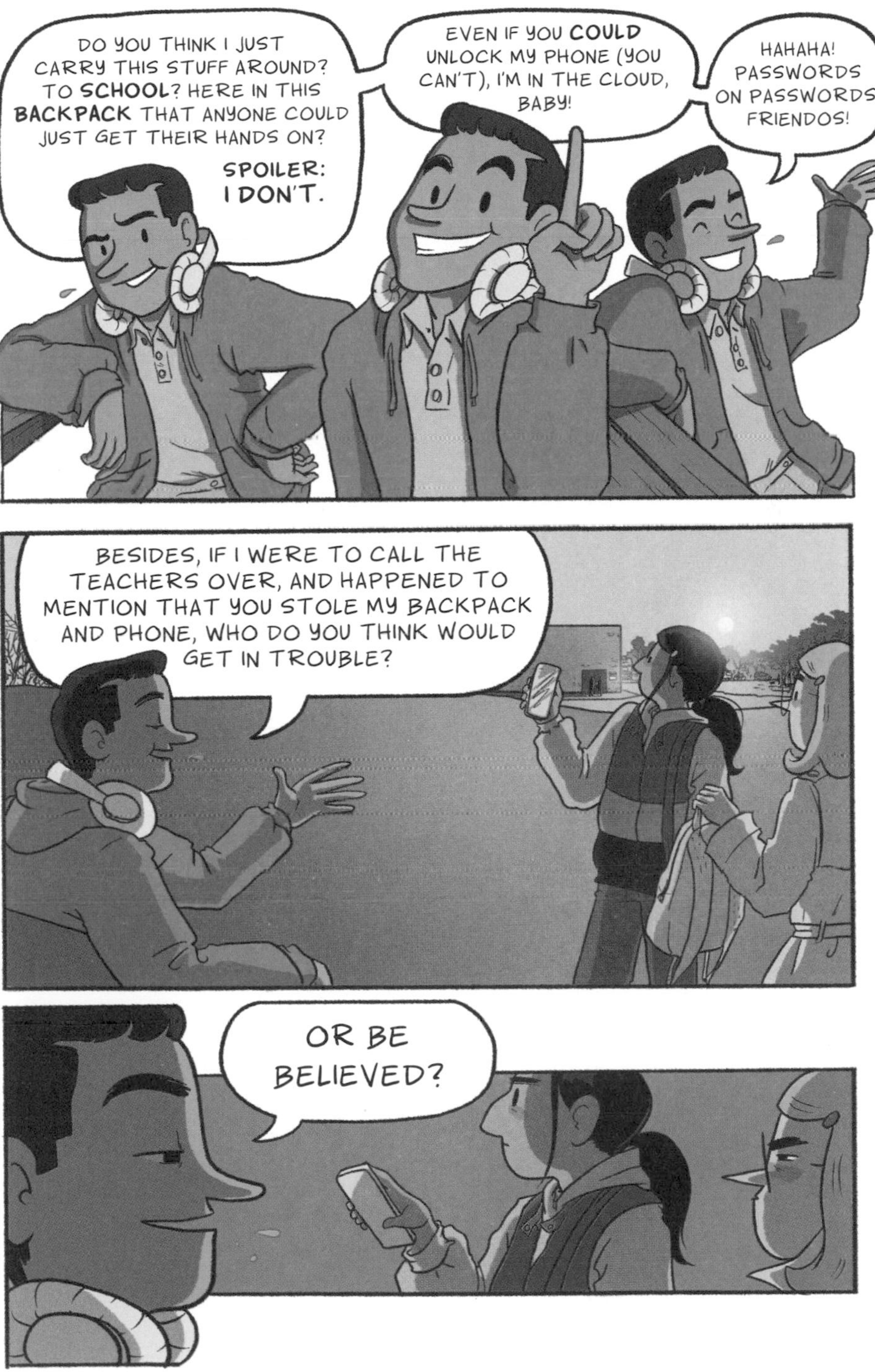
DO YOU THINK I JUST CARRY THIS STUFF AROUND? TO **SCHOOL**? HERE IN THIS **BACKPACK** THAT ANYONE COULD JUST GET THEIR HANDS ON?
SPOILER: I DON'T.
EVEN IF YOU **COULD** UNLOCK MY PHONE (YOU CAN'T), I'M IN THE CLOUD, BABY!
HAHAHA! PASSWORDS ON PASSWORDS, FRIENDOS!
BESIDES, IF I WERE TO CALL THE TEACHERS OVER, AND HAPPENED TO MENTION THAT YOU STOLE MY BACKPACK AND PHONE, WHO DO YOU THINK WOULD GET IN TROUBLE?
OR BE BELIEVED?

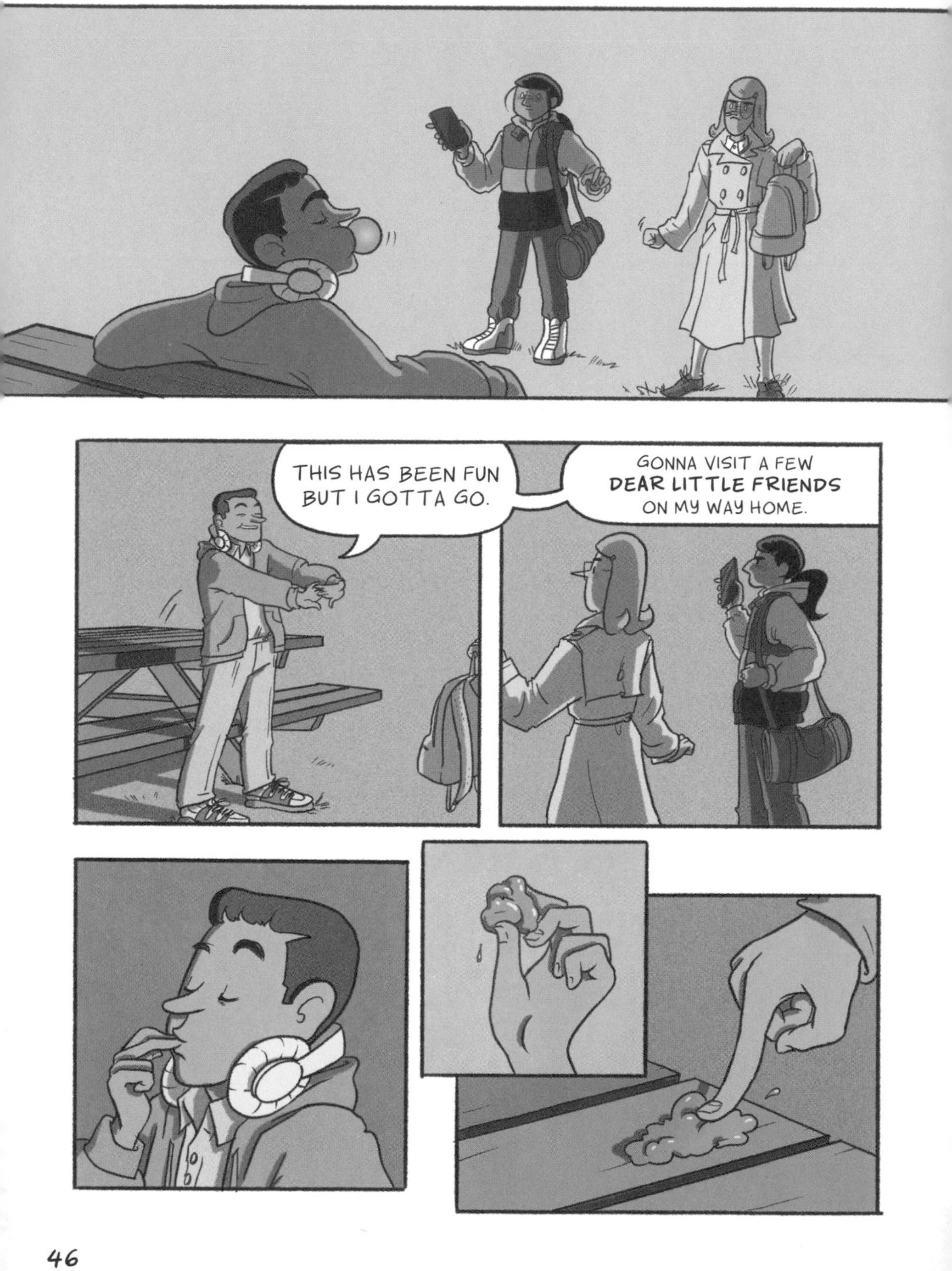
THIS HAS BEEN FUN BUT I GOTTA GO.
GONNA VISIT A FEW **DEAR LITTLE FRIENDS** ON MY WAY HOME.

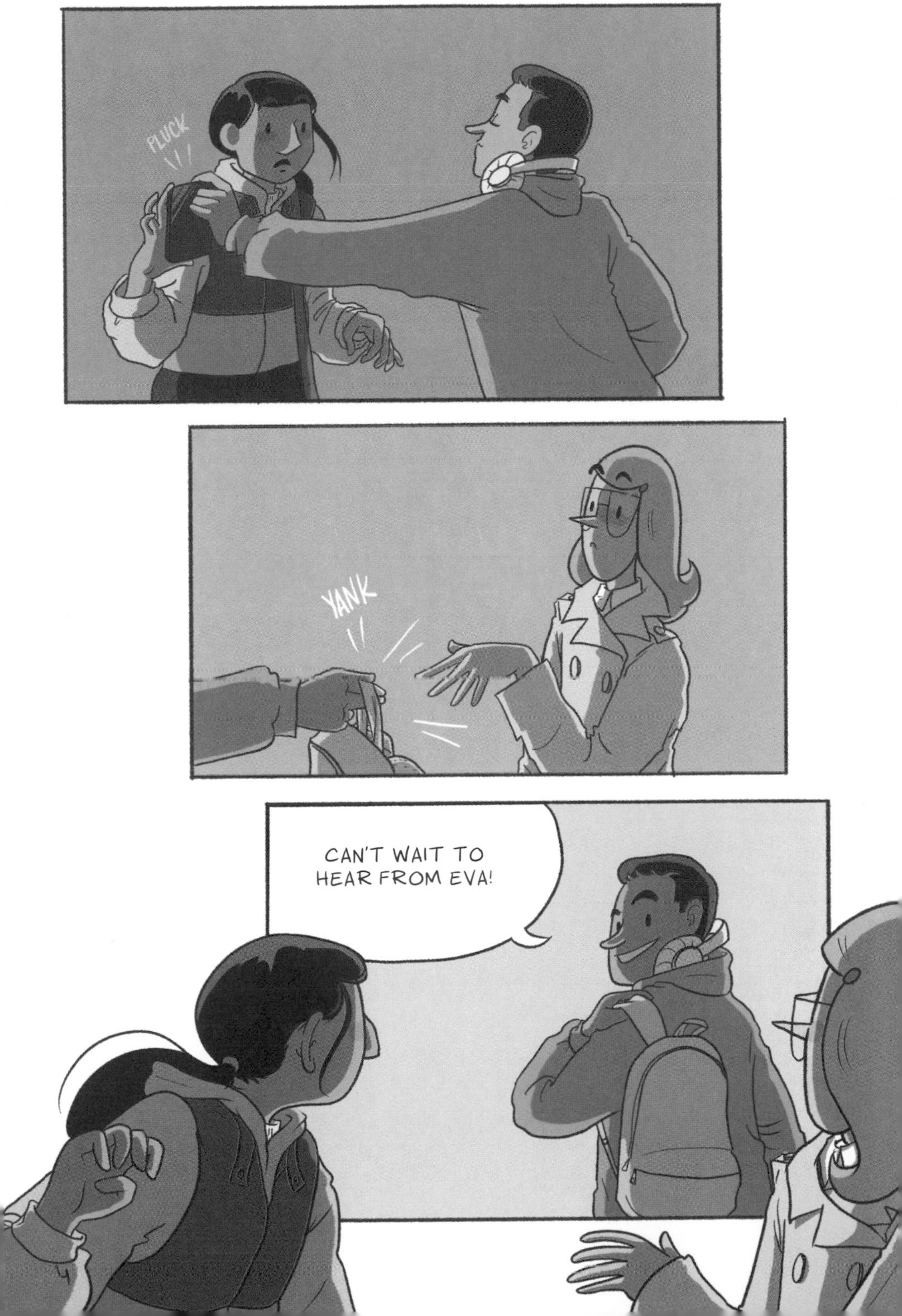
PLUCK
YANK
CAN'T WAIT TO
HEAR FROM EVA!

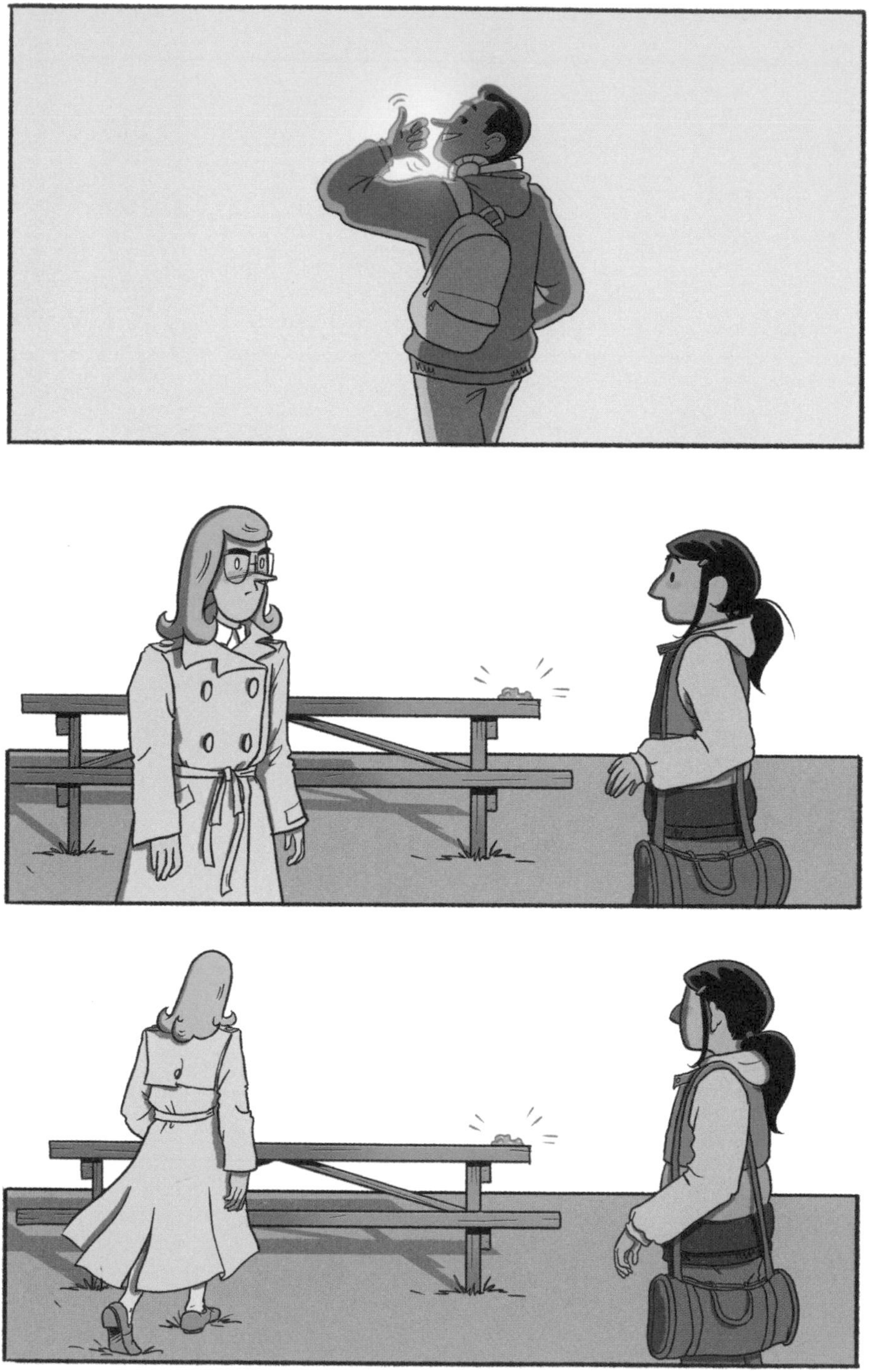

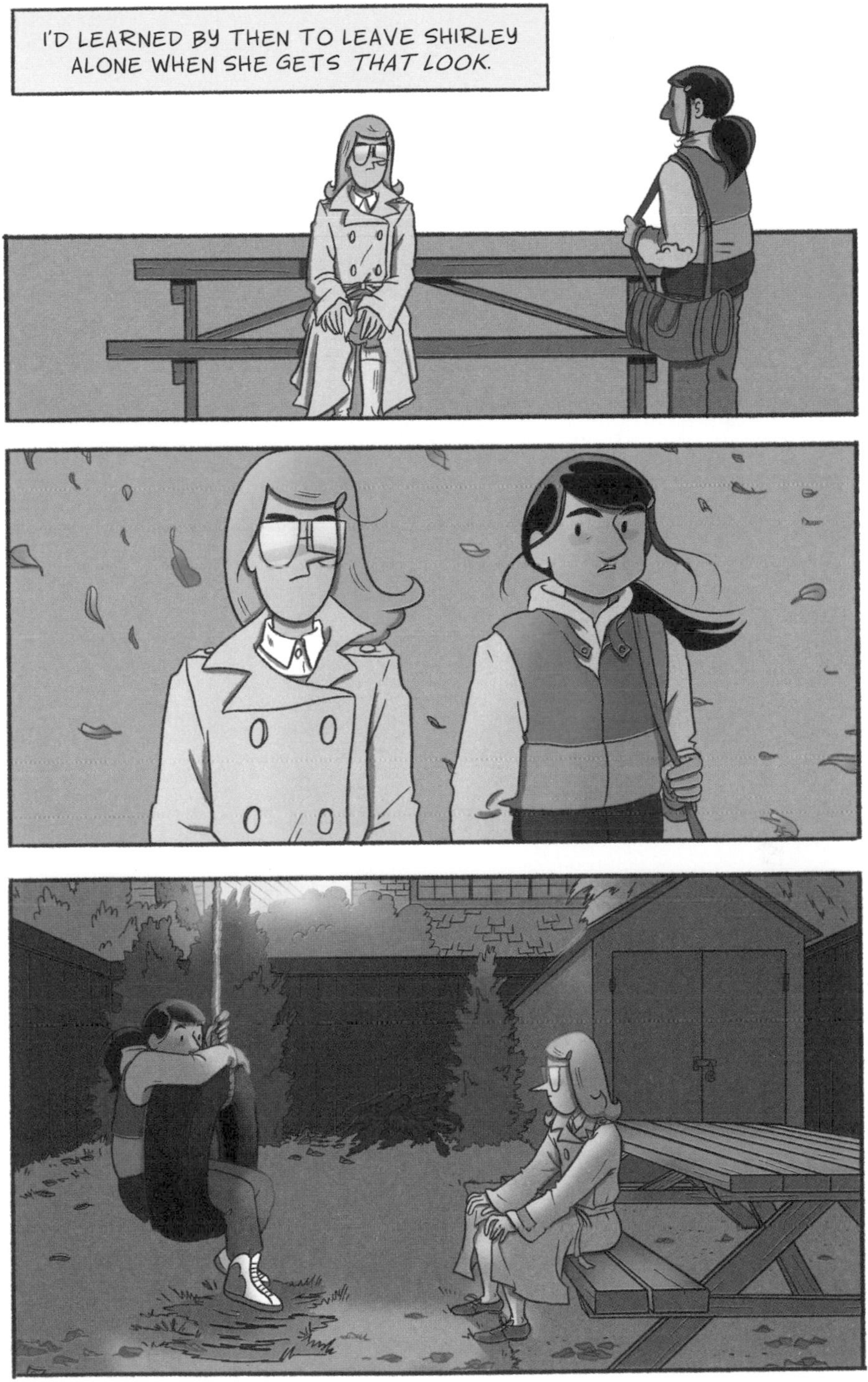
I'D LEARNED BY THEN TO LEAVE SHIRLEY ALONE WHEN SHE GETS *THAT LOOK*.

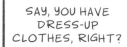
SAY, YOU HAVE DRESS-UP CLOTHES, RIGHT?

UH, YEAH. THERE'S A BOX OF OLD SHIRTS AND HATS PLUS SOME DRESSES 'N' THINGS MY MOM GOT ME THAT I NEVER WEAR.

YOU WANT TO PLAY DRESS-UP?

YES.

SHIRLEY WAS LIKE THAT. OBSESSED ONE MINUTE, TOTALLY FORGETTING THE NEXT. WE SPENT THE REST OF THE AFTERNOON GOOFING OFF IN COSTUMES.

AND IF ANY CLOTHES WERE MISSING WHEN I PACKED THEM UP AGAIN, I DIDN'T NOTICE.

Chapter 3

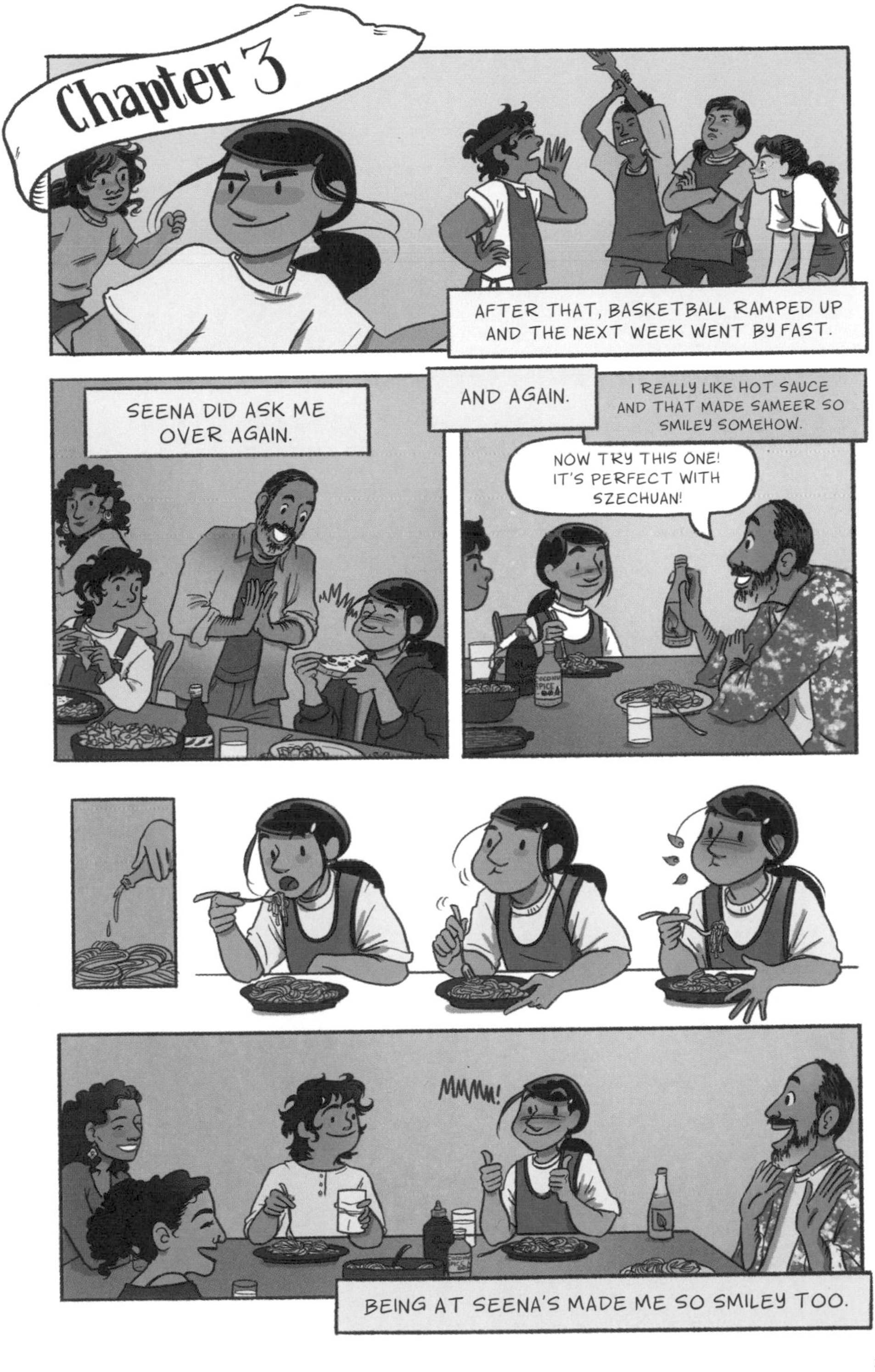
AFTER THAT, BASKETBALL RAMPED UP AND THE NEXT WEEK WENT BY FAST.
SEENA DID ASK ME OVER AGAIN.
AND AGAIN.
I REALLY LIKE HOT SAUCE AND THAT MADE SAMEER SO SMILEY SOMEHOW.
NOW TRY THIS ONE! IT'S PERFECT WITH SZECHUAN!
MMMM!
BEING AT SEENA'S MADE ME SO SMILEY TOO.

WITH PRACTICES OVER NOON-HOUR AND AFTER SCHOOL, I BARELY SAW SHIRLEY OUTSIDE OF CLASS.

I DIDN'T KNOW WHAT SHIRLEY DID DURING THOSE PRACTICES . . .

OH, PRACTICING VIOLIN, OR WORKING ON OPEN CASES. I HAVE A FEW EXPERIMENTS ON THE GO.

I WANTED TO ASK ABOUT EVA MAKWA'S CASE,

...

BUT SHIRLEY HAD SEEMED SO UPSET BY CHUCK THAT I DIDN'T WANT TO BRING IT UP.

SOMETIMES THERE WERE CASES SHIRLEY COULDN'T SOLVE, AND ANYBODY WHO LIKES WINNING KNOWS IT'S NO FUN TALKING ABOUT YOUR LOSSES.

CHUCK BEAT HER, AND EACH DAY I WONDERED IF THIS WAS THE DAY WE'D HEAR SOME TERRIBLE NEWS ABOUT EVA.

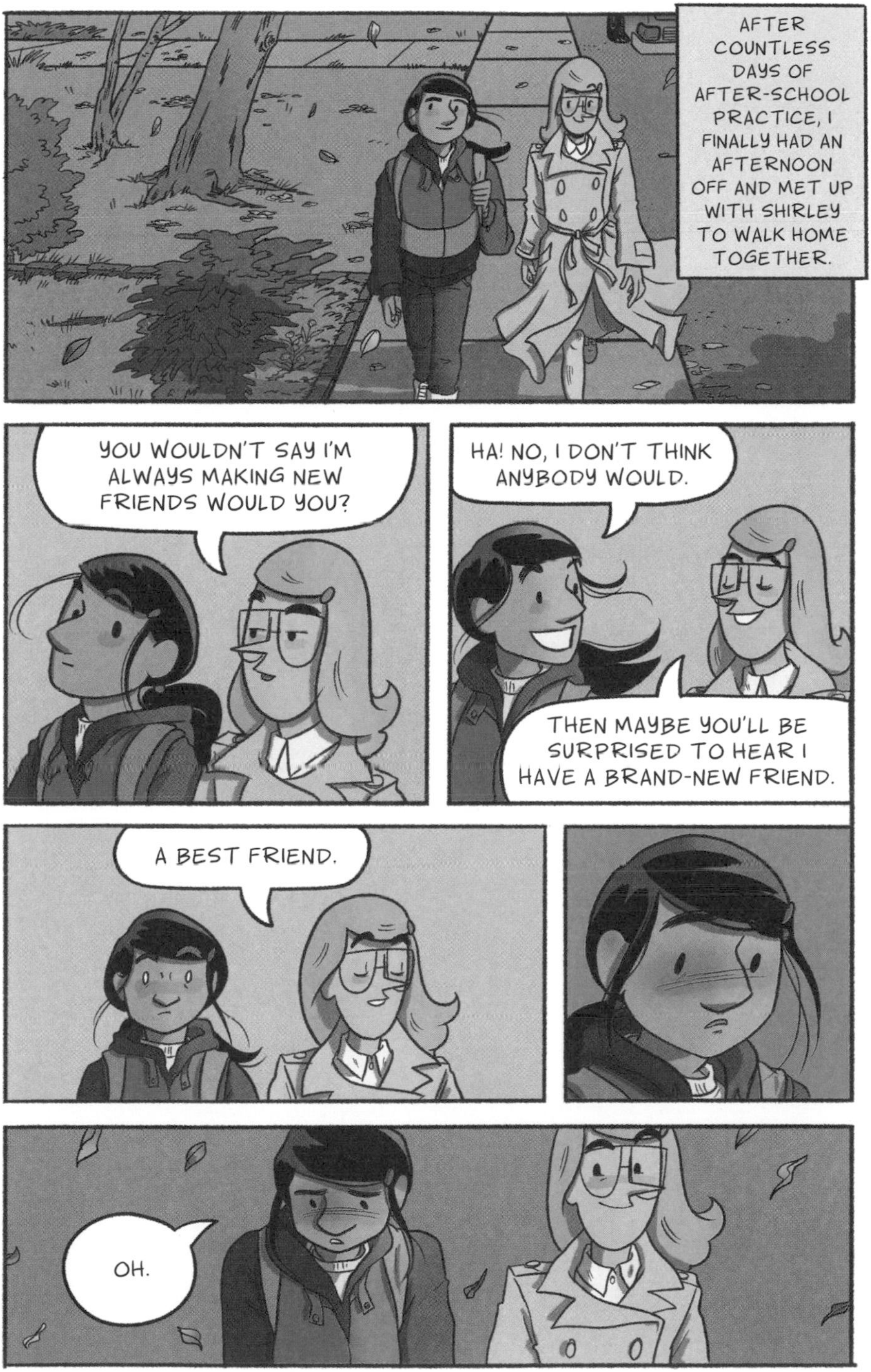
AFTER COUNTLESS DAYS OF AFTER-SCHOOL PRACTICE, I FINALLY HAD AN AFTERNOON OFF AND MET UP WITH SHIRLEY TO WALK HOME TOGETHER.
YOU WOULDN'T SAY I'M ALWAYS MAKING NEW FRIENDS WOULD YOU?
HA! NO, I DON'T THINK ANYBODY WOULD.
THEN MAYBE YOU'LL BE SURPRISED TO HEAR I HAVE A BRAND-NEW FRIEND.
A BEST FRIEND.
OH.

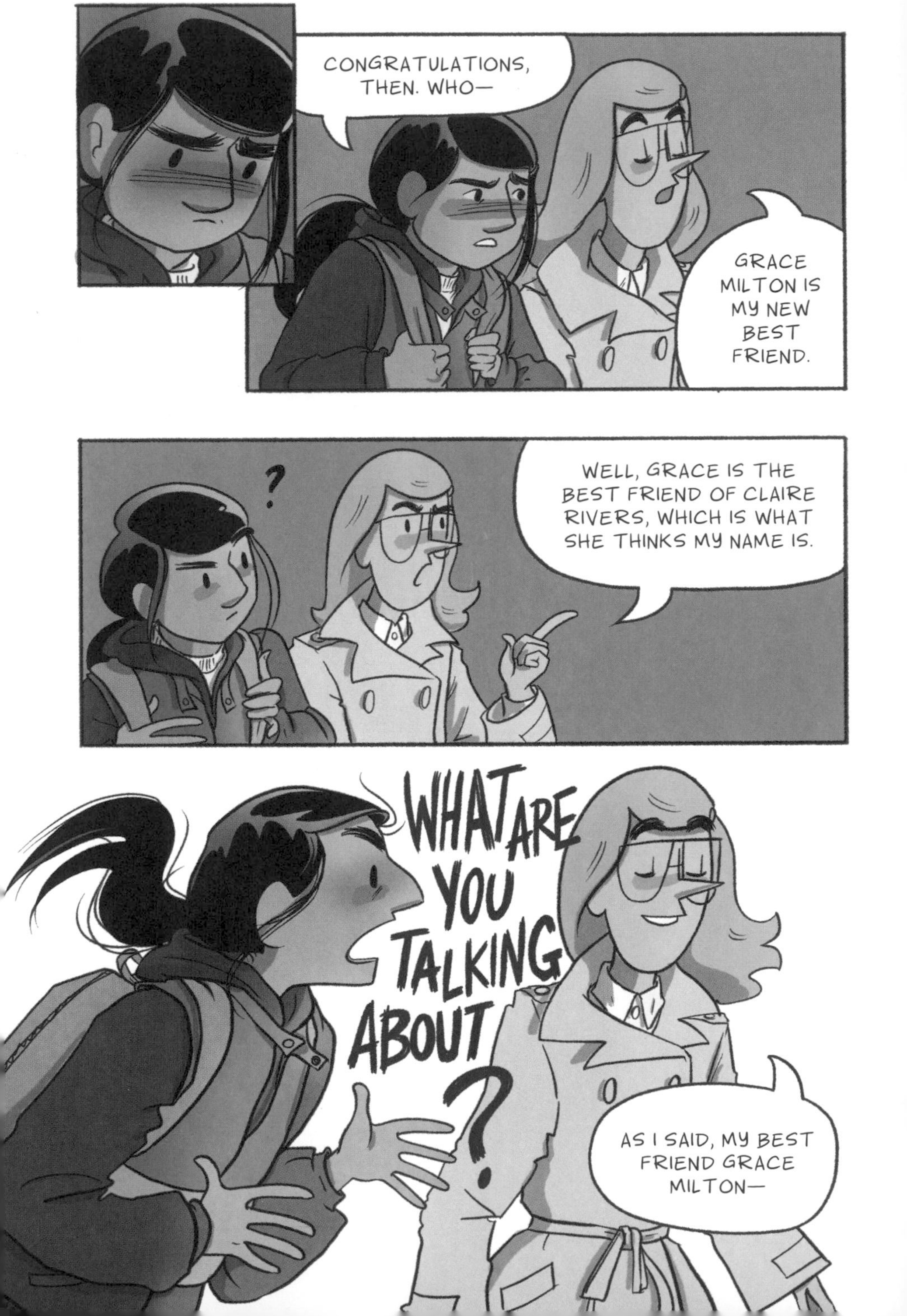
CONGRATULATIONS, THEN. WHO—
GRACE MILTON IS MY NEW BEST FRIEND.
?
WELL, GRACE IS THE BEST FRIEND OF CLAIRE RIVERS, WHICH IS WHAT SHE THINKS MY NAME IS.
WHAT ARE YOU TALKING ABOUT?
AS I SAID, MY BEST FRIEND GRACE MILTON—

WELL, GRACE MILTON (FRENCH HORN) HAS STRUCK UP A VERY CLOSE FRIENDSHIP IN HER AFTER-SCHOOL BAND WITH A YOUNG AND (IF I DO SAY SO) VERY TALENTED VIOLINIST WHO JOINED UP LATE.

people together

JUST THIS WEEK IN FACT!

CLAIRE SOMETHING?

CLAP

CLAIRE RIVERS.

IT'S VERY HANDY TO SNAP UP A VALID STUDENT ID OR TWO AS THEY GO MISSING FROM TIME TO TIME, WAHEED.

I NEVER LEAVE A LOST-AND-FOUND WITHOUT SOMETHING OF VALUE. I GOT THIS FROM THE ONE AT THE PUBLIC LIBRARY.

SAINT·THERESA'S
ACADEMY FOR PRESTIGIOUS YOUNGSTERS
student identification

CLAIRE RIVERS
AGE: 10 | GRADE: 5
Claire Rivers*
SIGNATURE

I GUESS YOU KINDA LOOK LIKE THIS . . .

BUT CHUCK KNOWS YOU! AND WHAT YOU LOOK LIKE! DID YOU GO TO THEIR HOUSE?

IT WAS CRITICAL THAT I GO TO THEIR HOUSE, WAHEED.

YANK

FUN FACT: CLAIRE'S FAVORITE GAME IS HIDE-AND-SEEK. I NOW KNOW THE MILTON HOUSE LIKE THE BACK OF MY HAND.

DON'T LOOK SO WORRIED.

SOMEONE LIKE CHUCK DOES NOT PAY ATTENTION TO HIS YOUNGER SISTER OR HER FRIENDS.

BESIDES, YOU DIDN'T KNOW ME TO SEE ME, SO WHY WOULD HE?

I WOULD KNOW YOU TO SEE YOU.

YOU DIDN'T THE OTHER DAY. AFTER YOUR BASKETBALL PRACTICE.

WHAT?

AUDREY, HOW COME YOU DIDN'T JOIN BAND?

I CAN BARELY CLAP MY HANDS TO A BEAT! BESIDES, I DON'T HAVE TIME FOR ANOTHER PRACTICE...

WHO HAS TIME?!

MY SISTER PLAYS FLUTE.

I HATE THE FLUTE!

YOU HATE EVERYTHING.

HA! YOU DO.

HA HA HA

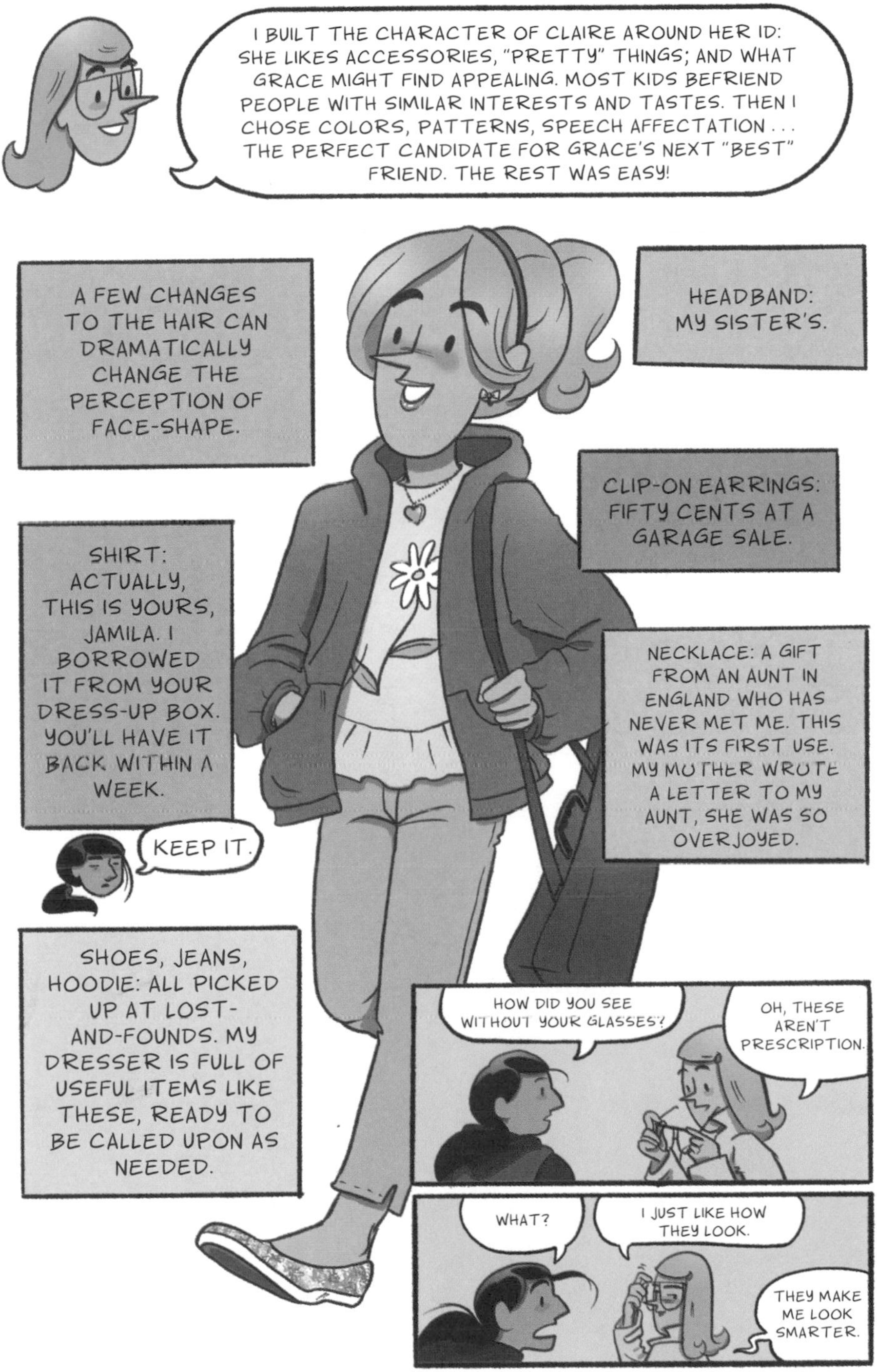
I BUILT THE CHARACTER OF CLAIRE AROUND HER ID: SHE LIKES ACCESSORIES, "PRETTY" THINGS; AND WHAT GRACE MIGHT FIND APPEALING. MOST KIDS BEFRIEND PEOPLE WITH SIMILAR INTERESTS AND TASTES. THEN I CHOSE COLORS, PATTERNS, SPEECH AFFECTATION . . . THE PERFECT CANDIDATE FOR GRACE'S NEXT "BEST" FRIEND. THE REST WAS EASY!
A FEW CHANGES TO THE HAIR CAN DRAMATICALLY CHANGE THE PERCEPTION OF FACE-SHAPE.
HEADBAND: MY SISTER'S.
CLIP-ON EARRINGS: FIFTY CENTS AT A GARAGE SALE.
SHIRT: ACTUALLY, THIS IS YOURS, JAMILA. I BORROWED IT FROM YOUR DRESS-UP BOX. YOU'LL HAVE IT BACK WITHIN A WEEK.
NECKLACE: A GIFT FROM AN AUNT IN ENGLAND WHO HAS NEVER MET ME. THIS WAS ITS FIRST USE. MY MOTHER WROTE A LETTER TO MY AUNT, SHE WAS SO OVERJOYED.
KEEP IT.
SHOES, JEANS, HOODIE: ALL PICKED UP AT LOST-AND-FOUNDS. MY DRESSER IS FULL OF USEFUL ITEMS LIKE THESE, READY TO BE CALLED UPON AS NEEDED.
HOW DID YOU SEE WITHOUT YOUR GLASSES?
OH, THESE AREN'T PRESCRIPTION.
WHAT?
I JUST LIKE HOW THEY LOOK.
THEY MAKE ME LOOK SMARTER.

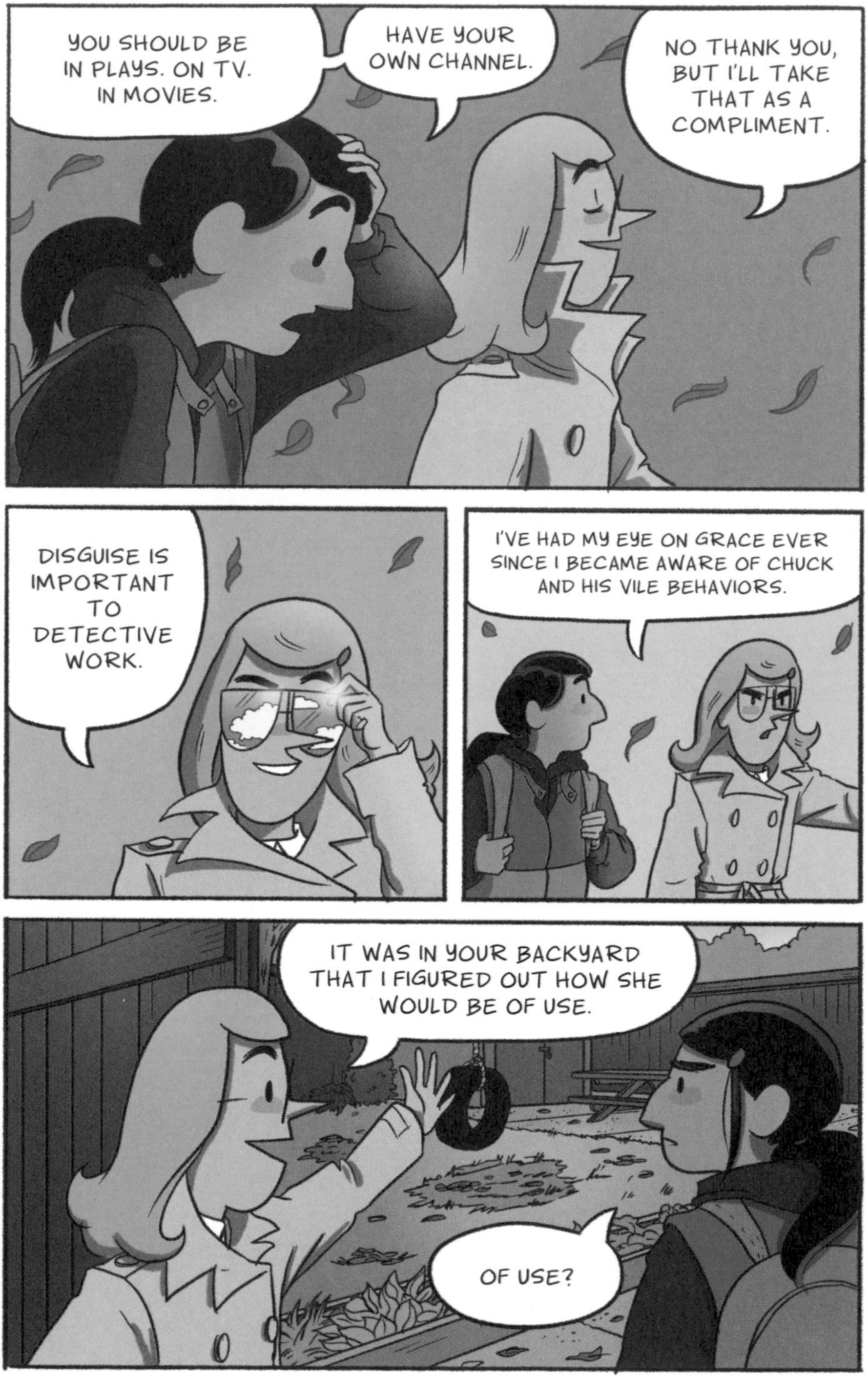
YOU SHOULD BE IN PLAYS. ON TV. IN MOVIES.
HAVE YOUR OWN CHANNEL.
NO THANK YOU, BUT I'LL TAKE THAT AS A COMPLIMENT.
DISGUISE IS IMPORTANT TO DETECTIVE WORK.
I'VE HAD MY EYE ON GRACE EVER SINCE I BECAME AWARE OF CHUCK AND HIS VILE BEHAVIORS.
IT WAS IN YOUR BACKYARD THAT I FIGURED OUT HOW SHE WOULD BE OF USE.
OF USE?

WILL YOUR MOM LET YOU SLEEP OVER AT MY PLACE THIS WEEKEND?

SINCE THE SUMMER, MY MOM AND I HAVE GOTTEN A LOT CLOSER.

SHE PLAYS HORSE WITH ME IN THE DRIVEWAY SOMETIMES

AND SHE'S SHOWING ME AND FAROOQ HOW TO MAKE NIHARI, OUR FAVORITE STEW.

STRANGERS AND DRIVERS AND CYCLIST LISTS AND HOVERBOARDS AND WHEELIE SHOES A... ...ND SE EGWAYS AND ROLL... ...ER BL ...ADES ...AND TRA... ...FIC A...

SHE'S STILL PARANOID ABOUT ME BEING OUT IN THE CITY.

BUT SHE SEEMS TO TRUST ME WITH SHIRLEY.

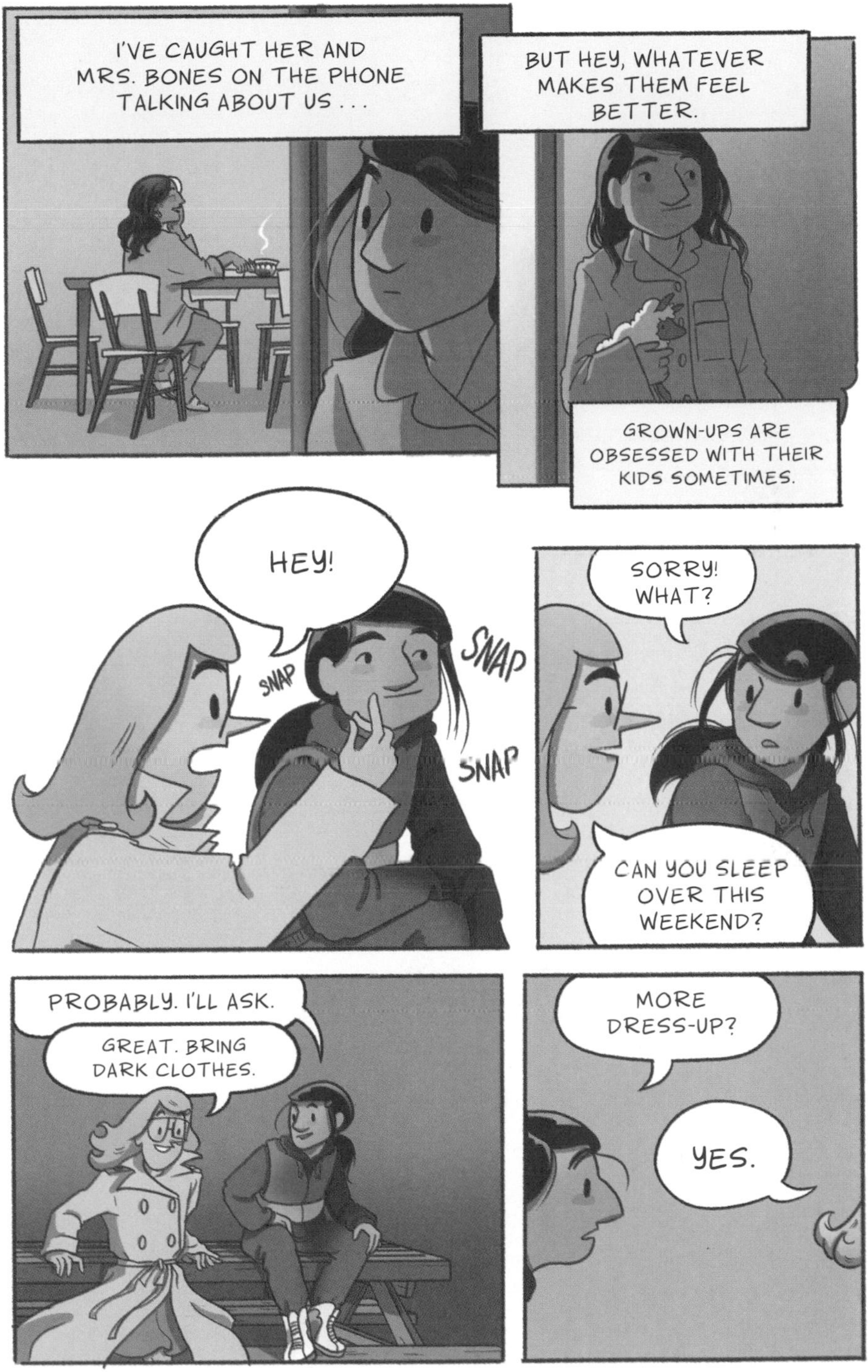
I'VE CAUGHT HER AND MRS. BONES ON THE PHONE TALKING ABOUT US . . .
BUT HEY, WHATEVER MAKES THEM FEEL BETTER.
GROWN-UPS ARE OBSESSED WITH THEIR KIDS SOMETIMES.
HEY!
SNAP
SNAP
SNAP
SORRY! WHAT?
CAN YOU SLEEP OVER THIS WEEKEND?
PROBABLY. I'LL ASK.
GREAT. BRING DARK CLOTHES.
MORE DRESS-UP?
YES.

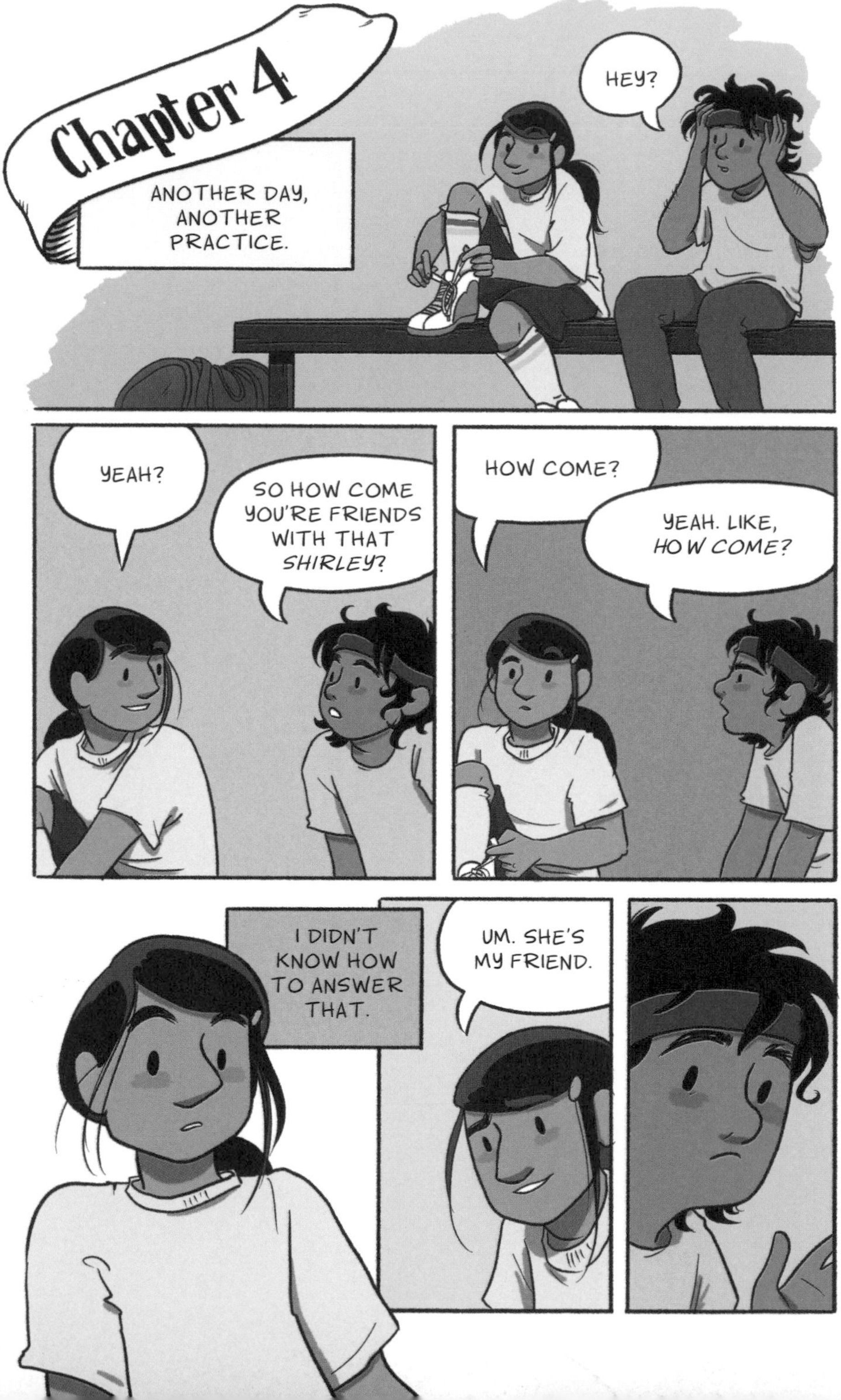
Chapter 4
ANOTHER DAY, ANOTHER PRACTICE.
HEY?
YEAH?
SO HOW COME YOU'RE FRIENDS WITH THAT SHIRLEY?
HOW COME?
YEAH. LIKE, HOW COME?
I DIDN'T KNOW HOW TO ANSWER THAT.
UM. SHE'S MY FRIEND.

WE MET AT A GARAGE SALE IN THE SUMMER AND OUR MOMS LET US GO OUT ALONE IF WE PLAYED TOGETHER . . .

OOOOOOOOOOHHHHHHH

OKAY, I GET IT.

I DIDN'T THINK SHE DID. GET IT.

WHY?

SHE JUST SEEMS . . . NOT LIKE YOU. BUT IF YOUR MOMS MADE YOU HANG OUT, I GET IT. MY AUNTY HAS A KID THAT MY MOM MAKES ME HANG WITH WHEN SHE'S OVER.

WE'RE NOT FRIENDS, BUT SHE'S *FINE*.

THAT'S NOT REALLY—

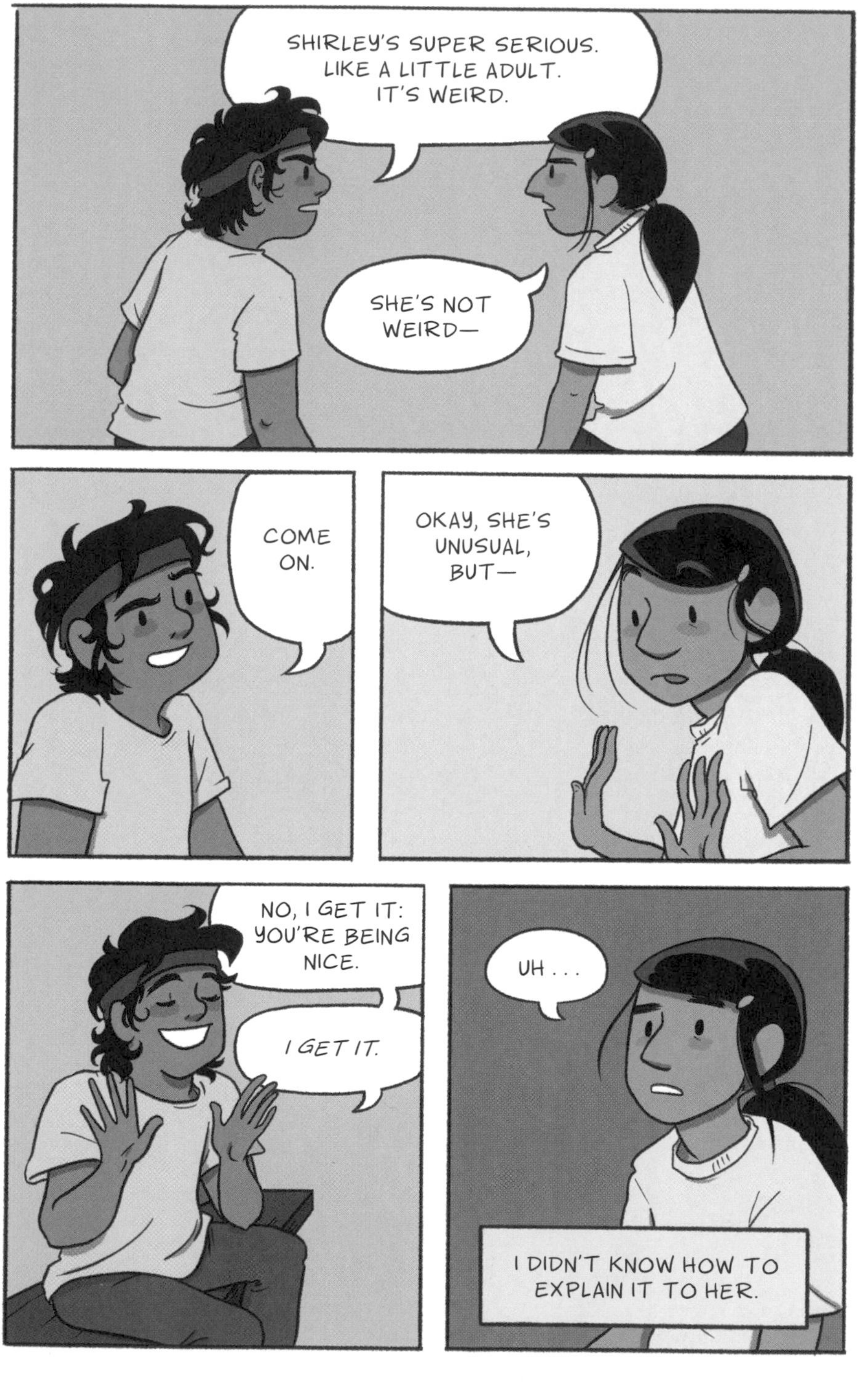
SHIRLEY'S SUPER SERIOUS. LIKE A LITTLE ADULT. IT'S WEIRD.
SHE'S NOT WEIRD—
COME ON.
OKAY, SHE'S UNUSUAL, BUT—
NO, I GET IT: YOU'RE BEING NICE.
I GET IT.
UH . . .
I DIDN'T KNOW HOW TO EXPLAIN IT TO HER.

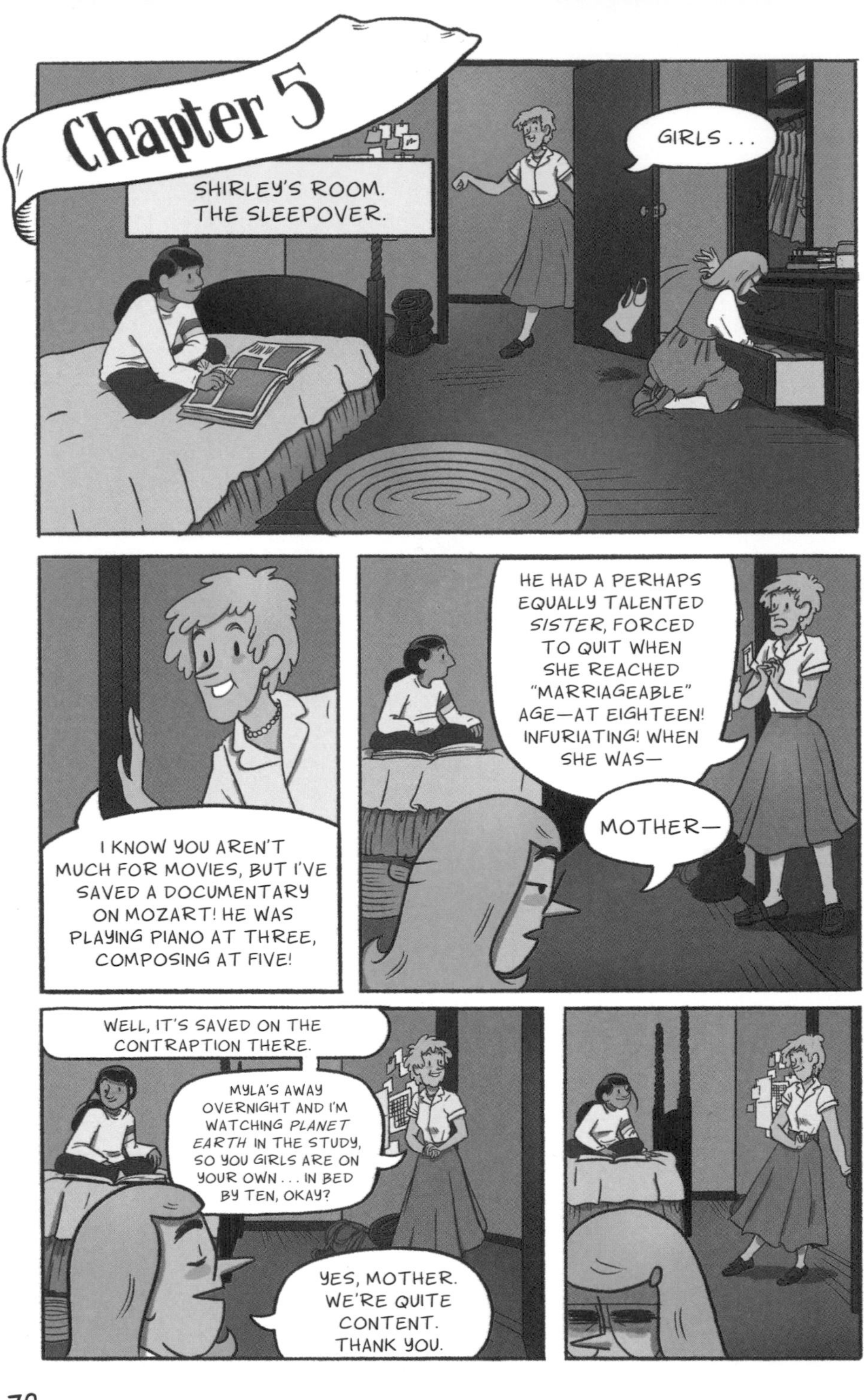
Chapter 5
SHIRLEY'S ROOM. THE SLEEPOVER.
GIRLS . . .
I KNOW YOU AREN'T MUCH FOR MOVIES, BUT I'VE SAVED A DOCUMENTARY ON MOZART! HE WAS PLAYING PIANO AT THREE, COMPOSING AT FIVE!
HE HAD A PERHAPS EQUALLY TALENTED *SISTER*, FORCED TO QUIT WHEN SHE REACHED "MARRIAGEABLE" AGE—AT EIGHTEEN! INFURIATING! WHEN SHE WAS—
MOTHER—
WELL, IT'S SAVED ON THE CONTRAPTION THERE.
MYLA'S AWAY OVERNIGHT AND I'M WATCHING *PLANET EARTH* IN THE STUDY, SO YOU GIRLS ARE ON YOUR OWN . . . IN BED BY TEN, OKAY?
YES, MOTHER. WE'RE QUITE CONTENT. THANK YOU.

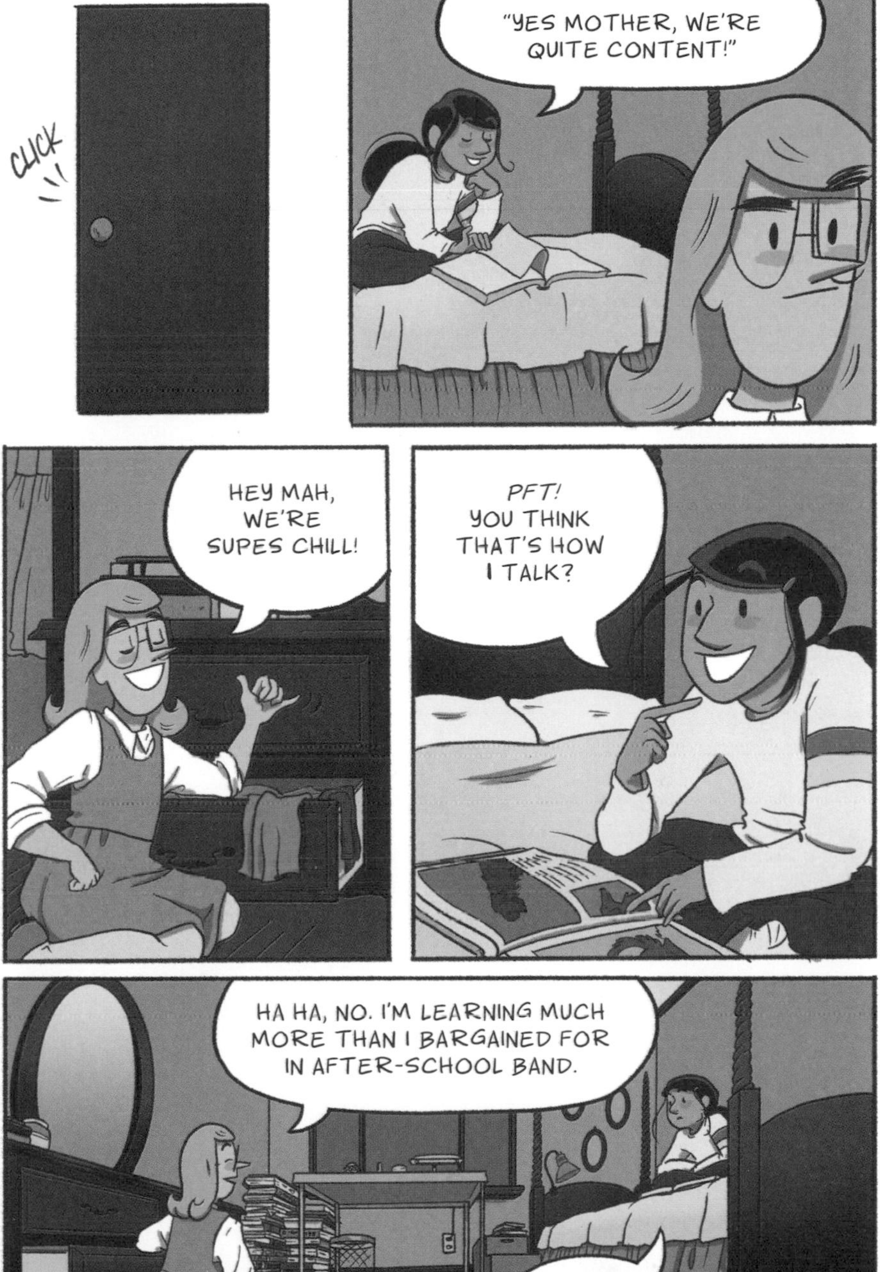
CLICK
"YES MOTHER, WE'RE QUITE CONTENT!"
HEY MAH, WE'RE SUPES CHILL!
PFT! YOU THINK THAT'S HOW I TALK?
HA HA, NO. I'M LEARNING MUCH MORE THAN I BARGAINED FOR IN AFTER-SCHOOL BAND.
NOT ABOUT VIOLIN?

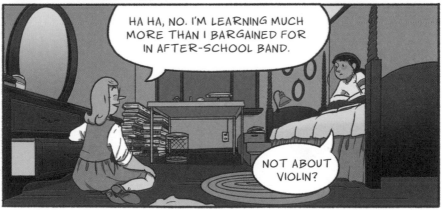

HA!

UNFORTUNATELY, THERE IS NOTHING FOR ME TO LEARN *MUSICALLY* IN AFTER-SCHOOL BAND.

BUT THE STUDY OF CHILDREN IS FASCINATING.

YOU ACT LIKE YOU AREN'T IN CLASS WITH OTHER KIDS ALL DAY!

ALL TOO WELL.

ALSO, **YOU** ARE A KID.

YOU KNOW THAT, RIGHT?

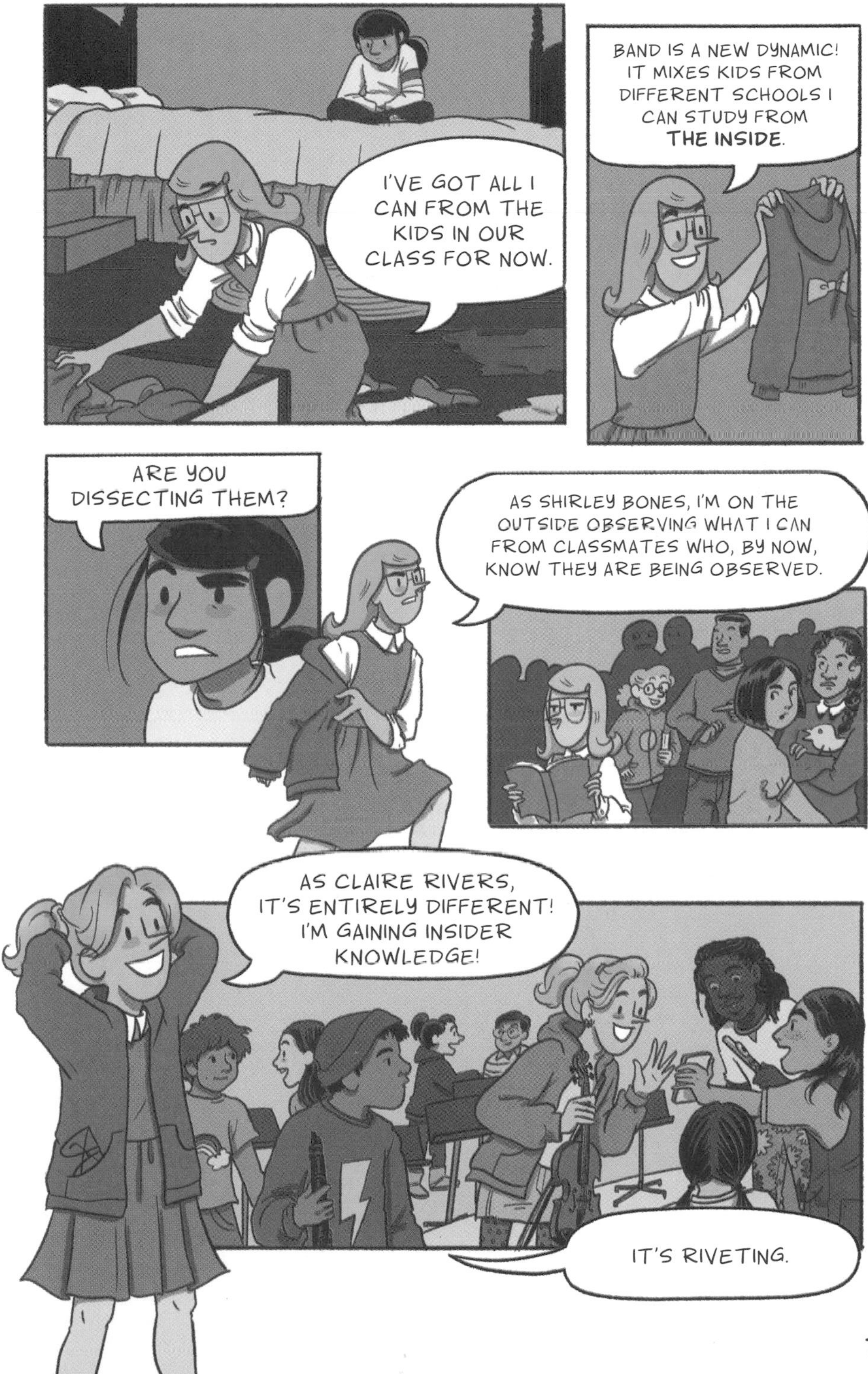
I'VE GOT ALL I CAN FROM THE KIDS IN OUR CLASS FOR NOW.
BAND IS A NEW DYNAMIC! IT MIXES KIDS FROM DIFFERENT SCHOOLS I CAN STUDY FROM **THE INSIDE**.
ARE YOU DISSECTING THEM?
AS SHIRLEY BONES, I'M ON THE OUTSIDE OBSERVING WHAT I CAN FROM CLASSMATES WHO, BY NOW, KNOW THEY ARE BEING OBSERVED.
AS CLAIRE RIVERS, IT'S ENTIRELY DIFFERENT! I'M GAINING INSIDER KNOWLEDGE!
IT'S RIVETING.

NOW YOU HAVE ALL THE COOL SLANG.

NOT **ALL**, BUT MY VOCABULARY HAS IMPROVED.

"IMPROVED"? YOU TALK BETTER THAN MOST OF OUR TEACHERS. YOU'RE ONLY GONNA GET WORSE.

BETTER AND WORSE ARE SUBJECTIVE. ALL ITERATIONS OF ENGLISH ARE VALID, AND SLANG CARRIES COMPLEX MEANINGS THAT CHARACTERIZE AND BOND GROUPS AND OFFER UNIQUE OPPORTUNITIES FOR EXPRESSION.

SLANG HAS VALUE EVEN THOUGH TEACHERS WILL NOT ACCEPT IT ON ASSIGNMENTS.

OH. OKAY.

WHAT?

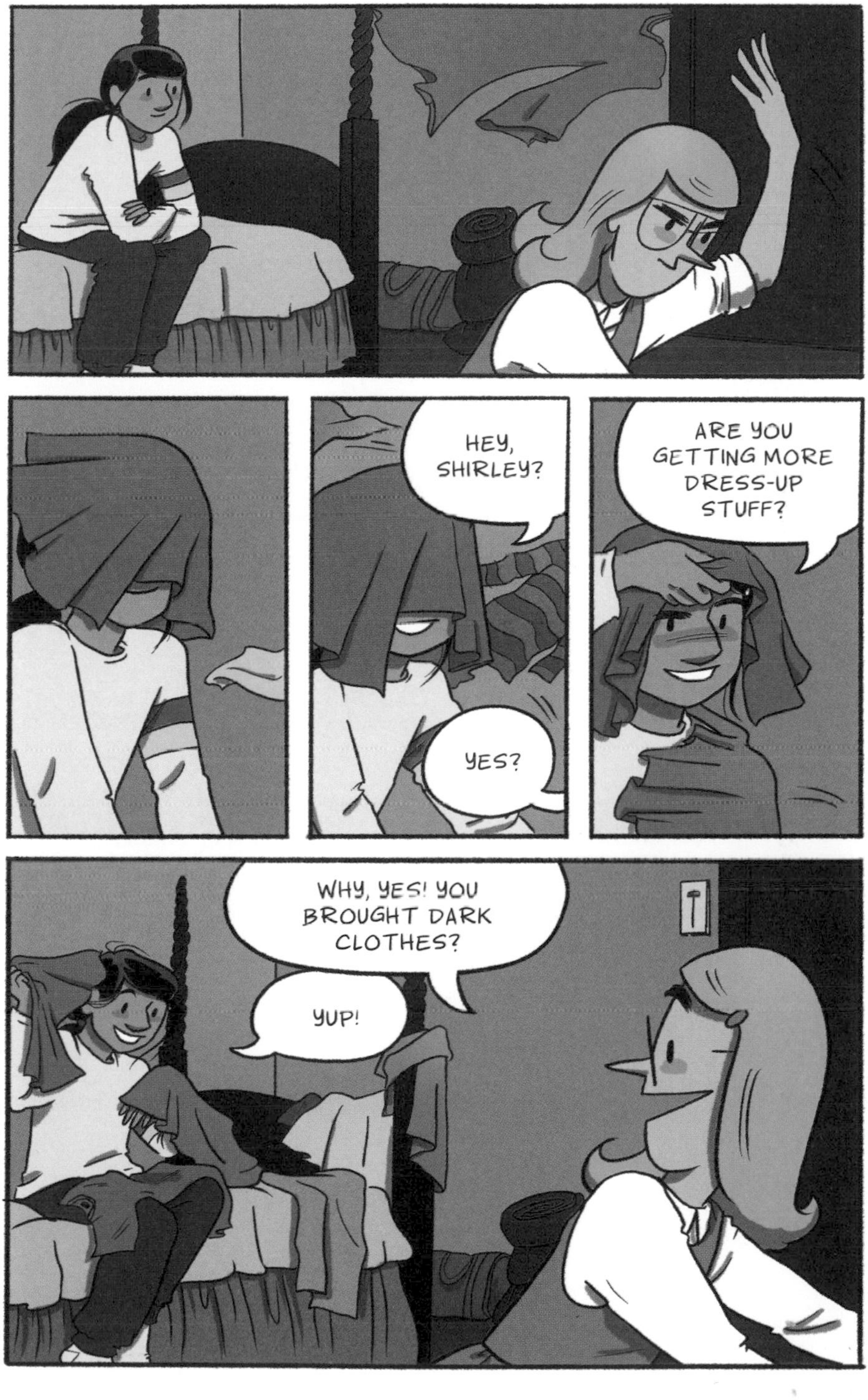
HEY, SHIRLEY?
YES?
ARE YOU GETTING MORE DRESS-UP STUFF?
WHY, YES! YOU BROUGHT DARK CLOTHES?
YUP!

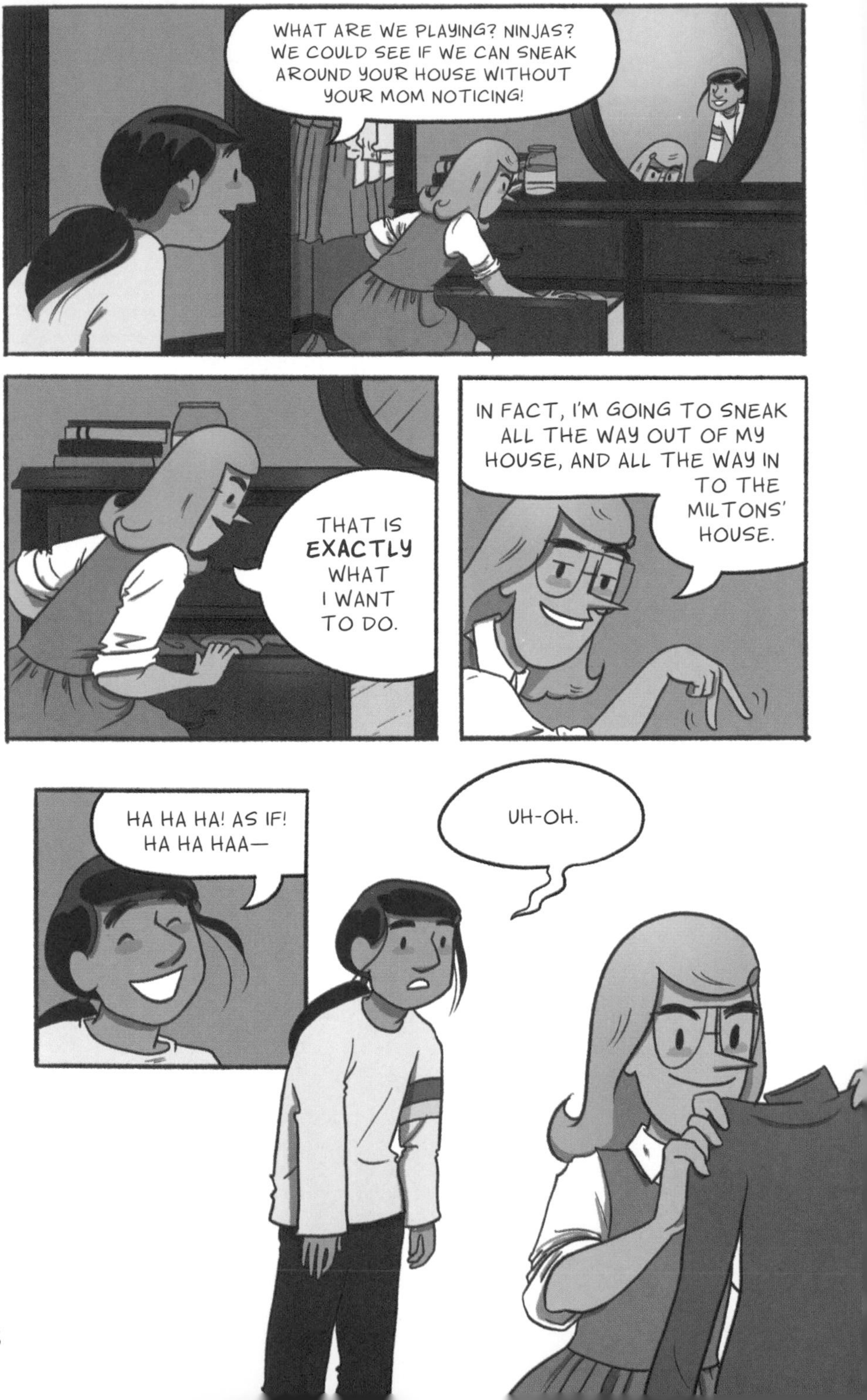
WHAT ARE WE PLAYING? NINJAS? WE COULD SEE IF WE CAN SNEAK AROUND YOUR HOUSE WITHOUT YOUR MOM NOTICING!
THAT IS **EXACTLY** WHAT I WANT TO DO.
IN FACT, I'M GOING TO SNEAK ALL THE WAY OUT OF MY HOUSE, AND ALL THE WAY IN TO THE MILTONS' HOUSE.
HA HA HA! AS IF! HA HA HAA—
UH-OH.

77

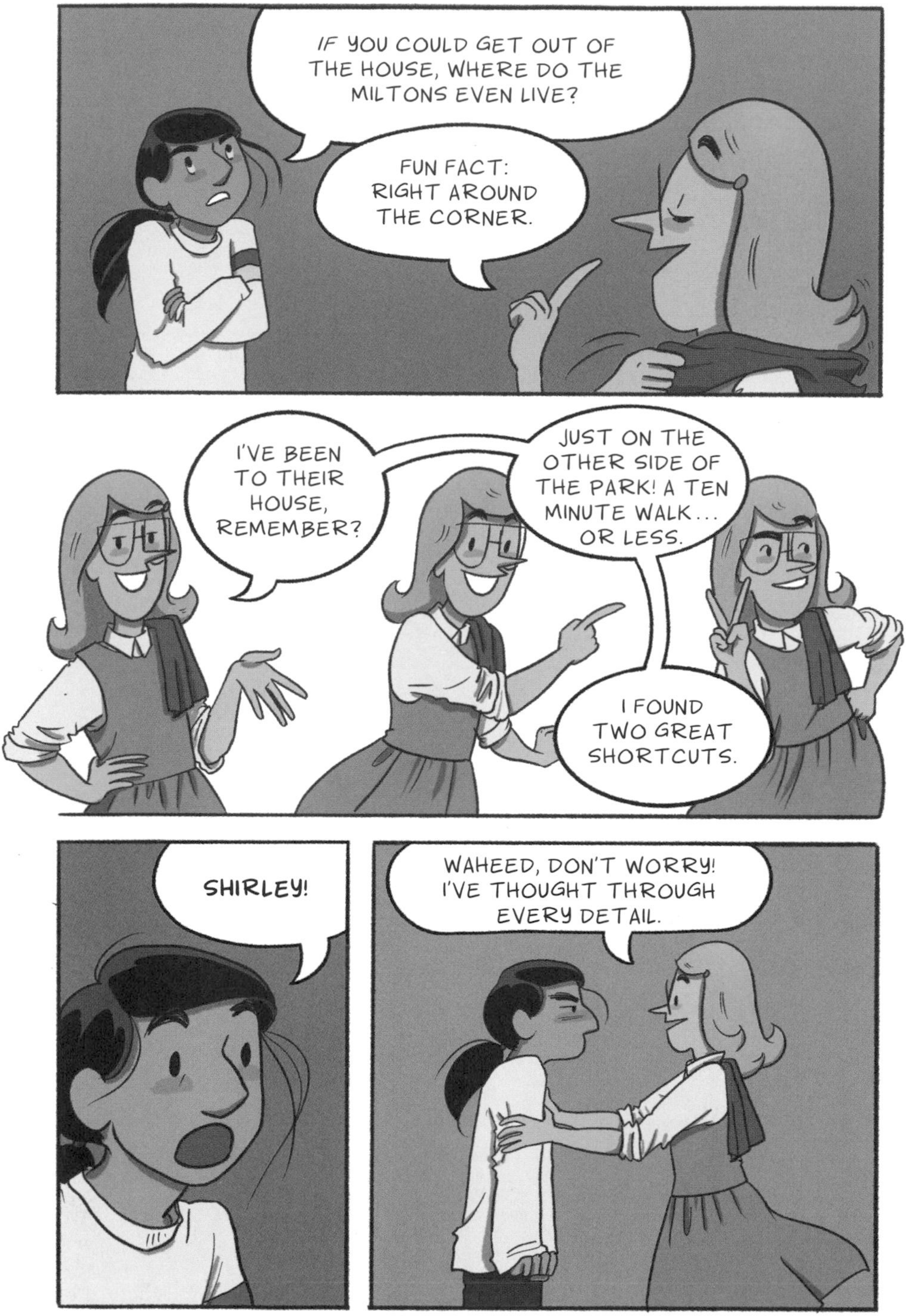
IF YOU COULD GET OUT OF THE HOUSE, WHERE DO THE MILTONS EVEN LIVE?
FUN FACT: RIGHT AROUND THE CORNER.
I'VE BEEN TO THEIR HOUSE, REMEMBER?
JUST ON THE OTHER SIDE OF THE PARK! A TEN MINUTE WALK... OR LESS.
I FOUND TWO GREAT SHORTCUTS.
SHIRLEY!
WAHEED, DON'T WORRY! I'VE THOUGHT THROUGH EVERY DETAIL.

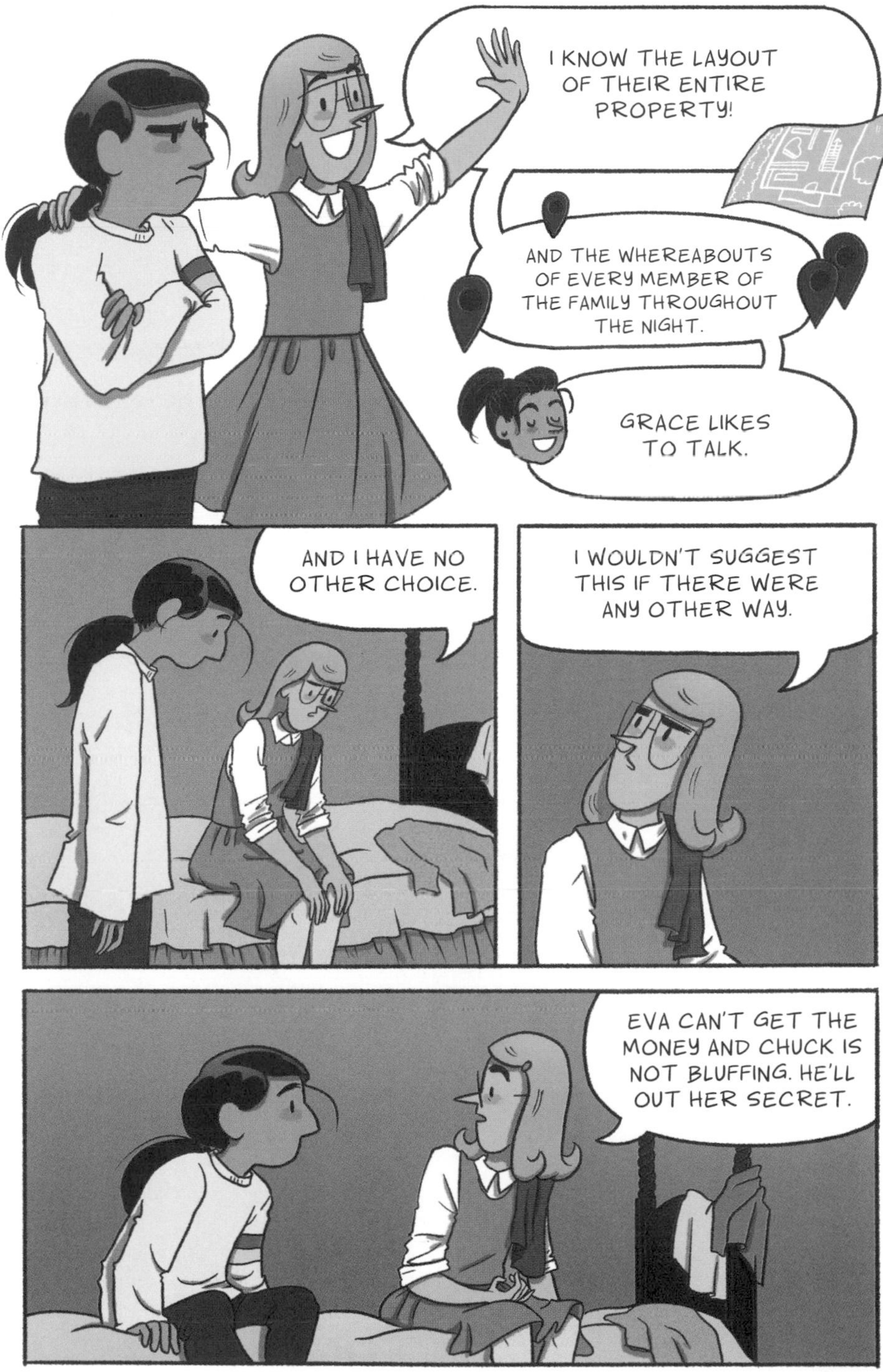
I KNOW THE LAYOUT OF THEIR ENTIRE PROPERTY!
AND THE WHEREABOUTS OF EVERY MEMBER OF THE FAMILY THROUGHOUT THE NIGHT.
GRACE LIKES TO TALK.
AND I HAVE NO OTHER CHOICE.
I WOULDN'T SUGGEST THIS IF THERE WERE ANY OTHER WAY.
EVA CAN'T GET THE MONEY AND CHUCK IS NOT BLUFFING. HE'LL OUT HER SECRET.

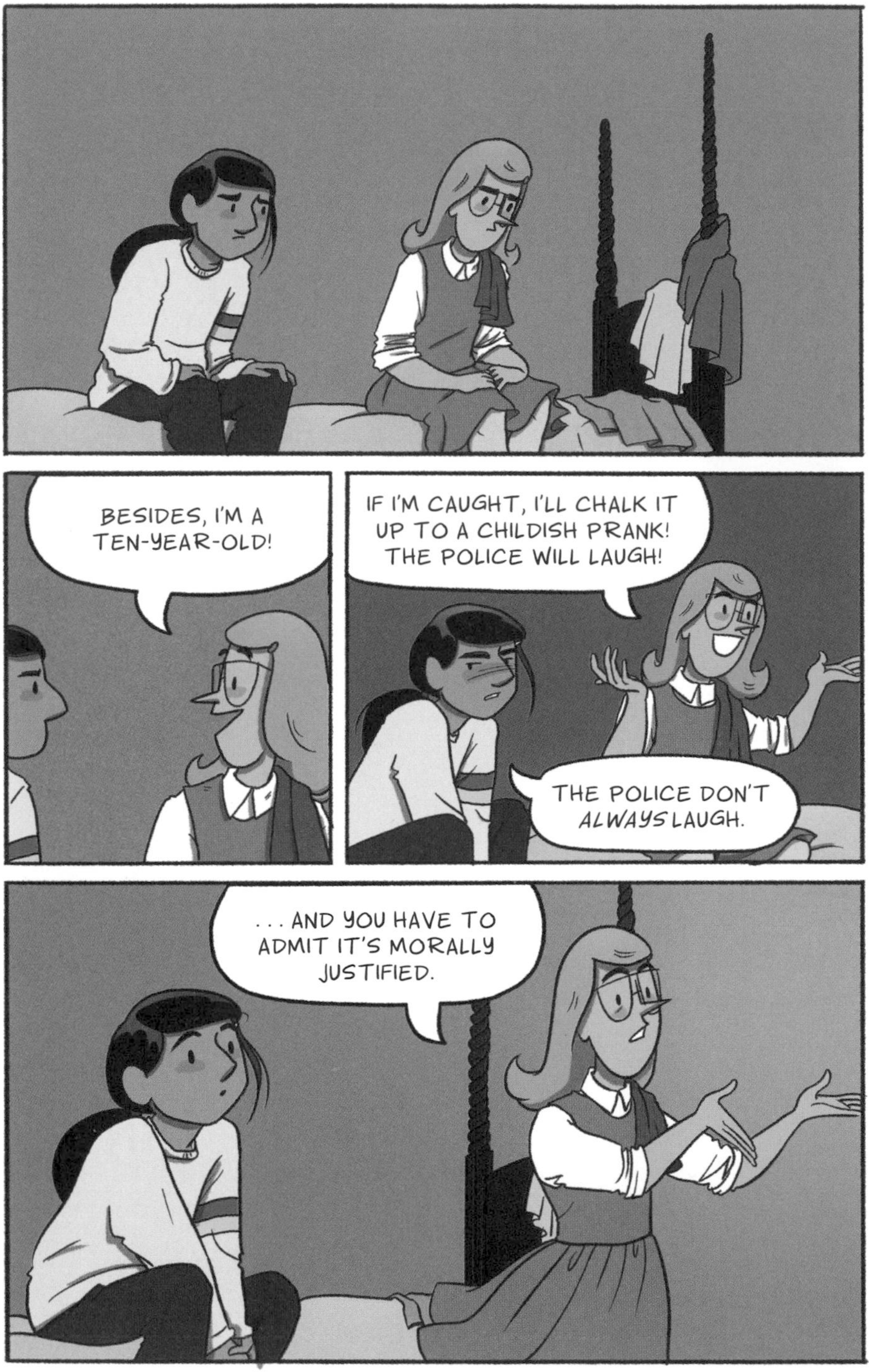
BESIDES, I'M A TEN-YEAR-OLD!
IF I'M CAUGHT, I'LL CHALK IT UP TO A CHILDISH PRANK! THE POLICE WILL LAUGH!
THE POLICE DON'T *ALWAYS* LAUGH.
. . . AND YOU HAVE TO ADMIT IT'S MORALLY JUSTIFIED.

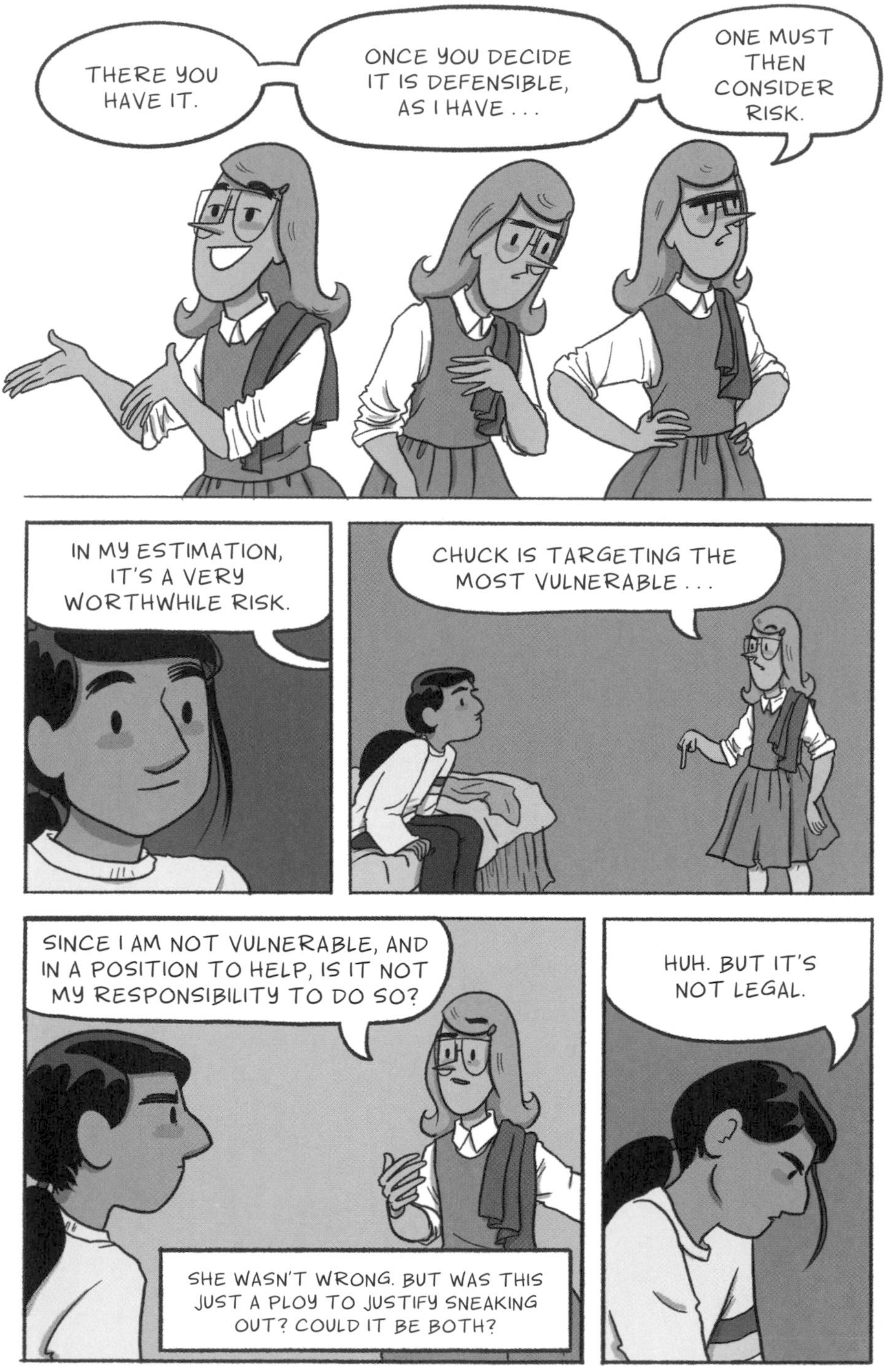
THERE YOU HAVE IT.
ONCE YOU DECIDE IT IS DEFENSIBLE, AS I HAVE . . .
ONE MUST THEN CONSIDER RISK.
IN MY ESTIMATION, IT'S A VERY WORTHWHILE RISK.
CHUCK IS TARGETING THE MOST VULNERABLE . . .
SINCE I AM NOT VULNERABLE, AND IN A POSITION TO HELP, IS IT NOT MY RESPONSIBILITY TO DO SO?
SHE WASN'T WRONG. BUT WAS THIS JUST A PLOY TO JUSTIFY SNEAKING OUT? COULD IT BE BOTH?
HUH. BUT IT'S NOT LEGAL.

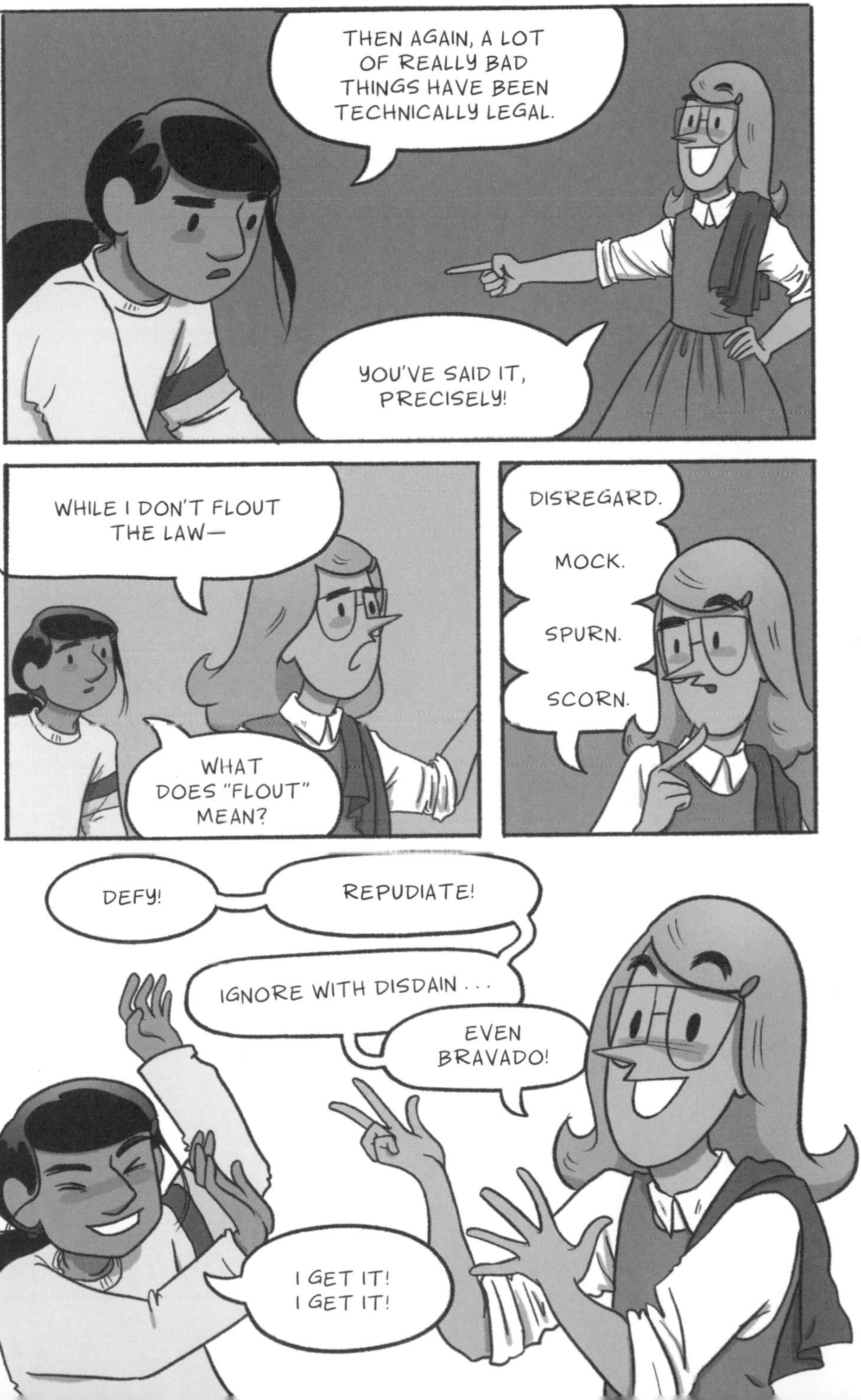
THEN AGAIN, A LOT OF REALLY BAD THINGS HAVE BEEN TECHNICALLY LEGAL.
YOU'VE SAID IT, PRECISELY!
WHILE I DON'T FLOUT THE LAW—
WHAT DOES "FLOUT" MEAN?
DISREGARD.
MOCK.
SPURN.
SCORN.
DEFY!
REPUDIATE!
IGNORE WITH DISDAIN . . .
EVEN BRAVADO!
I GET IT! I GET IT!

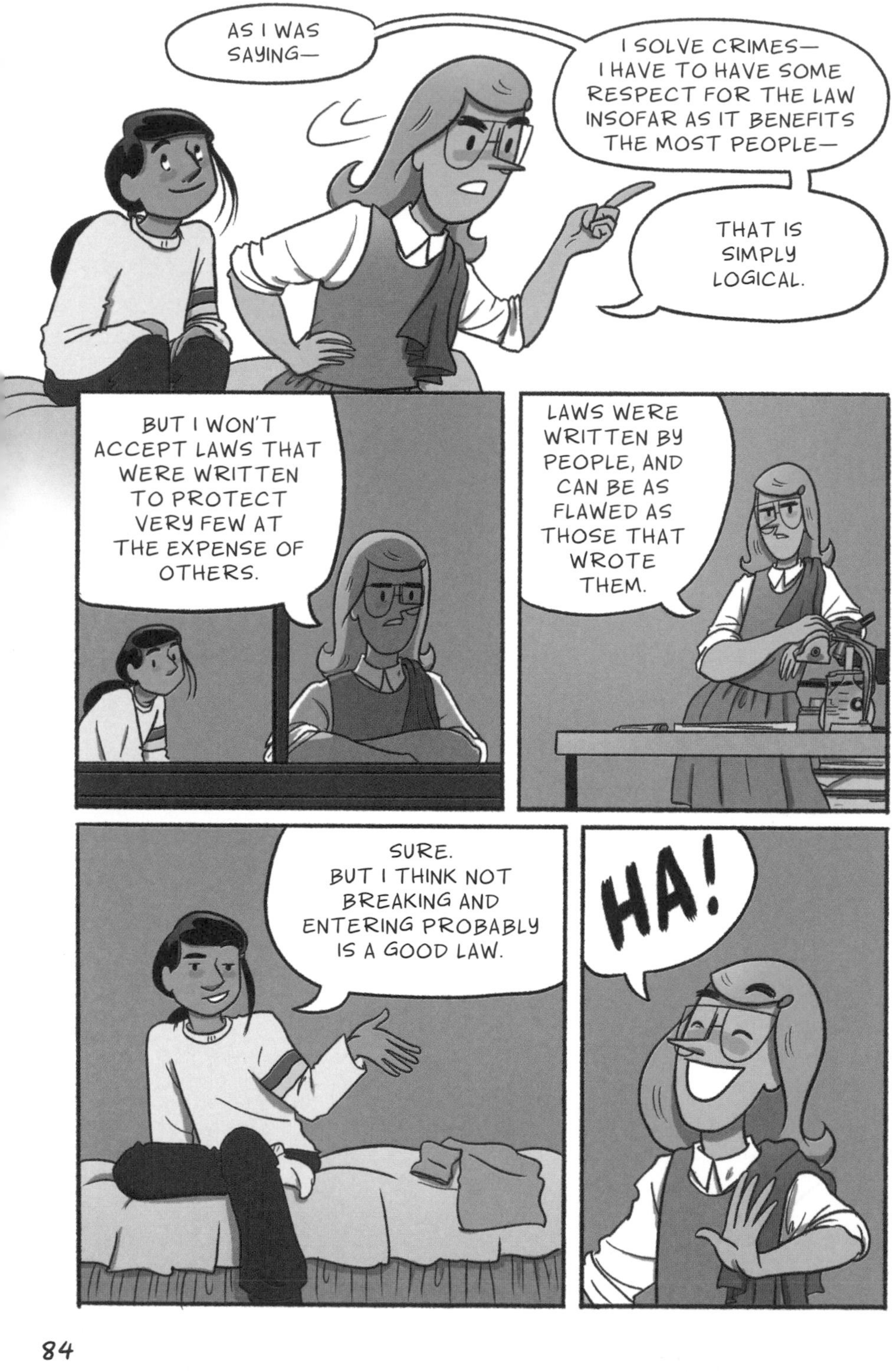
AS I WAS SAYING—
I SOLVE CRIMES— I HAVE TO HAVE SOME RESPECT FOR THE LAW INSOFAR AS IT BENEFITS THE MOST PEOPLE—
THAT IS SIMPLY LOGICAL.
BUT I WON'T ACCEPT LAWS THAT WERE WRITTEN TO PROTECT VERY FEW AT THE EXPENSE OF OTHERS.
LAWS WERE WRITTEN BY PEOPLE, AND CAN BE AS FLAWED AS THOSE THAT WROTE THEM.
SURE. BUT I THINK NOT BREAKING AND ENTERING PROBABLY IS A GOOD LAW.
HA!

86

87

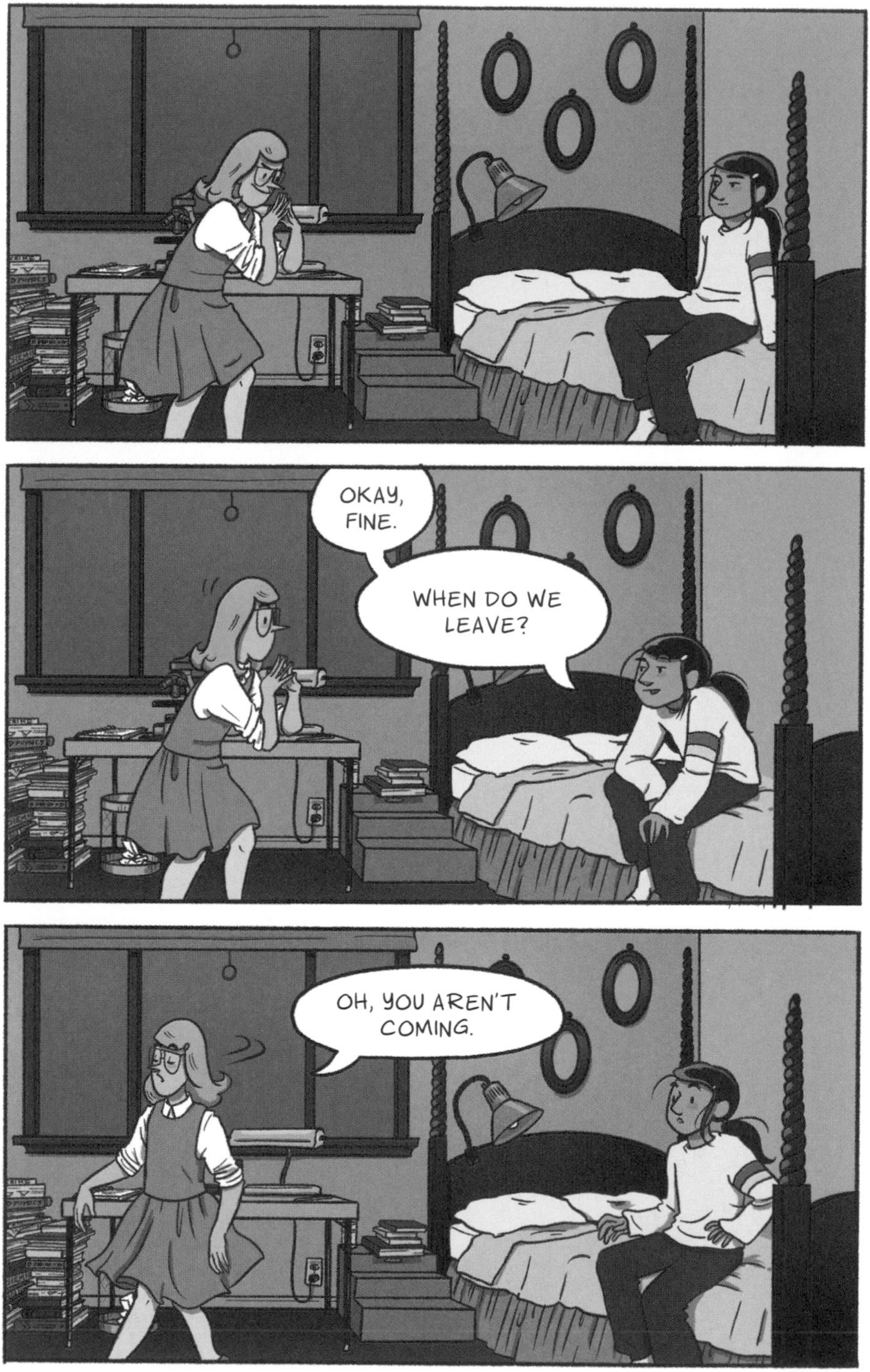
OKAY, FINE.
WHEN DO WE LEAVE?
OH, YOU AREN'T COMING.

89

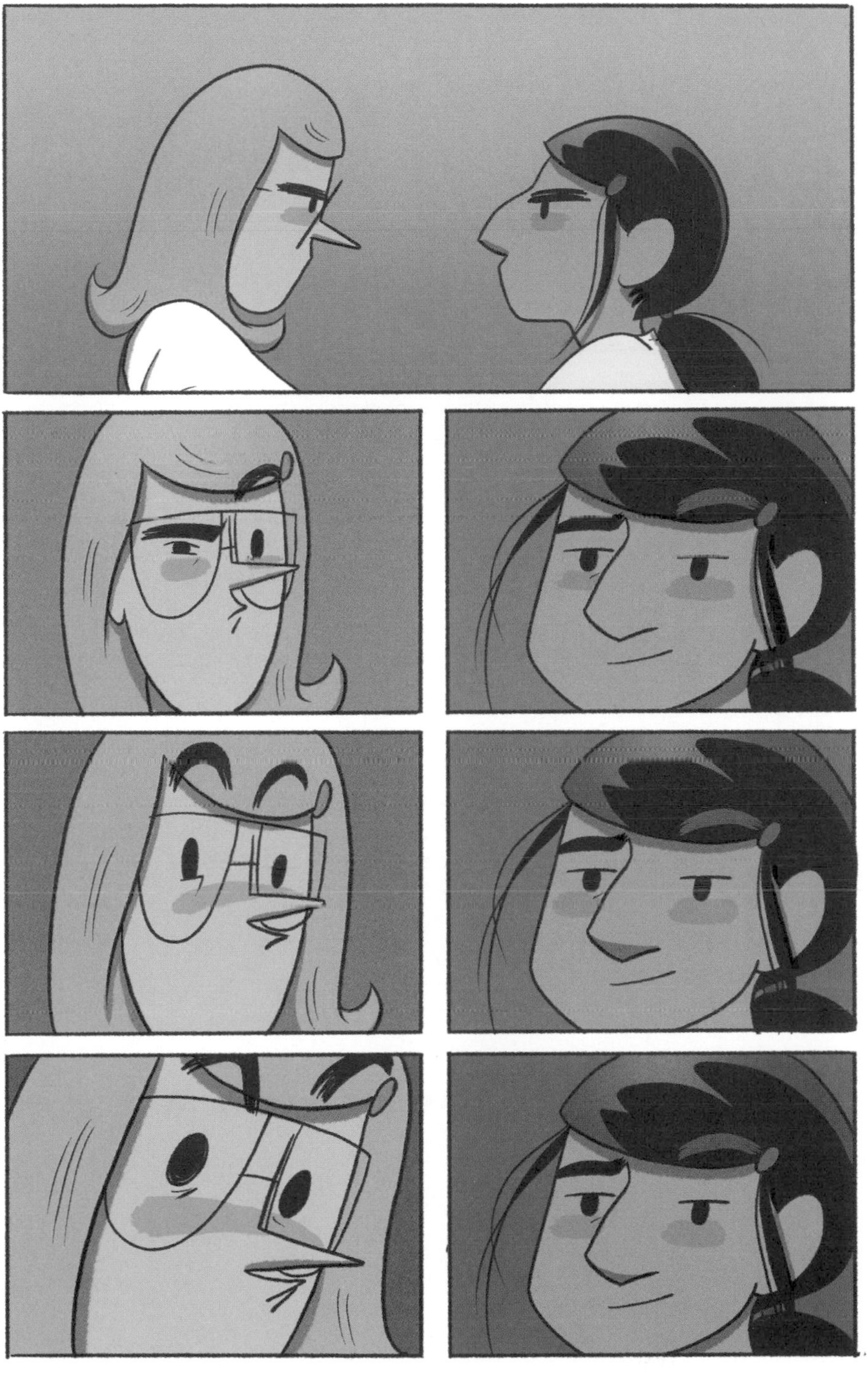

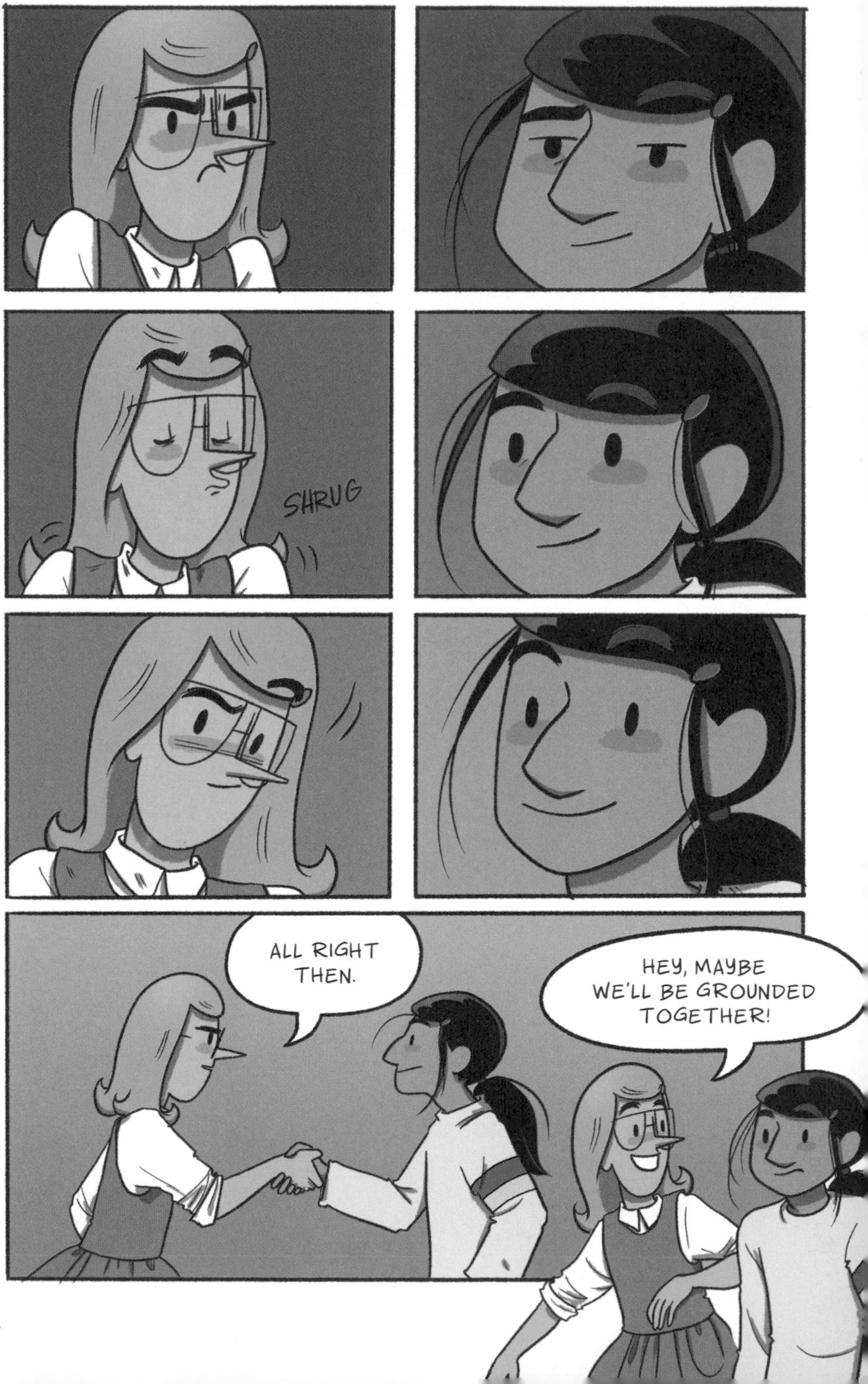
SHRUG
ALL RIGHT THEN.
HEY, MAYBE WE'LL BE GROUNDED TOGETHER!

Chapter 6

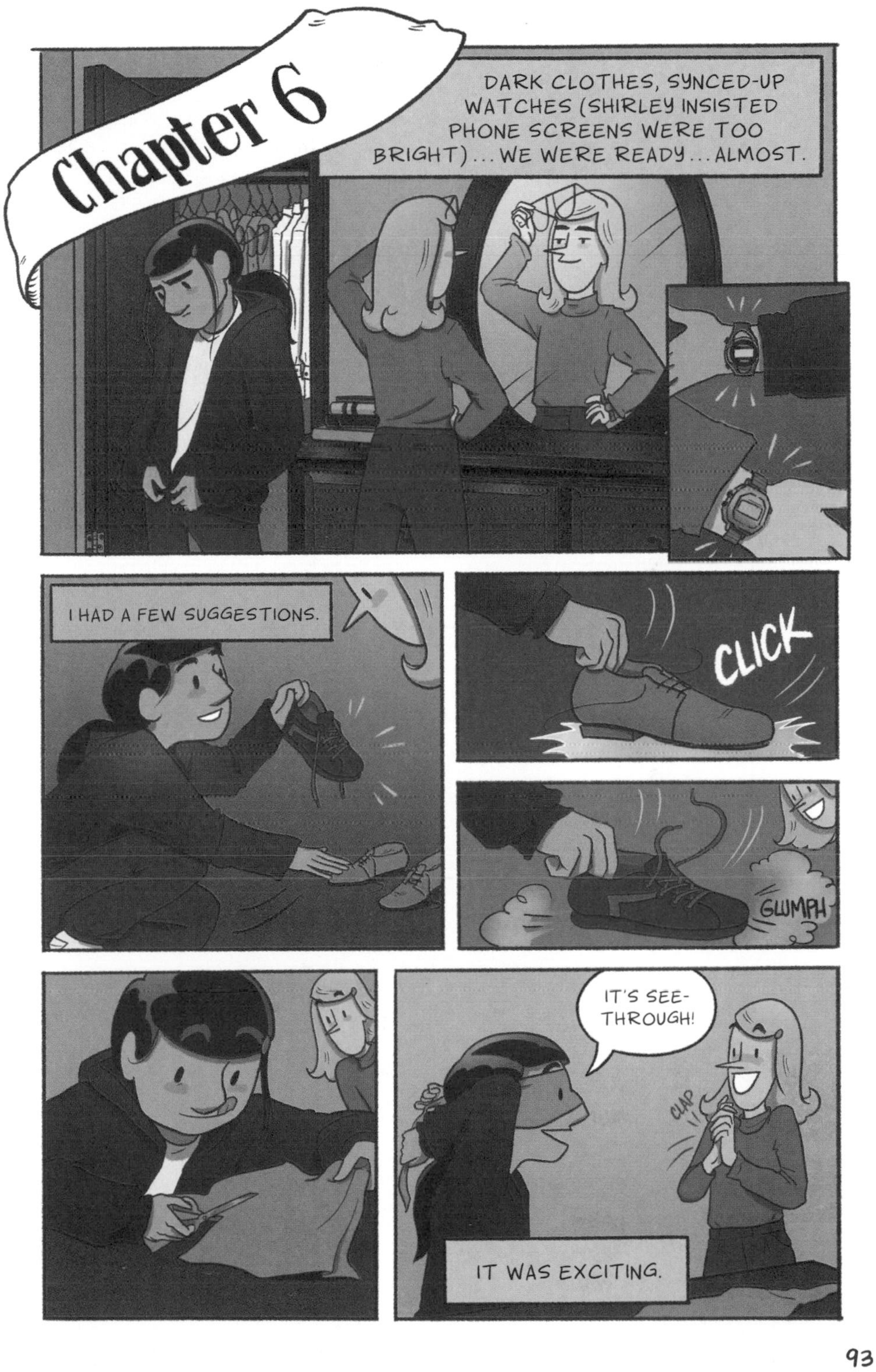
DARK CLOTHES, SYNCED-UP WATCHES (SHIRLEY INSISTED PHONE SCREENS WERE TOO BRIGHT) . . . WE WERE READY . . . ALMOST.
I HAD A FEW SUGGESTIONS.
CLICK
GLUMPH
IT'S SEE-THROUGH!
CLAP
IT WAS EXCITING.

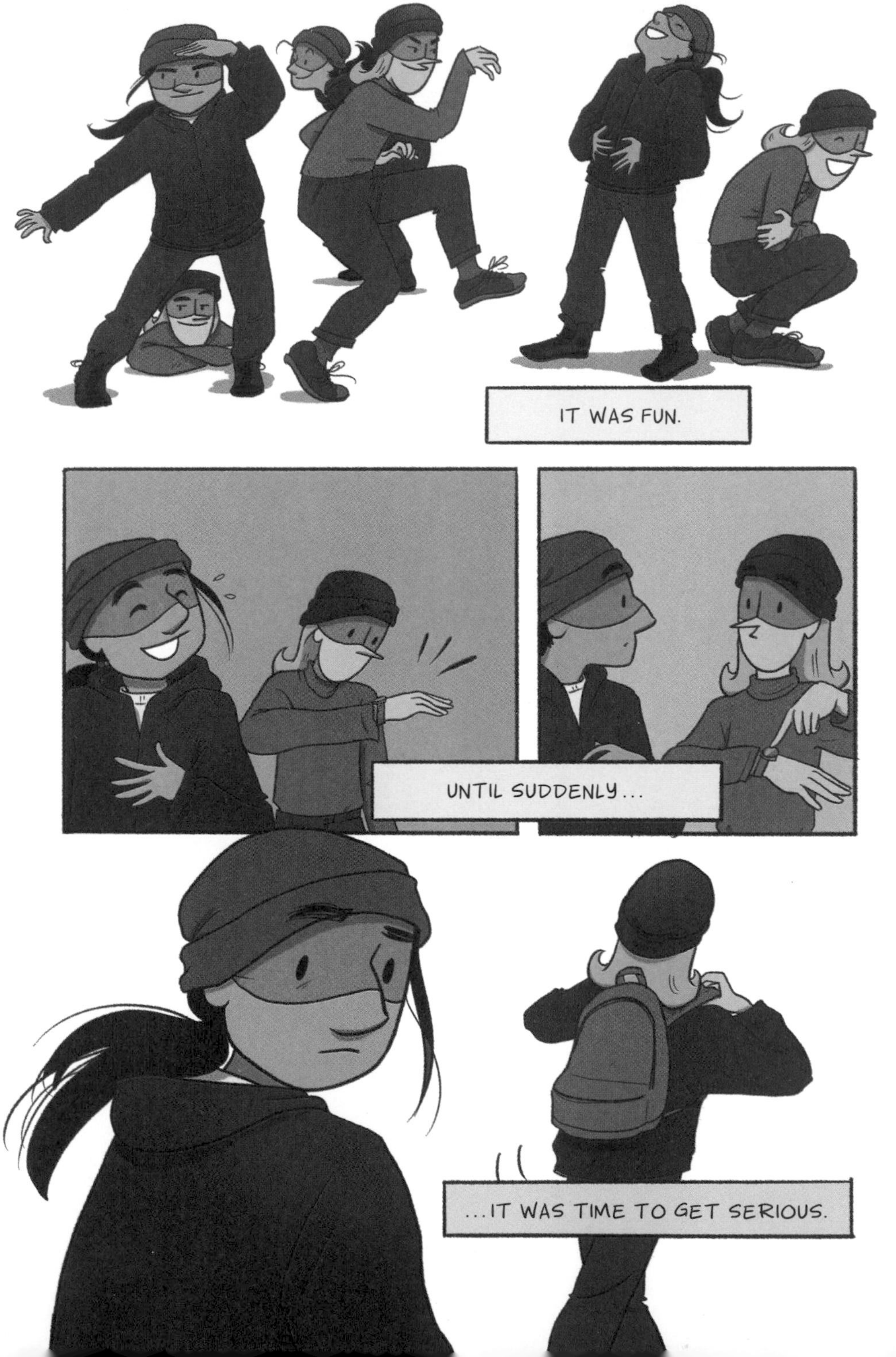
IT WAS FUN.
UNTIL SUDDENLY...
...IT WAS TIME TO GET SERIOUS.

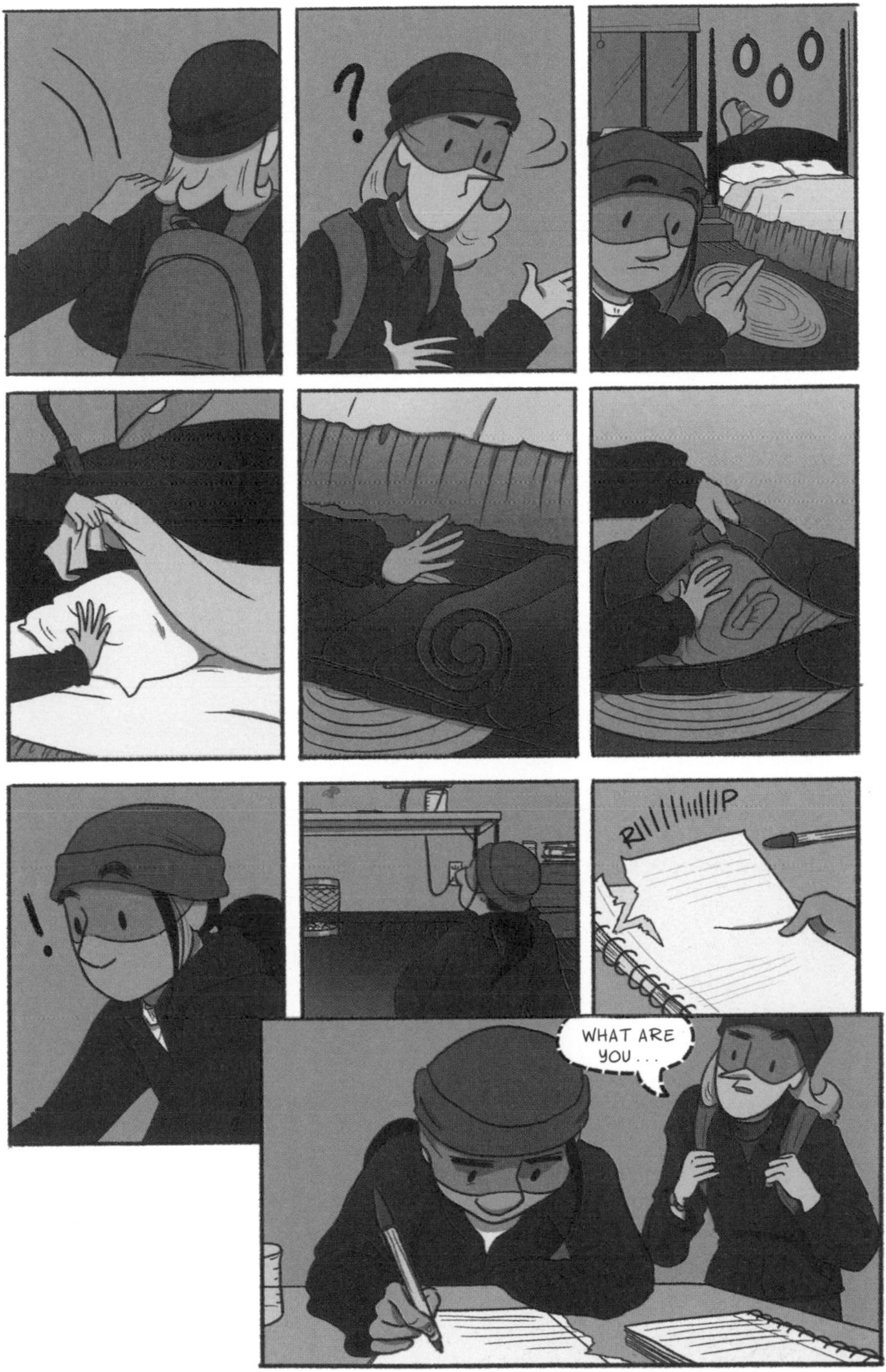
?
!
RIIIIIIIIIP
WHAT ARE YOU . . .

THE CLEVER JACKAL SNEAKS TOWARD ITS PREY...

BABY JACKALS ARE CALLED PUPS AND BEGIN HUNTING AS EARLY AS...

CREEEEEEEEKK

G'ROAN

KA-CHUNK

SHUMP

GETTING OUT OF THE HOUSE: ACHIEVED.

CLICK

BUT WHAT IF WE COULDN'T GET BACK IN?!

MIME TRANSLATION: WHERE'S THE BACK DOOR KEY???

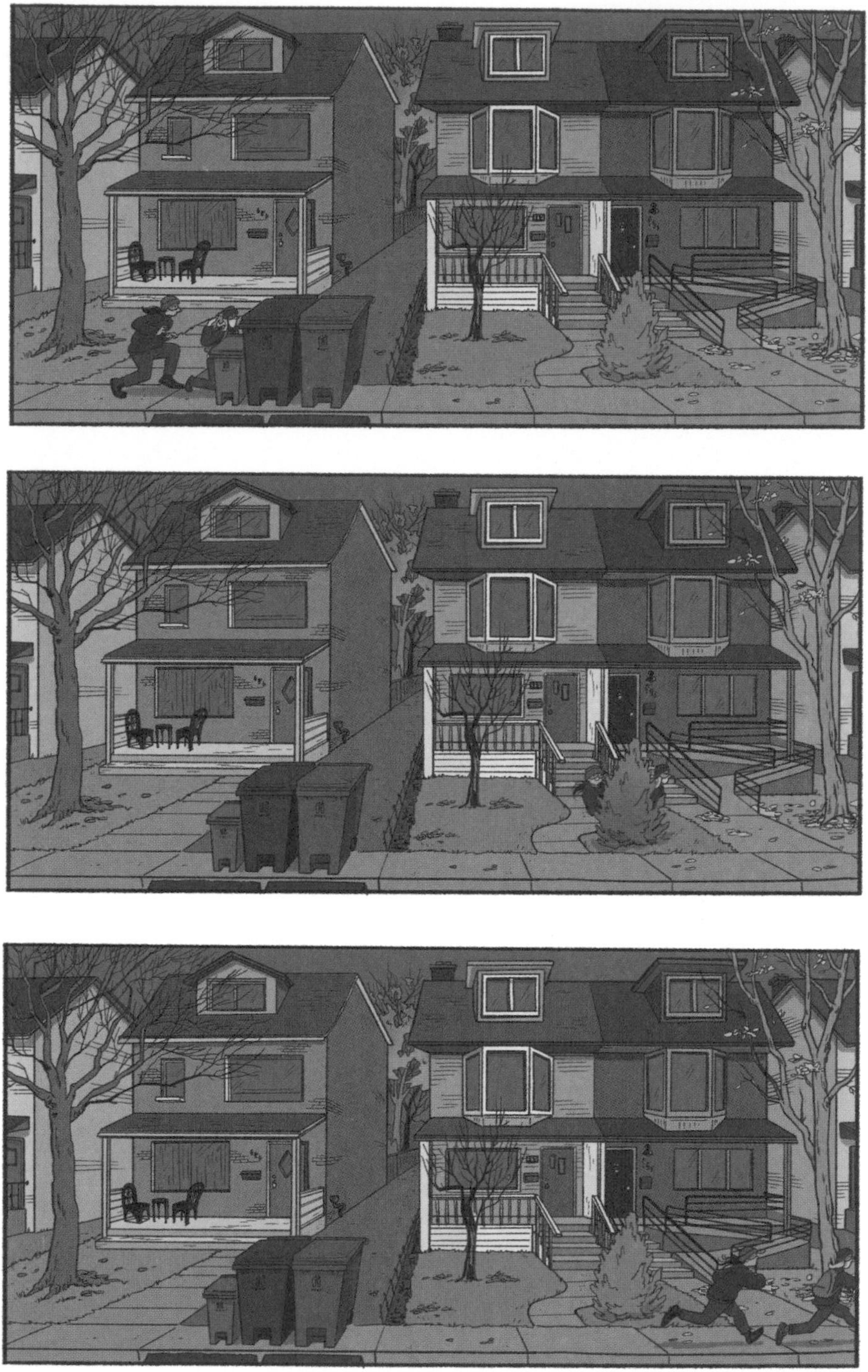

WHEW!

HERE. PUT THIS ON.

IF WE ARE SPOTTED WALKING AROUND IN MASKS AND SNEAK-WEAR, PEOPLE WILL KNOW WE'RE UP TO SOMETHING.

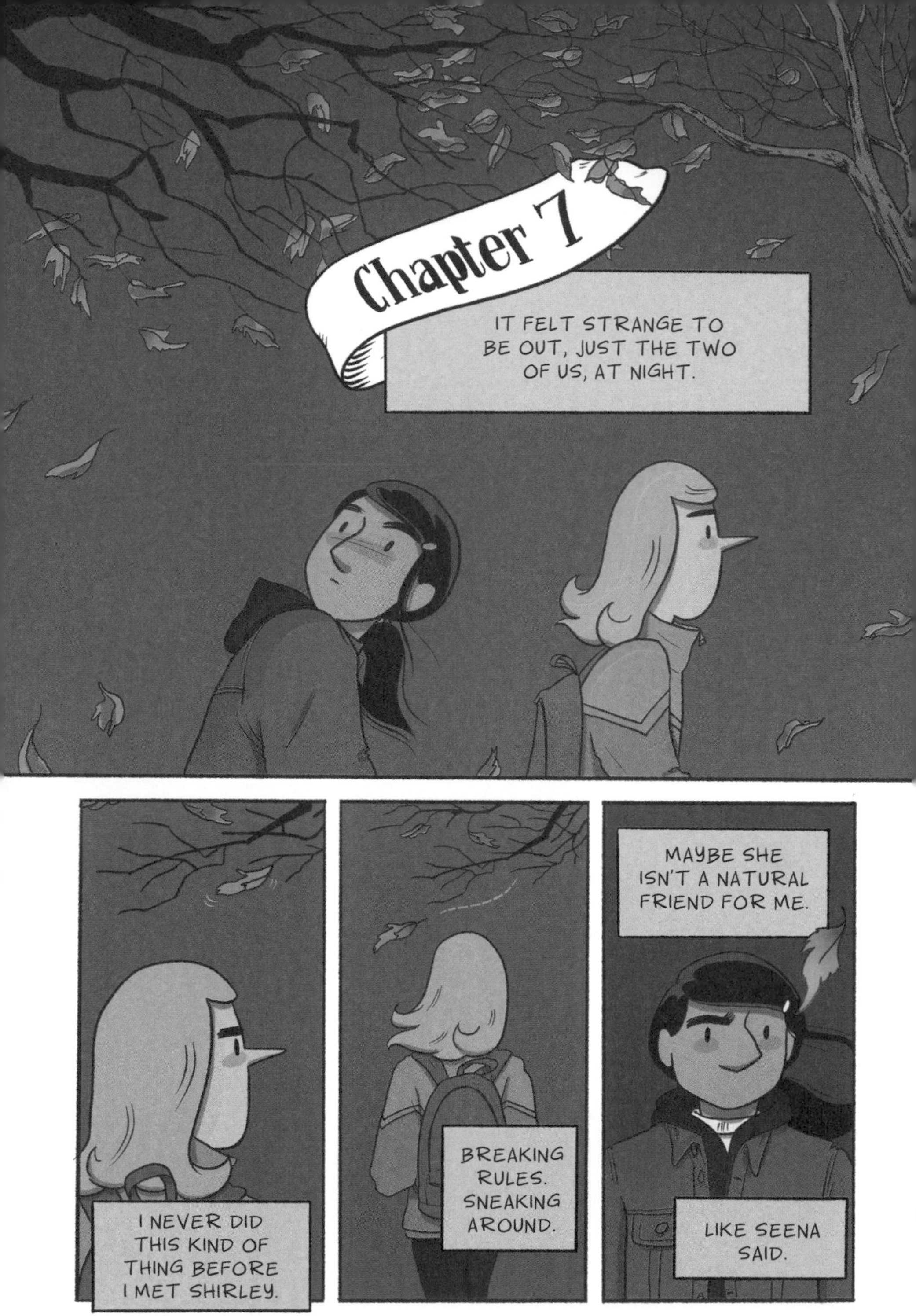
Chapter 7
IT FELT STRANGE TO BE OUT, JUST THE TWO OF US, AT NIGHT.
I NEVER DID THIS KIND OF THING BEFORE I MET SHIRLEY.
BREAKING RULES. SNEAKING AROUND.
MAYBE SHE ISN'T A NATURAL FRIEND FOR ME.
LIKE SEENA SAID.

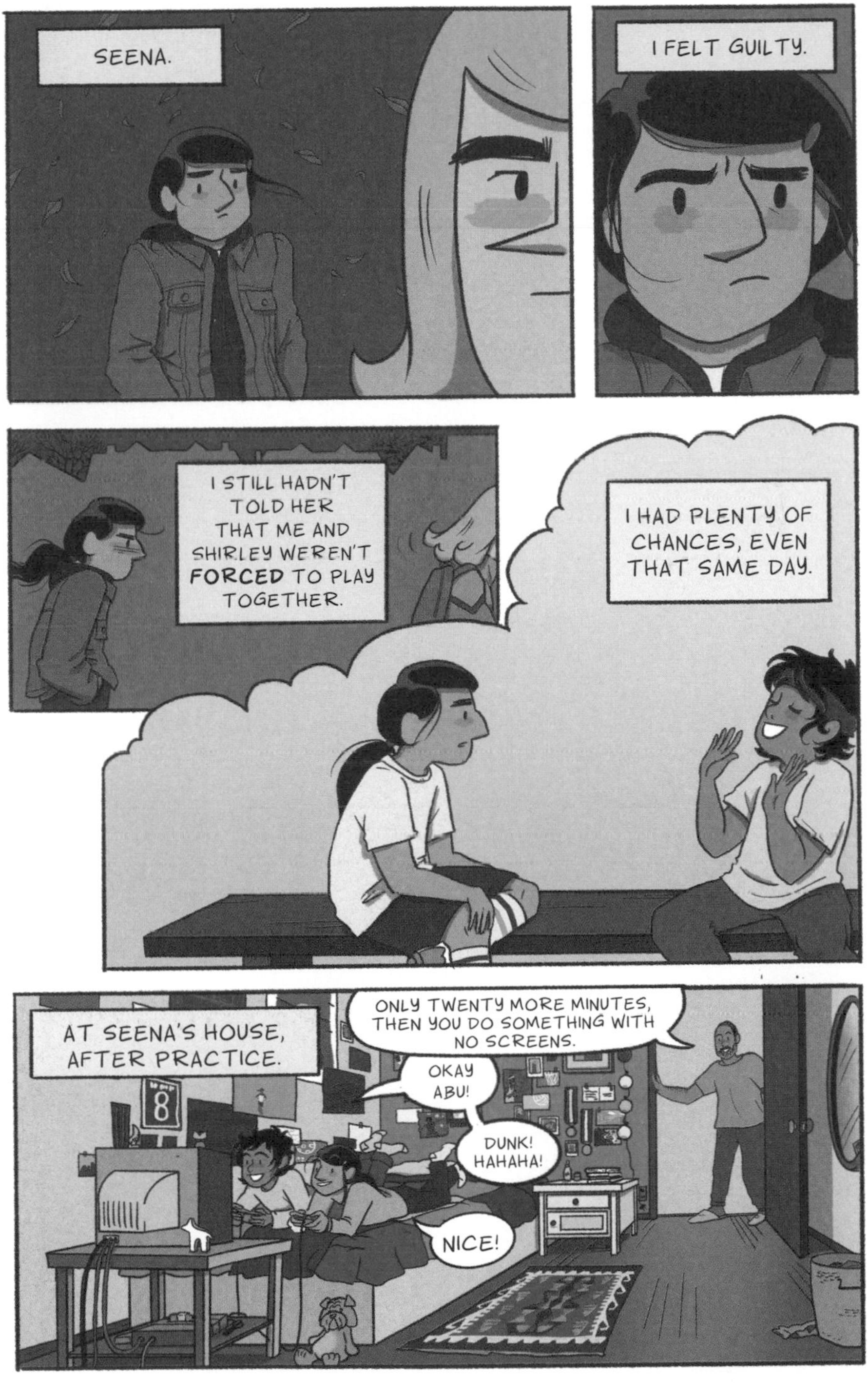
SEENA.
I FELT GUILTY.
I STILL HADN'T TOLD HER THAT ME AND SHIRLEY WEREN'T **FORCED** TO PLAY TOGETHER.
I HAD PLENTY OF CHANCES, EVEN THAT SAME DAY.
AT SEENA'S HOUSE, AFTER PRACTICE.
ONLY TWENTY MORE MINUTES, THEN YOU DO SOMETHING WITH NO SCREENS.
OKAY ABU!
DUNK! HAHAHA!
NICE!
8

I'D HATE TO BE FRIENDS WITH SOMEONE WHO ISN'T INTO BASKETBALL.

CLICK CLICK CLICK CLICK CLICK CLICK

MY SISTER'S BEST FRIEND DOESN'T CARE ABOUT MOVIES, AND THAT'S THE **ONLY** THING MY SISTER LIKES.

CLICK CLICK CLICK CLICK CLICK CLICK

WHAT DO THEY EVEN TALK ABOUT?!

THAT WOULD HAVE BEEN A GREAT TIME TO SAY SOMETHING.

HEH.

YEAH.

(NOT THAT.)

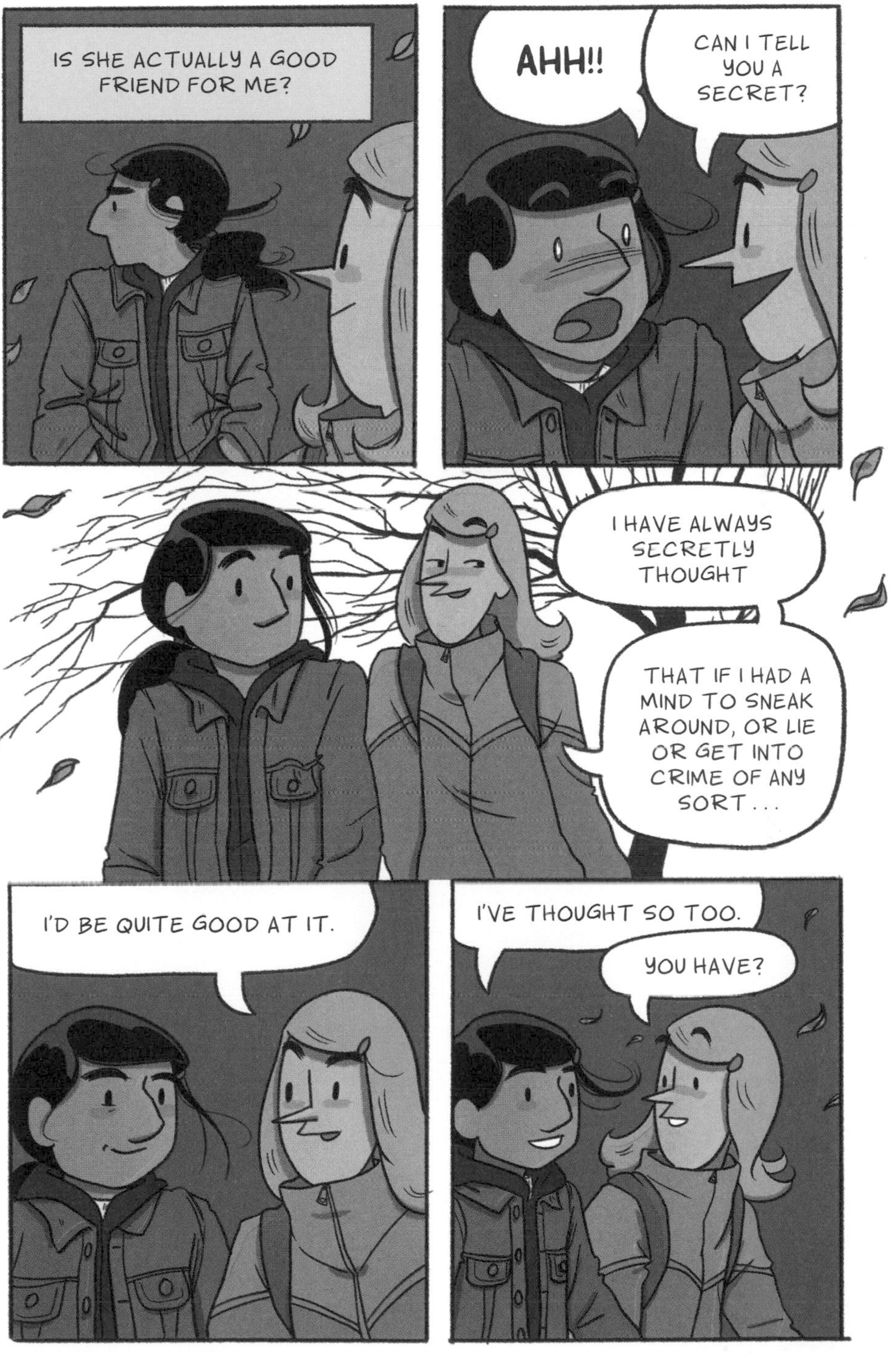
IS SHE ACTUALLY A GOOD FRIEND FOR ME?
AHH!!
CAN I TELL YOU A SECRET?
I HAVE ALWAYS SECRETLY THOUGHT
THAT IF I HAD A MIND TO SNEAK AROUND, OR LIE OR GET INTO CRIME OF ANY SORT . . .
I'D BE QUITE GOOD AT IT.
I'VE THOUGHT SO TOO.
YOU HAVE?

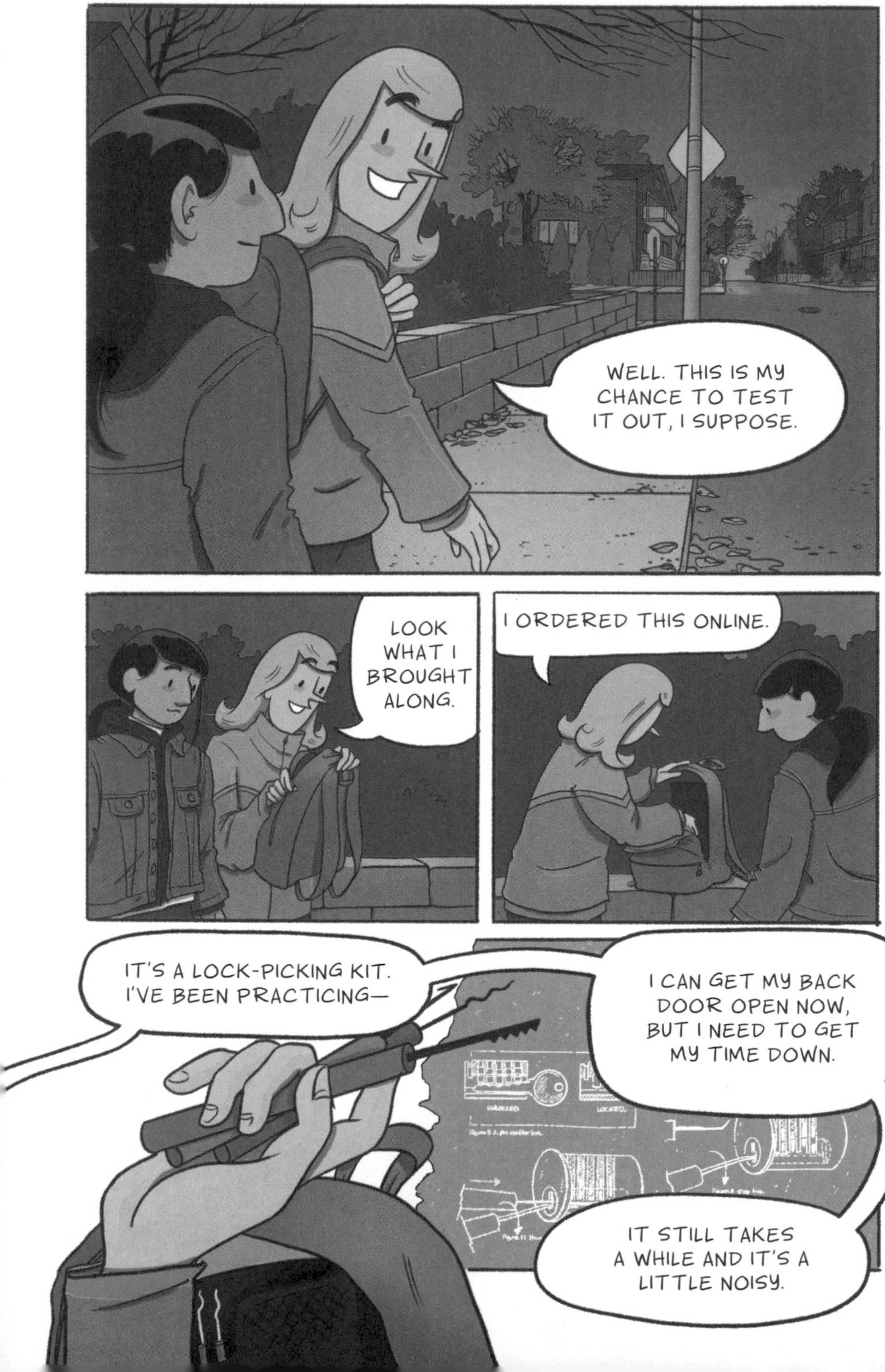
WELL. THIS IS MY CHANCE TO TEST IT OUT, I SUPPOSE.
LOOK WHAT I BROUGHT ALONG.
I ORDERED THIS ONLINE.
IT'S A LOCK-PICKING KIT. I'VE BEEN PRACTICING—
I CAN GET MY BACK DOOR OPEN NOW, BUT I NEED TO GET MY TIME DOWN.
UNLOCKED
LOCKED.
IT STILL TAKES A WHILE AND IT'S A LITTLE NOISY.

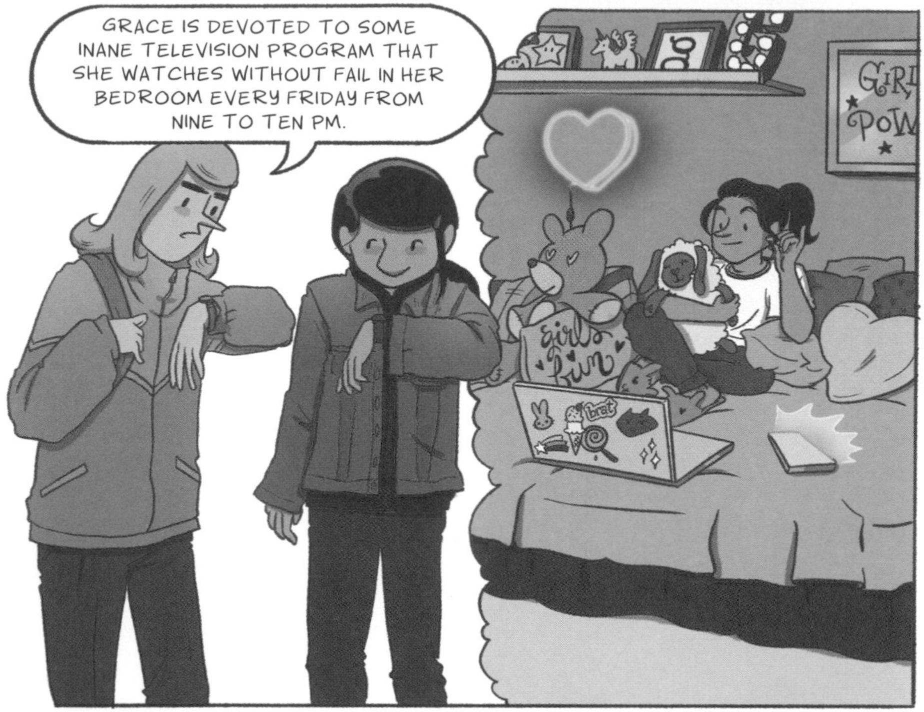
GRACE IS DEVOTED TO SOME INANE TELEVISION PROGRAM THAT SHE WATCHES WITHOUT FAIL IN HER BEDROOM EVERY FRIDAY FROM NINE TO TEN PM.
GIRL POW
girls run
brat

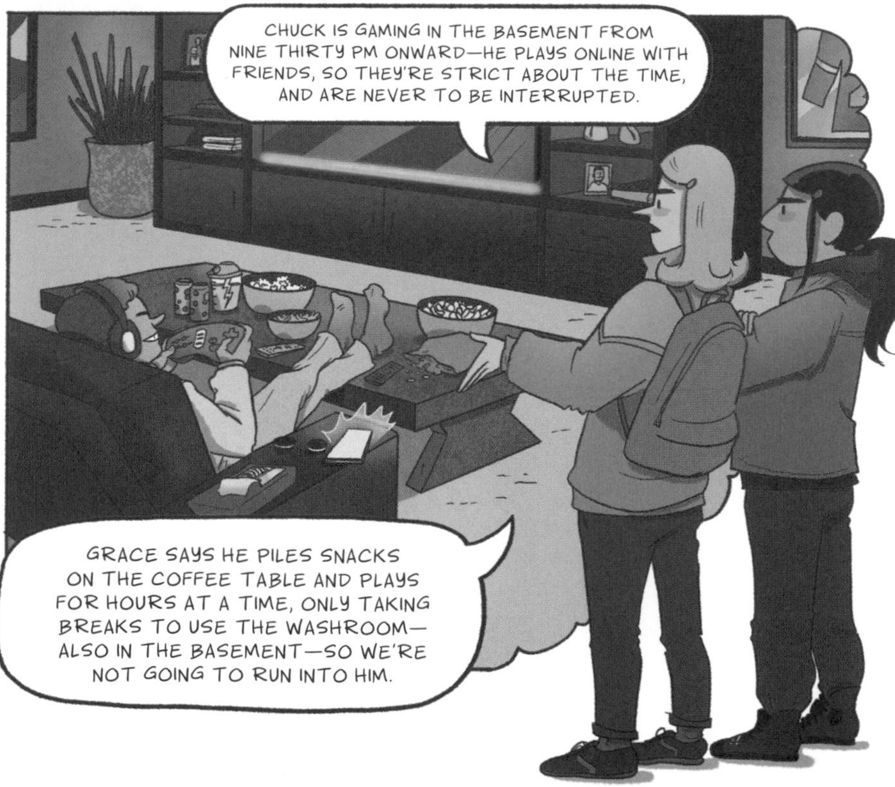
CHUCK IS GAMING IN THE BASEMENT FROM NINE THIRTY PM ONWARD—HE PLAYS ONLINE WITH FRIENDS, SO THEY'RE STRICT ABOUT THE TIME, AND ARE NEVER TO BE INTERRUPTED.
GRACE SAYS HE PILES SNACKS ON THE COFFEE TABLE AND PLAYS FOR HOURS AT A TIME, ONLY TAKING BREAKS TO USE THE WASHROOM—ALSO IN THE BASEMENT—SO WE'RE NOT GOING TO RUN INTO HIM.

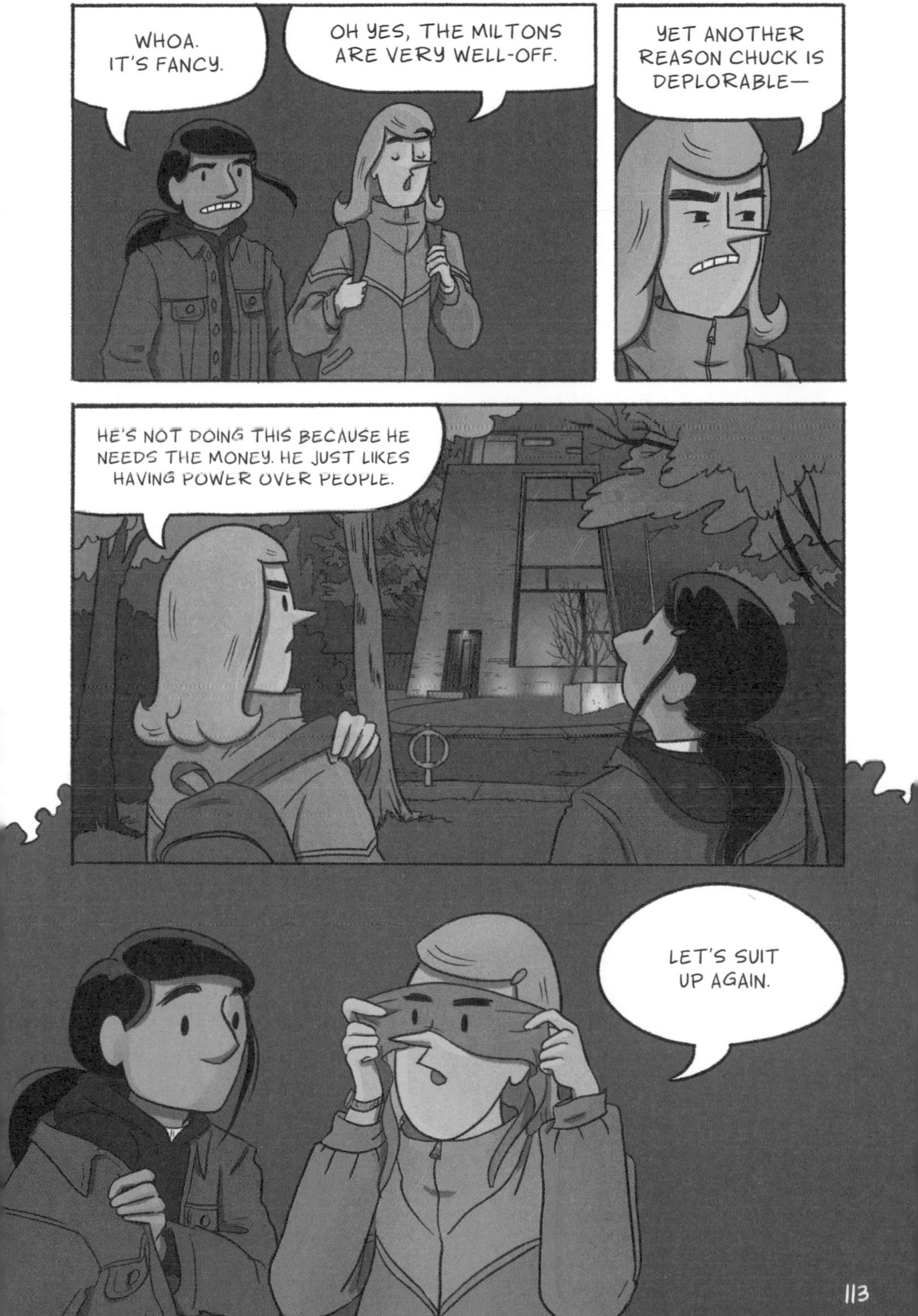
WHOA. IT'S FANCY.
OH YES, THE MILTONS ARE VERY WELL-OFF.
YET ANOTHER REASON CHUCK IS DEPLORABLE—
HE'S NOT DOING THIS BECAUSE HE NEEDS THE MONEY. HE JUST LIKES HAVING POWER OVER PEOPLE.
LET'S SUIT UP AGAIN.

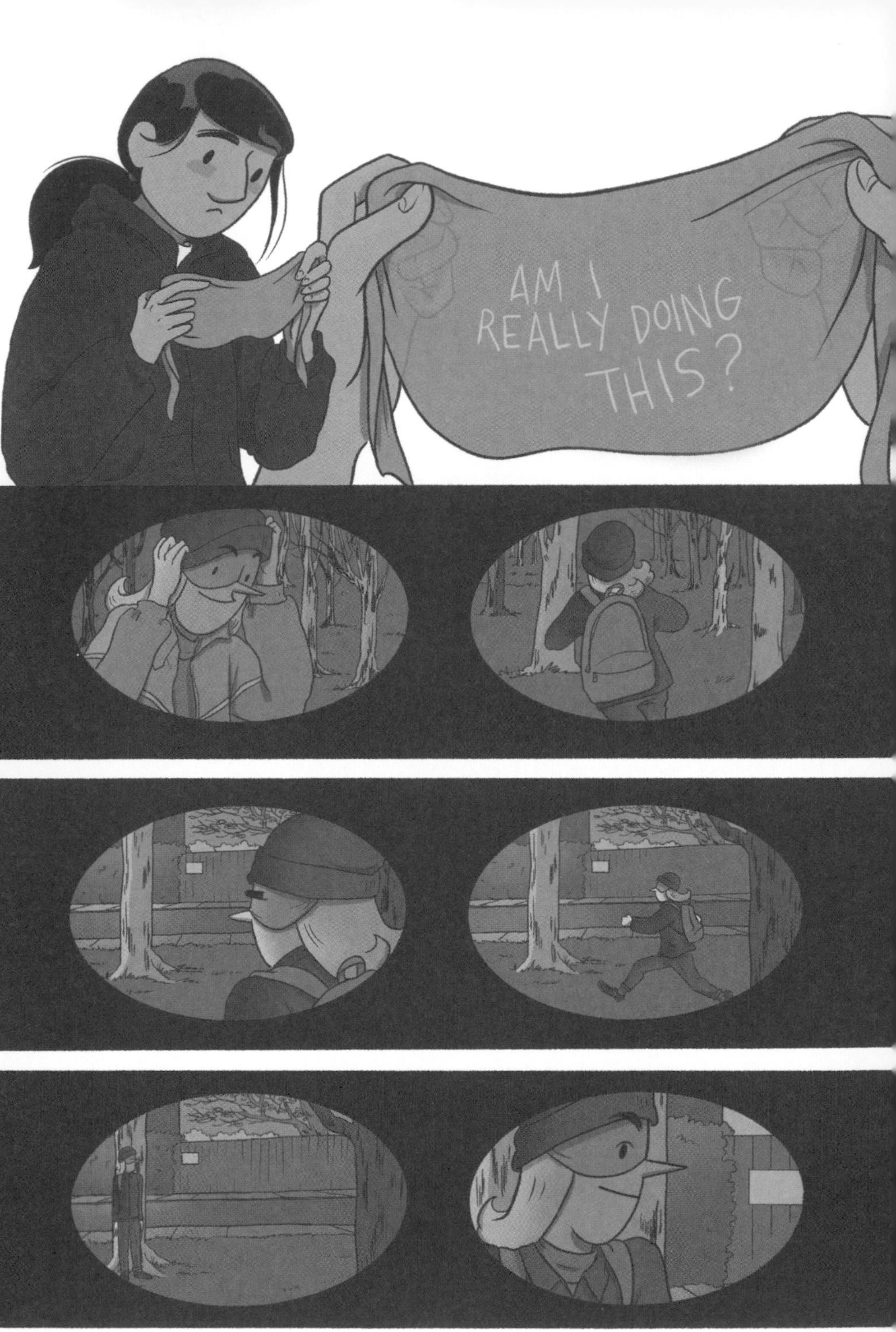
AM I REALLY DOING THIS?

WE GOT QUIET AGAIN.

SUDDENLY IT FELT **REAL**.

Chapter 8

WE WERE REALLY
DOING THIS.

BEWARE
OF
DOG

SHIRLEY'S WHISPER WAS
ALMOST SILENT. LIKE
THE VOICE OF A MOTH.

THE SIGN
IS A FAKE.

THEY WANT TO SCARE
PEOPLE OFF BUT DON'T
WANT TO HAVE TO TAKE
CARE OF A REAL DOG.

I BET YOUR "BEST FRIEND" GRACE GAVE YOU THE CODE?

SHE DID A VERY BAD JOB OF HIDING IT.

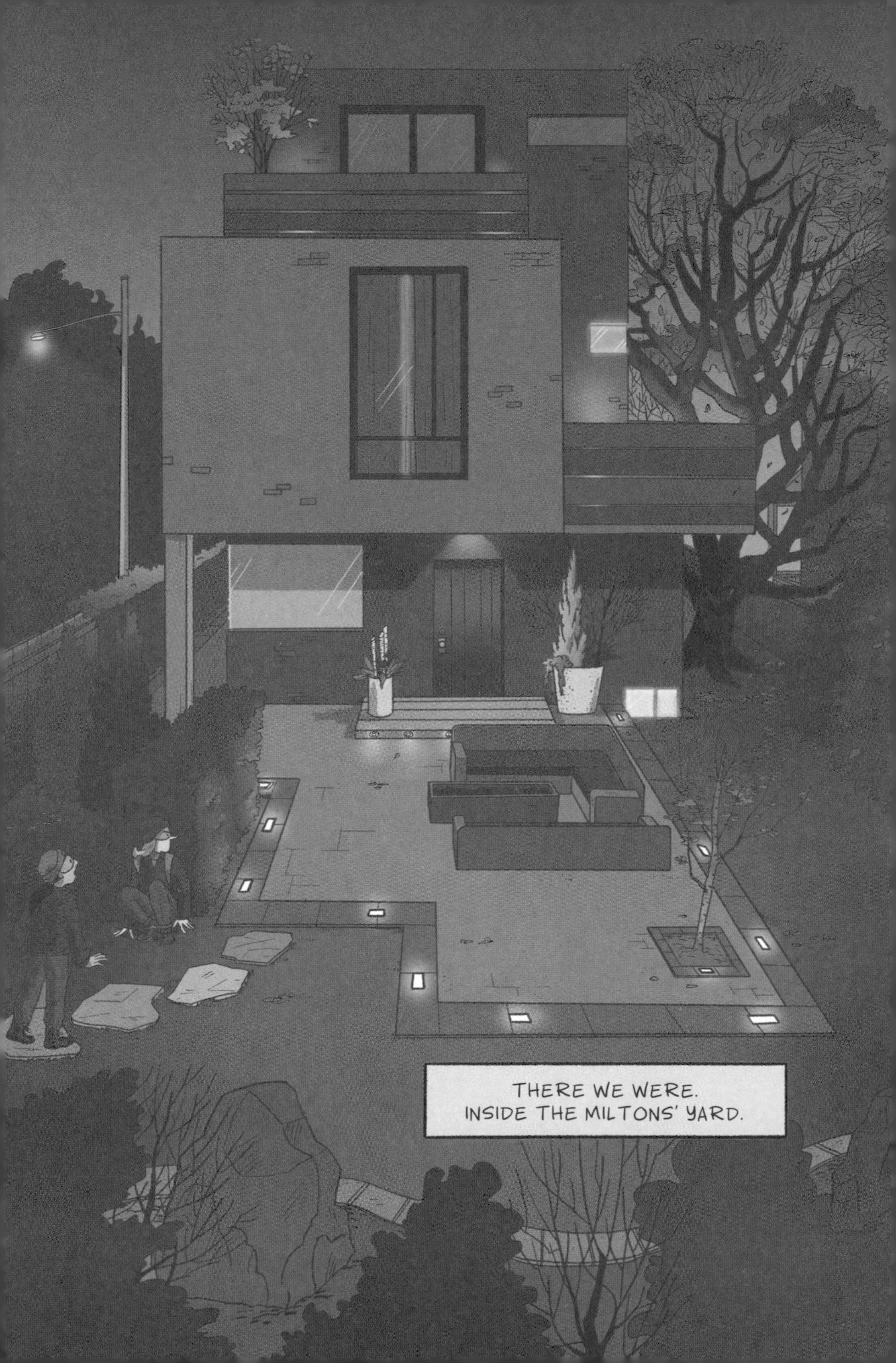
THERE WE WERE.
INSIDE THE MILTONS' YARD.

SHIRLEY SEEMED
SO CONFIDENT.

I COULDN'T HELP FEELING LIKE
WE WEREN'T ALONE.

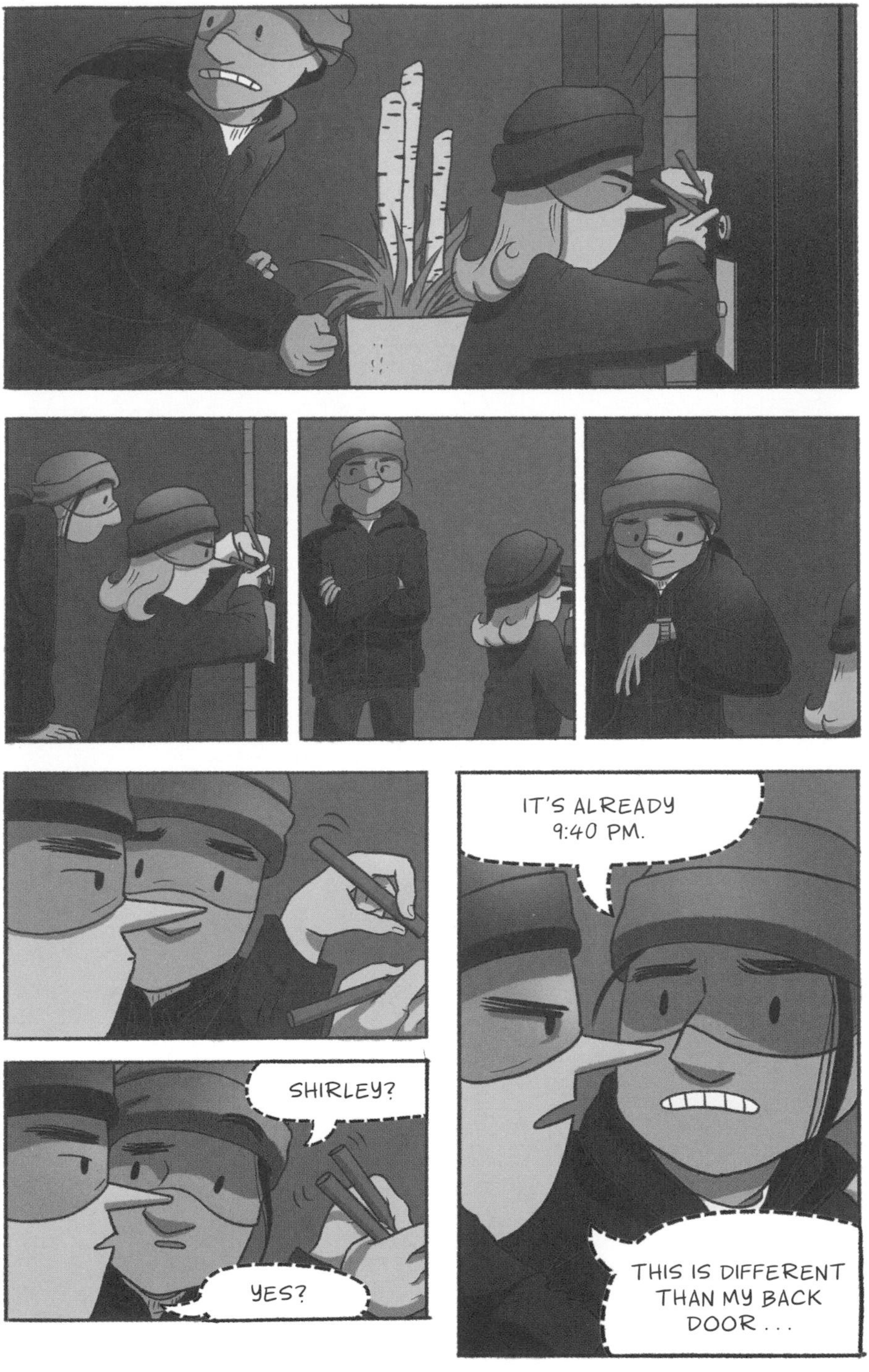
IT'S ALREADY 9:40 PM.
SHIRLEY?
YES?
THIS IS DIFFERENT THAN MY BACK DOOR . . .

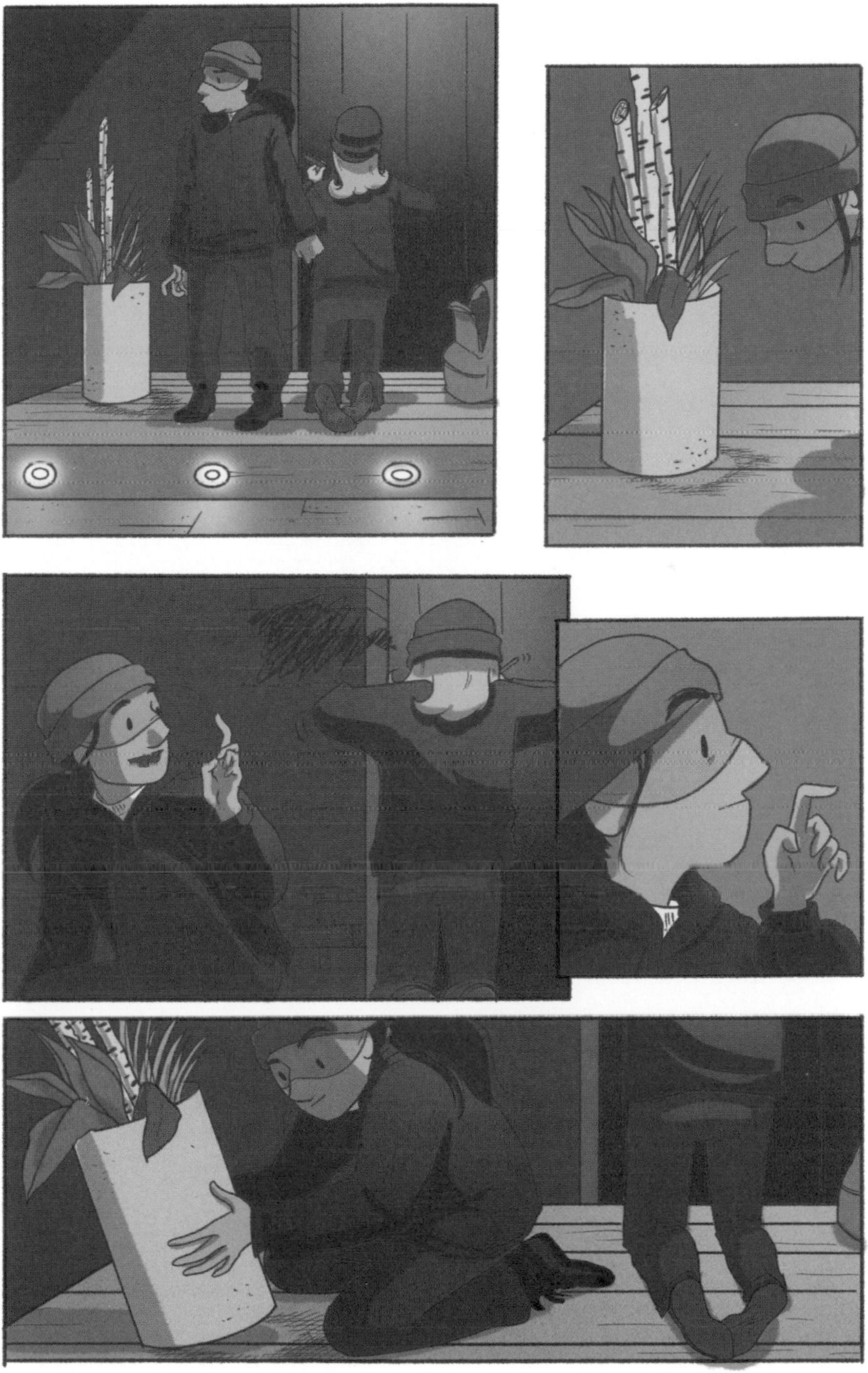

PLEASE DON'T BUMP ME
WHILE I'M DOING THIS.

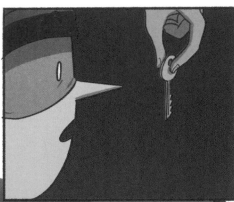

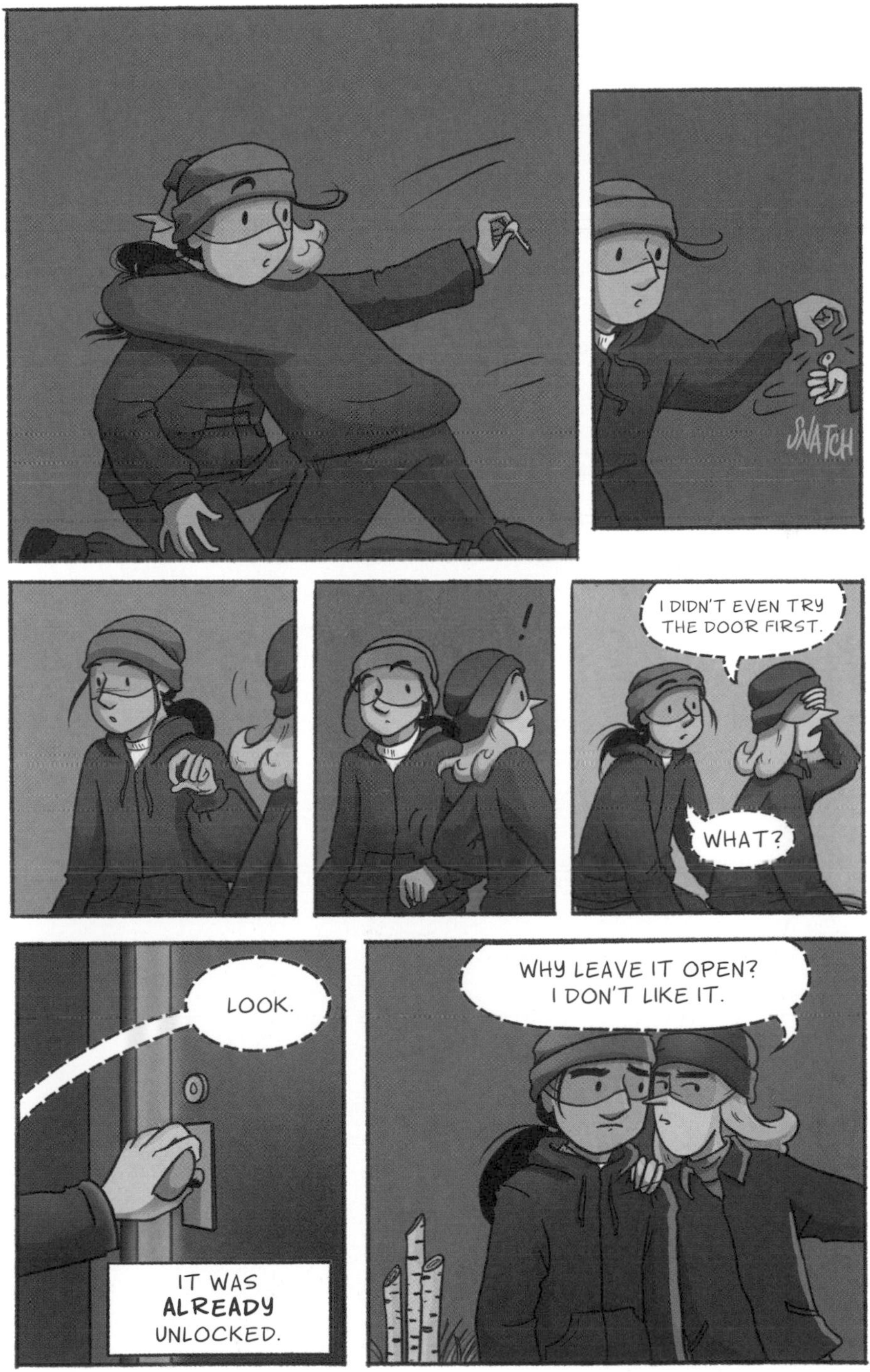
SNATCH
!
I DIDN'T EVEN TRY THE DOOR FIRST.
WHAT?
LOOK.
IT WAS **ALREADY** UNLOCKED.
WHY LEAVE IT OPEN? I DON'T LIKE IT.

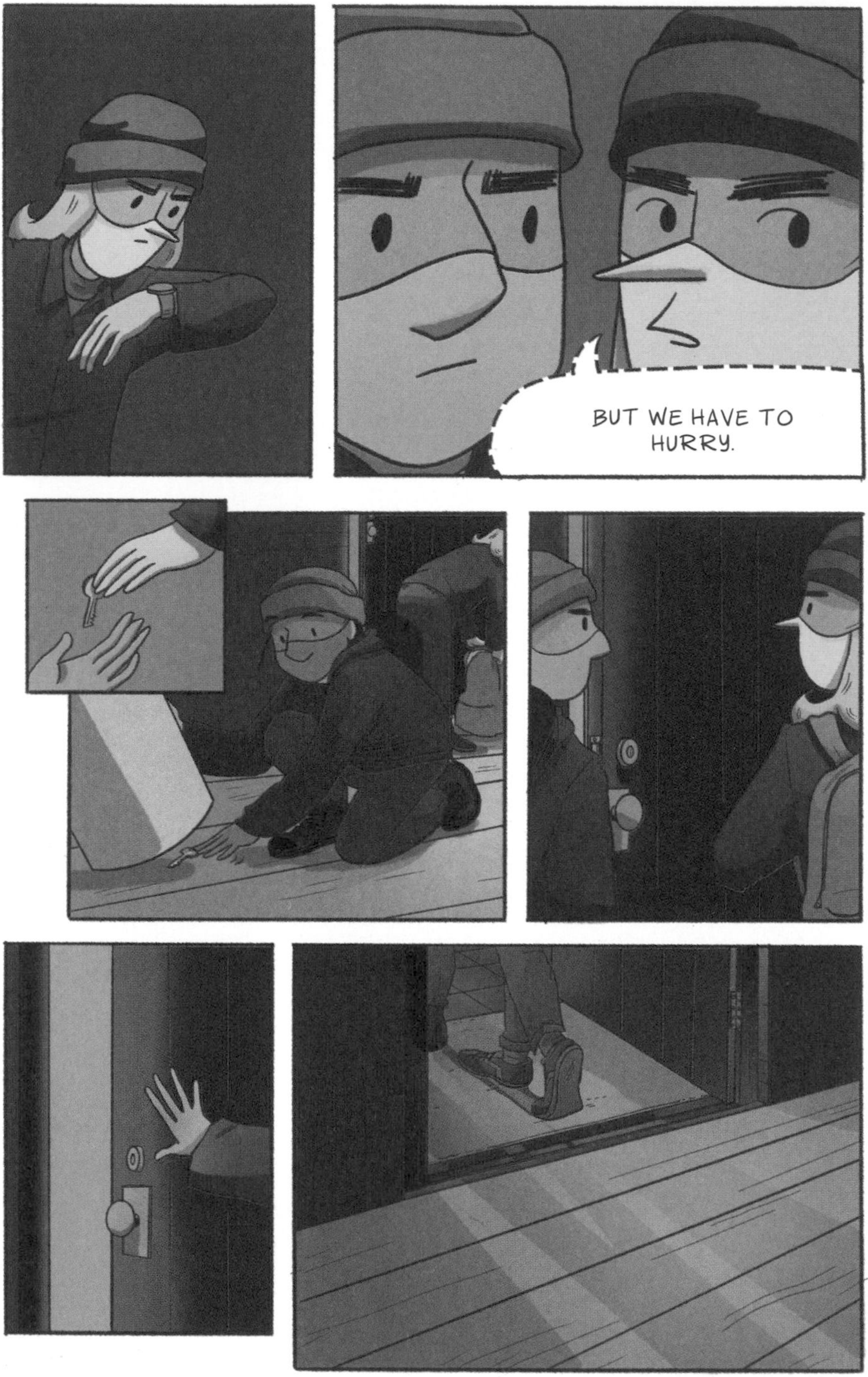
BUT WE HAVE TO
HURRY.

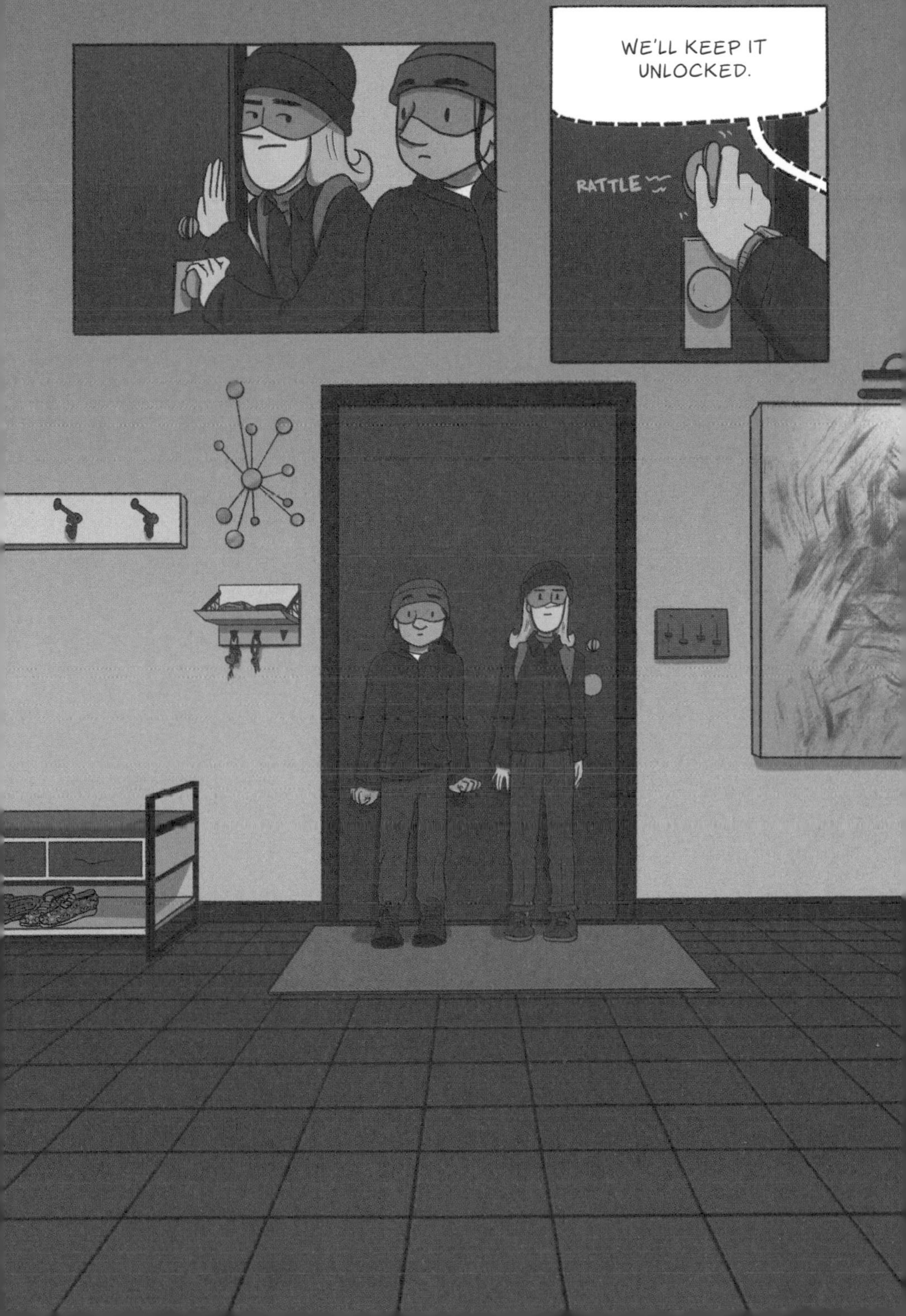
WE'LL KEEP IT UNLOCKED.
RATTLE

Chapter 9

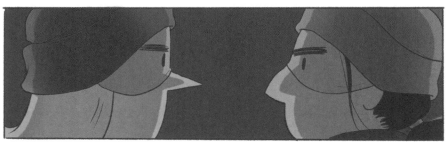

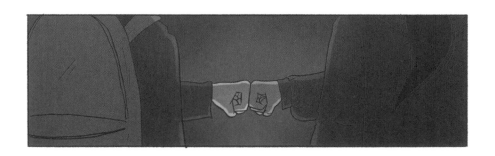

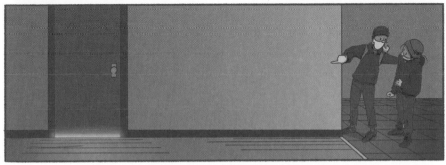

THAT'S THE STAIRS TO THE BASEMENT...

WHERE CHUCK...

IS PLAYING VIDEO GAMES.

SHIRLEY ONLY USED HAND GESTURES, BUT I KNEW EXACTLY WHAT SHE MEANT.

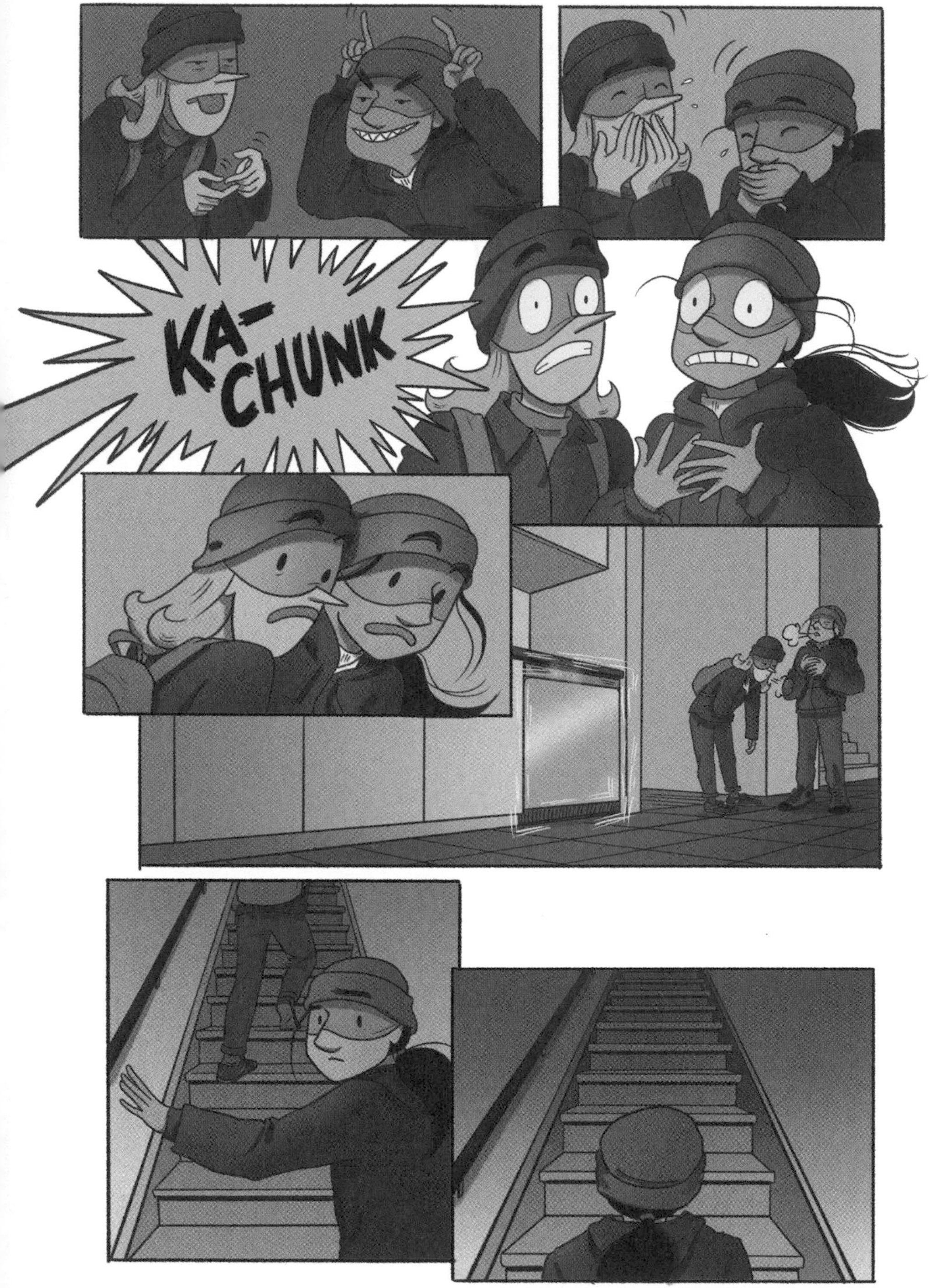
KA-CHUNK

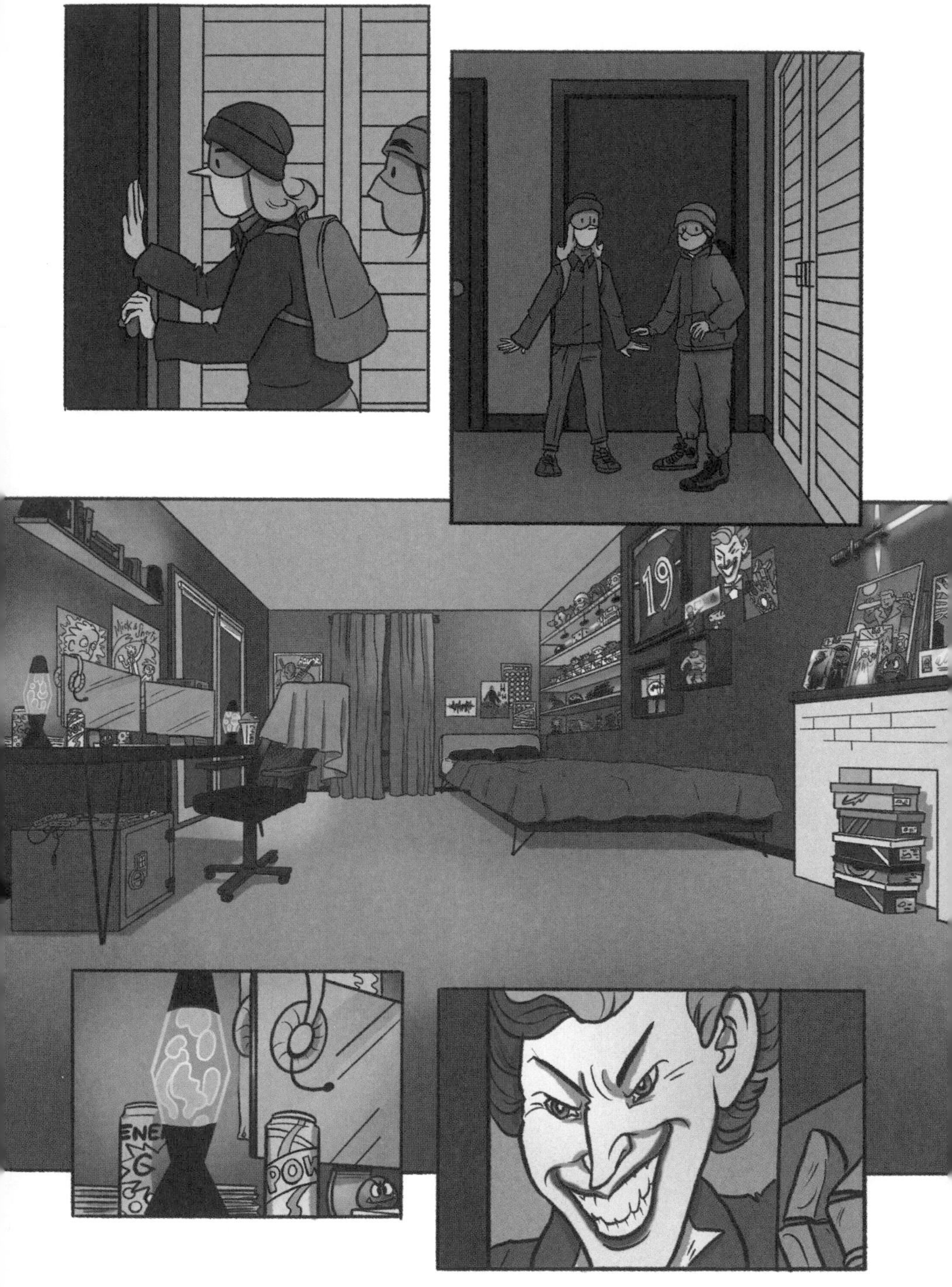
19

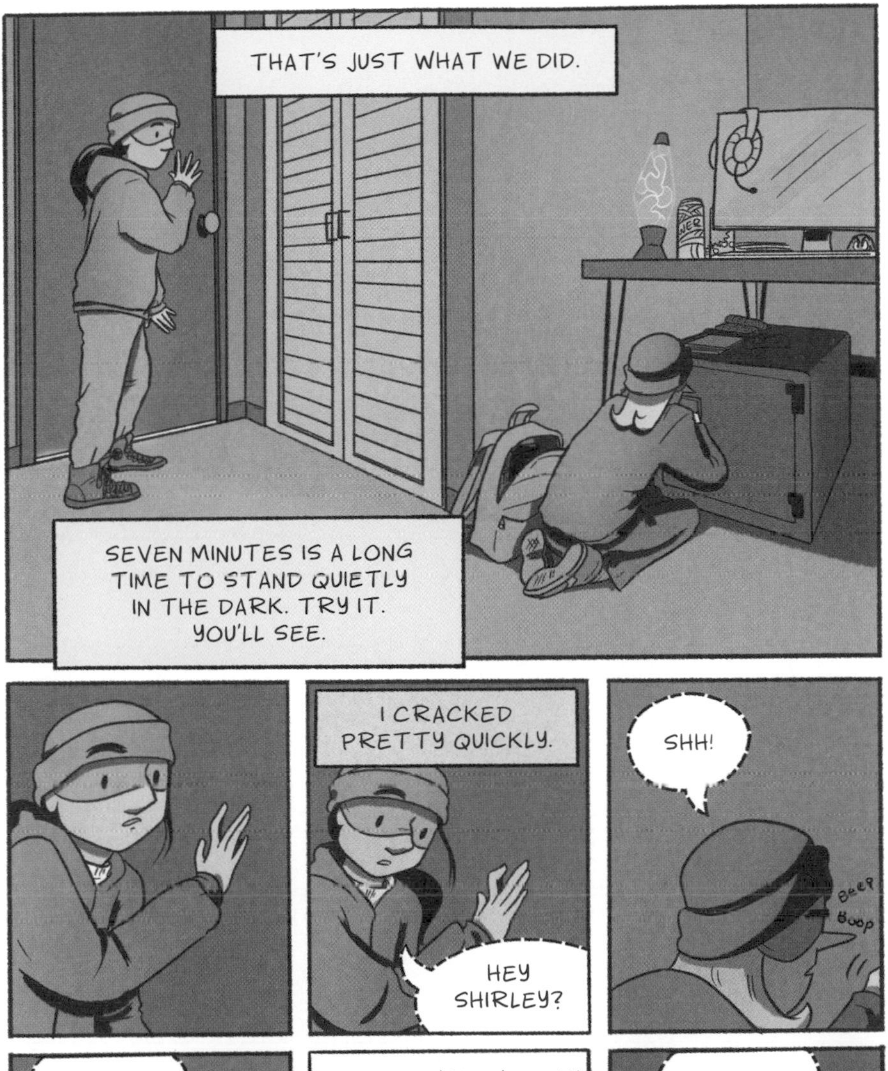
THAT'S JUST WHAT WE DID.
SEVEN MINUTES IS A LONG TIME TO STAND QUIETLY IN THE DARK. TRY IT. YOU'LL SEE.
I CRACKED PRETTY QUICKLY.
HEY SHIRLEY?
SHH!
Beep
Boop
YES?
YOU KNOW HOW I PLAY BALL WITH SEENA?
MM-HMM.

I'VE GONE TO HER HOUSE A FEW TIMES TOO.

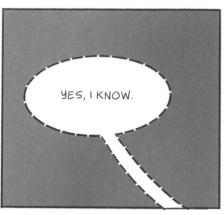

YES, I KNOW.

YOU DO?

BY THEN, I SHOULDN'T HAVE BEEN SURPRISED.

OKAY. WELL, SHE WAS ASKING ABOUT YOU.

AND SHE GOT IT IN HER MIND THAT WE WERE . . .

YES?

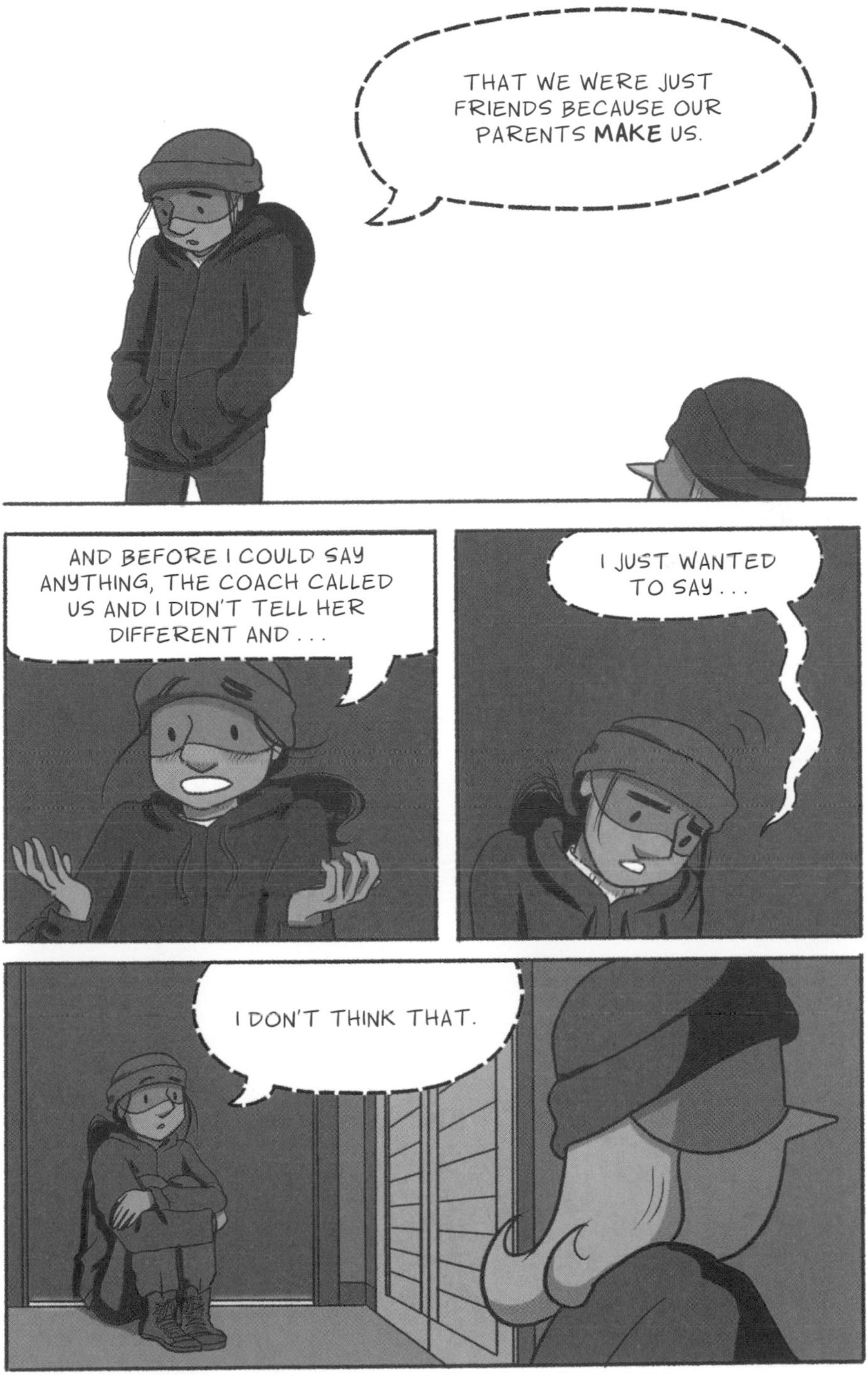
THAT WE WERE JUST FRIENDS BECAUSE OUR PARENTS **MAKE** US.
AND BEFORE I COULD SAY ANYTHING, THE COACH CALLED US AND I DIDN'T TELL HER DIFFERENT AND . . .
I JUST WANTED TO SAY . . .
I DON'T THINK THAT.

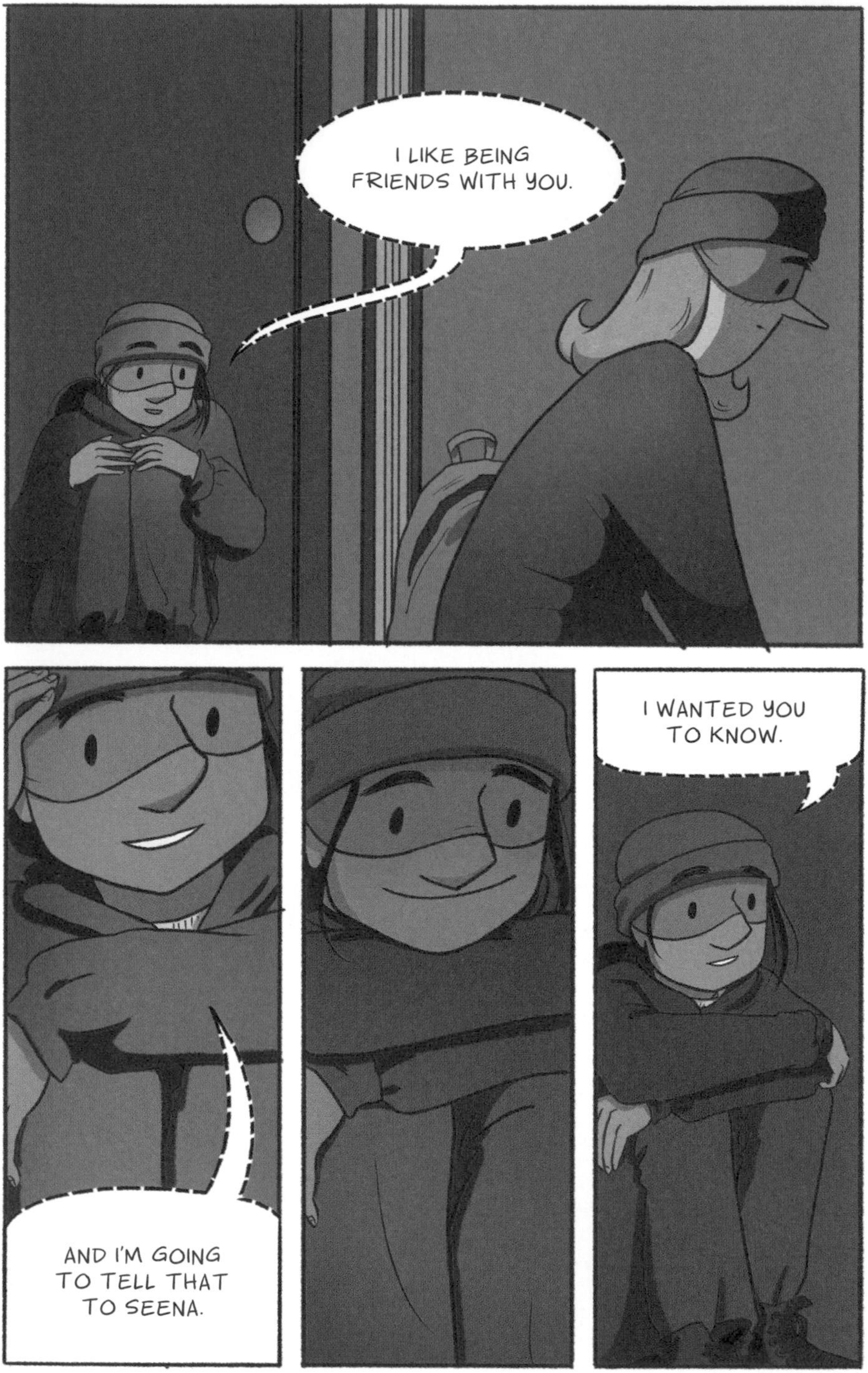
I LIKE BEING FRIENDS WITH YOU.
I WANTED YOU TO KNOW.
AND I'M GOING TO TELL THAT TO SEENA.

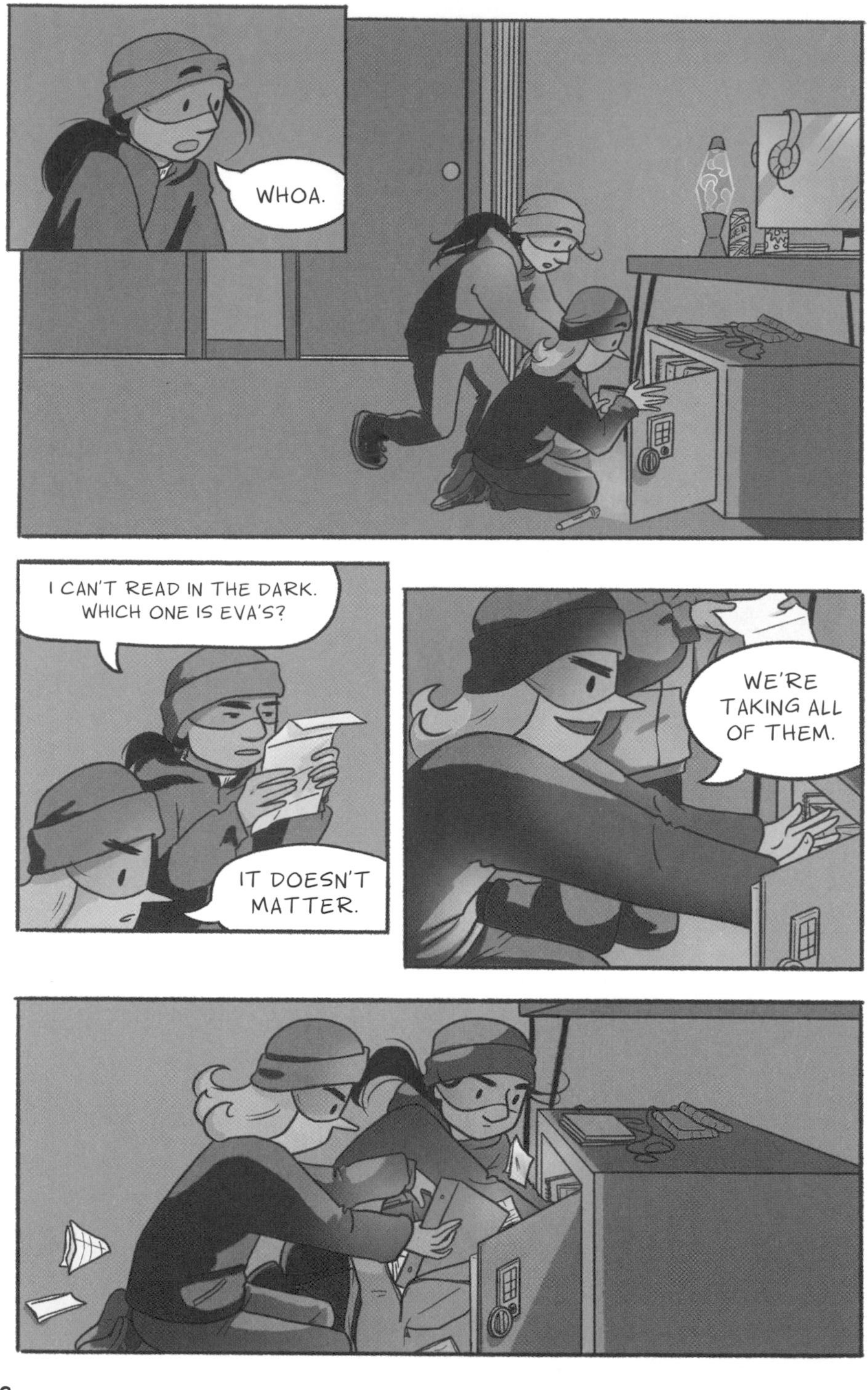
WHOA.
I CAN'T READ IN THE DARK. WHICH ONE IS EVA'S?
IT DOESN'T MATTER.
WE'RE TAKING ALL OF THEM.

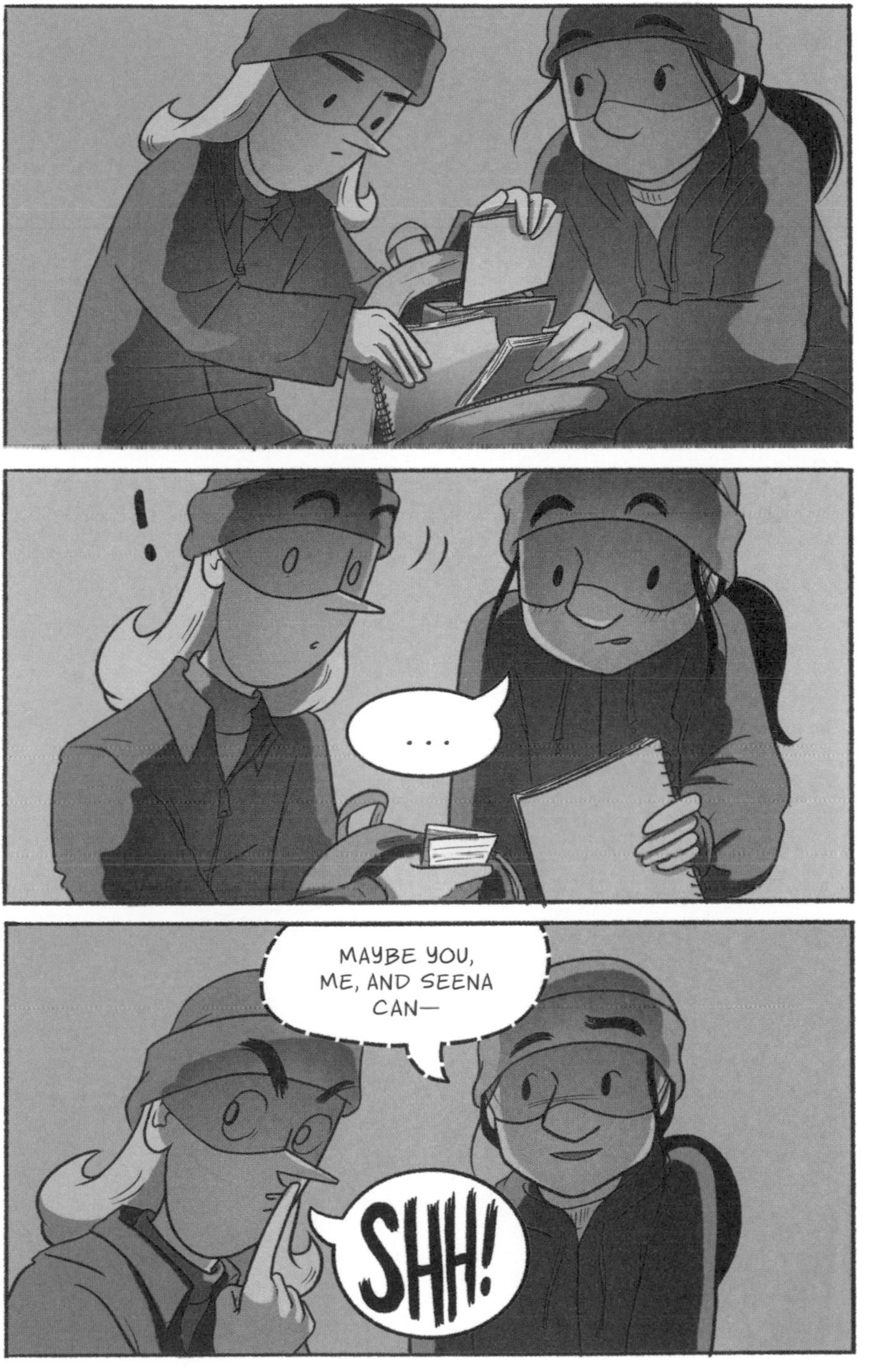
!
. . .
MAYBE YOU, ME, AND SEENA CAN—
SHH!

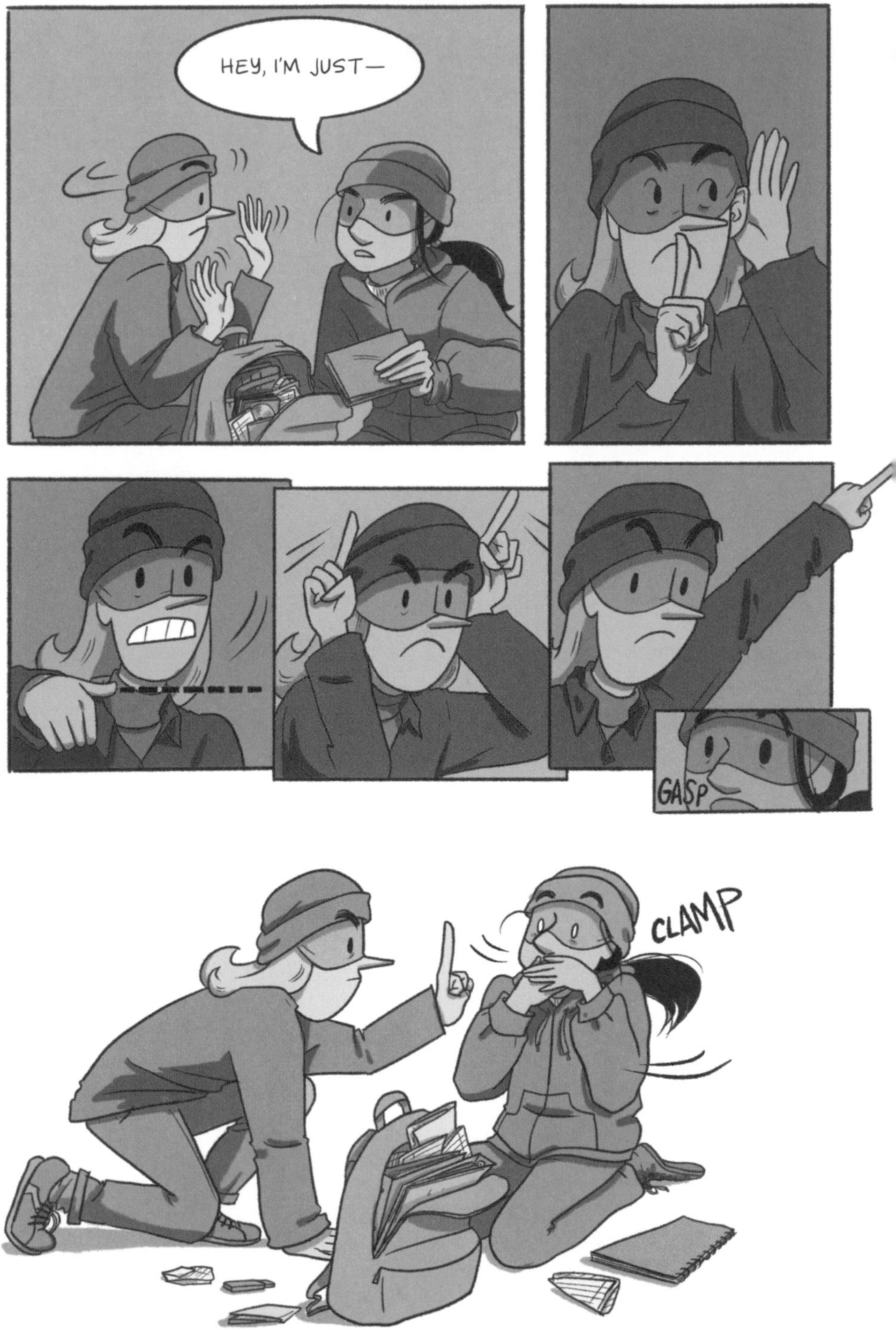
HEY, I'M JUST—
GASP
CLAMP

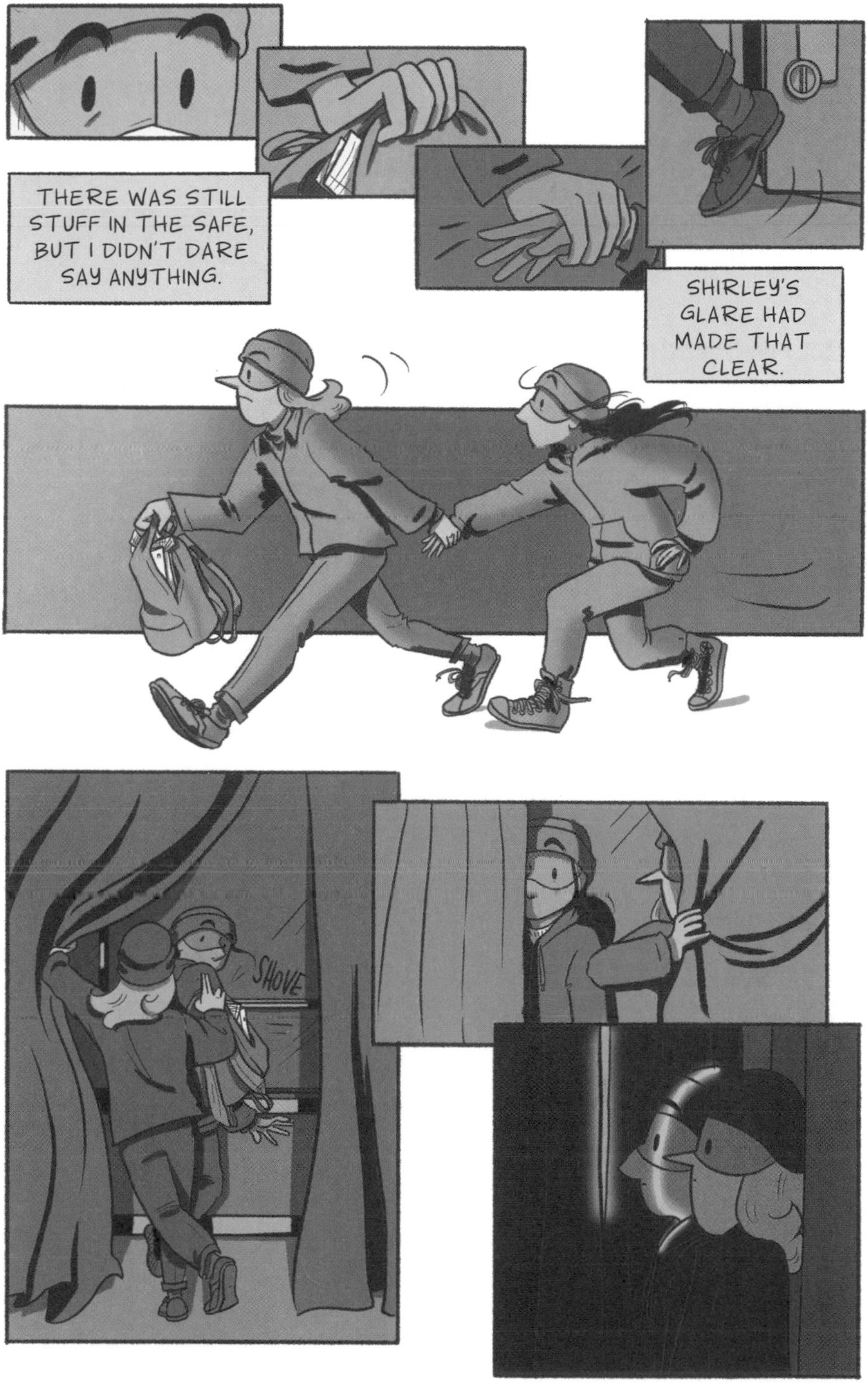

THERE WAS STILL STUFF IN THE SAFE, BUT I DIDN'T DARE SAY ANYTHING.
SHIRLEY'S GLARE HAD MADE THAT CLEAR.
SHOVE

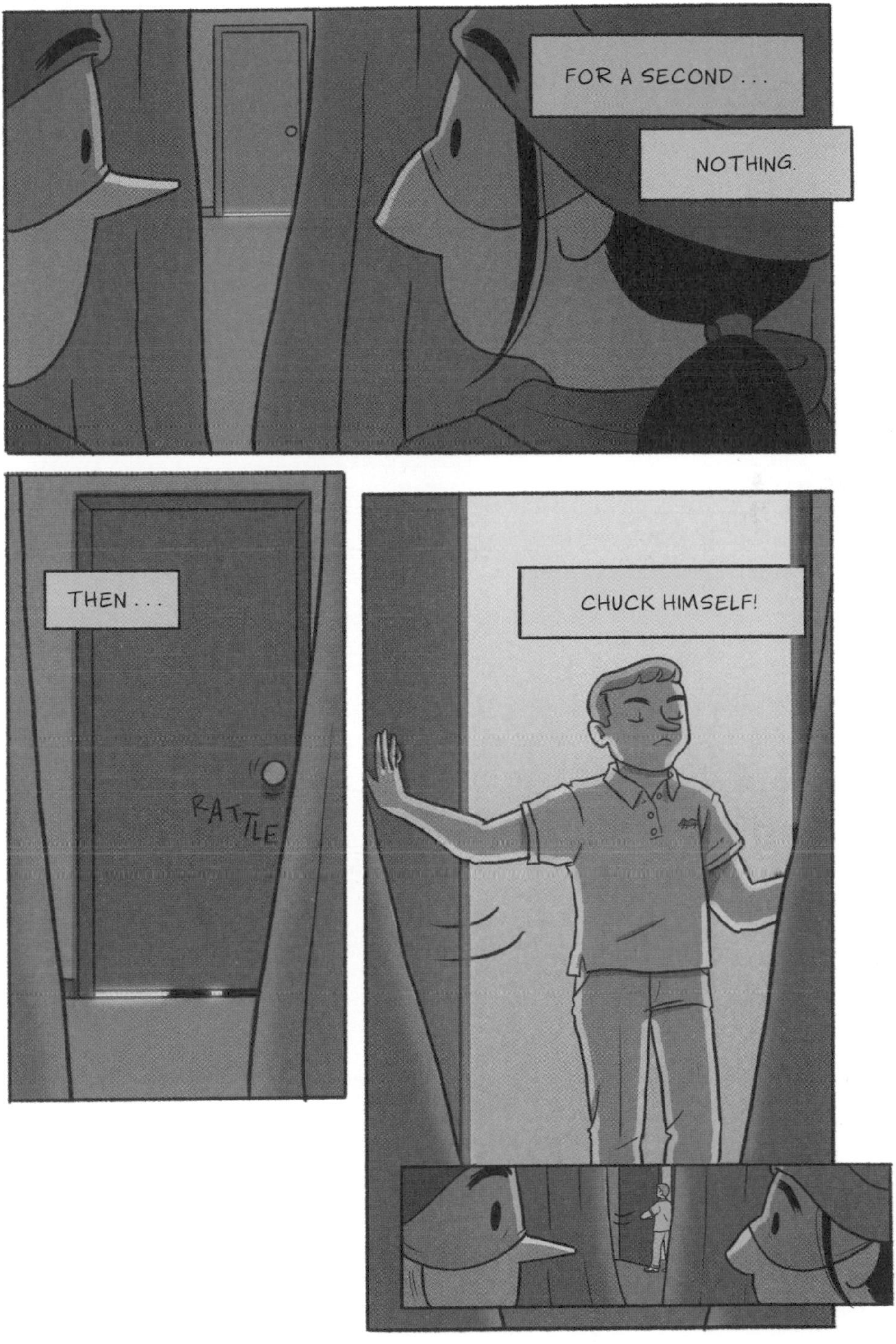
FOR A SECOND . . .
NOTHING.
THEN . . .
RATTLE
CHUCK HIMSELF!

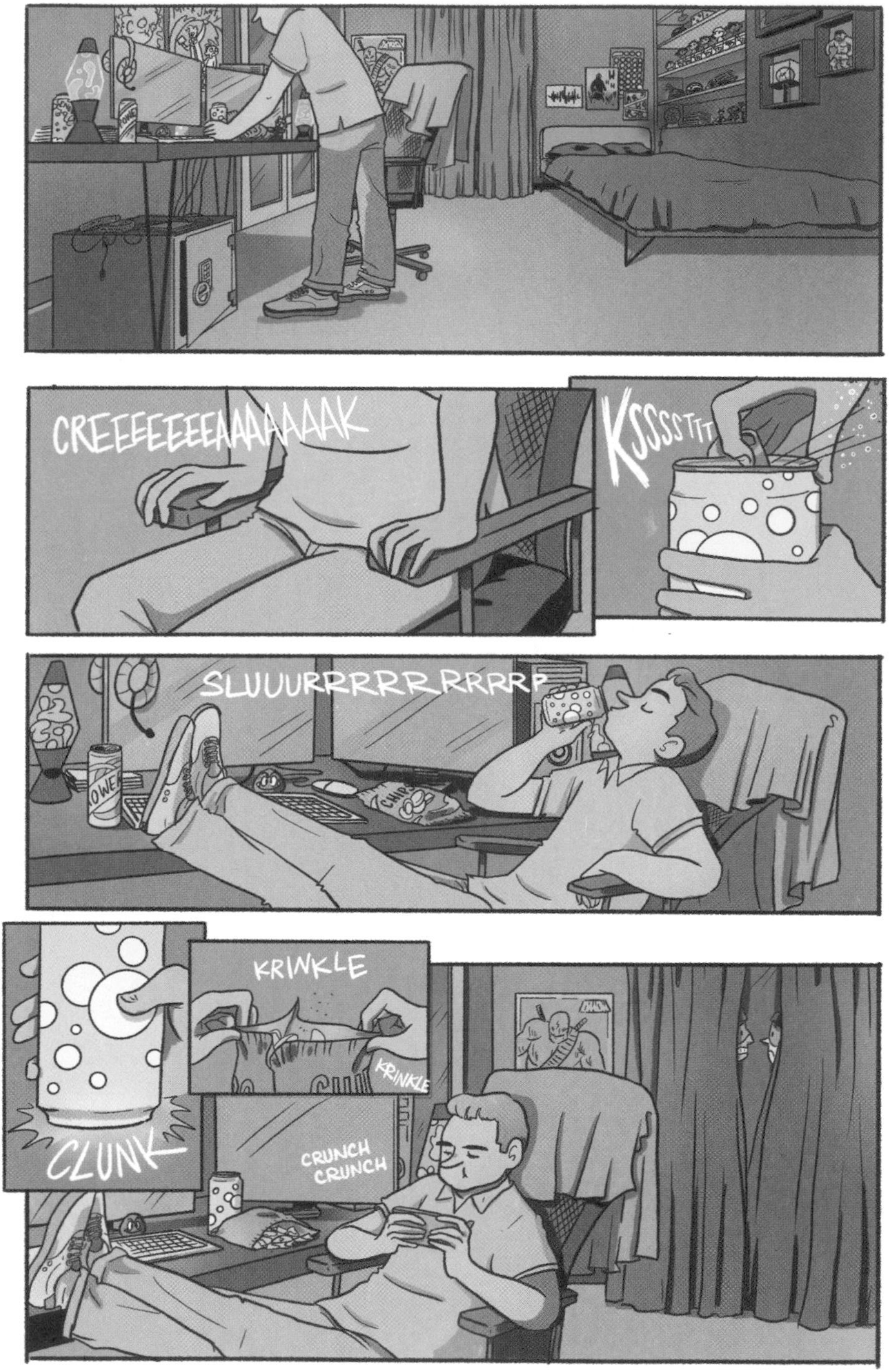
CREEEEEEEAAAAAAAK
KSSSSTTT
SLUUURRRRRRRRP
KRINKLE
KRINKLE
CLUNK
CRUNCH
CRUNCH

MINUTES PASSED. I DON'T KNOW HOW MANY.

A PART OF ME WANTED TO STEP OUT AND CONFESS,

BUT SHIRLEY GAVE ME A LITTLE HAND SQUEEZE OF CONFIDENCE, AND A LOOK THAT SOMEHOW REASSURED ME: SHE'S GOT THIS.

I FELT CONFIDENCE AND EXCITEMENT FLOOD BACK INTO ME.

WE GOT THIS.

WHAT WOULD WE DO IF CHUCK SAW THE SAFE?
KNOWING SHIRLEY, SHE ALREADY HAD A PLAN, BUT SINCE SHE COULDN'T TELL ME, I NEEDED MY OWN.
SSSSLLUUURRRPP
BURP
WHILE CHUCK CHEWED AND SMACKED AND SLURPED (SO GROSS), I PLANNED:
PLAN A:
chuck sees open safe.
I PUNCH CHUCK.
I get creamed.
BAD PLAN.

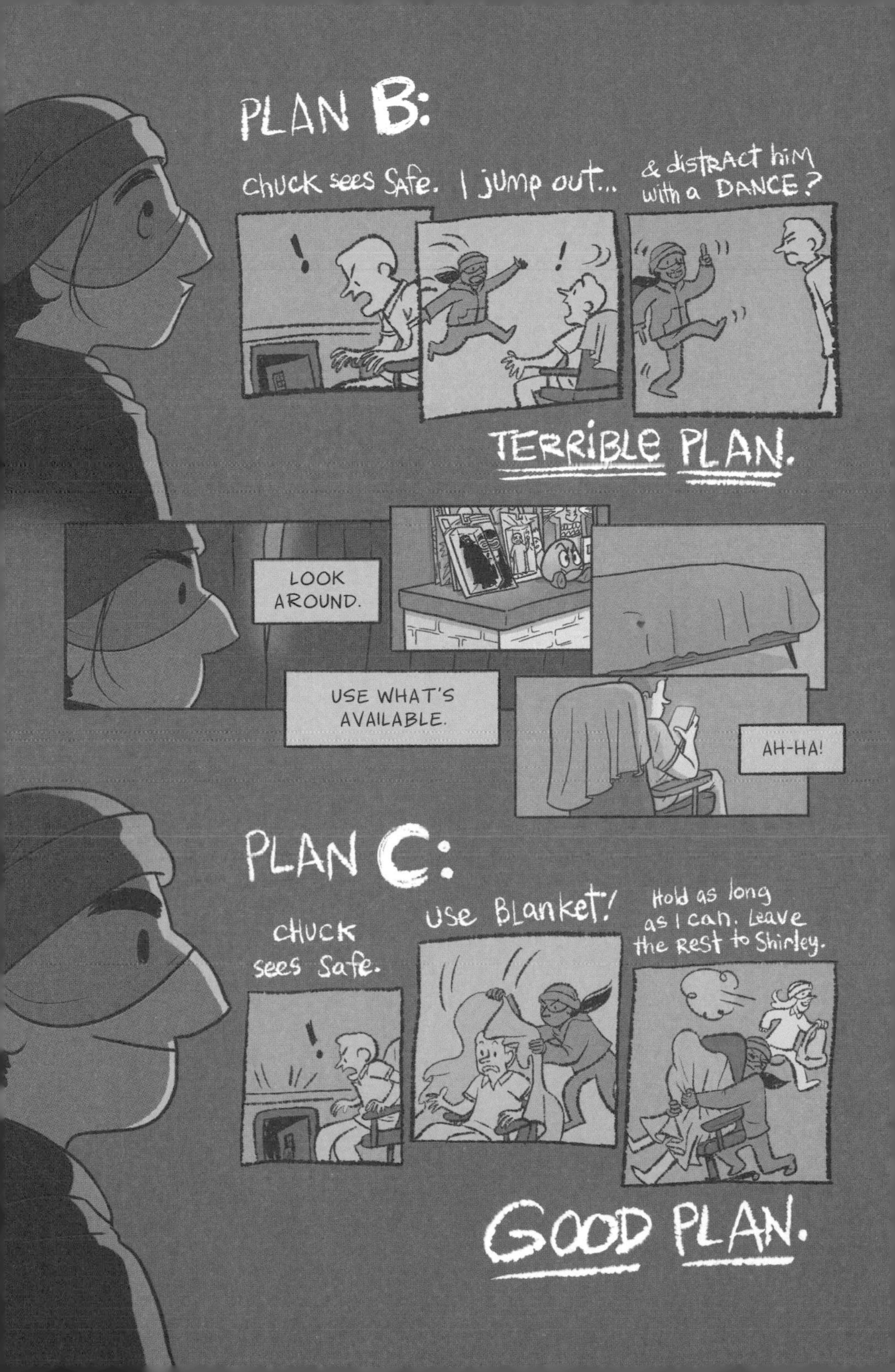
PLAN B:
chuck sees Safe.
I jump out...
& distRAct him with a DANCE?
TERRIBLE PLAN.
LOOK AROUND.
USE WHAT'S AVAILABLE.
AH-HA!
PLAN C:
CHUCK sees Safe.
use BLanket!
Hold as long as I can. Leave the Rest to Shirley.
GOOD PLAN.

I FIGURED ONCE HE FINISHED THE SODA, MAYBE THEN HE'D LEAVE.

TO PASS THE TIME I TRIED TO FIGURE HOW MANY MORE SIPS 'TIL IT WAS DONE . . .

I GUESSED NINE.

151

155

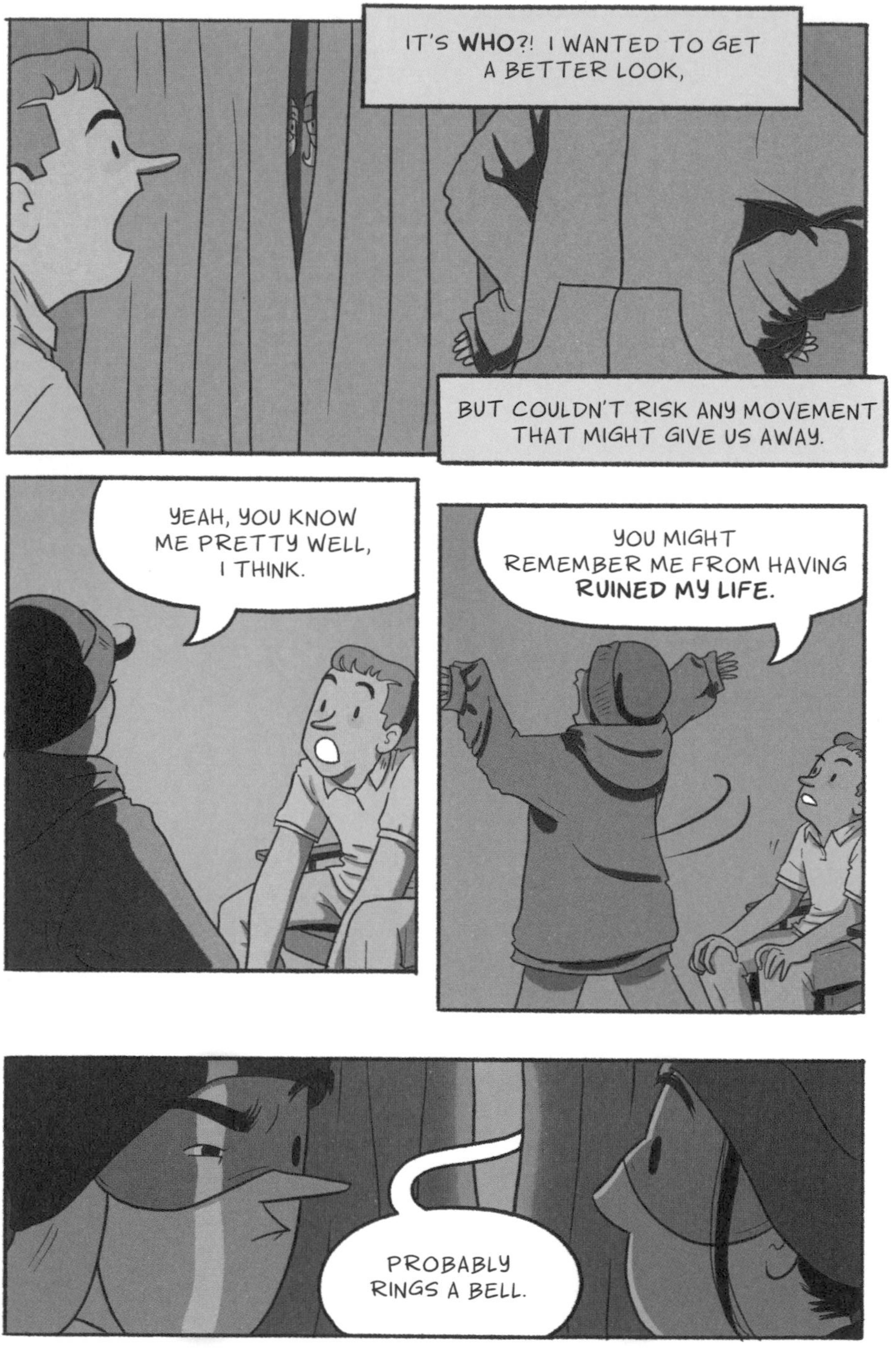
IT'S WHO?! I WANTED TO GET A BETTER LOOK,
BUT COULDN'T RISK ANY MOVEMENT THAT MIGHT GIVE US AWAY.
YEAH, YOU KNOW ME PRETTY WELL, I THINK.
YOU MIGHT REMEMBER ME FROM HAVING RUINED MY LIFE.
PROBABLY RINGS A BELL.

I HAD BEGGED YOU NOT TO SEND IT OUT

ER

AND YOU LAUGHED IN MY FACE,

HEH HUR

LIKE YOU'RE TRYING TO LAUGH NOW

BUT I CAN SEE YOU SHAKING, YOU EEL.

NOT SO FUNNY WHEN I'M IN YOUR HOUSE,

WHEN I DON'T HAVE ANYTHING ELSE TO LOSE.

IS IT?

IS IT FUNNY?

CHUCK?

JAB

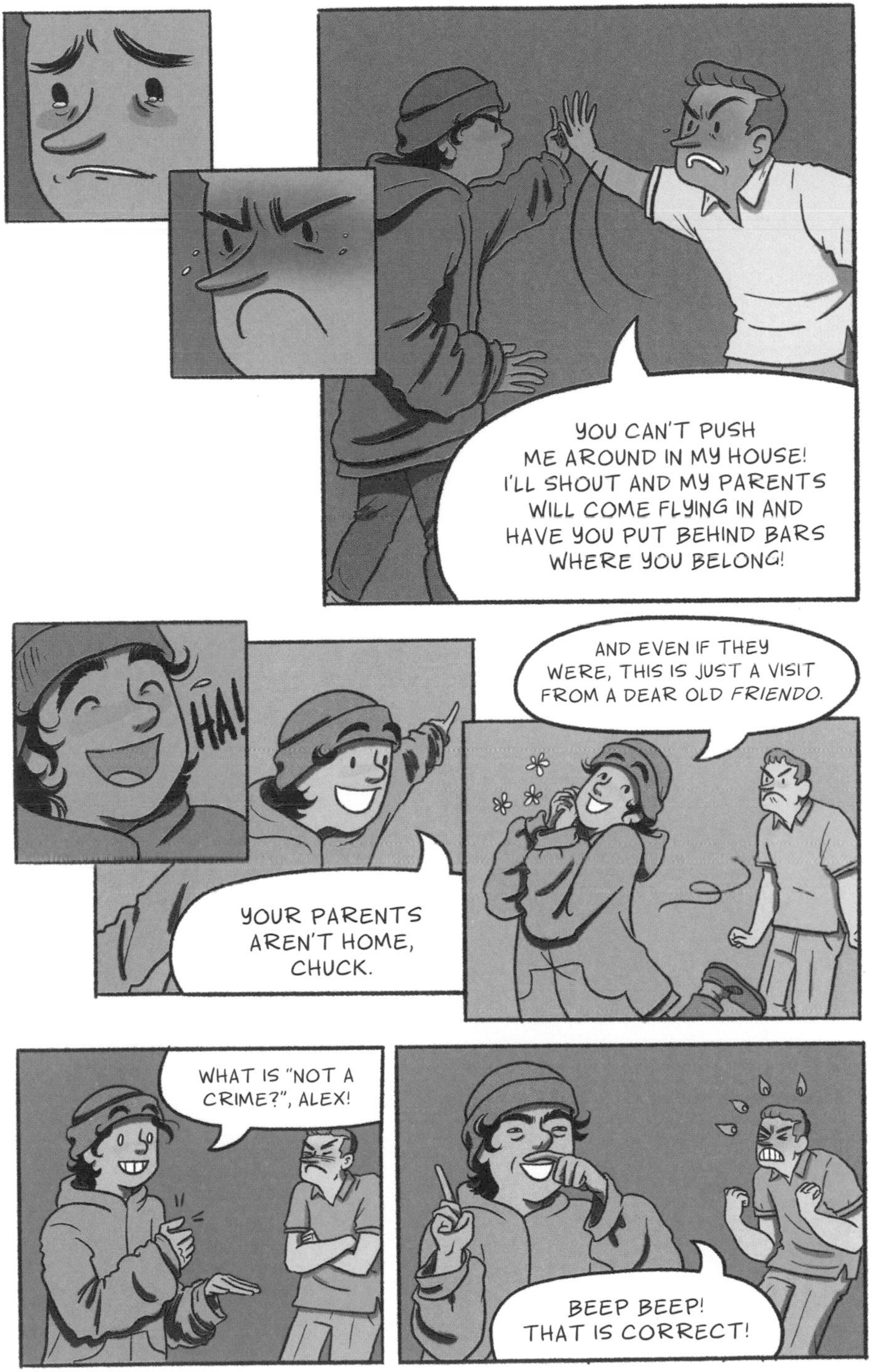
YOU CAN'T PUSH ME AROUND IN MY HOUSE! I'LL SHOUT AND MY PARENTS WILL COME FLYING IN AND HAVE YOU PUT BEHIND BARS WHERE YOU BELONG!
HA!
YOUR PARENTS AREN'T HOME, CHUCK.
AND EVEN IF THEY WERE, THIS IS JUST A VISIT FROM A DEAR OLD *FRIENDO*.
WHAT IS "NOT A CRIME?", ALEX!
BEEP BEEP! THAT IS CORRECT!

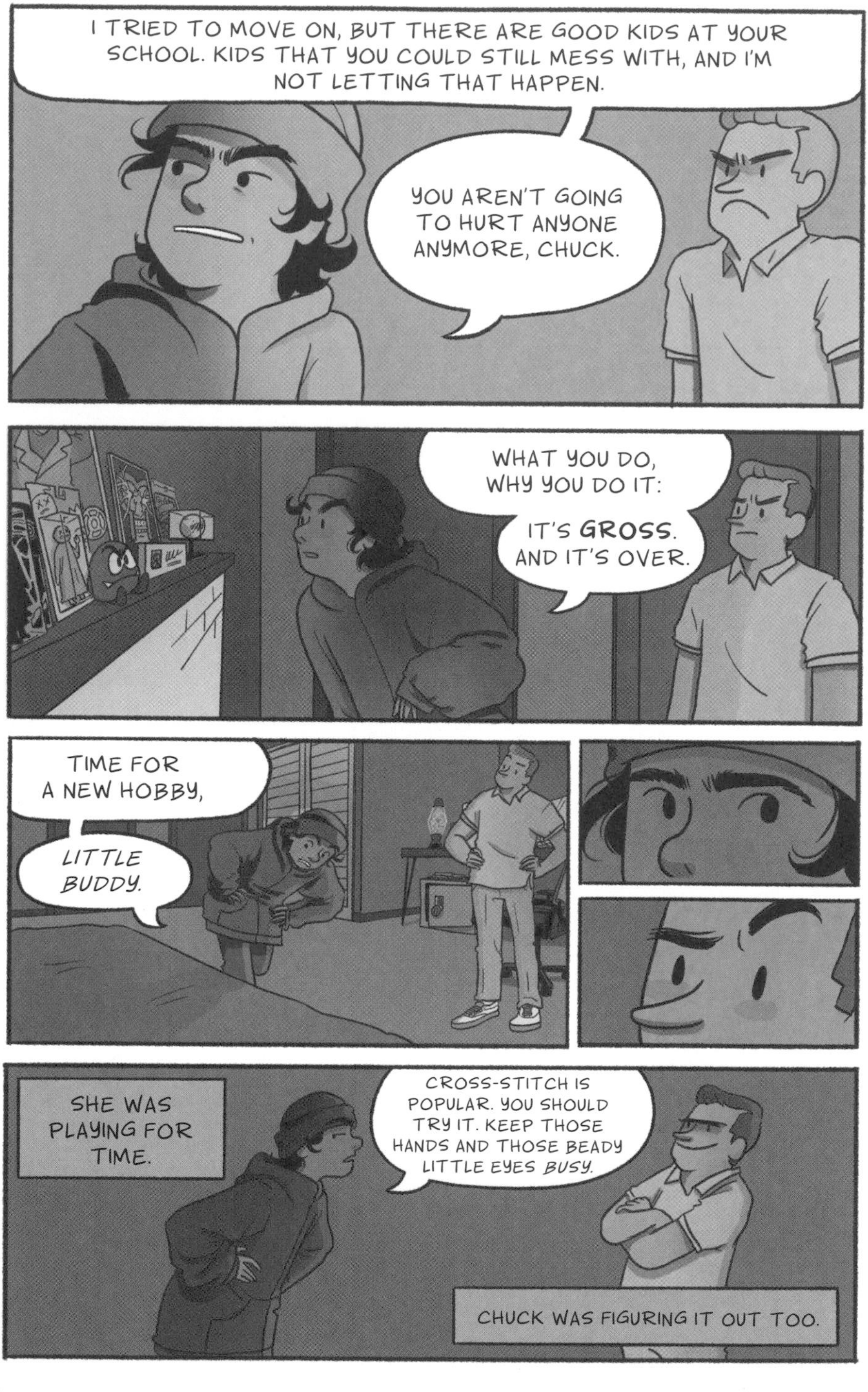
I TRIED TO MOVE ON, BUT THERE ARE GOOD KIDS AT YOUR SCHOOL. KIDS THAT YOU COULD STILL MESS WITH, AND I'M NOT LETTING THAT HAPPEN.
YOU AREN'T GOING TO HURT ANYONE ANYMORE, CHUCK.
WHAT YOU DO, WHY YOU DO IT:
IT'S **GROSS**. AND IT'S OVER.
TIME FOR A NEW HOBBY,
LITTLE BUDDY.
SHE WAS PLAYING FOR TIME.
CROSS-STITCH IS POPULAR. YOU SHOULD TRY IT. KEEP THOSE HANDS AND THOSE BEADY LITTLE EYES *BUSY*.
CHUCK WAS FIGURING IT OUT TOO.

HEH HEH HEH

UH-OH.

BIG WORDS, BIG WORDS.

ANYTHING ELSE YOU WANT TO MONOLOGUE ABOUT WHILE YOU LOOK AROUND FOR SOMETHING TO PIN ON ME?

I'LL TAKE "STALLING" FOR 1000, ALEX!

168

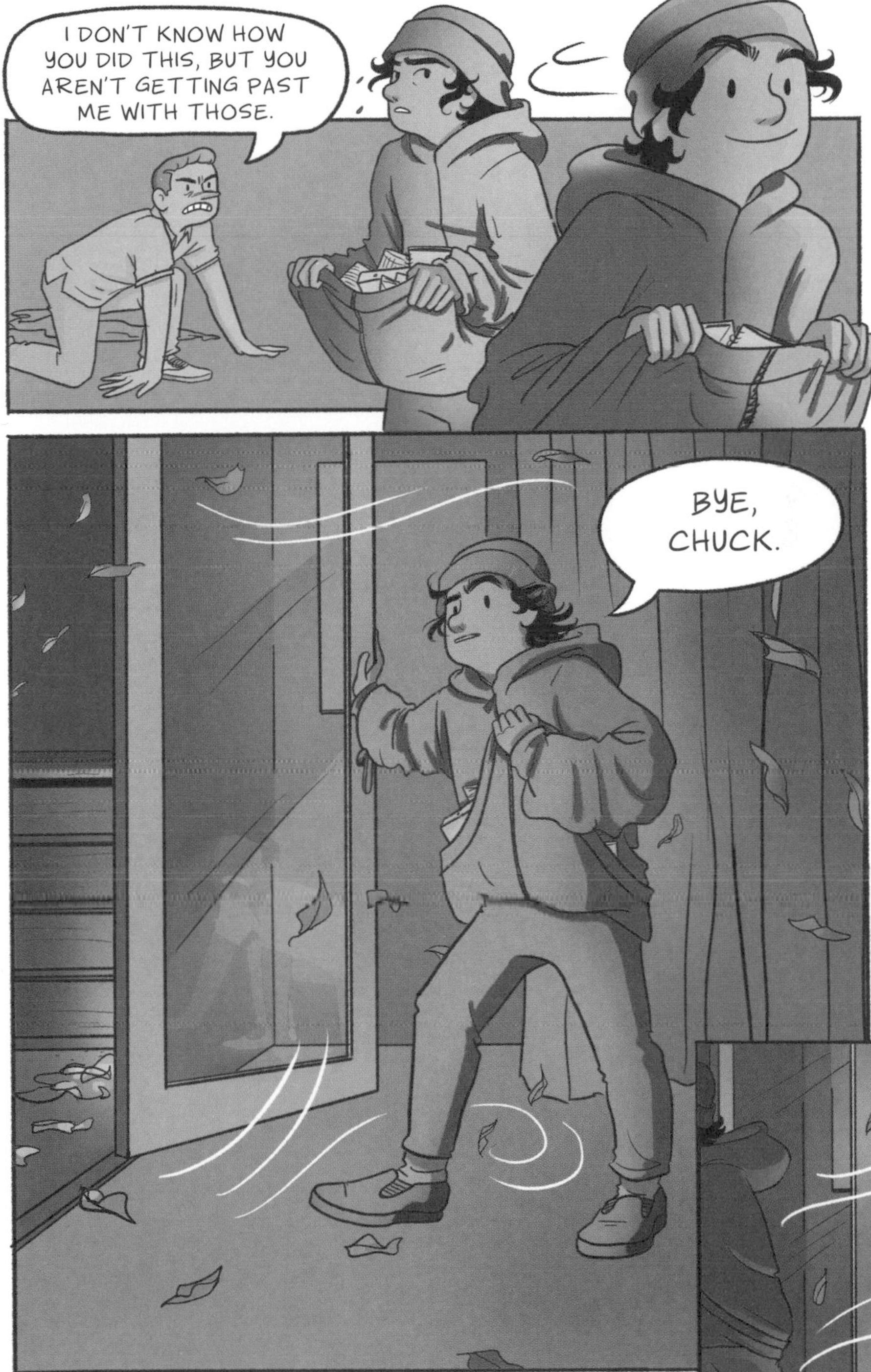
I DON'T KNOW HOW YOU DID THIS, BUT YOU AREN'T GETTING PAST ME WITH THOSE.
BYE, CHUCK.

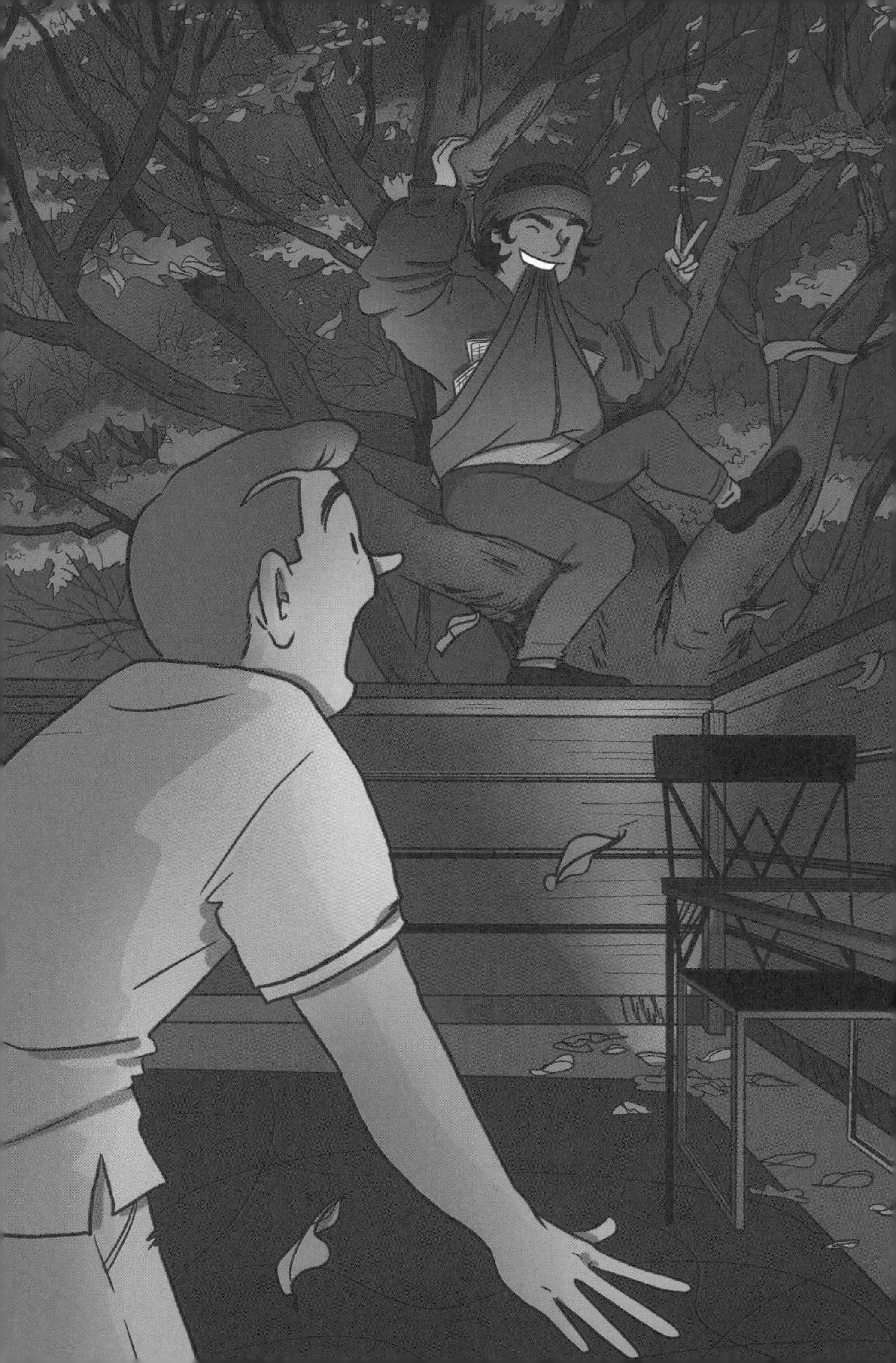

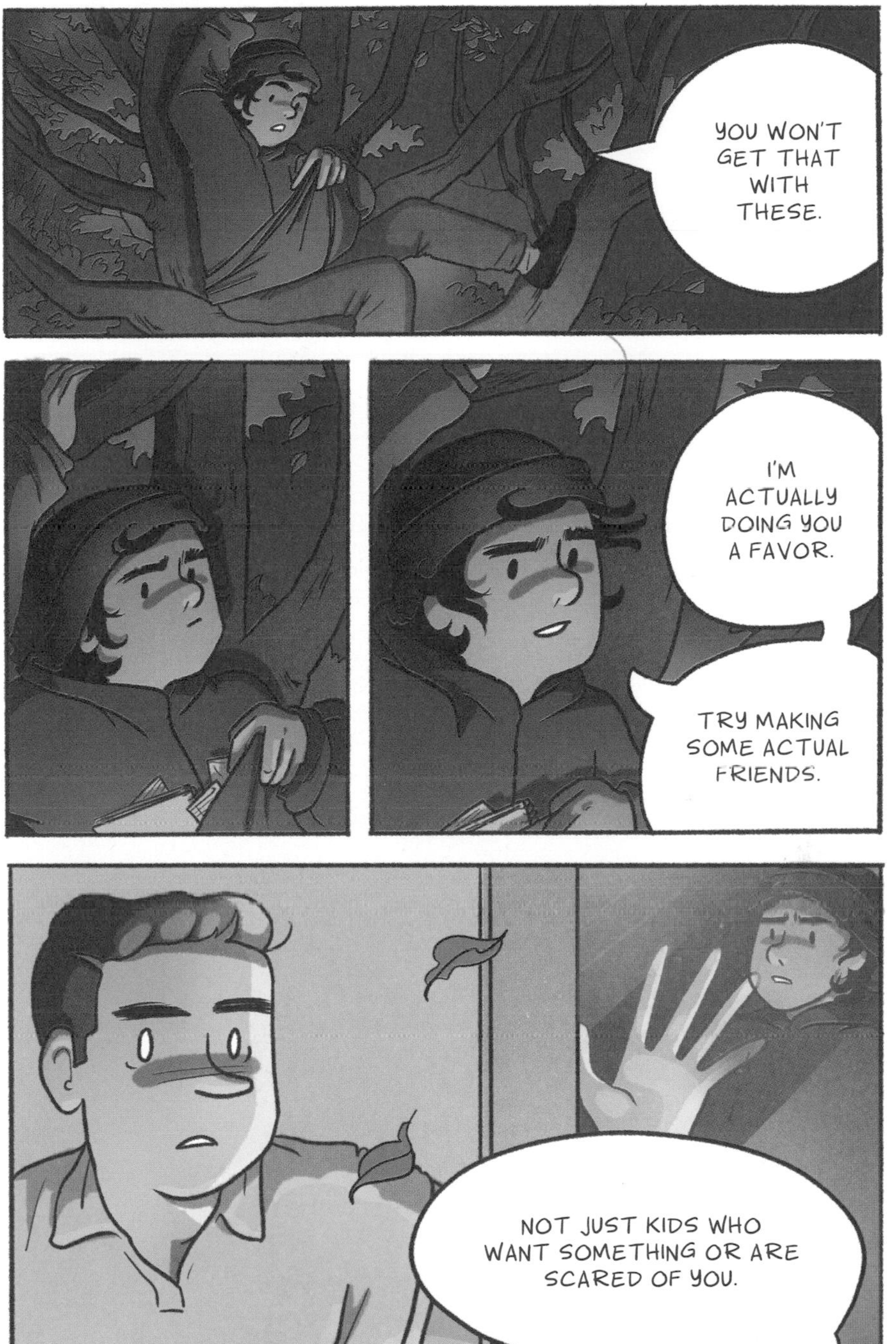
YOU WON'T GET THAT WITH THESE.
I'M ACTUALLY DOING YOU A FAVOR.
TRY MAKING SOME ACTUAL FRIENDS.
NOT JUST KIDS WHO WANT SOMETHING OR ARE SCARED OF YOU.

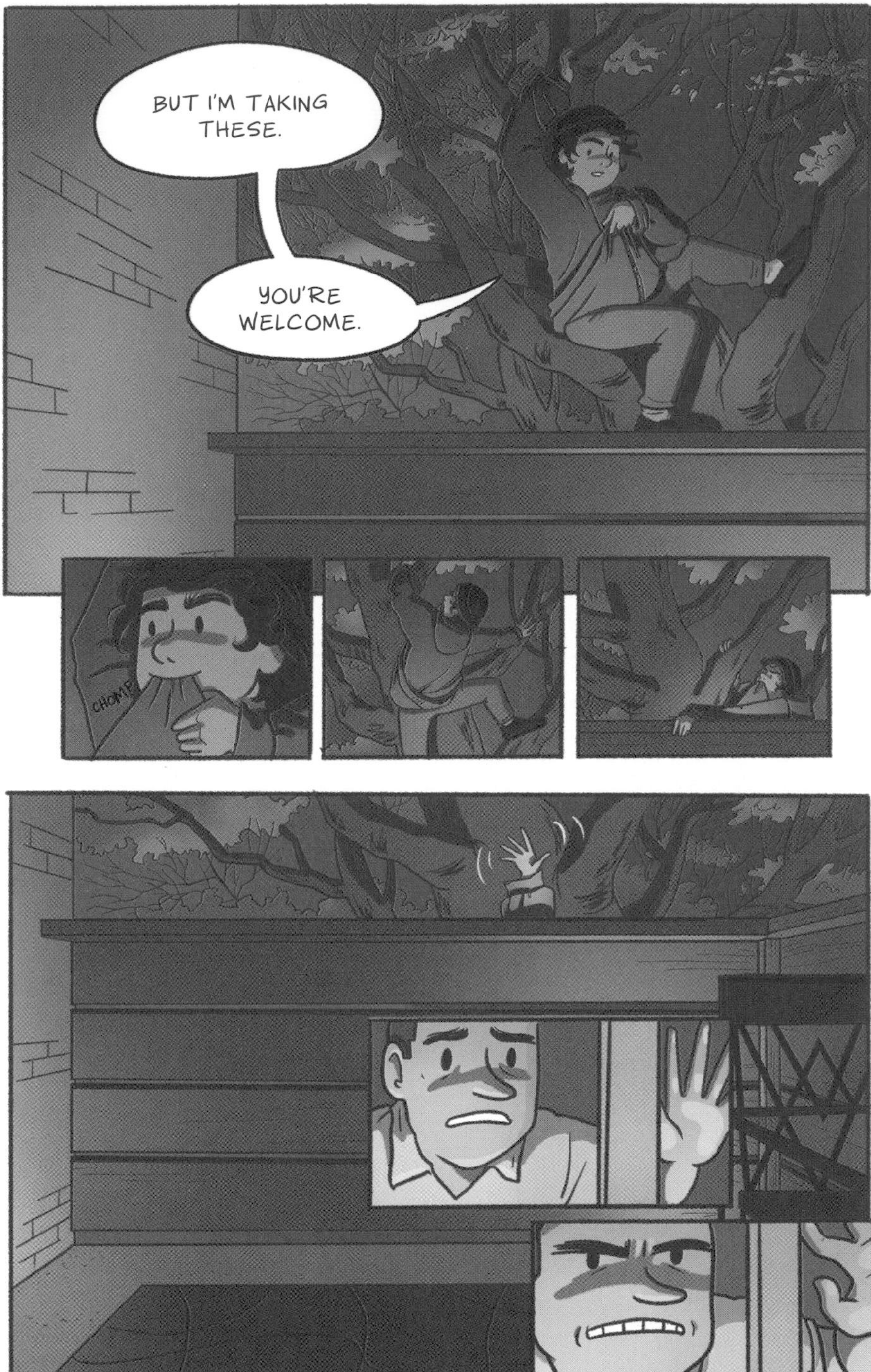
BUT I'M TAKING THESE.
YOU'RE WELCOME.
CHOMP

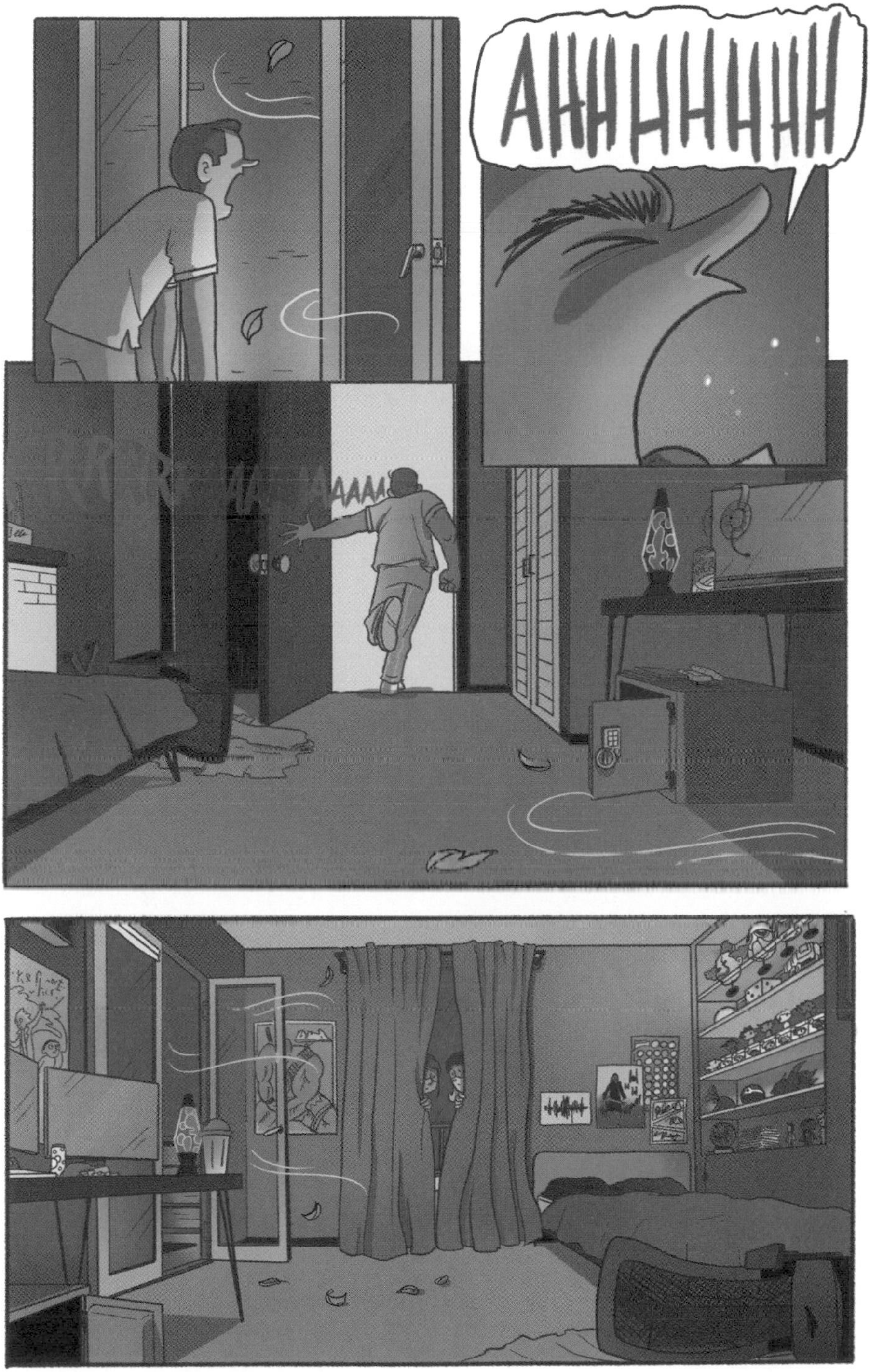
AHHHHHHH

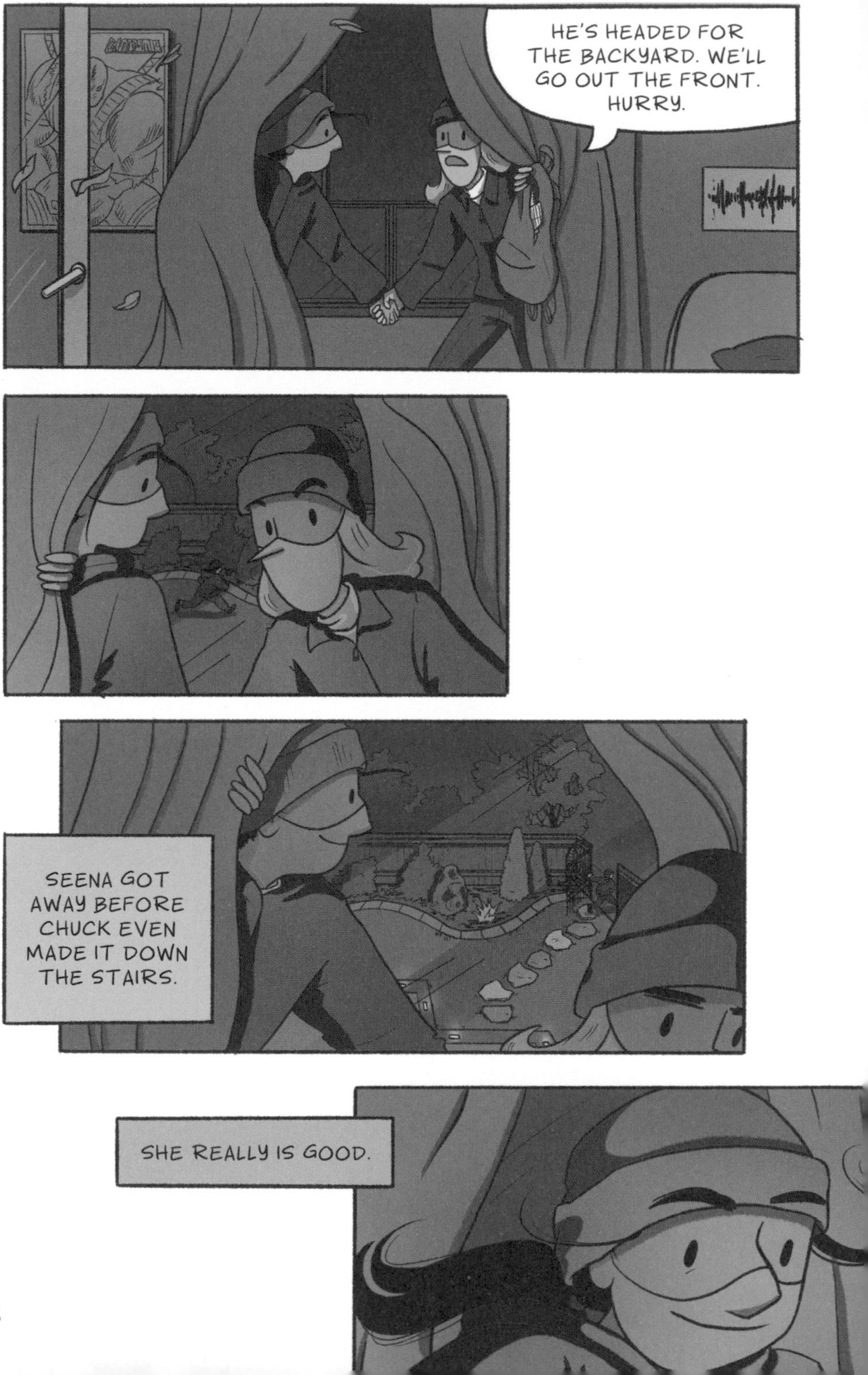
HE'S HEADED FOR THE BACKYARD. WE'LL GO OUT THE FRONT. HURRY.
SEENA GOT AWAY BEFORE CHUCK EVEN MADE IT DOWN THE STAIRS.
SHE REALLY IS GOOD.

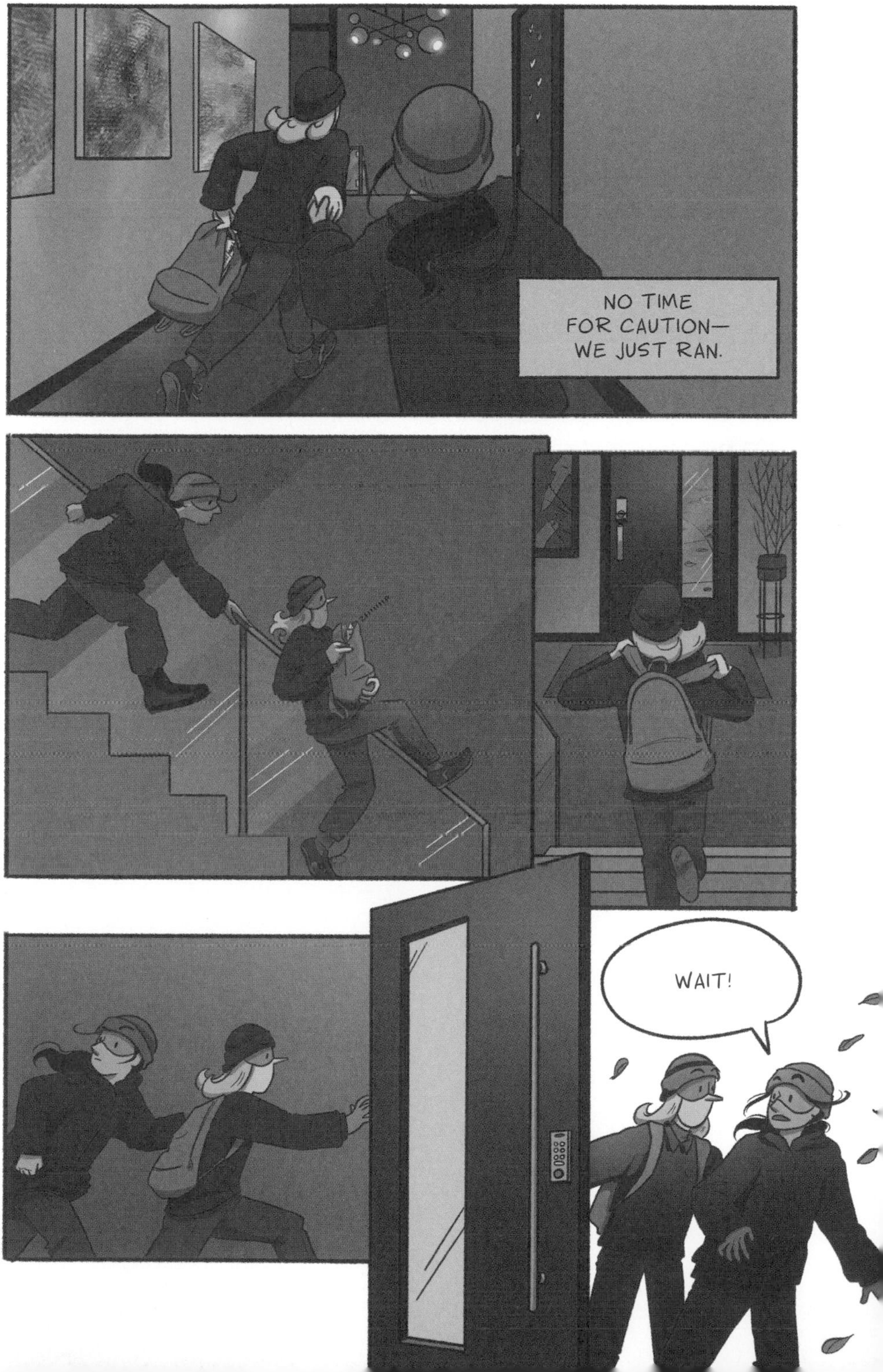
NO TIME
FOR CAUTION—
WE JUST RAN.
WAIT!

179

IN SHIRLEY'S YARD, WE FINALLY STOPPED TO CATCH OUR BREATH. WE WEREN'T IN THE CLEAR YET.

PANT PANT

WE ESCAPED CHUCK'S, BUT THERE WERE OTHER WAYS TO GET CAUGHT.

WE CHECKED OUR WATCHES—

THE WHOLE EPISODE BARELY TOOK AN HOUR!

MASKS OFF—LESS QUESTIONS IF SOMEONE IS UP.

A CLICK.

A STEP.

A SNORE.

zZZZ

CLUNK

AND WE WERE BACK.

AS IF WE'D NEVER LEFT.

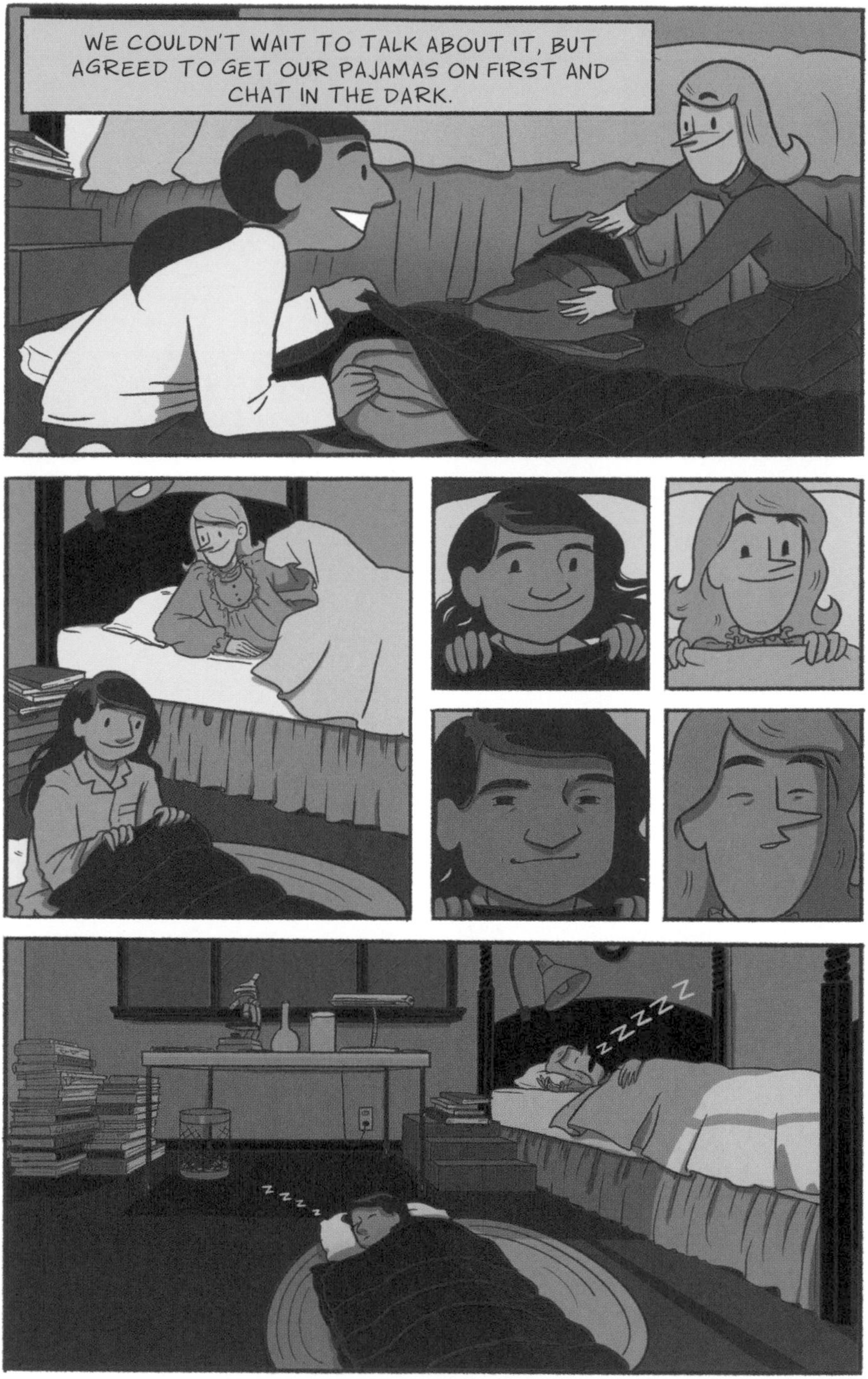
WE COULDN'T WAIT TO TALK ABOUT IT, BUT AGREED TO GET OUR PAJAMAS ON FIRST AND CHAT IN THE DARK.
ZZZZZZ
ZZZZ

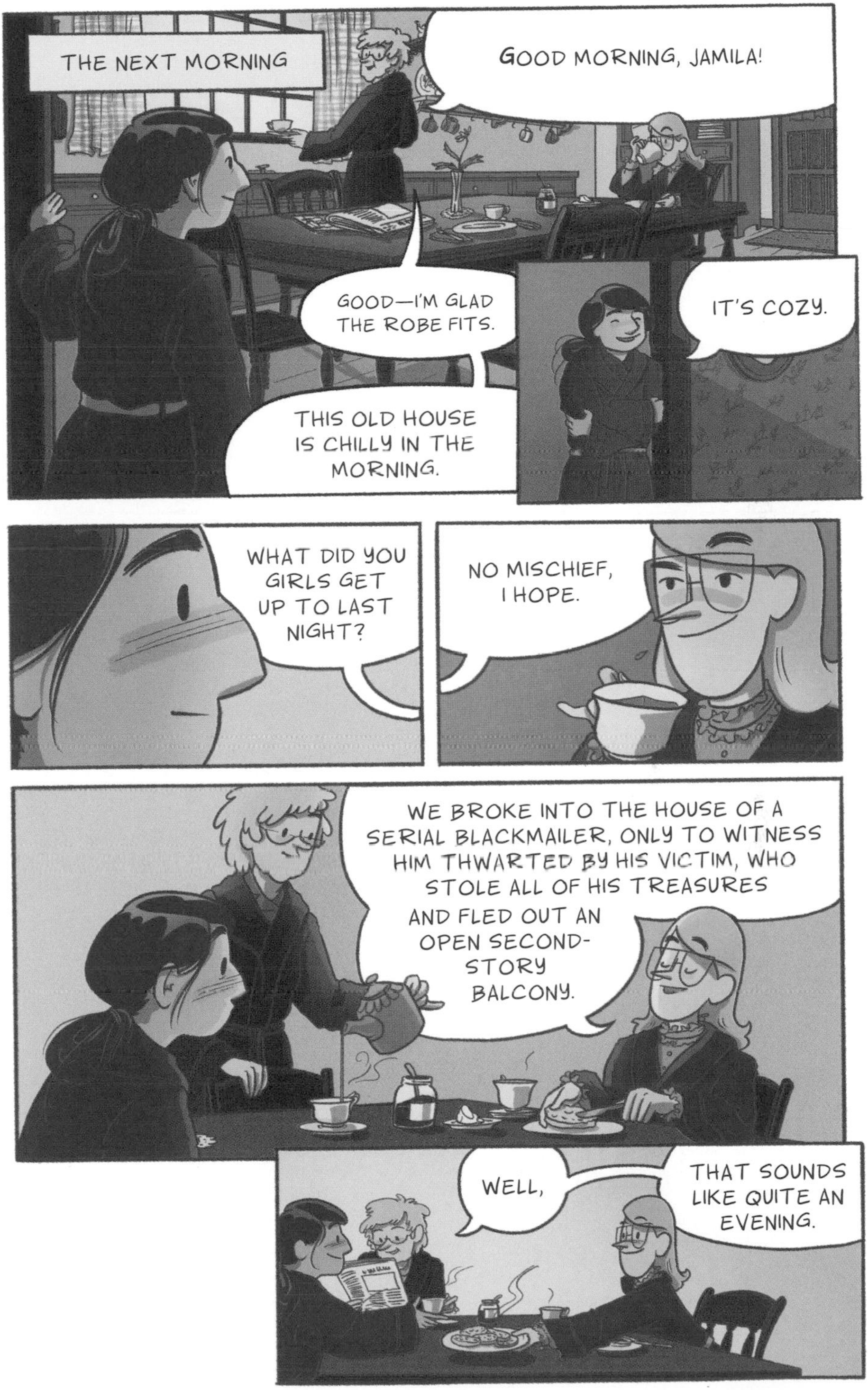
THE NEXT MORNING
GOOD MORNING, JAMILA!
GOOD—I'M GLAD THE ROBE FITS.
THIS OLD HOUSE IS CHILLY IN THE MORNING.
IT'S COZY.
WHAT DID YOU GIRLS GET UP TO LAST NIGHT?
NO MISCHIEF, I HOPE.
WE BROKE INTO THE HOUSE OF A SERIAL BLACKMAILER, ONLY TO WITNESS HIM THWARTED BY HIS VICTIM, WHO STOLE ALL OF HIS TREASURES
AND FLED OUT AN OPEN SECOND-STORY BALCONY.
WELL,
THAT SOUNDS LIKE QUITE AN EVENING.

THE LUCKY THING IS YOU GET TO HAVE MORE THAN ONE FRIEND.

DID EVERYBODY KNOW THIS? IT'S FUNNY I WAS JUST FIGURING IT OUT.

I COULDN'T STOP THINKING ABOUT SEENA . . .

AFTER BREAKFAST ON SATURDAY, SHIRLEY AND I TALKED ABOUT WHAT DO TO WITH ALL OF THE EVIDENCE WE STOLE.

WE HAVE THE FOLLOWING OPTIONS: DESTROY THEM OR RETURN THEM.

BUT RETURN THEM TO WHO? A BUNCH OF PEOPLE COULD BE INVOLVED—HOW DO WE KNOW WHICH KID WAS CHUCK'S TARGET?

185

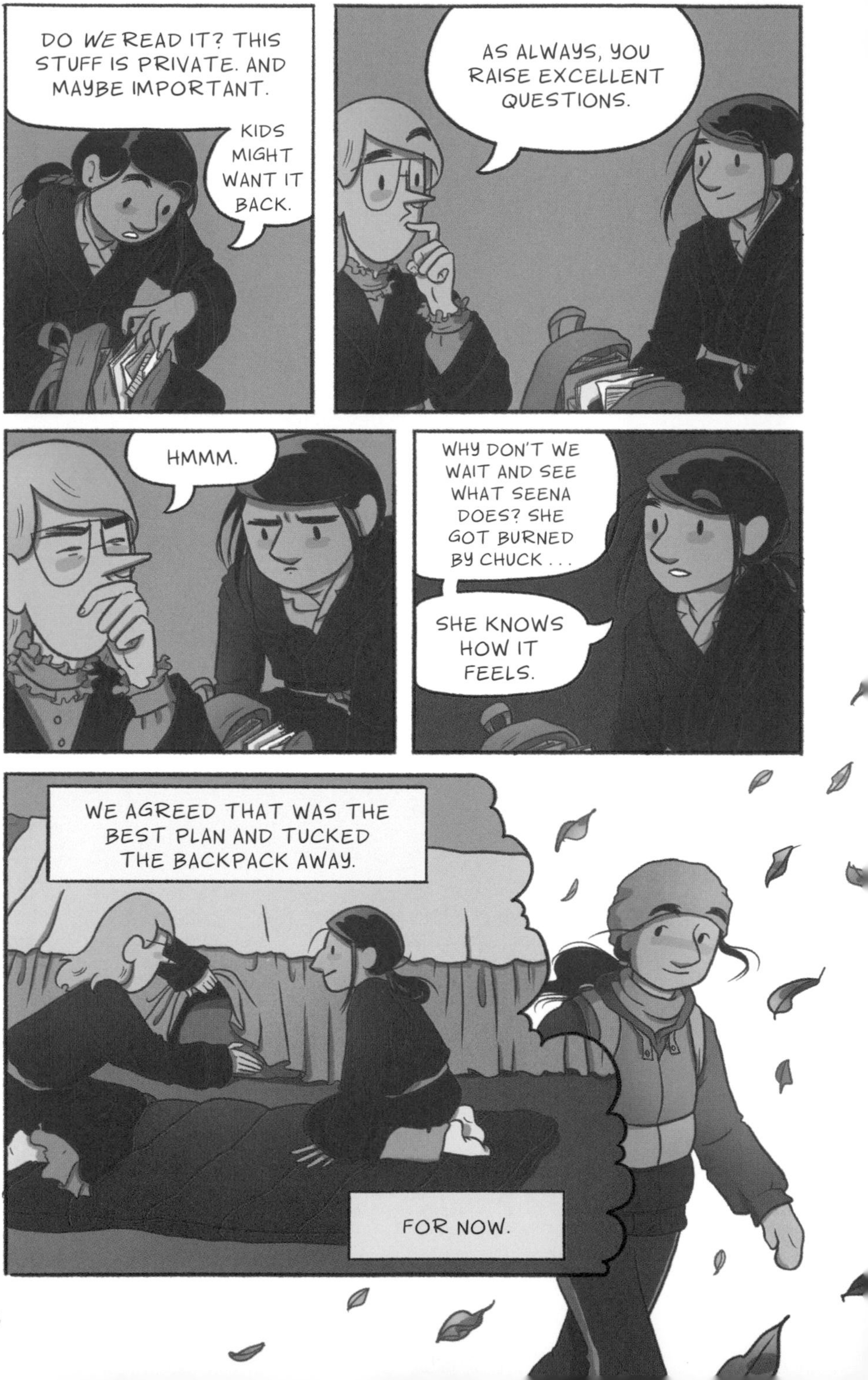
DO WE READ IT? THIS STUFF IS PRIVATE. AND MAYBE IMPORTANT.
KIDS MIGHT WANT IT BACK.
AS ALWAYS, YOU RAISE EXCELLENT QUESTIONS.
HMMM.
WHY DON'T WE WAIT AND SEE WHAT SEENA DOES? SHE GOT BURNED BY CHUCK . . .
SHE KNOWS HOW IT FEELS.
WE AGREED THAT WAS THE BEST PLAN AND TUCKED THE BACKPACK AWAY.
FOR NOW.

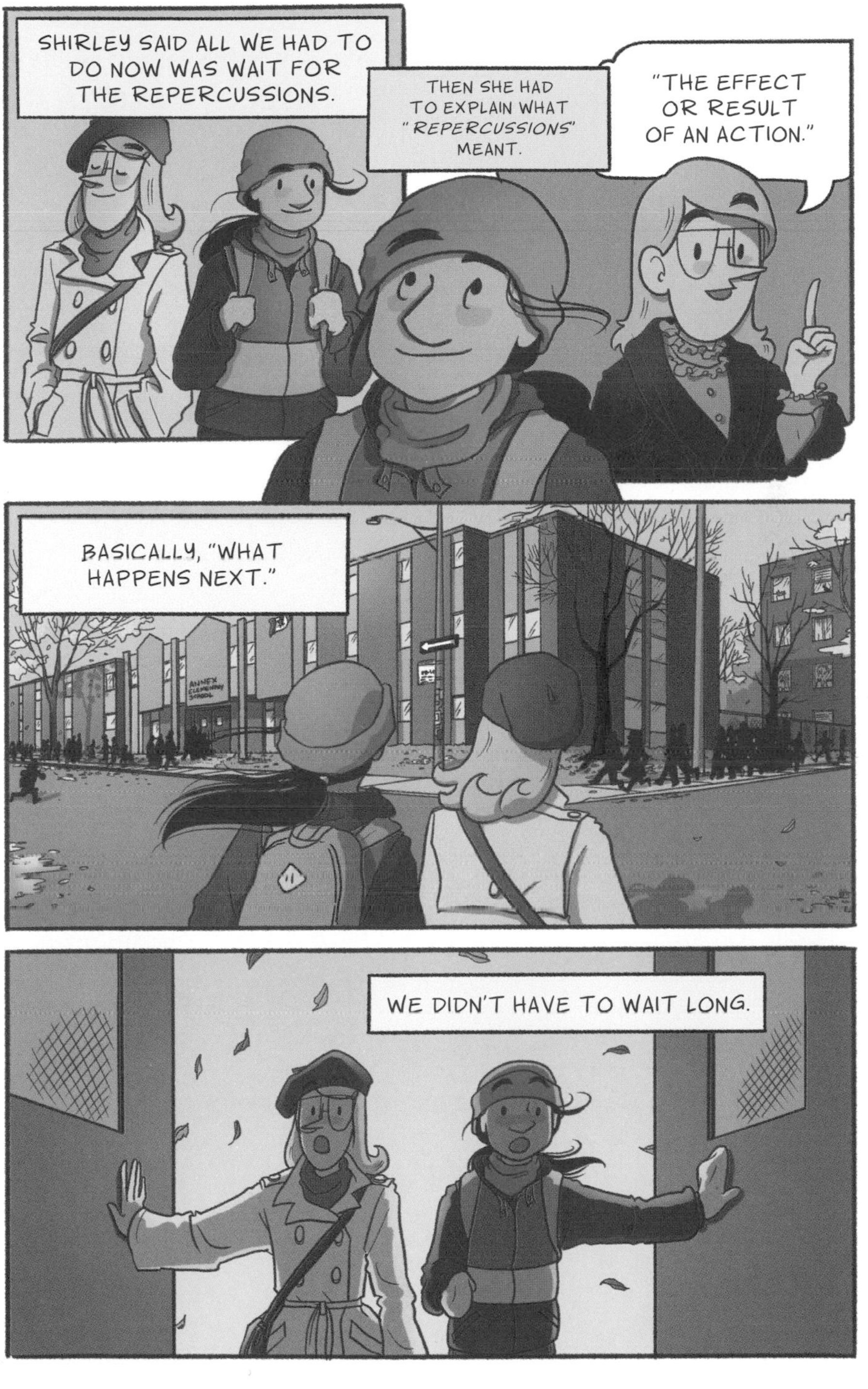
SHIRLEY SAID ALL WE HAD TO DO NOW WAS WAIT FOR THE REPERCUSSIONS.
THEN SHE HAD TO EXPLAIN WHAT "REPERCUSSIONS" MEANT.
"THE EFFECT OR RESULT OF AN ACTION."
BASICALLY, "WHAT HAPPENS NEXT."
WE DIDN'T HAVE TO WAIT LONG.

THE HALLWAY WAS *BUZZING.*

WHAT'S GOING ON?

YOU KNOW CHUCK? THAT AWESOME SIXTH GRADER WHO ALWAYS HAS CANDY?

SURE. WHAT ABOUT HIM?

HE GOT BROKEN INTO! AT HIS HOUSE!

RRRRIIIIINNGGGG

HOW DID YOU HEAR THIS?

I GOTTA GO!

EVERYBODY KNOWS!

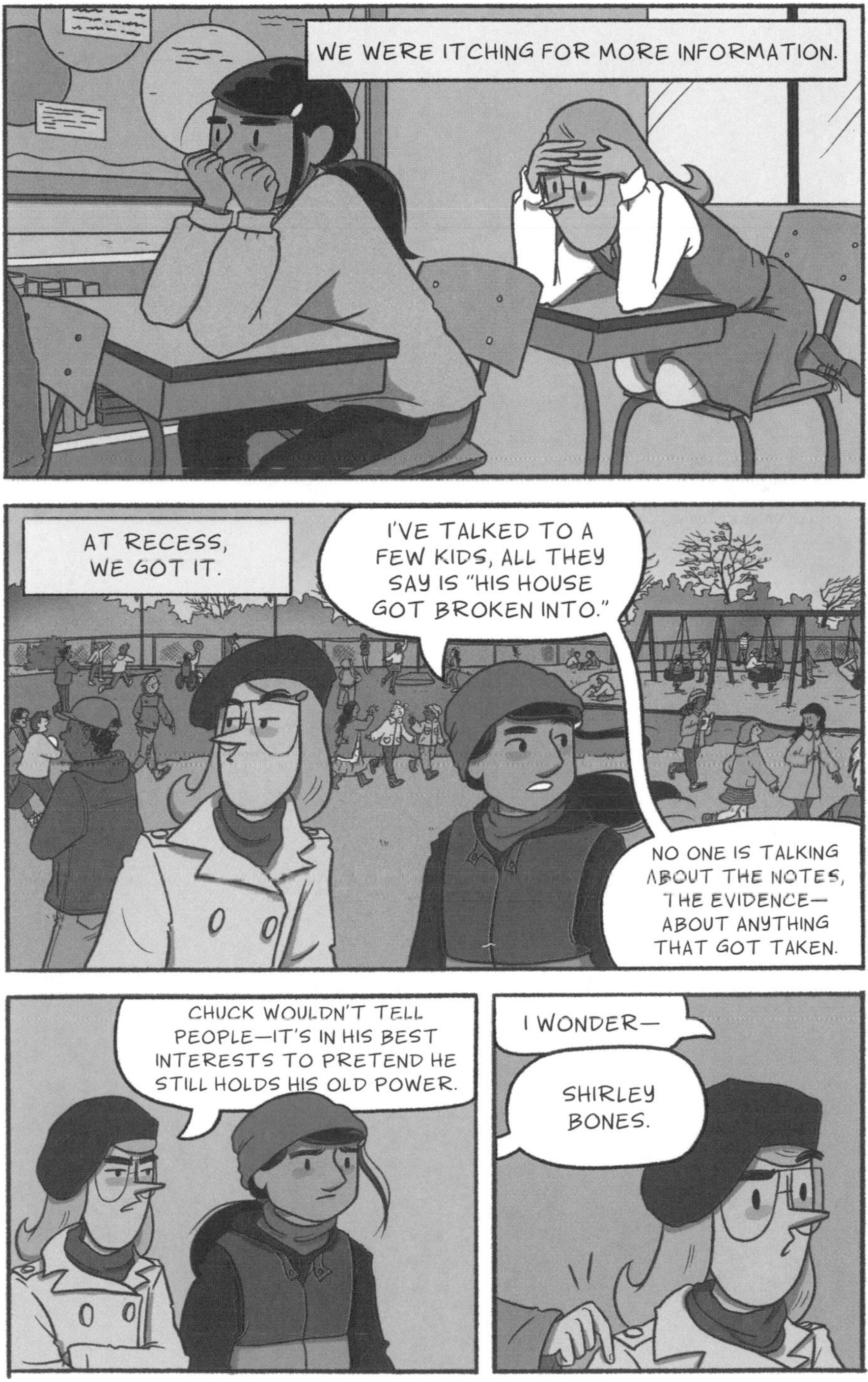
WE WERE ITCHING FOR MORE INFORMATION.
AT RECESS, WE GOT IT.
I'VE TALKED TO A FEW KIDS, ALL THEY SAY IS "HIS HOUSE GOT BROKEN INTO."
NO ONE IS TALKING ABOUT THE NOTES, THE EVIDENCE— ABOUT ANYTHING THAT GOT TAKEN.
CHUCK WOULDN'T TELL PEOPLE—IT'S IN HIS BEST INTERESTS TO PRETEND HE STILL HOLDS HIS OLD POWER.
I WONDER—
SHIRLEY BONES.

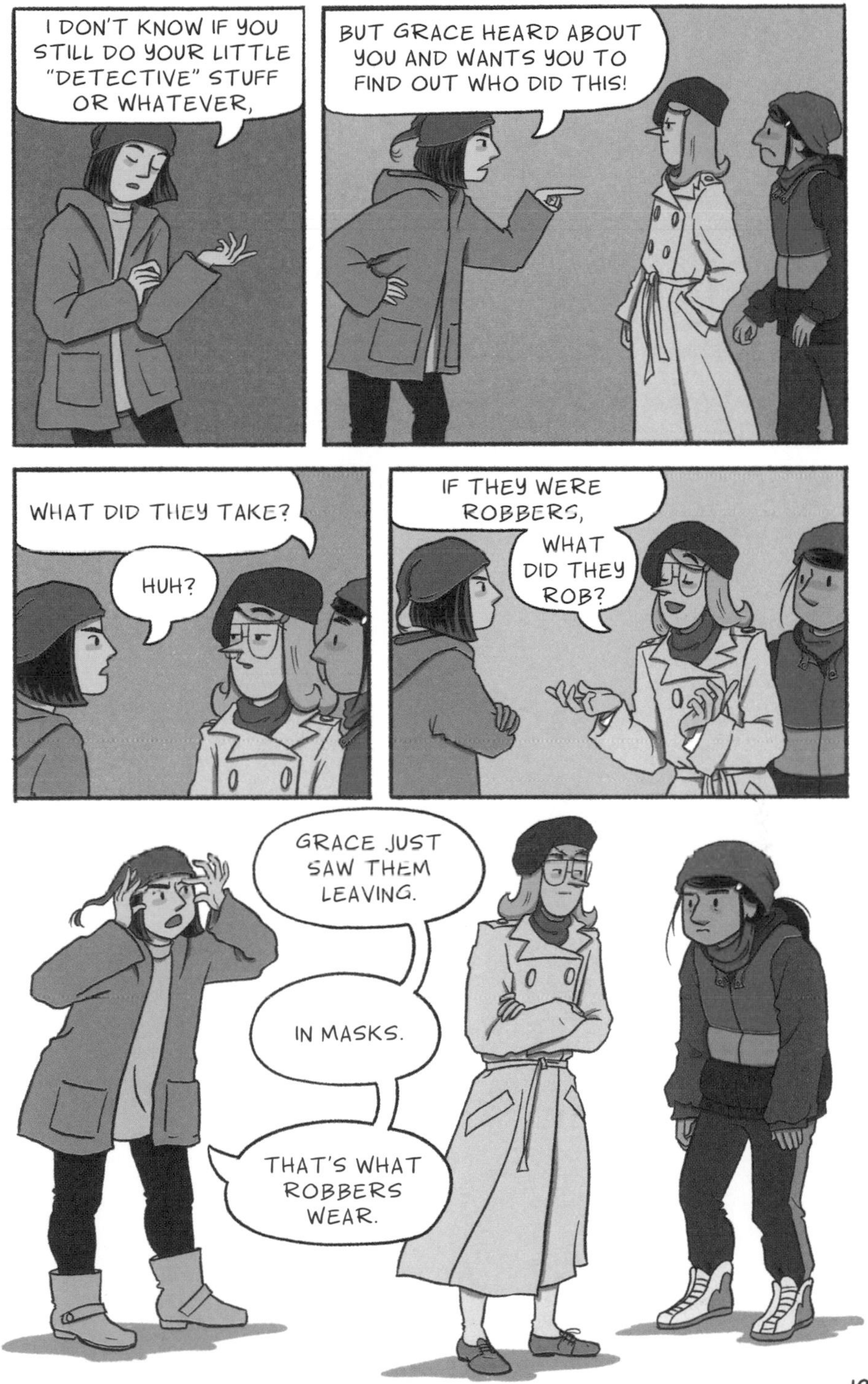
I DON'T KNOW IF YOU STILL DO YOUR LITTLE "DETECTIVE" STUFF OR WHATEVER,
BUT GRACE HEARD ABOUT YOU AND WANTS YOU TO FIND OUT WHO DID THIS!
WHAT DID THEY TAKE?
HUH?
IF THEY WERE ROBBERS,
WHAT DID THEY ROB?
GRACE JUST SAW THEM LEAVING.
IN MASKS.
THAT'S WHAT ROBBERS WEAR.

HER BROTHER CHUCK'S DOOR WAS OPEN,

BUT WHEN SHE TOLD HIM WHAT SHE SAW, HE SAID SHE WAS JUST MAKING IT UP FOR ATTENTION!

HE TOLD HER TO SHUT UP ABOUT IT AND THAT SHE BETTER NOT TELL ANYBODY.

SHE'S TRYING TO HELP HIM!

SO THE DESCRIPTION IS TWO KIDS, ONE HAS A DARK PONYTAIL?

NOD

UH-HUH.

NOTHING ELSE?

NUH-UH.

KID IN A MASK, WITH A DARK PONYTAIL . . .

THAT COULD BE ANYONE . . .

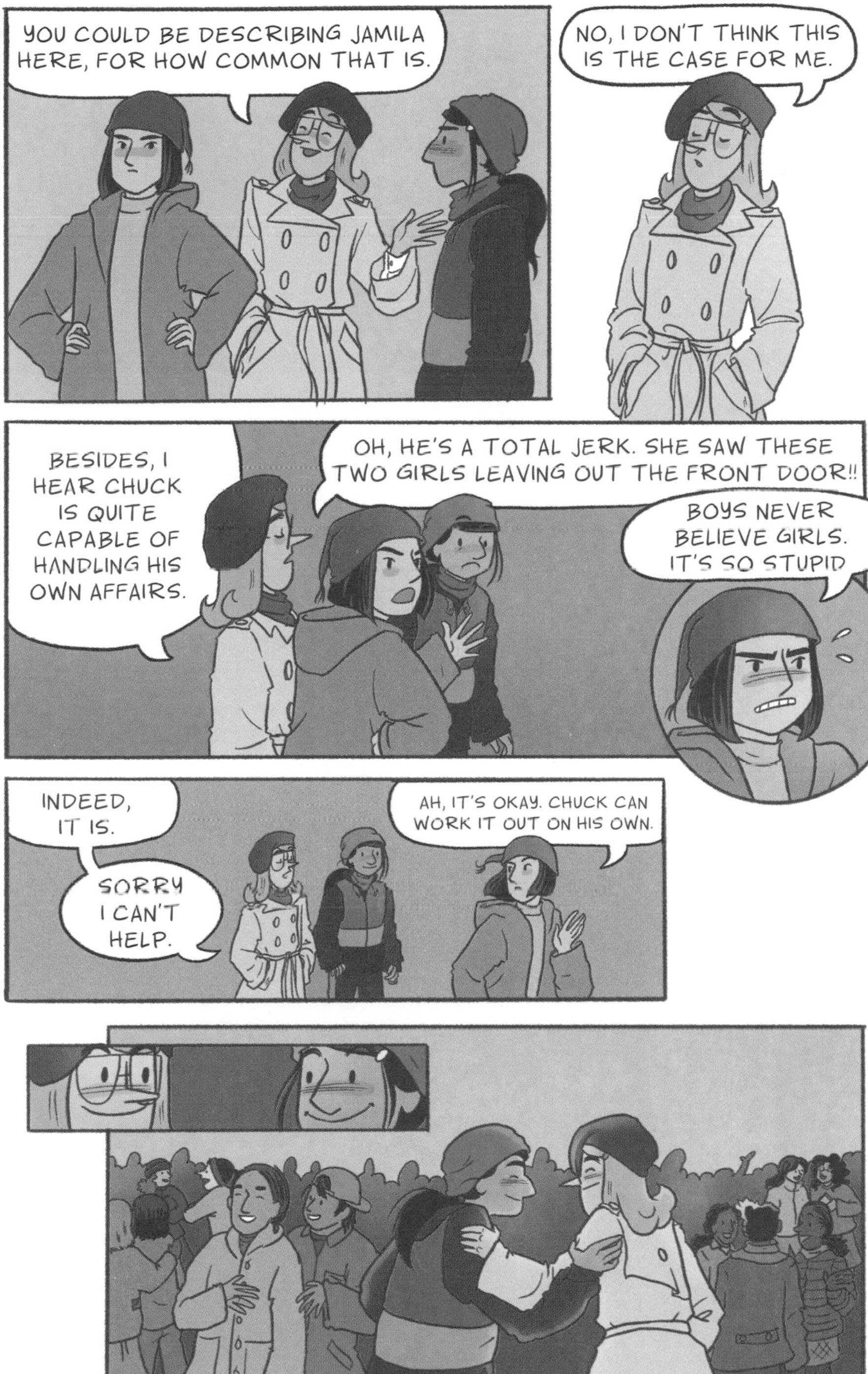
YOU COULD BE DESCRIBING JAMILA HERE, FOR HOW COMMON THAT IS.
NO, I DON'T THINK THIS IS THE CASE FOR ME.
BESIDES, I HEAR CHUCK IS QUITE CAPABLE OF HANDLING HIS OWN AFFAIRS.
OH, HE'S A TOTAL JERK. SHE SAW THESE TWO GIRLS LEAVING OUT THE FRONT DOOR!!
BOYS NEVER BELIEVE GIRLS. IT'S SO STUPID
INDEED, IT IS.
SORRY I CAN'T HELP.
AH, IT'S OKAY. CHUCK CAN WORK IT OUT ON HIS OWN.

Chapter 12

I TEXTED SEENA TO MEET ME HERE. WHERE IS SHE? HOW LONG'S THE WALK FROM HER SCHOOL? TEN MINUTES? FIFTEEN?

ANNEX ELEMENTARY. AFTER SCHOOL, OUTSIDE THE GYM.

YOU'RE NERVOUS.

I DON'T KNOW WHAT TO SAY! HOW DO I EXPLAIN THAT WE WERE THERE?

MAYBE YOU SHOULD STAY AND HELP ME EXPLAIN.

YES, MY FAMOUS TACT AND DELICACY WILL HELP.

I THINK YOU NEED TO DO THIS ON YOUR OWN. AT LEAST AT FIRST. MAYBE I'LL JOIN YOU IN A BIT.

ARG! WE DON'T EVEN KNOW HER BIG SECRET! WHAT'S ON CHUCK'S VIDEO?

SHE'S AT A NEW SCHOOL THIS YEAR, RIGHT?

YEAH . . .

HAVE YOU EVER ASKED HER ABOUT HER OLD SCHOOL?

SHE DOESN'T SEEM TO WANT TO TALK ABOUT IT . . .

HMM.

194

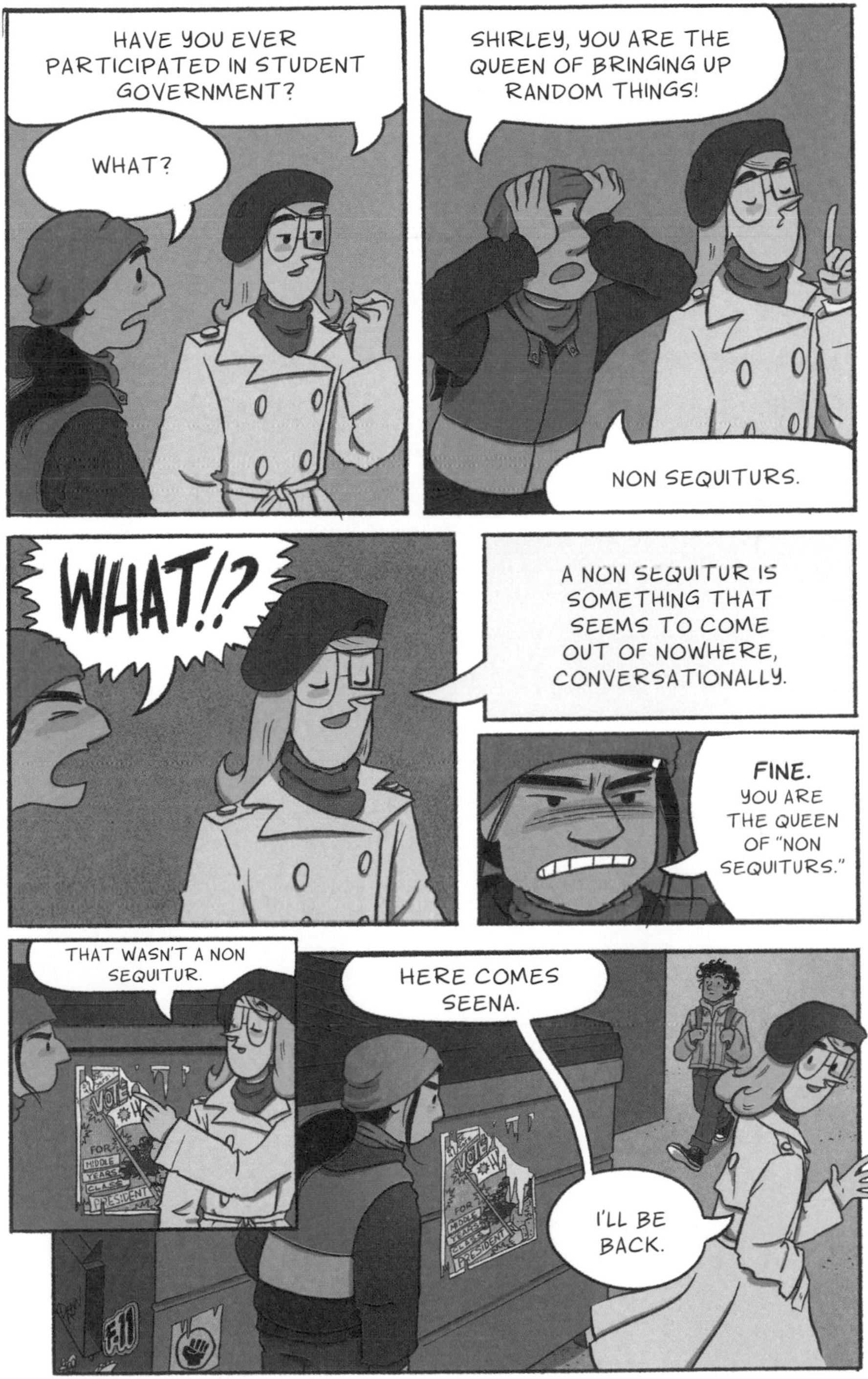
HAVE YOU EVER PARTICIPATED IN STUDENT GOVERNMENT?
WHAT?
SHIRLEY, YOU ARE THE QUEEN OF BRINGING UP RANDOM THINGS!
NON SEQUITURS.
WHAT!?
A NON SEQUITUR IS SOMETHING THAT SEEMS TO COME OUT OF NOWHERE, CONVERSATIONALLY.
FINE. YOU ARE THE QUEEN OF "NON SEQUITURS."
THAT WASN'T A NON SEQUITUR.
HERE COMES SEENA.
I'LL BE BACK.
VOTE
FOR MIDDLE YEARS CLASS PRESIDENT

UH OH.

IS THIS YOU?

YEAH . . .

WAIT, IS YOUR OLD SCHOOL **MY** SCHOOL?

YUP.

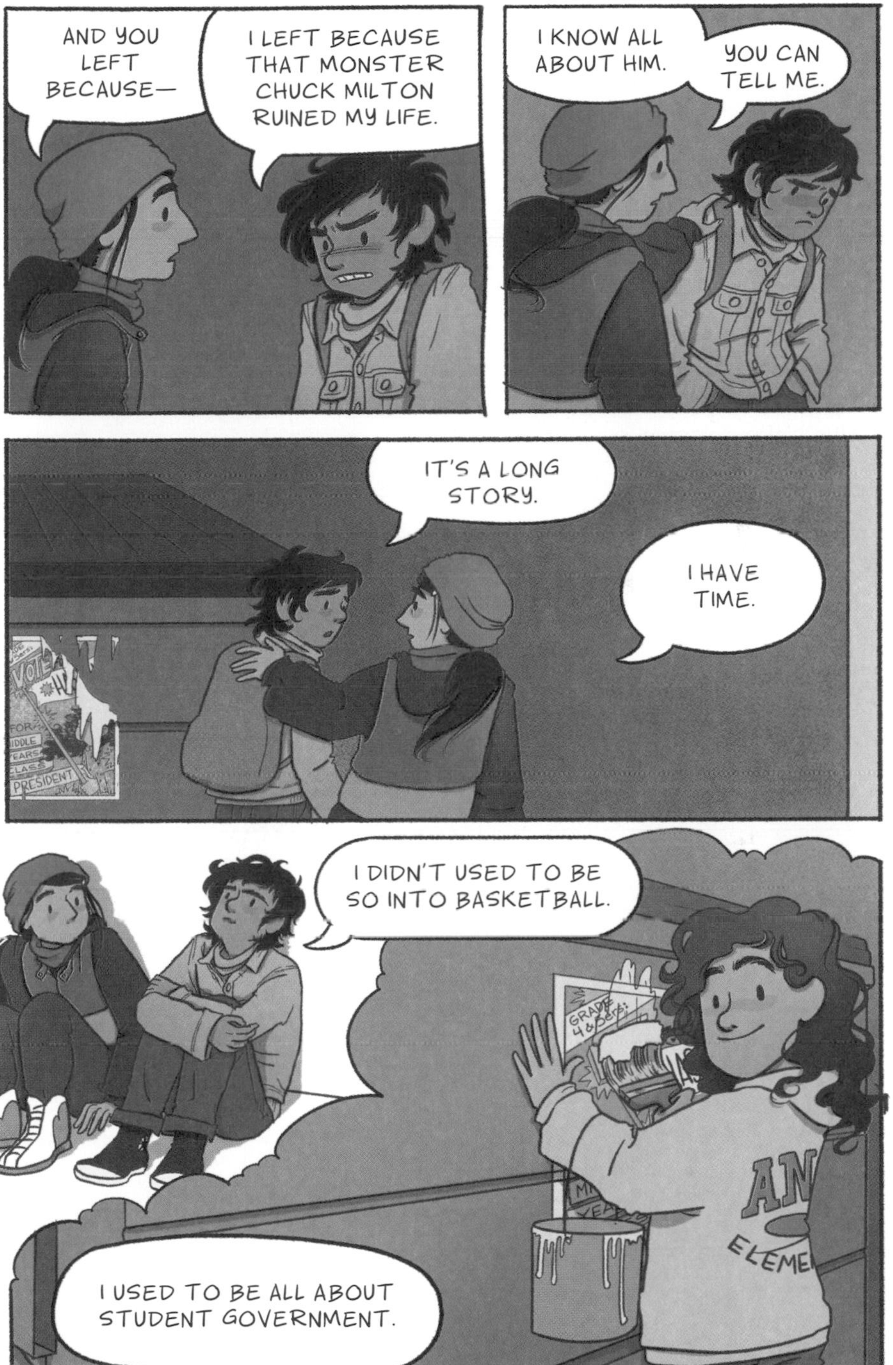
AND YOU LEFT BECAUSE—
I LEFT BECAUSE THAT MONSTER CHUCK MILTON RUINED MY LIFE.
I KNOW ALL ABOUT HIM.
YOU CAN TELL ME.
IT'S A LONG STORY.
I HAVE TIME.
I DIDN'T USED TO BE SO INTO BASKETBALL.
I USED TO BE ALL ABOUT STUDENT GOVERNMENT.

IN GRADE FOUR—TWO YEARS AGO—I RAN FOR MIDDLE YEARS PRESIDENT—THEY REPRESENT GRADES FOUR AND FIVE—

AND I WON.

I'D GO WITH THE UPPER YEARS' PRESIDENT TO A MONTHLY STAFF MEETING AND TELL THE TEACHERS AND PRINCIPAL WHAT STUDENTS WANT.

USUAL STUFF YOU WON'T EVER GET LIKE LONGER RECESS AND NO TESTS . . .

TOP STUDENT REQUESTS
• NO TESTS, EVER.
• 5 RECESSES PER DAY.
• TEACHERS NICER, NEVER MEAN.
• MORE FUN CLASSES (GYM, ART, DRAMA)
• PIZZA DAY EVERY DAY

NEW TO CANADA? TORONTO?? THIS SCHOOL??? JOIN US!!! · SIGN UP·

BUT ALSO WE STARTED THE NEWCOMERS CLUB FOR KIDS WHO JUST MOVED TO CANADA,

WHICH HAD A SPIN-OFF: THE INTERNATIONAL LUNCH CLUB— THAT WAS REALLY POPULAR IN THE END—

WHO IS YOUR COUNCILLOR? MP? MPP? MAYOR? PREMIER?

CAUSES YOU CAR
· BLM · MMIW
· FOOD JUSTICE
· INDIGENOUS SOVE
·   MATE CHA

STOP CLIMATE

AND SOCIAL JUSTICE CLUB, WHERE WE WRITE REPRESENTATIVES AND TALK ABOUT OTHER WAYS KIDS CAN PROTEST.

YOU STARTED THOSE?

DO YOU KNOW MRS. LEZAMA?

THAT'S MY TEACHER! SHE'S REALLY GOOD. SHE WAS SO NICE WHEN I FIRST STARTED THIS YEAR.

YEAH, SHE'S GREAT.

ALL THOSE CLUBS NEED A TEACHER SUPERVISOR AND SHE HELPED SO MUCH

AND GOT OTHER GOOD TEACHERS INVOLVED TOO.

SHE WAS THE ONE WHO FIRST SUGGESTED I RUN, BACK WHEN I WAS IN HER CLASS.

STUDENT GOVERNMENT COULD BE A GREAT PLACE TO HONE YOUR SKILLS, SEENA.

HONE?

SHARPEN.

YOU HAVE GOOD IDEAS, A SENSE OF COMMUNITY, AND NATURAL LEADERSHIP SKILLS.

WE NEED ALL THE GOOD LEADERS WE CAN GET.

BEFORE I RAN, I SAT IN ON SOME STUDENT GOVERNMENT MEETINGS TO CHECK IT OUT, BUT THE KIDS SEEMED WAY OLDER. IT WAS REAL INTIMIDATING—

ESPECIALLY TO KIDS MY AGE.

SO ONCE I WAS ELECTED, I PUSHED FOR MORE YOUNG PEOPLE,

BY ADDING A JR. VICE PRESIDENT...

... WHICH **CHUCK** WON.

AFTER GETTING ELECTED, HE GOT REALLY OUT OF HAND.

THE VICE PRESIDENT WAS SUPPOSED TO GET MORE KIDS **INVOLVED**.

CHUCK JUST WANTED MORE KIDS TO ORDER AROUND.

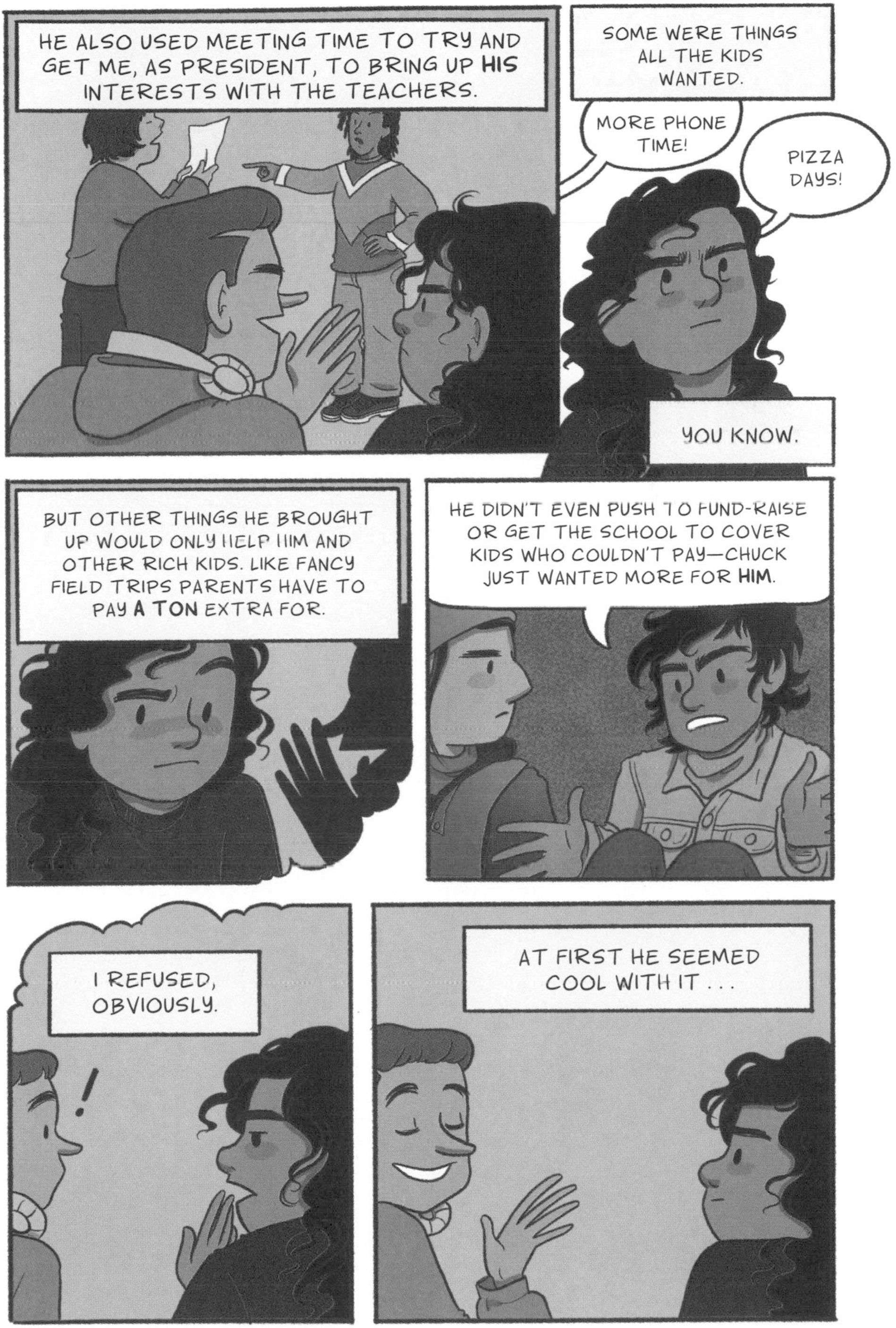
HE ALSO USED MEETING TIME TO TRY AND GET ME, AS PRESIDENT, TO BRING UP **HIS** INTERESTS WITH THE TEACHERS.
SOME WERE THINGS ALL THE KIDS WANTED.
MORE PHONE TIME!
PIZZA DAYS!
YOU KNOW.
BUT OTHER THINGS HE BROUGHT UP WOULD ONLY HELP HIM AND OTHER RICH KIDS. LIKE FANCY FIELD TRIPS PARENTS HAVE TO PAY **A TON** EXTRA FOR.
HE DIDN'T EVEN PUSH TO FUND-RAISE OR GET THE SCHOOL TO COVER KIDS WHO COULDN'T PAY—CHUCK JUST WANTED MORE FOR **HIM**.
I REFUSED, OBVIOUSLY.
!
AT FIRST HE SEEMED COOL WITH IT . . .

BUT THEN I'D FIND OUT HE WAS TALKING TO THE TEACHERS—

TELLING THEM THAT I WASN'T LISTENING TO HIM, THAT I WASN'T "REPRESENTING STUDENT NEEDS" ON COUNCIL.

MOST OF THE TEACHERS KNEW ME WELL ENOUGH TO KNOW THIS WASN'T TRUE.

BUT SOME TEACHERS— ONES WHO DIDN'T COME TO THE MONTHLY MEETINGS THEMSELVES, OR THE FEW WHO HADN'T SUPPORTED MY CLUBS— WERE LISTENING.

I JUST DON'T HAVE BULLETIN BOARD SPACE TO SPARE FOR THESE "SPECIAL INTEREST" GROUPS—

MRS. WHITE, IT'S A *STUDENT* CLUB. ANYONE CAN JOIN—

HE WAS PLANTING SEEDS.

THEN IT WAS GRADE FIVE—LAST YEAR. I WAS VOTED IN AS MIDDLE GRADE PRESIDENT AGAIN!

AFTER A YEAR OF EXPERIENCE, I WAS CONFIDENT, AND READY!

CHUCK WASN'T HAPPY. HE MADE VICE PRESIDENT AGAIN, BUT THAT WASN'T ENOUGH. HE WANTED THE TOP SPOT.

THE YEAR WAS GOOD AT FIRST! THE NEW UPPER YEARS' CABINET WERE COOL AND REALLY NICE TO ME.

SHE'S SO CUTE!

HANG OUT WITH US!

YOU'RE SO SMART FOR YOUR AGE!

THEY TREATED ME KINDA LIKE A PET . . .

AND I ADMIT I LIKED THE ATTENTION.

MY PARENTS WERE HAPPY—THEY LET ME SPEND WAY MORE UNSUPERVISED TIME WITH MY NEW OLDER FRIENDS,

ASSUMING WE WERE DOING GOVERNMENT STUFF.

BUT HALF THE TIME THE GIRLS WANTED TO HANG OUT BY CORNER STORES, GETTING SLUSHIES . . .

AND AS I FOUND OUT,

STEALING STUFF.

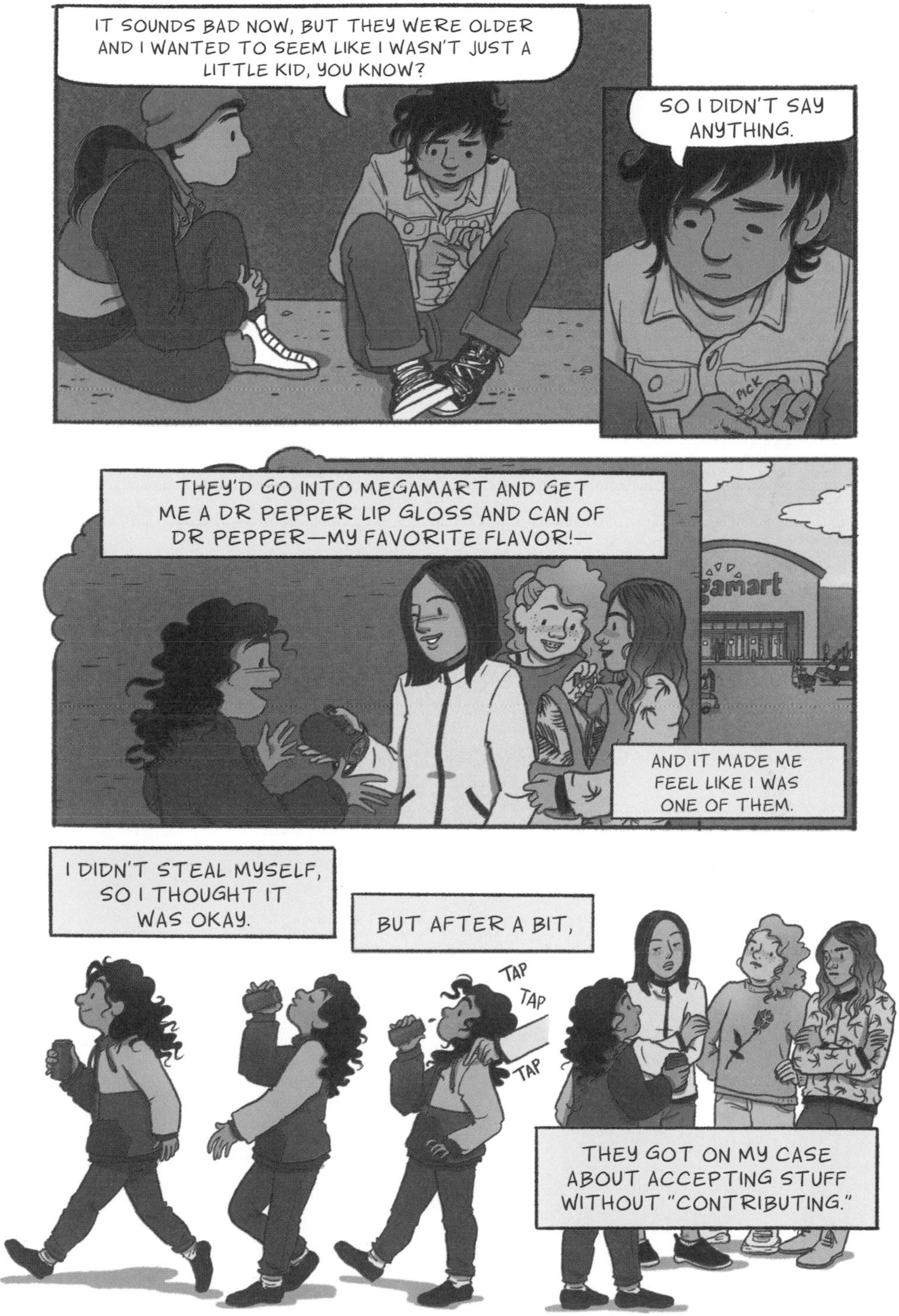
IT SOUNDS BAD NOW, BUT THEY WERE OLDER AND I WANTED TO SEEM LIKE I WASN'T JUST A LITTLE KID, YOU KNOW?
SO I DIDN'T SAY ANYTHING.
PICK
THEY'D GO INTO MEGAMART AND GET ME A DR PEPPER LIP GLOSS AND CAN OF DR PEPPER—MY FAVORITE FLAVOR!—
gamart
AND IT MADE ME FEEL LIKE I WAS ONE OF THEM.
I DIDN'T STEAL MYSELF, SO I THOUGHT IT WAS OKAY.
BUT AFTER A BIT,
TAP
TAP
TAP
THEY GOT ON MY CASE ABOUT ACCEPTING STUFF WITHOUT "CONTRIBUTING."

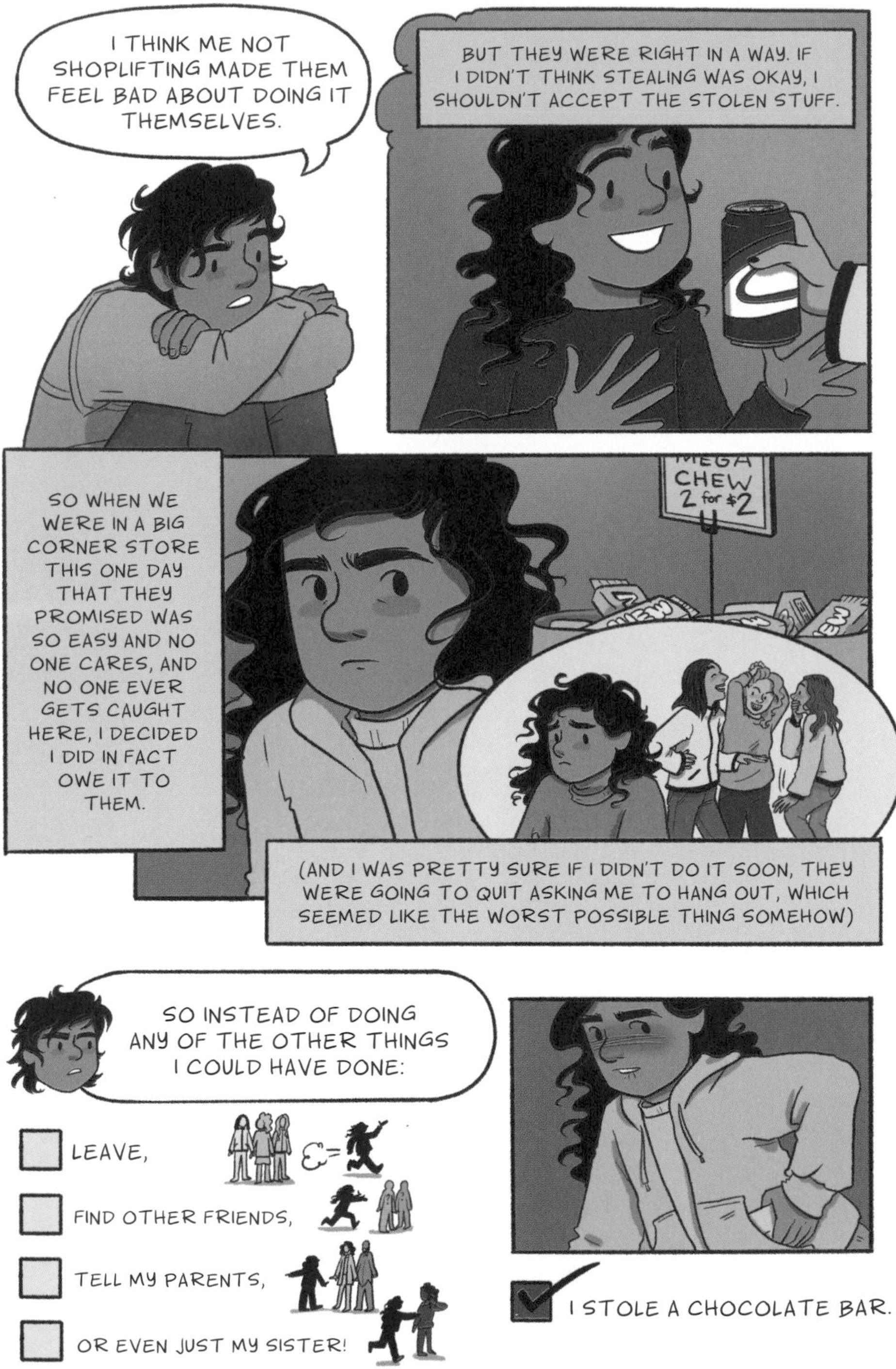

I THINK ME NOT SHOPLIFTING MADE THEM FEEL BAD ABOUT DOING IT THEMSELVES.
BUT THEY WERE RIGHT IN A WAY. IF I DIDN'T THINK STEALING WAS OKAY, I SHOULDN'T ACCEPT THE STOLEN STUFF.
SO WHEN WE WERE IN A BIG CORNER STORE THIS ONE DAY THAT THEY PROMISED WAS SO EASY AND NO ONE CARES, AND NO ONE EVER GETS CAUGHT HERE, I DECIDED I DID IN FACT OWE IT TO THEM.
MEGA CHEW 2 for $2
(AND I WAS PRETTY SURE IF I DIDN'T DO IT SOON, THEY WERE GOING TO QUIT ASKING ME TO HANG OUT, WHICH SEEMED LIKE THE WORST POSSIBLE THING SOMEHOW)
SO INSTEAD OF DOING ANY OF THE OTHER THINGS I COULD HAVE DONE:
LEAVE,
FIND OTHER FRIENDS,
TELL MY PARENTS,
OR EVEN JUST MY SISTER!
I STOLE A CHOCOLATE BAR.

WAS IT A CHOMPO BAR?

SORRY!

I JUST—

SORRY. GO ON.

I STOLE A MEGA-CHEW, IF YOU MUST KNOW, AND TWO BIG BUBS.

CANDY UPDATES **MEGA-CHEW**

VERY CHEWY, TOOTH-BREAKING CARAMEL WITH CHOCOLATE AND POINTY TOFFEE PIECES. IF YOU HATE THE DENTIST: AVOID. MAY GLUE MOUTH SHUT.

BIG BUB REALLY BAD BUBBLE GUM. WITH REALLY CORNY COMIC STRIPS. COLLECT 1500 COMICS TO GET A SLINGSHOT. SHOOT THE GUM AT YOUR ENEMIES, KILLING THEM PROBABLY. THAT'S HOW HARD IT IS.

UNLESS THERE ARE MORE QUESTIONS, I'LL CONTINUE?

PLEASE GO ON.

I IMMEDIATELY GOT CAUGHT.

APPARENTLY THE GIRLS TRIED TO WARN ME THE SHOPKEEPER WAS WATCHING,

BUT I WAS NERVOUS AND DIDN'T SEE.

ALL I KNOW IS THAT THE SECOND SHE CAUGHT ME,

THEY WERE GONE.

AND THEY STAYED GONE AS THE SHOPKEEPER AND HER HUSBAND CALLED MY PARENTS.

THEY DIDN'T TEXT WHILE I WAITED FOR MY PARENTS TO PICK ME UP.

THEY DIDN'T MESSAGE ME IN ANY WAY WHEN I WAS CRYING, LISTENING TO MY PARENTS APOLOGIZE TO THE SHOPKEEPERS...

AND BEING **FILMED** BY SOME BRAT

WHO SOLD THE VIDEO TO CHUCK.

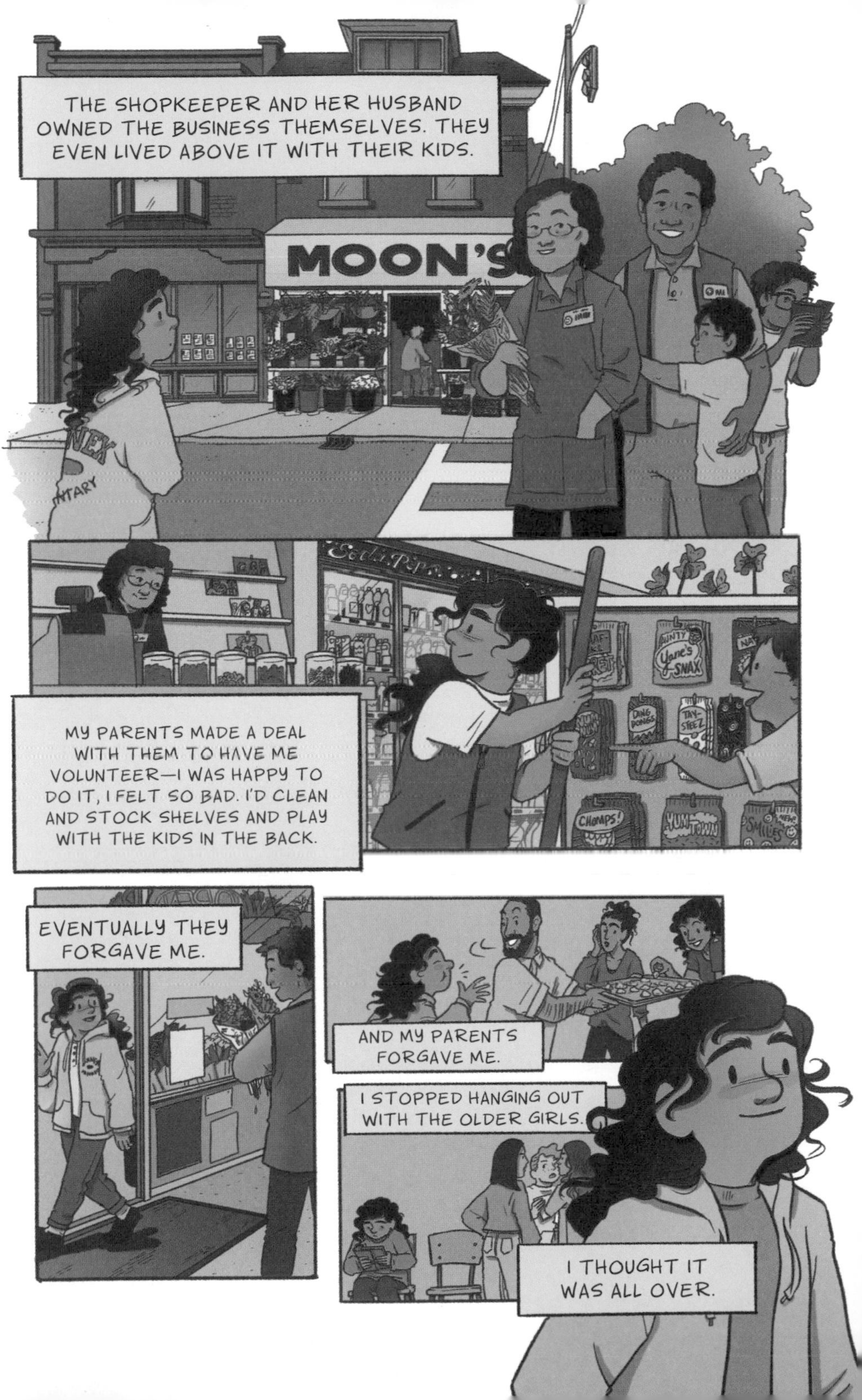
THE SHOPKEEPER AND HER HUSBAND OWNED THE BUSINESS THEMSELVES. THEY EVEN LIVED ABOVE IT WITH THEIR KIDS.
MOON'S
MY PARENTS MADE A DEAL WITH THEM TO HAVE ME VOLUNTEER—I WAS HAPPY TO DO IT, I FELT SO BAD. I'D CLEAN AND STOCK SHELVES AND PLAY WITH THE KIDS IN THE BACK.
AUNTY Yane's SNAX
DING DONGS
TAY-STEEZ
CHOMPS!
YUM TOWN
SMILIES
EVENTUALLY THEY FORGAVE ME.
AND MY PARENTS FORGAVE ME.
I STOPPED HANGING OUT WITH THE OLDER GIRLS.
I THOUGHT IT WAS ALL OVER.

I WAS WRONG.

DING

UNKNOWN NAME

TAP

THE VIDEO WAS COMPLETE WITH DRAMATIC FREEZE-FRAMES, SOUND EFFECTS, AND HEADLINES.

WAH! WAH! BOO HOO! LEADERSHIP SKILLS? UP FOR DEBATE.

PRESIDENT? MORE LIKE THIEF

STEALS FROM SMALL, LOCAL BUSINESS!

PRESIDENT HYPOCRITE

DING

DING

DING

I HAD TO HAND IT TO HIM, "PRESIDENT HYPOCRITE" COULD CATCH ON . . . IF THE VIDEO EVER GOT OUT.

If you don't respond, this goes out.

Tell anyone, this goes out.

The whole school sees it.

Tell anyone, this goes out.

The whole school sees it.

What do you want?

• • •

HE WANTED TO MEET.

HE'S GOOD.

HE DOESN'T PUT HIS NAME IN WRITING. DOESN'T DO ANYTHING THAT COULD GET HIM CAUGHT. HE DIDN'T WANT MONEY—NOT FROM ME. SOMETHING MORE COMPLICATED.

VOTE for HASEENA
FOR MIDDLE YEARS CLASS PRESIDENT

IT'S EASY, *PAL*!

HANG OUT WITH THE UPPER YEARS' GOVERNMENT GIRLS!

THEY'RE YOUR *FRIENDS*, AREN'T THEY?

DO WHAT YOU DO ANYWAY: HANG OUT! GRAB A SLUSHIE.

AND WHEN THEIR STICKY FINGERS COME OUT,

YOU TAKE THAT NEAT LITTLE PHONE OF YOURS, AND GET YOURSELF A NICE LITTLE VIDEO.

AND YOU SEND IT TO ME.

211

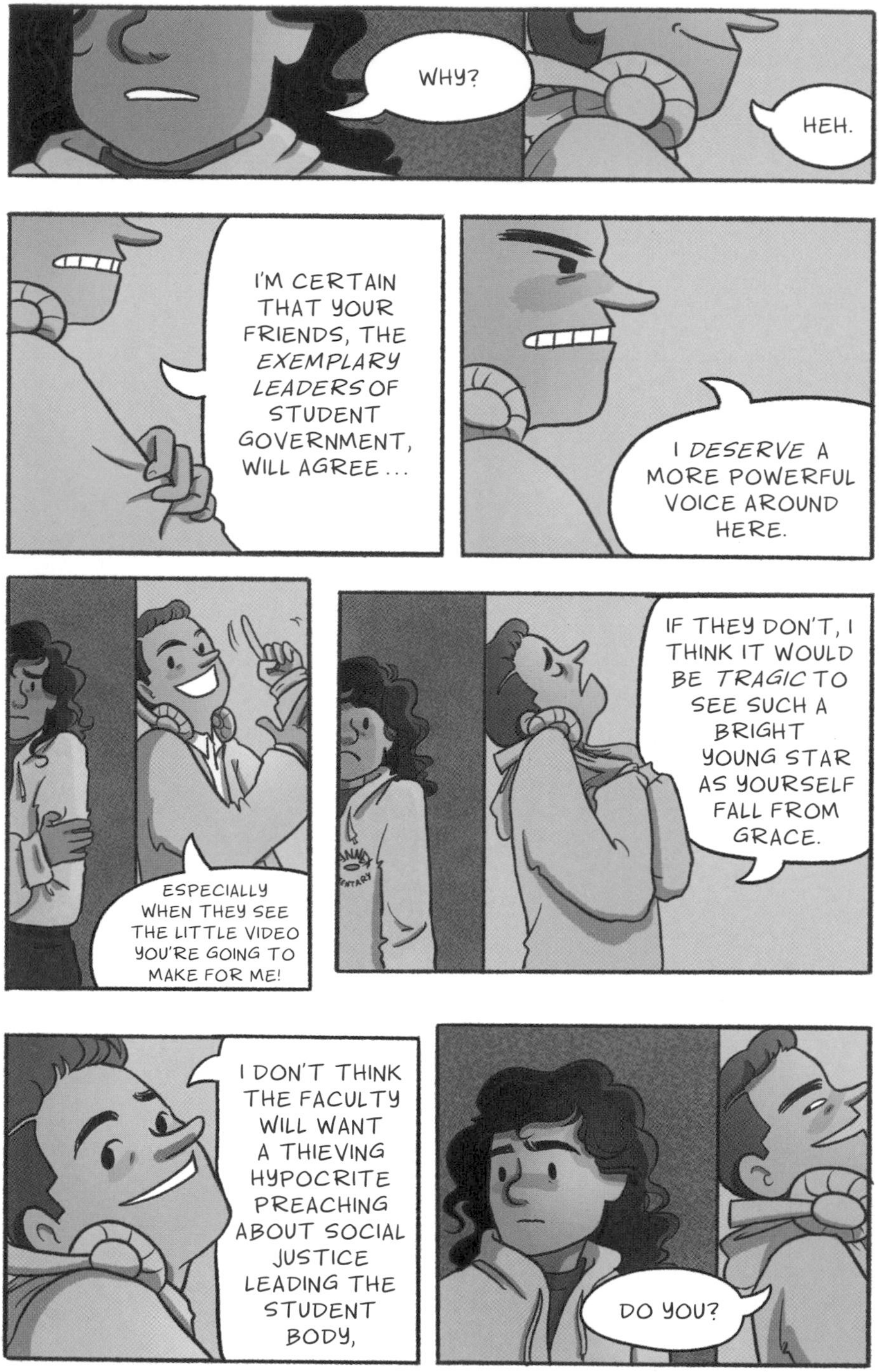
WHY?
HEH.
I'M CERTAIN THAT YOUR FRIENDS, THE *EXEMPLARY LEADERS* OF STUDENT GOVERNMENT, WILL AGREE . . .
I *DESERVE* A MORE POWERFUL VOICE AROUND HERE.
ESPECIALLY WHEN THEY SEE THE LITTLE VIDEO YOU'RE GOING TO MAKE FOR ME!
IF THEY DON'T, I THINK IT WOULD BE *TRAGIC* TO SEE SUCH A BRIGHT YOUNG STAR AS YOURSELF FALL FROM GRACE.
I DON'T THINK THE FACULTY WILL WANT A THIEVING HYPOCRITE PREACHING ABOUT SOCIAL JUSTICE LEADING THE STUDENT BODY,
DO YOU?

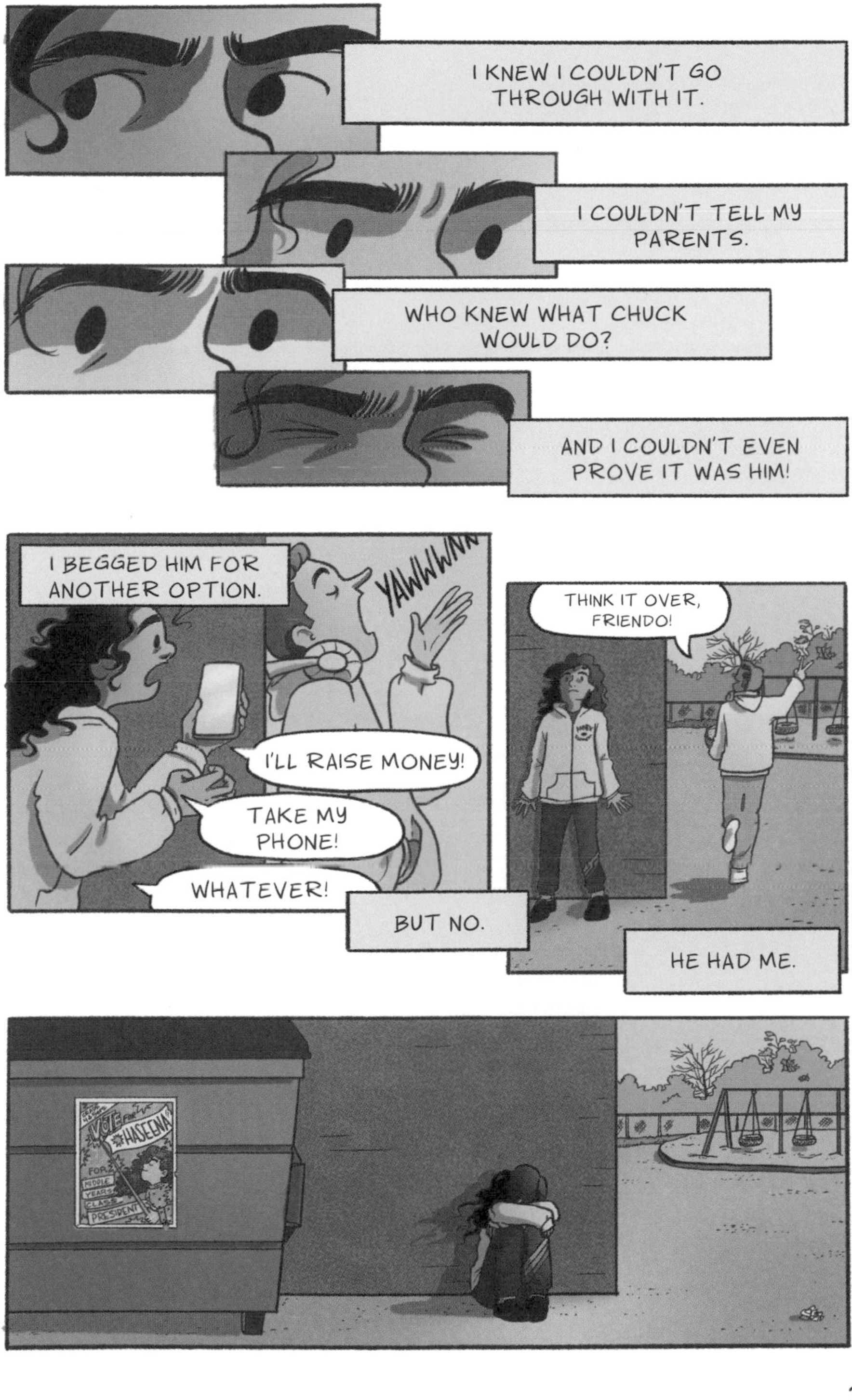
I KNEW I COULDN'T GO THROUGH WITH IT.
I COULDN'T TELL MY PARENTS.
WHO KNEW WHAT CHUCK WOULD DO?
AND I COULDN'T EVEN PROVE IT WAS HIM!
I BEGGED HIM FOR ANOTHER OPTION.
YAWWWNN
I'LL RAISE MONEY!
TAKE MY PHONE!
WHATEVER!
BUT NO.
THINK IT OVER, FRIENDO!
HE HAD ME.

SO I DID NOTHING.

HE RELEASED THE VIDEO.

ANNOUNCEMENT:
THERE HAS BEEN A CHANGE IN THE MIDDLE GRADE CABINET...

I LOST EVERYTHING.

CHUCK TOOK MY PLACE AS MIDDLE GRADE PRESIDENT.

SO HE GOT EVERYTHING HE WANTED.

SCHOOL WAS MISERABLE.

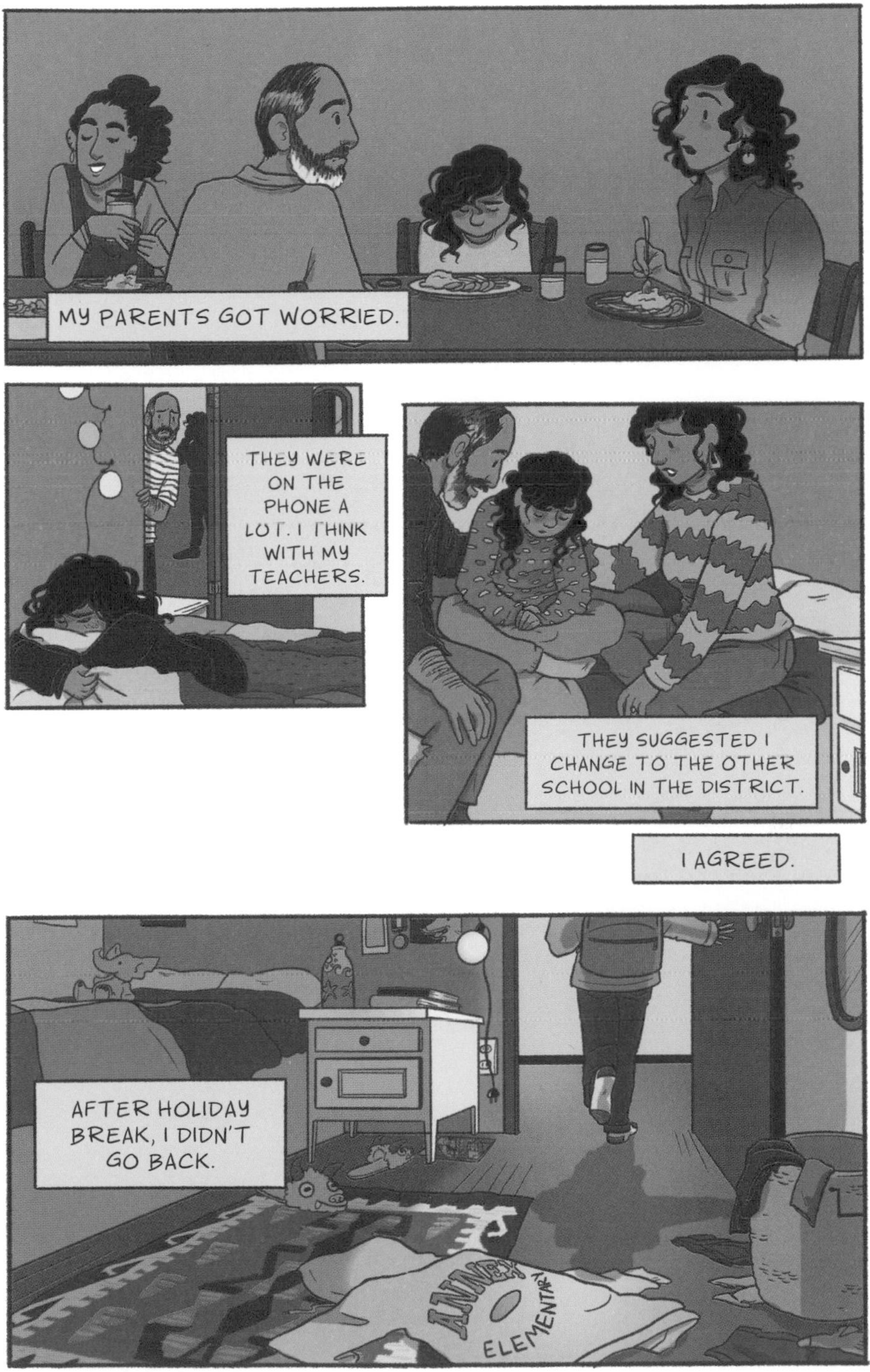
MY PARENTS GOT WORRIED.
THEY WERE ON THE PHONE A LOT. I THINK WITH MY TEACHERS.
THEY SUGGESTED I CHANGE TO THE OTHER SCHOOL IN THE DISTRICT.
I AGREED.
AFTER HOLIDAY BREAK, I DIDN'T GO BACK.

Chapter 13

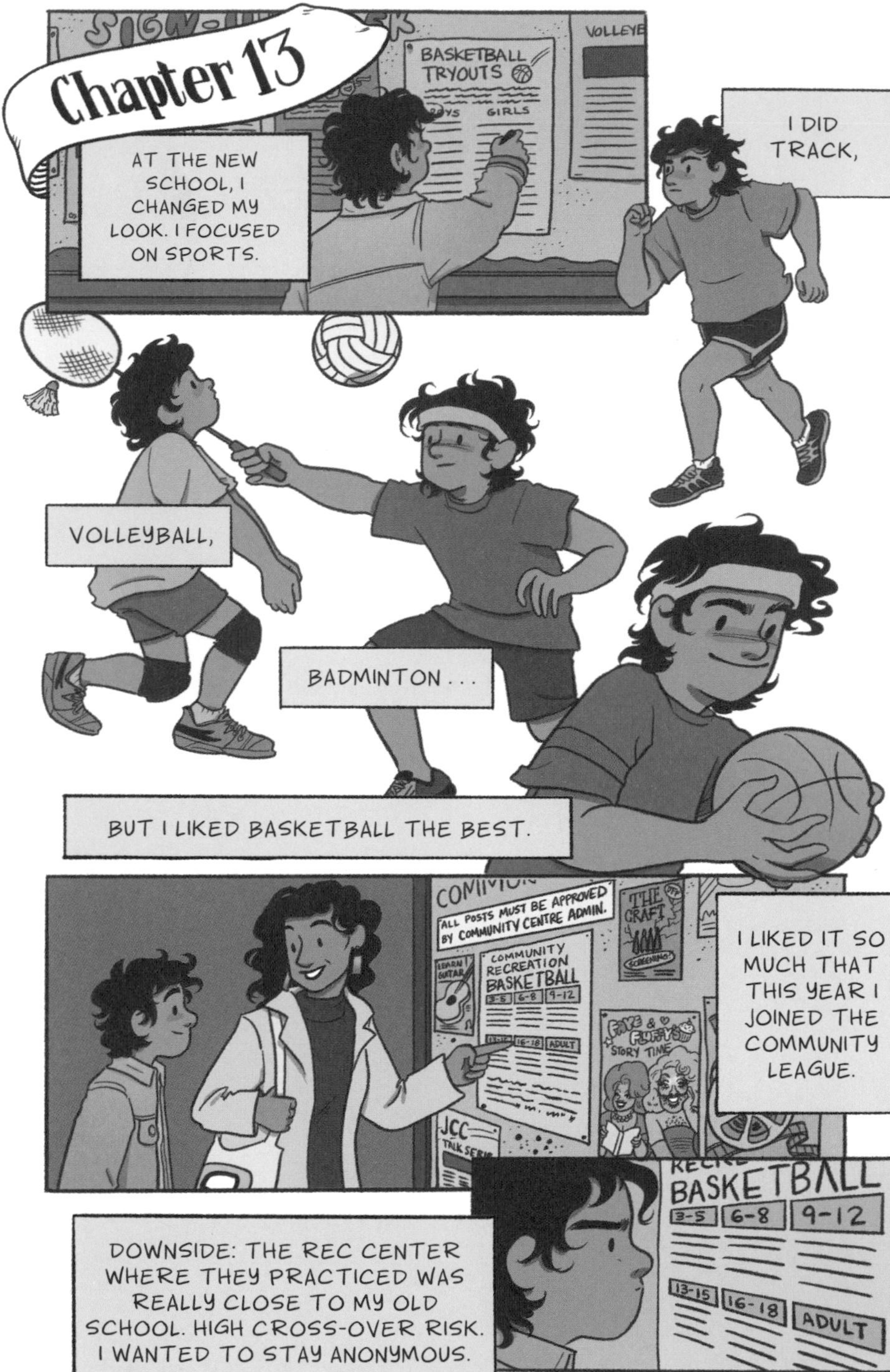

BASKETBALL TRYOUTS
GIRLS
AT THE NEW SCHOOL, I CHANGED MY LOOK. I FOCUSED ON SPORTS.
I DID TRACK,
VOLLEYBALL,
BADMINTON . . .
BUT I LIKED BASKETBALL THE BEST.
ALL POSTS MUST BE APPROVED BY COMMUNITY CENTRE ADMIN.
COMMUNITY RECREATION BASKETBALL
3-5
6-8
9-12
13-15
16-18
ADULT
THE CRAFT
STORY TIME
I LIKED IT SO MUCH THAT THIS YEAR I JOINED THE COMMUNITY LEAGUE.
BASKETBALL
DOWNSIDE: THE REC CENTER WHERE THEY PRACTICED WAS REALLY CLOSE TO MY OLD SCHOOL. HIGH CROSS-OVER RISK. I WANTED TO STAY ANONYMOUS.

I DON'T KNOW IF YOU'LL GET ALONG.

WHO CARES!

YOUR FRIENDS DON'T ALL HAVE TO BE FRIENDS WITH EACH OTHER!

THEY DON'T?

NO WAY! WHEN I WENT HERE I HAD DEBATE FRIENDS, STUDENT GOVERNMENT FRIENDS, LUNCH CLUB FRIENDS . . . SOME OF THEM COULDN'T STAND EACH OTHER!

BUT SHIRLEY AND I ALREADY HAVE SOMETHING IN COMMON.

WE BOTH LIKE YOU.

WHAT'S THAT?

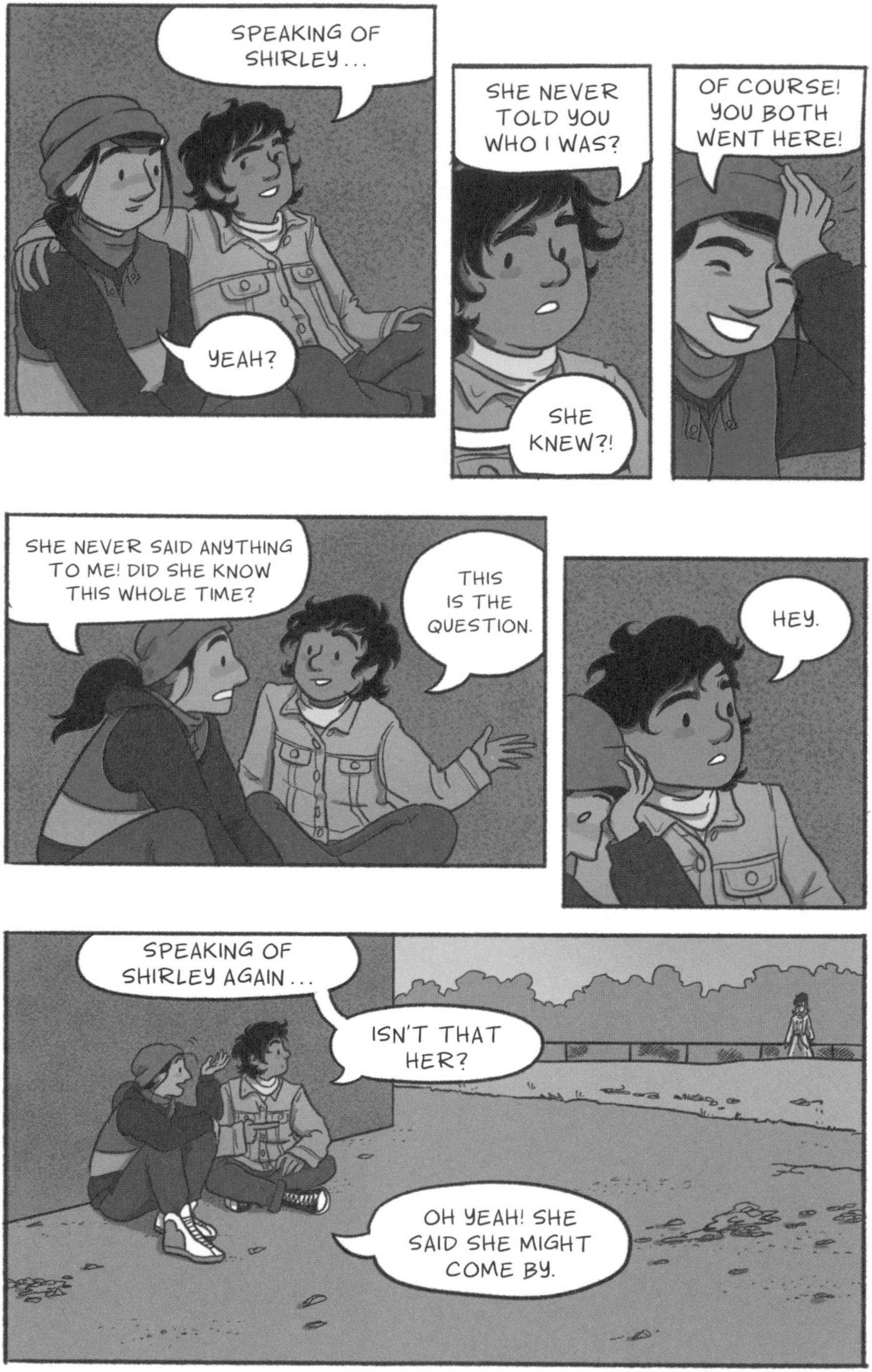
SPEAKING OF SHIRLEY...
YEAH?
SHE NEVER TOLD YOU WHO I WAS?
SHE KNEW?!
OF COURSE! YOU BOTH WENT HERE!
SHE NEVER SAID ANYTHING TO ME! DID SHE KNOW THIS WHOLE TIME?
THIS IS THE QUESTION.
HEY.
SPEAKING OF SHIRLEY AGAIN...
ISN'T THAT HER?
OH YEAH! SHE SAID SHE MIGHT COME BY.

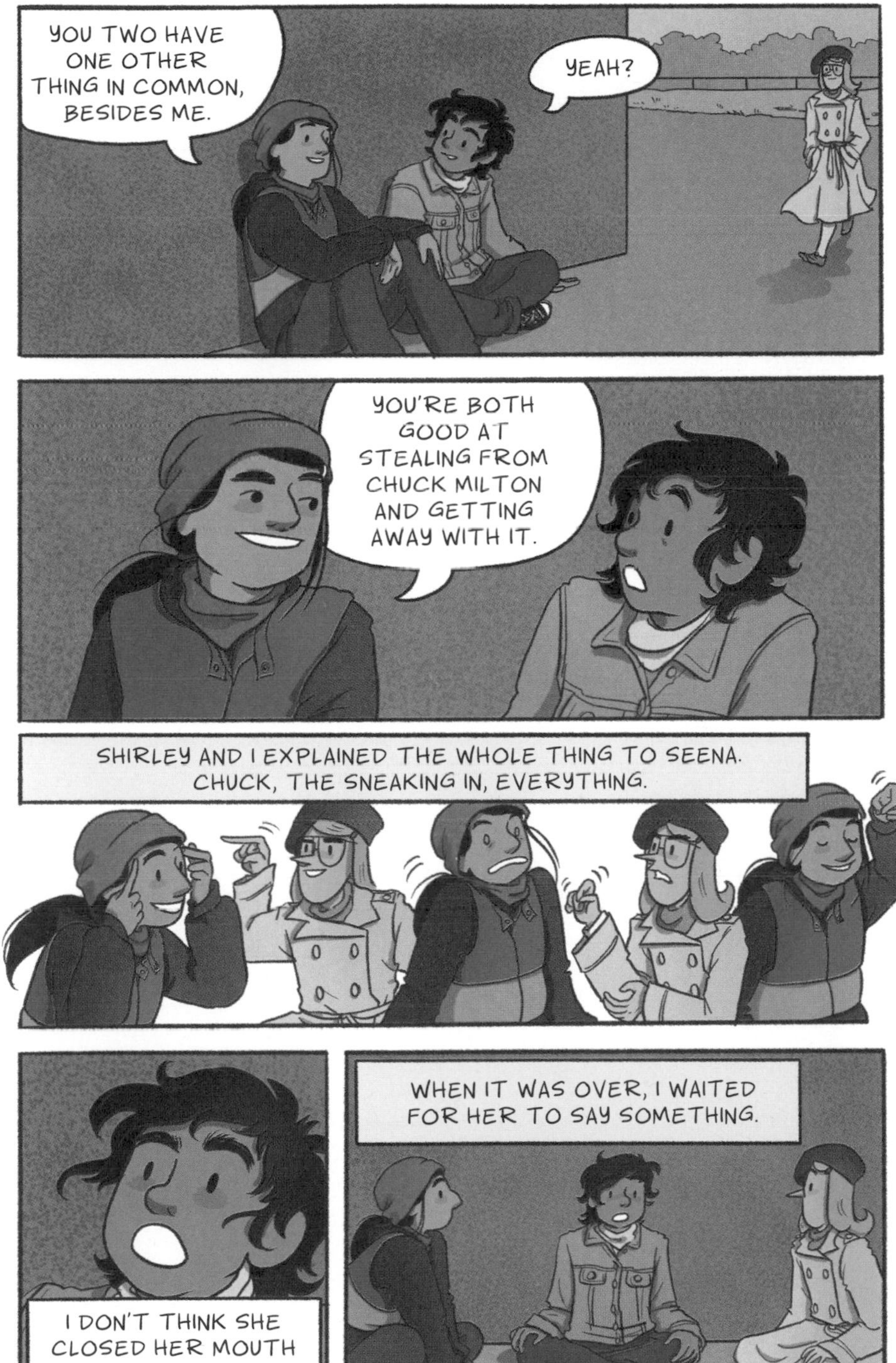

YOU TWO HAVE ONE OTHER THING IN COMMON, BESIDES ME.
YEAH?
YOU'RE BOTH GOOD AT STEALING FROM CHUCK MILTON AND GETTING AWAY WITH IT.
SHIRLEY AND I EXPLAINED THE WHOLE THING TO SEENA. CHUCK, THE SNEAKING IN, EVERYTHING.
I DON'T THINK SHE CLOSED HER MOUTH THE WHOLE TIME.
WHEN IT WAS OVER, I WAITED FOR HER TO SAY SOMETHING.

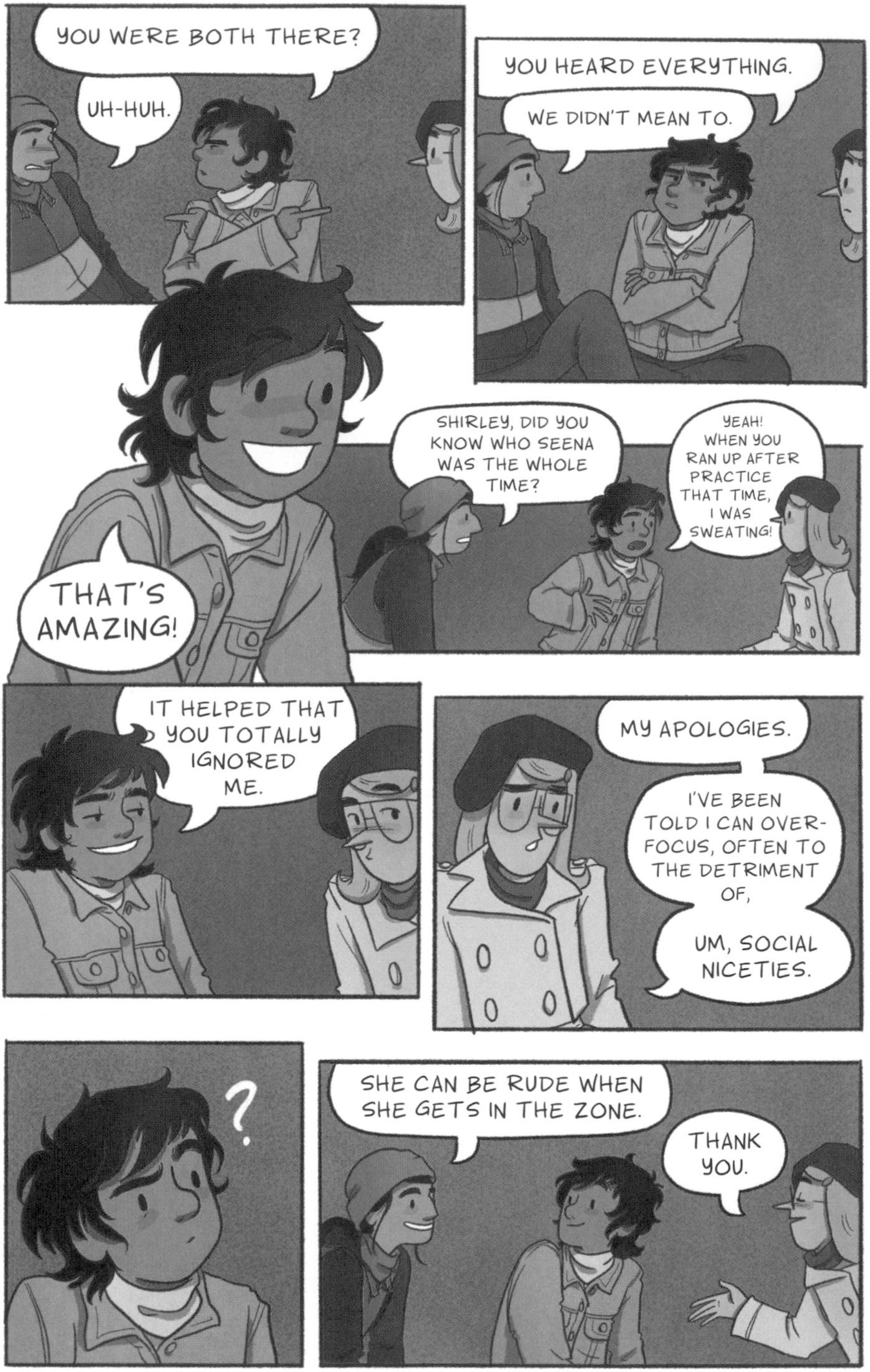
YOU WERE BOTH THERE?
UH-HUH.
YOU HEARD EVERYTHING.
WE DIDN'T MEAN TO.
THAT'S AMAZING!
SHIRLEY, DID YOU KNOW WHO SEENA WAS THE WHOLE TIME?
YEAH! WHEN YOU RAN UP AFTER PRACTICE THAT TIME, I WAS SWEATING!
IT HELPED THAT YOU TOTALLY IGNORED ME.
MY APOLOGIES.
I'VE BEEN TOLD I CAN OVER-FOCUS, OFTEN TO THE DETRIMENT OF,
UM, SOCIAL NICETIES.
?
SHE CAN BE RUDE WHEN SHE GETS IN THE ZONE.
THANK YOU.

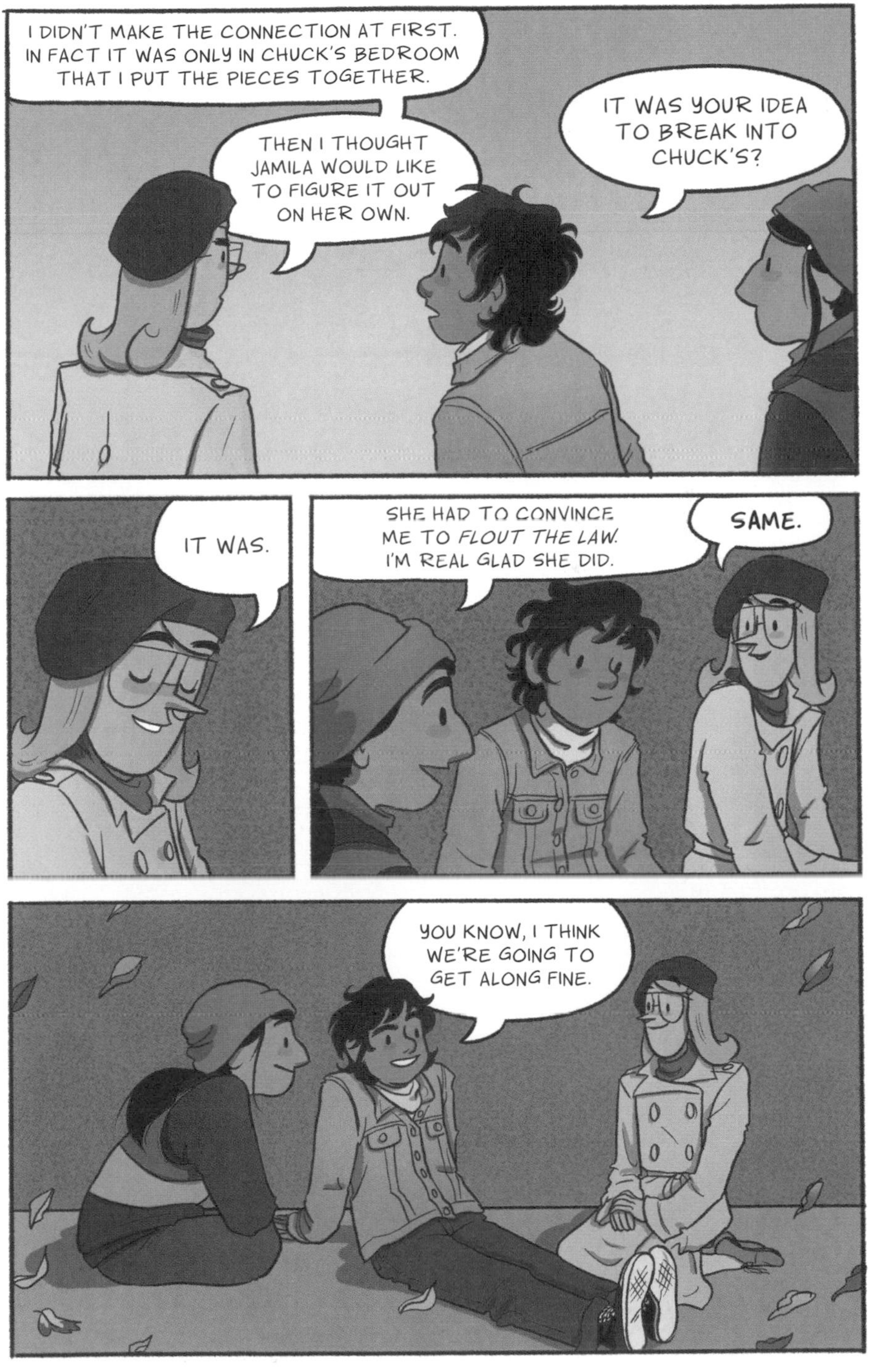

I DIDN'T MAKE THE CONNECTION AT FIRST. IN FACT IT WAS ONLY IN CHUCK'S BEDROOM THAT I PUT THE PIECES TOGETHER.
THEN I THOUGHT JAMILA WOULD LIKE TO FIGURE IT OUT ON HER OWN.
IT WAS YOUR IDEA TO BREAK INTO CHUCK'S?
IT WAS.
SHE HAD TO CONVINCE ME TO *FLOUT THE LAW.* I'M REAL GLAD SHE DID.
SAME.
YOU KNOW, I THINK WE'RE GOING TO GET ALONG FINE.

Chapter 14

WE WOUND UP GIVING SEENA EVERYTHING WE GOT FROM CHUCK'S.

IF YOU FIGURE IT OUT AND NEED HELP...

INDEED!

I DON'T KNOW WHAT I'M GONNA DO WITH THIS YET.

IT TOOK HER A WHILE.

I GOT IT!

ABOUT A WEEK LATER:

LOOKS LIKE SEENA DECIDED.

SHE SURE DID.

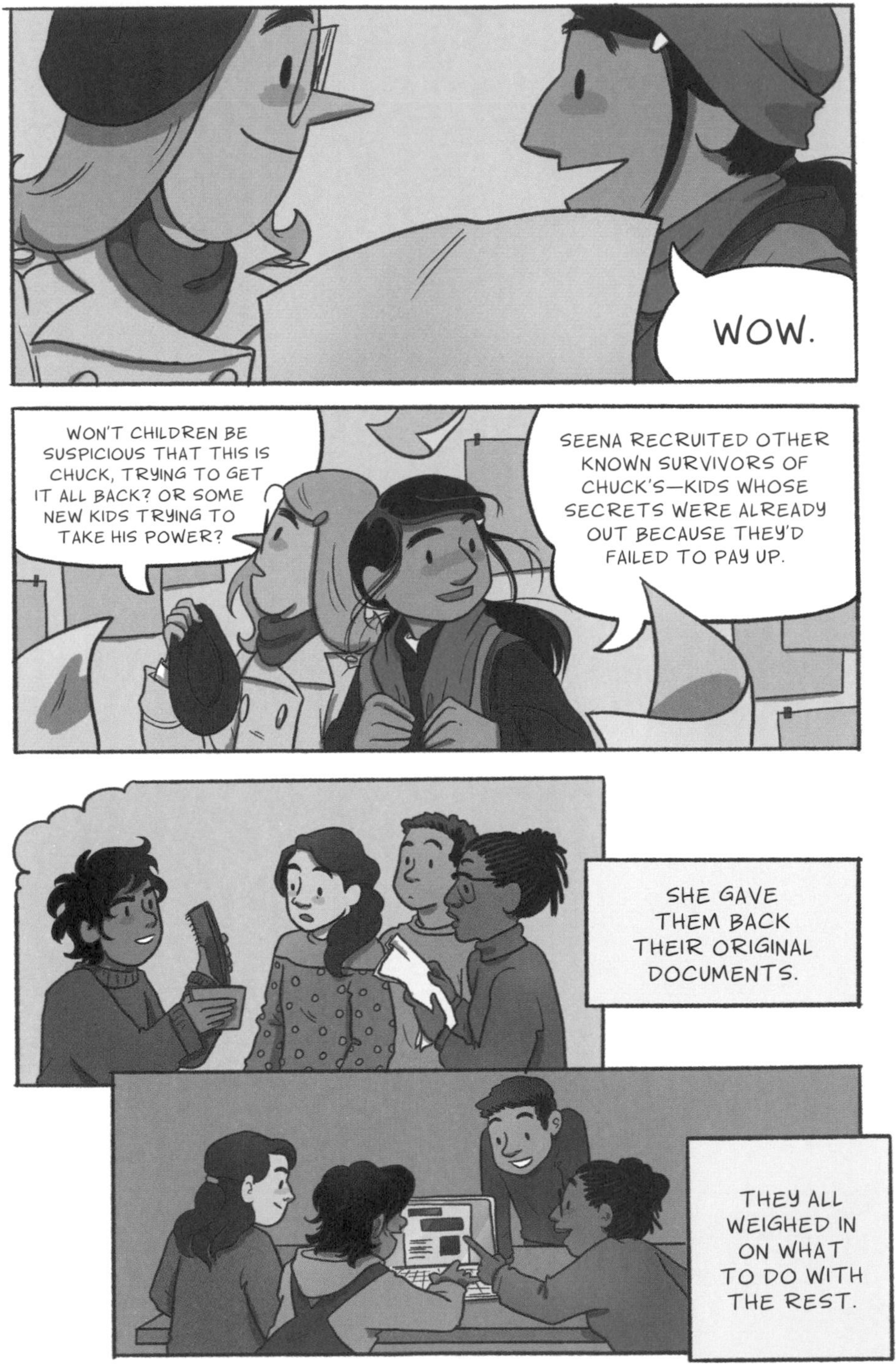
WOW.
WON'T CHILDREN BE SUSPICIOUS THAT THIS IS CHUCK, TRYING TO GET IT ALL BACK? OR SOME NEW KIDS TRYING TO TAKE HIS POWER?
SEENA RECRUITED OTHER KNOWN SURVIVORS OF CHUCK'S—KIDS WHOSE SECRETS WERE ALREADY OUT BECAUSE THEY'D FAILED TO PAY UP.
SHE GAVE THEM BACK THEIR ORIGINAL DOCUMENTS.
THEY ALL WEIGHED IN ON WHAT TO DO WITH THE REST.

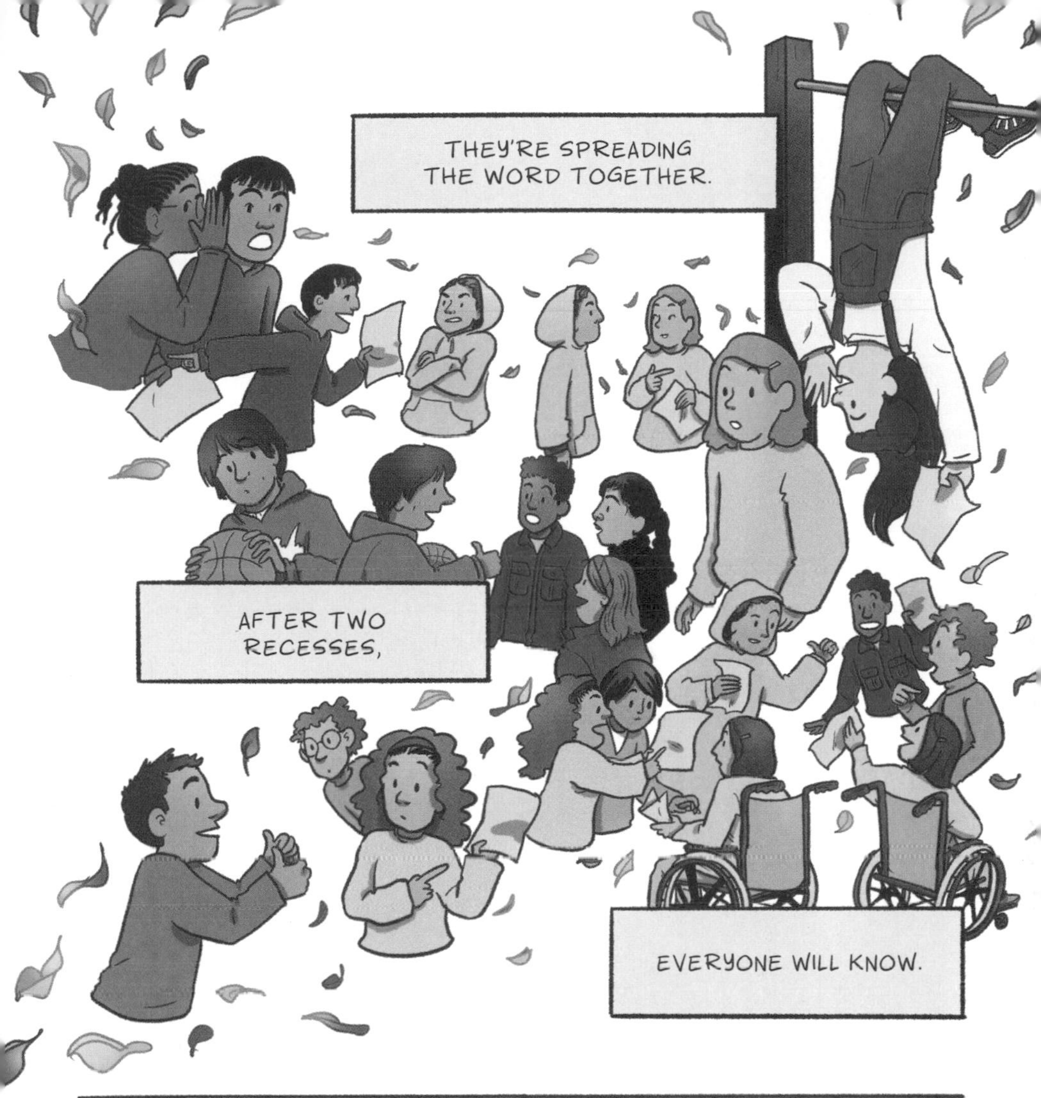
THEY'RE SPREADING THE WORD TOGETHER.
AFTER TWO RECESSES,
EVERYONE WILL KNOW.

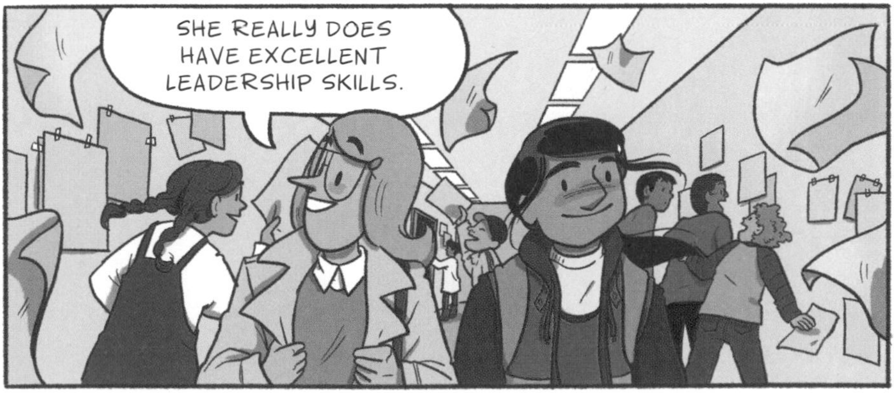
SHE REALLY DOES HAVE EXCELLENT LEADERSHIP SKILLS.

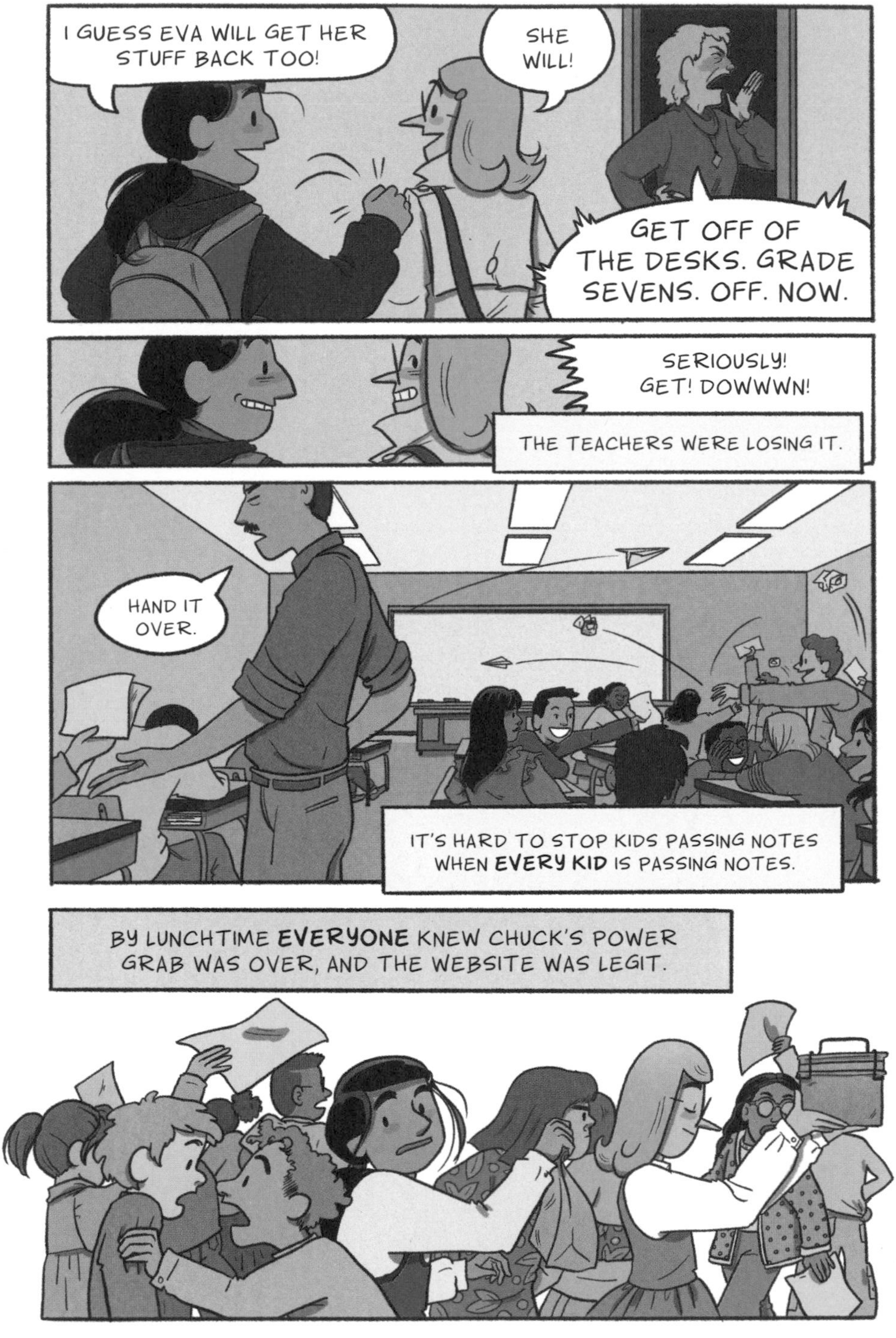
I GUESS EVA WILL GET HER STUFF BACK TOO!
SHE WILL!
GET OFF OF THE DESKS. GRADE SEVENS. OFF. NOW.
SERIOUSLY! GET! DOWWWN!
THE TEACHERS WERE LOSING IT.
HAND IT OVER.
IT'S HARD TO STOP KIDS PASSING NOTES WHEN **EVERY KID** IS PASSING NOTES.
BY LUNCHTIME **EVERYONE** KNEW CHUCK'S POWER GRAB WAS OVER, AND THE WEBSITE WAS LEGIT.

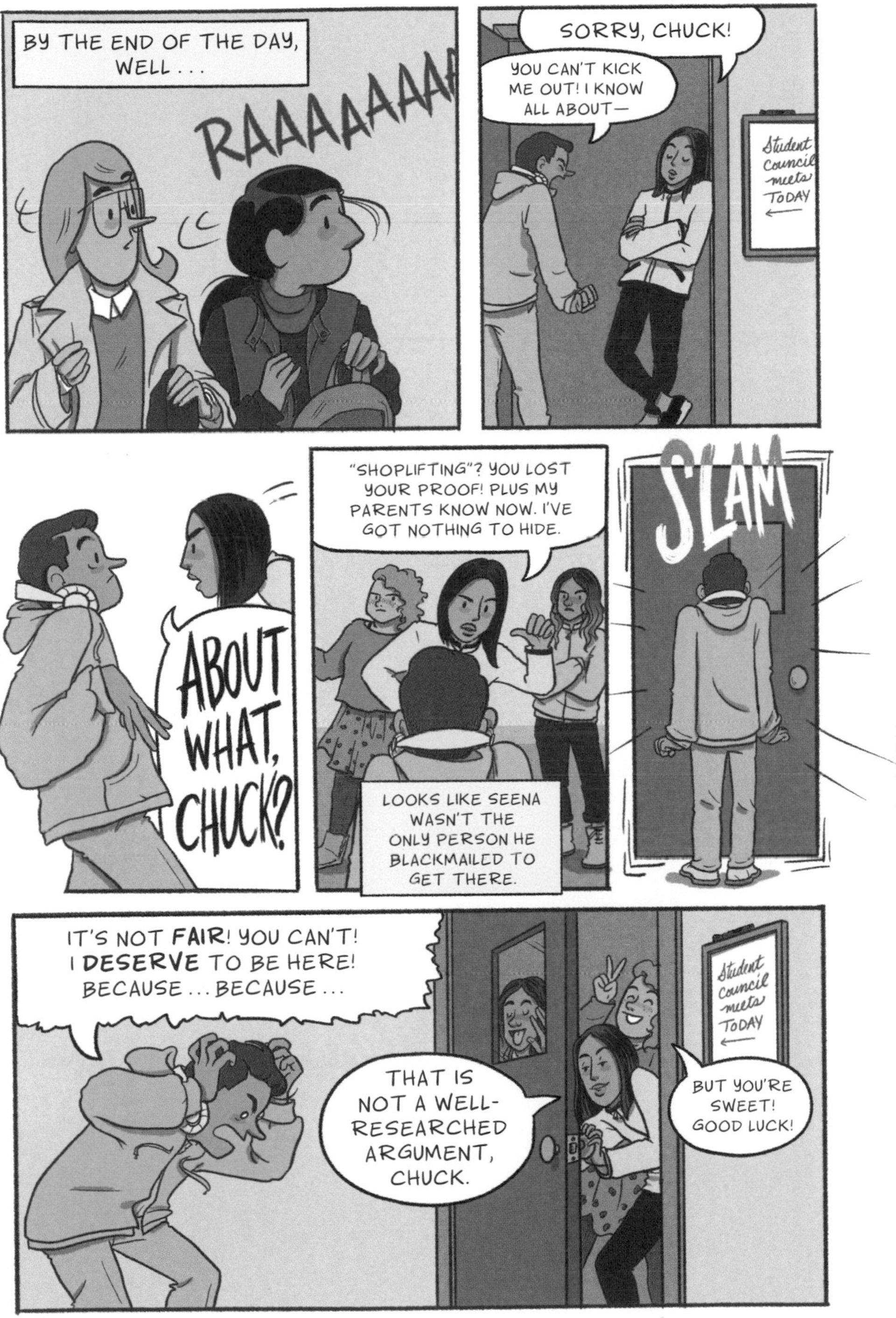
BY THE END OF THE DAY, WELL . . .
RAAAAAAAR
SORRY, CHUCK!
YOU CAN'T KICK ME OUT! I KNOW ALL ABOUT—
Student council meets TODAY
ABOUT WHAT, CHUCK?
"SHOPLIFTING"? YOU LOST YOUR PROOF! PLUS MY PARENTS KNOW NOW. I'VE GOT NOTHING TO HIDE.
LOOKS LIKE SEENA WASN'T THE ONLY PERSON HE BLACKMAILED TO GET THERE.
SLAM
IT'S NOT FAIR! YOU CAN'T! I DESERVE TO BE HERE! BECAUSE . . . BECAUSE . . .
THAT IS NOT A WELL-RESEARCHED ARGUMENT, CHUCK.
Student council meets TODAY
BUT YOU'RE SWEET! GOOD LUCK!

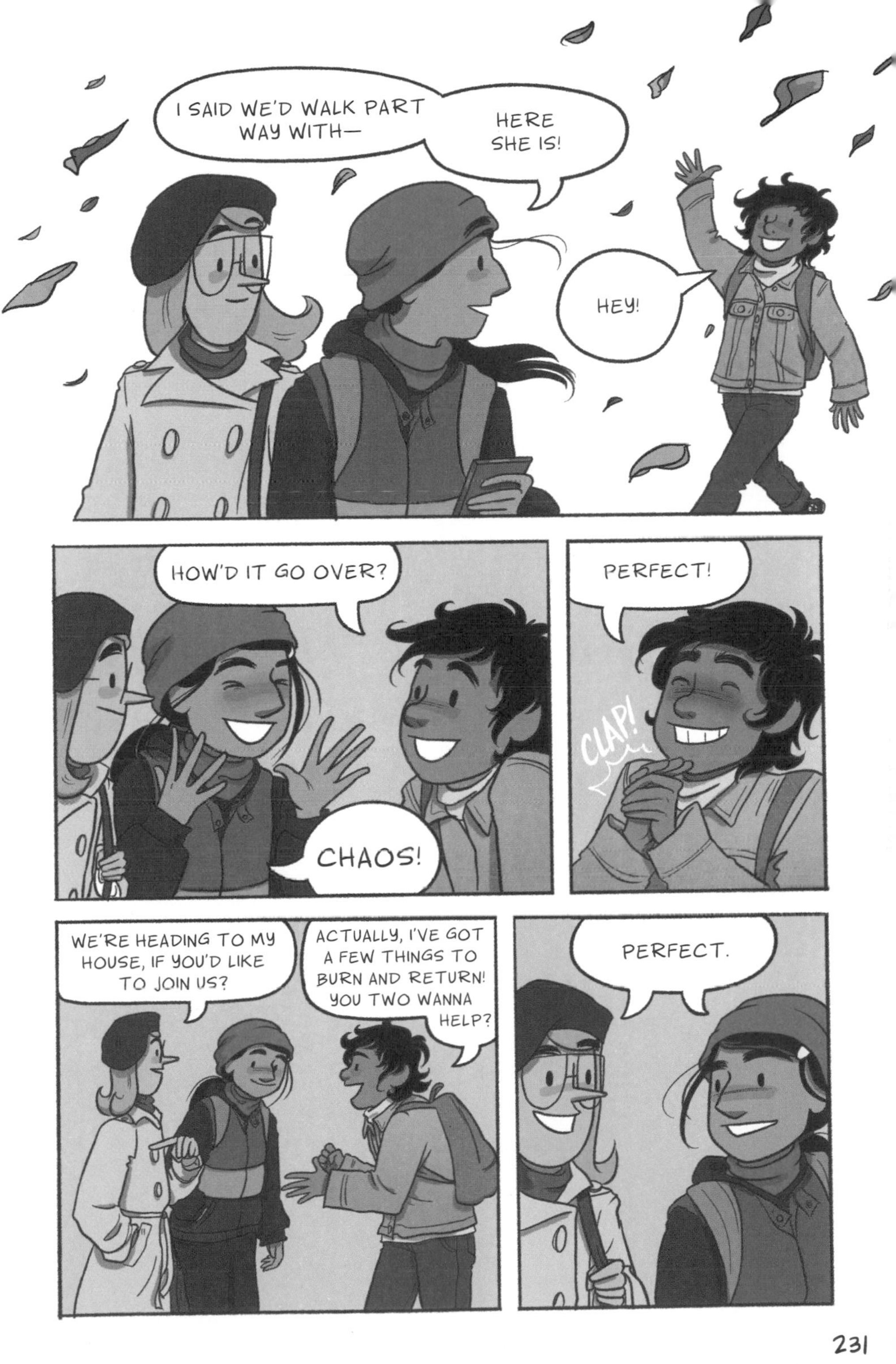
I SAID WE'D WALK PART WAY WITH—
HERE SHE IS!
HEY!
HOW'D IT GO OVER?
CHAOS!
PERFECT!
CLAP!
WE'RE HEADING TO MY HOUSE, IF YOU'D LIKE TO JOIN US?
ACTUALLY, I'VE GOT A FEW THINGS TO BURN AND RETURN! YOU TWO WANNA HELP?
PERFECT.

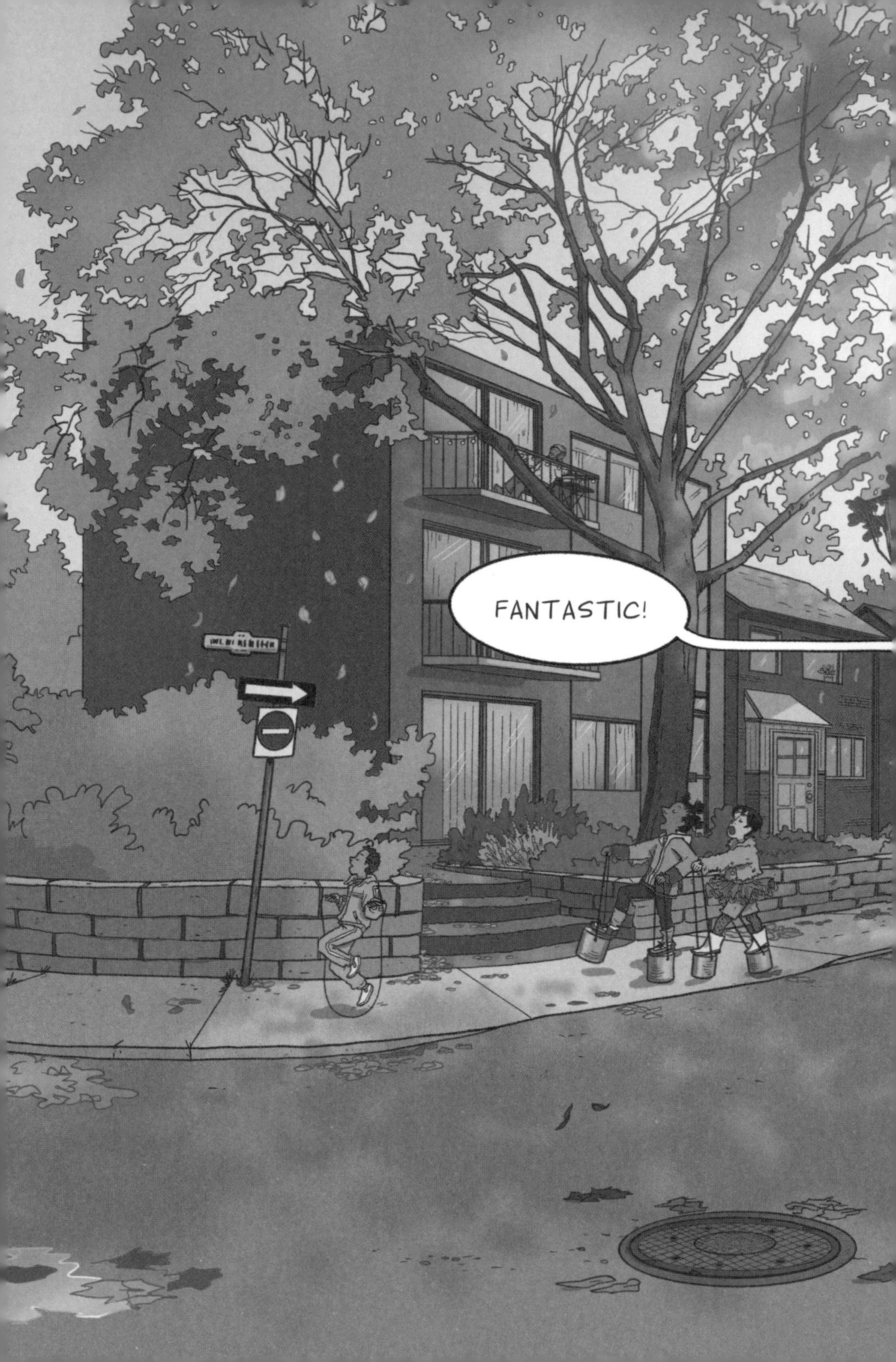
FANTASTIC!

ACKNOWLEDGMENTS

This story is inspired by "The Adventure of Charles Augustus Milverton" and Sir Arthur Conan Doyle's Sherlock Holmes series, which are largely wonderful, but also reflect the biases and prevailing ideas (good, bad, and terrible) of the times in which they were written. It's our job as readers to delight in the good, name the bad, and reject the terrible so we don't repeat those ideas in our work or in our lives. Do all of your reading with an open heart and a detective's discerning eye.

Tremendous thanks to the incredible people whose input, support, and existence was critical to the creation of this book: Anjali Singh, Ayesha Pande Literary, Dana Chidiac, Jenny Kelly, everyone at Dial & Penguin Kids (US & Canada), Mary Verhoeven, who flatted this book, the Spruce Bruce, Lindsay Cochrane, everyone at Royspace in Melbourne, Jossamy Goo, Alioo Edy, Nick Sharp-Paul, Ben Vains, Amy Wood, Steph Guthrie, Lil' Frenchie Westgate, and everyone else I have forgotten. Thank you!

Special thanks to the real Sameer and Aisha, who let me turn two friends into an imaginary family; Dana Woodward, whose contribution is immeasurable; the incredible kindness and joy of the late Carol Ens; my mom, Lottie; and the people of the city of Toronto who fight and advocate every day to make it livable for *everyone*.